KIDNAPPED BY THE MAN SHE LOVED!

"If I live through this, I'll see Lucas Sanger hang!" Lindsay closed her eyes. Exhausted and weakened by the drugs, she slept.

Hands shook her awake. Alarmed, Lindsay opened her eyes and focused on Lucas.

"Don't ever touch me again," she whispered between swollen lips.

"Come on, Lindsay, you can't escape my touching you, so why try?"

She whirled on him and with her fingers spread, she attacked him, reaching for his face, trying to scratch his eyes out, hurt him, draw blood, as he had done to her. But her wrists were grasped and drawn behind her and held tightly. A deep laugh escaped Lucas's throat as he looked into her face. He held her tightly against his chest, her arms pinned behind her.

The contact of their bodies had an effect Lindsay was not prepared for. She felt as though an electric shock coursed through her body. She weakened and Lucas felt her body go lax . . . .

We will send you a free catalog on request. Any titles not in your local book store can be purchased by mail. Send the price of the book plus 50¢ shipping charge to Tower Books, P.O. Box 270, Norwalk, Connecticut 06852.

Titles currently in print are available for industrial and sales promotion at reduced rates. Address inquiries to Tower Publications, Inc., Two Park Avenue, New York, New York 10016, Attention: Premium Sales Department.

COLORADO WOMAN

Patricia Greenlaw

TOWER BOOKS  NEW YORK CITY

To:

Dan and Nancy

Karol and Dave

All of whom helped me,

All of whom I love . . . .

A TOWER BOOK

Published by

Tower Publications, Inc.
Two Park Avenue
New York, N.Y. 10016

Copyright © 1980 by Tower Publications

All rights reserved
Printed in the United States

Prologue

The whine of wheels, the groaning of aged wood and the driver yelling at the tired horses were the first sounds Ned heard alerting him to Lindsay's arrival. He ran from the saloon and stopped in the middle of the dusty street. The stagecoach creaked around a corner. Through the noise of the slowly waking town Ned heard the driver yell to the passengers, "We're here folks!"

Ned began running toward the stopped coach. He turned the corner and stopped dead. His mouth and throat felt parched, his skin looked grey with the coating of dust mixed with sweat. He swept his hat off and wiped his arm across his brow. He licked his lips several times and placed the worn hat back on his head. Then he stood, watching the people getting off the coach. He rubbed his hands up and down his pants, cleaning his sweaty palms and trying to look calm.

A woman carrying a large basket passed beside the coach and her billowing skirt caught on the greasy wheel hub. She stammered in anger before the driver noticed and came to her aid. Ned lowered his eyes and smiled as the driver tried to calm the very irritated young woman. She wanted everyone to know her dress was ruined. It had cost a lot of money and she would make sure her husband talked to the stage lines about compensating her for this dreadful accident.

The woman finally walked away murmuring about the negligence of men today and the dangers of stagecoaches coming directly into town. Ned focused his attention on the coach. The driver returned to the open door and raised his arms to help someone down. The guard tossed several pieces of baggage to the ground and Ned's heart began to pound wildly. He glanced sideways, sure someone could hear his heart. A flash of red caught his eye and he swung his head around, his eyes locked on the disembarking passenger.

All sound diminished, all other passengers disappeared and Ned's world stopped as he watched the little girl stand beside the coach, shake the clinging dust from her skirt and shyly peer around her. Turning quickly, she walked across the street to the hotel and stood on the porch, her chin trembling and her eyes bright with unshed tears.

Ned gulped in several breaths of air, straightened his hat and slowly walked toward her.

* * *

Lindsay glanced around her. The dust was thick and she licked her lips. Suddenly she spotted the big man walking toward her and stood stock still. He was so big—bigger than her father and she always thought her father the biggest man in the world. The man's feet plodded through the dust kicking up clouds that lapped at his pants. He was watching her. She backed up slowly, her tiny hands clutching her worn dress. The wall of the hotel stopped her progress and she waited, almost as scared as that fateful day she spotted the Indians riding toward her home.

He was coming toward her too fast, everything was happening too fast. Lindsay wanted to run, cry, scream, anything but stand here and wait but she did nothing except watch her uncle come closer. He reached the porch, propped one big foot on the worn planks, and leaned toward her, resting an arm on his leg. He said nothing, only smiled. She stared at him, their eyes locked in frightened anticipation. A tear slipped down her cheek and she angrily brushed at it. He still had not spoken but his eyes were shining. Lindsay raised her chin and sniffed. Why didn't he say something? Maybe daddy was right. Maybe this man doesn't like children. Maybe he only spits tobacco juice and smokes, maybe he hates children . . . that's it . . . he hates me and he's trying to think of a way to get rid of me.

Her thoughts were jumbled and she was trying hard to

keep from crying. She turned her head and looked around. A few men were standing behind her uncle, watching her and smiling. She sniffed and the tears began to fall down her dusty cheeks. She wiped her arm across her face as a sob escaped. How much longer would she have to stand here and be stared at? How much longer could she take not knowing what was going to happen to her? How would she ever live without her mother? She lowered her head and cried. The porch groaned under the weight of her big uncle. Her head snapped up as she heard his footsteps approaching her. She pressed back against the wall, pushing hard against the rough wood, trying to disappear into the planks. He stood directly in front of her now, his arms at his sides, his fingers clenched. He was still smiling. "If you're that pretty covered with dust, you're gonna be beautiful in your new clothes."

She said nothing, only watched him. He did have a nice smile and such pretty, shining eyes.

He bent down on one knee and slowly held his arms out to her. She stiffened. Her eyes clenched shut and the tears began sliding down her dirty face again. She had no one else in the world now. Maybe he wouldn't hurt her. Didn't he say something about new clothes? Why would he buy me anything if he didn't care about me? Maybe I should give him a chance. She opened her eyes and looked at him through misty tears. He was in the same position, still smiling. She began walking slowly toward his outstretched arms. She stopped when she reached his hands and stared into his face.

Ned wanted to reach out and grab this little girl who was trying so hard to be brave but he knew that would frighten her. She had to come to him. Hurry, Lindsay, come into my arms, I'll keep you safe, he thought. I think I already love you. He watched the myriad of emotions sweep across her face. She was fighting so hard to remain aloof and brave. How long could a five-year-old child hold out? Watching this one she could probably hold out forever. He spoke, ever so softly, ever so lovingly, "Lindsay, honey, you're home."

She hung her head and walked into the circle of his arms. He hugged her close to his chest. She could feel his heart pounding. He began caressing her head, murmuring to her. He held her for several minutes until her tears were spent. When she was through crying he stood and taking her hand proudly led her into the hotel for food and rest.

The next day they left Durango for her new home. Ned chatted endlessly about the ranch, his hopes and dreams for her, his plans to buy more cattle and start a herd for her. He talked as though she were a grown woman, not a mere child.

Linday tried to listen to him but her mind was exhausted and try as she might she could not concentrate on her uncle's words. Her eyes would close, her mind would wander back to the fateful day and Ned's talk would fade as though he slowly disappeared down a long tunnel. Ned seemed not to notice her disinterest in his rambling talk and continued on.

After several hours of riding, they crested a hill and Lindsay glimpsed her first view of her new home. Her green eyes widened in surprise as she stared at the large gambrel roof log house, windows reflecting sunlight, and tall pine trees swaying gently. A dark vine, interspersed with fuscia flowers, snaked along the porch railing and tumbled onto the ground.

An ocean of lawn surrounded the house with a weathered log fence standing guard. Behind the house, supporting a carved Lazy Hat brand, stood a bleached barn surrounded by more fencing and containing several horses pawing and snorting in anger at being confined. Two bunkhouses stood behind the barn, one with a tin roof extending over the ground. Several men were working under this roof and Lindsay could hear the clang of metal. Behind the ranch the land rolled toward hills broken by a silver river murmuring down from the hills. The river burst into a pool of clear, emerald water, then narrowed and continued its long journey to the sea. Beyond the river Lindsay could see the cattle. A vast amount of brown and white animals chewing contentedly on the lush grass. To the west the land bumped into the mountains, tall, erect, massive, and uneven.

"Do you like it, Lindsay?" Ned asked.

She lowered her eyes and nodded her head shyly. From

here it looked like the most beautiful place on earth, but her home had been beautiful and safe once too. Now she didn't have anybody to love her.

As the wagon creaked to a stop in front of the gate, Zuni, the housekeeper, ran down the porch steps, her hands gripping her large white apron. Lindsay climbed down and stood against the wagon for support. She glanced around. Men were walking up to her uncle, laughing, talking, chewing tobacco. They all watched her.

Zuni approached her slowly, her arms out, "Cariña, cariña!"

Although Lindsay had no idea what Zuni said she liked this woman. She walked slowly to her and Zuni hugged her. For the first time in many months Lindsay felt safe, secure.

She was ushered into the house, her uncle explaining to the waiting help that she was tired and hungry and would meet them all later.

She was led through an entry which smelled of fresh beeswax. A mirror hung on one wall. A clothes tree leaned crookedly against another wall, three umbrellas and a limp hat hung from its arms. Sunlight filtered through the parlor windows bouncing off empty glasses and amber-filled bottles scattered on a sideboard. Above the fireplace, dominating the room, hung a portrait of a beautiful, dark-eyed woman. A large dining room, filled to capacity with an oak table and several chairs, stood across from the parlor. Inviting windows faced the mountains, encouraging a little nose to press against their coolness . . . and dream.

Through a back door in the dining room Lindsay could see the kitchen with its spicy, tangy odors dominating the house. The floor of quarry stone was squeaky clean and the back door stood ajar, allowing her to glimpse clothes hanging on a line, enveloped in sunlight, blowing in the breeze.

Lindsay smiled to herself. Maybe this wasn't going to be such a bad place to live after all. She glanced up at her uncle who was holding her hand and leading her up the stairs. He most certainly was not the fire-breathing dragon she had conjured in her mind. All the stories her father had told her about Ned couldn't be true. Even if they were Ned seemed to like her. Lindsay was too young to understand her father's jealousy toward his brother, his hatred of his brother's courage, his lifestyle, and looks. When Lindsay was born she had Ned's eyes, the same color, the same twinkle. It was not easy for her father to accept this. In many ways he didn't, so Lindsay turned to her mother for kindness and love.

If any doubt nagged at her about liking her new home it quickly dissipated after she was gently pushed into her bedroom. She stood just inside the doorway, her eyes twinkling. A lacy white canopy hung from the top of the bed and brightly colored pillows lay on a white quilt. A warm shawl was draped over the back of a rocking chair, impatiently waiting for a little girl. A breeze, puffing through the open casement, played with the fluffy curtains. A dresser and mirror displayed a comb and brush and a shimmering lace cloth trickled down its shiny brown side. A closet, its door slightly open, protected a myriad of colorful garments. Lindsay ran around the room touching everything, examining the clothes, asking over and over if this was really all for her.

Ned laughed, "No matter what their age females seem to come alive at the sight of new clothes."

The first few months after her arrival, Lindsay had nightmares every night. She saw the faces of her parents, arrows hideously piercing their bodies, their convulsions of pain, and her own discovery of their death. But always, loving arms embraced her and held her close until she slept. Eventually the nightmares became less and less frequent and she slept the night through.

Lindsay learned to ride like the wind, swim, herd cattle, put up fences, and grow vegetables in her garden. Ricco Manfretti, the leather-faced old ranch hand, an expert horseman, taught her to ride and Jonas Fields, his senior, taught her to swim and fish.

For her first birthday at the ranch, Ricco gave her a puppy . . . a straggly, long-haired, reddish mutt with a funny little nose. She named her Angel. Not to be outdone, Jonas gave her a kitten . . . grey with a black spot on its face. She named him Devil.

Uncle Ned grumbled under his breath at all this attention

and gift giving but when everyone had gone to their bunks, he brought out his gifts. One year it was a hand-carved saddle with silver trim on the hoods and a pair of leather riding gloves, another year it ws an emerald necklace and earrings to match. Zuni chuckled at this gift, arguing to his glowering face that Lindsay was only nine years old. Ned shuffled his feet and turned back to watch Lindsay place the jewelry on her neck and ears.

But most of her gifts from Uncle Ned were horses and cattle. He wanted her to have a good start in cattle ranching and by the age of eighteen she had more cattle than many of the cattle ranchers around Durango. She had six of her own horses and rode each one, but her favorite was Regalo, a chestnut stallion who pawed at the wind and hammered out circles in the corral, frightening the dogs. He was sort of like Lindsay, Ricco thought.

As Lindsay grew up it was obvious she was becoming a real beauty. Red hair hung down to the middle of her back with so much natural curl she cursed it under her breath, wishing for a way to straighten it. When she perspired or it rained, tight little curls would hug her face and neck. Her eyes were large—a pale shade of green—turning dark when she was excited or mad. Her skin was milky, creamy soft with cheeks of burnished copper. The Irish in her seemed to override any other blood lines. Her pugged nose teased her oval face while pouty lips taunted the men. Her supple, lithe body, long legs, tiny waist, and firm breasts drew many admiring stares but Lindsay paid no attention to men. If anybody pressed too close she threatened to tell her uncle.

Lindsay had a stubborn streak and clothing was one of the few things she argued about frequently with her uncle. She always wore pants when she rode and she never rode sidesaddle. "Not ladylike," Ned grumbled, "My Lindsay is a lady—she should ride like one."

She hated billowing dresses with those silly corsets. Being so tiny she had no need for them or the other restricting accoutrements she refused to wear. Ned tried to entice her into many dresses with bows and yards of lace or the newest style from France but Lindsay balked. "Do you want me to look like all the other women around Uncle Ned?" And Ned would concede again. He certainly didn't want Lindsay to look like anyone but Lindsay.

Julie Starn was a friend of Lindsay's. The two girls enjoyed each other's company—but they were completely opposite in regard to their clothing. Julie was constantly buying the newest styles and colors, even if they weren't flattering to her—ribbons for her hair, combs with jewels for special occasions, and jewelry to match.

One afternoon, while visiting the Tyler ranch, Julie again brought up Lindsay's dressing habits.

"Lindsay, I do declare, if you aren't the strangest thing about your dressing habits." Fluttering her eyelashes and giggling behind her hand, she went on "You know, if you would only try and dress more like a woman and less like a man you might have a better time."

Lindsay looked at her and smiled. "Julie, you know how I feel about all those silly doodads that women are supposed to wear to make them look beautiful. They're plain uncomfortable."

Walking to the window she continued, "Why can't we be ourselves and wear . . . well, wear long pants and serape and be accepted the same as a man?"

Julie giggled. "Why, Lindsay Tyler, I swear if you ain't got some of the strangest notions in that head. Well, all I have to say is, I'm thrilled to death to be a woman and dress in all the newest styles and flirt and dance with a handsome man until I'm breathless!" Getting up and placing her bonnet on her bouncing blond curls she continued, "I just know if you was to dress different, you, too, could be a belle of the ball, but I guess I really should be happy since if you was to dress like me I might have too much competition."

Giggling, she blew Lindsay a kiss. "I really must be going now, love. My pa will be awful mad if I don't get home before dinner is ready." She opened Lindsay's bedroom door, whisked around the corner, and down the stairs.

Through the glass, Lindsay could see her take the reins of her horse from the post, climb into the buckboard, and start down the trail.

"Oh, darn," she said, wiping her hand across her brow and pushing a straggly curl from her forehead, "Just cause I wear pants doesn't mean I feel like a man." Continuing to herself, "Well, if a man doesn't like the way I dress, then I guess he can just not look at me." But she also felt something. There was something in her that was blossoming—a part of her that ached and yearned.

And it made her moody.

Chapter 1

Lindsay stretched languidly, savoring the feel of the cool grass against her hot skin. She plucked a blade of grass and put it in her mouth as she turned to her horse. She remembered the day she first saw her beautiful Regalo.

Ricco had trained and broken him as a colt. When she turned sixteen, Ned had presented him to her. She remembered standing on the porch of the ranch house staring at this beautiful animal, then slowly approaching him, touching his nose, talking softly. Within minutes Lindsay had him saddled and trotted him to the entrance of the yard. Leaning down, she opened the gate. It seemed as if she had been riding Regalo all her life. Her hair bounced down from its cluster of curls, her pants flapped around her legs. She bent low over the horse's powerful outstretched neck. Her heart pounded madly as they made their way over sagebrush and rock. They became one. Sweat poured from Regalo's flanks. Lindsay could feel it cooling her thighs too. There was a communion of wind, speed, muscle, and heartbeat. Finally, she pulled him up, his nostrils flaring. Her hair had completely fallen and both horse and rider were glistening. She touched him gently on his damp neck. They knew each other—and that's the way it was with Lindsay and her chestnut stallion.

The cool grass felt good. Regalo whinnied. She raised

herself and walked to him. He raised his head and softly snorted, seeming to sense it was time to go.

"Come on, Regalo," she said with a sigh, "I guess we better start back or everyone will be out looking for us."

She led the horse to a low outcropping of rocks. She perched on the rocks and jumped on Regalo's back. She rode bareback and since she wasn't very tall, she struggled clumsily to mount the large stallion. Once there, all clumsiness gave way to graceful confidence. She turned the horse's head toward home and Regalo cantered off.

* * *

"You know, Jonas," Ned said. "I think I'll take Lindsay into Durango for a few days. She seems to be kinda restless lately."

Ned walked slowly to the barn, waiting to open the gate for Lindsay who was coming over the rise.

Jonas slowly crawled down from his perch on the fence and rubbed his stiff knees. "God, I'm getting old. Was a time, not long ago, I could outwork any fella on this place."

"You ole cuss, there ain't a varmint in these parts that'll ever be able to keep up with you."

Both men walked to the barn and waited for Lindsay and Regalo to finish the last fifty yards. They looked to the west gate, anticipating her bright smile and tinkling laugh. But both men had noticed a new moodiness in her. Although they never talked about it, it gnawed at them.

"You know, Jonas, Lindsay is one of the best things that ever happened to me. But I think she's gonna need more than me before too much longer. She's all grown up now and every once in a while I see that look in her eyes. I haven't met a man yet that could handle her . . . I sometimes worry if there is one."

"Ah, Ned," Jonas said scratching his head and squinting into the sun, "she's not that grow'd up. And even if she was, she wouldn't leave you—us—no how."

"Yes, sir, Jonas, I think I'll take her into Durango for a few days of shopping. Maybe some fun. Yes, sir." His eyes softened as he watched Lindsay's flushed face. "I think she just might enjoy a break in the routine."

"What are you two talking about now?" Lindsay asked absentmindedly from her horse. She stroked the stallion's back and turned to them. Her long hair fell about her shoulders, the sun reflecting its gold highlights. She turned to her uncle and wiped her hands on her pants. A smile played at her lips as she cocked her head.

"Uncle Ned, you and Jonas spend too much time just sitting around. You're going to have to get busy. You're letting this place get too rundown." At that she ran off, glancing at them over her shoulders and giggling.

Both Ned and Jonas looked at each other and winked. They used to race her when she was younger and they too were younger. But in the last few years she had gotten faster and they had gotten slower.

* * *

"Uncle Ned," Lindsay breathed excitedly, "look at all the people here. It's been so long since I've been here I had almost forgotten how big Durango is!"

Lindsay was escorted into town by Ned, Jonas, Ricco, and a small assemblage of range hands. They spent one week in town and Lindsay bought several day dresses, a couple of party gowns, three new riding outfits, shoes, and several chemises. Uncle Ned tried to talk her into a new gown "direct from Paris" with seed pearls sewn on the bodice and a short, flaring train, but Lindsay would have no part of it.

They ate at Hatties and gorged themselves on hot cornbread, bacon, strawberry jam, goat cheese, and boysenberry pie. She watched the men betting on who could hit most of the swinging bottles that were tied to a tree. A man with a long pole would tap the bottles, setting them in motion before each contestant stepped up to take his turn.

One day, while she and Ricco were watching this contest, a lithe, deeply tanned man wearing a flat-crowned hat sauntered up, placed some money on the rickety little table, and quietly stood back to wait his turn. Each man put up five dollars, betting against any others that wanted to beat him.

He had to shoot all six of the small, glass bottles that hung from wires from the tree. When one bottle was shot another was tied in its place. An expert shot from Kansas had hit four bottles earlier. But four wasn't enough and the betting kitty was full.

Finally, it was the stranger's turn. He stood on the mark, drew his gun, and shattered all of the swinging bottles. He holstered his smoking gun, turned to the speechless man handling the money, took his winnings and walked off. He tipped his hat on his way through the astonished crowd. His eye caught Lindsay's and he winked. A murmur broke the silence. There was much conjecture about the man. Lindsay was stunned. All she could think of was what an arrogant, swaggering man he was, not like the men at the ranch at all. But soon he was out of her mind as her attention was directed by Durango's other magic. She watched the men and how they treated their horses. At night she and Ned, Ricco and Jonas would take walks, listening to the loud banter coming from the saloon and laughing when someone came bouncing out the double doors. The week was fun filled and Lindsay would tumble into bed each night and fall into an exhausted sleep.

One evening while Ned, Jonas, and Ricco had gone to the saloon for a drink and some looks at some loose women, Lindsay went down to the lobby of the hotel to sit and watch the people strolling by. She was bored with sitting in her room alone. Although she had been given strict instructions not to leave the hotel, she wasn't ordered to stay in her room. After donning a light shawl and running a brush through her hair she walked to the lobby. Sitting on a bench behind a post, she straightened her skirts and surveyed the room.

The lobby was quiet. A lantern hung behind the desk and another sat on a table by the door. A cool breeze blew through the open door rustling her skirts. Ribald remarks from drunken men rode the breeze to her. The desk clerk's head hung forward limply as though supported by a weak spring and every few seconds a snore escaped his throat. After each snore, his head straightened on his neck, then slowly bobbed until it again hung sideways. Lindsay smiled and was soon engrossed with counting the seconds until a snore escaped.

She heard a noise behind her. She turned and looked directly into the eyes of the swaggering man from the bottle shooting contest. He was openly appraising her and Lindsay tugged at her skirt, frowning at him as a blush crept into her cheeks. She turned sharply back to watch the desk clerk.

Soon another man came through the doorway, looked around, and then walked swiftly to the man sitting behind Lindsay.

"Lucas, he's waiting."

The man rose from the chair. Lindsay glanced at him and thought, too bad he's so arrogant, he really is rather handsome.

Both men walked toward the door, but as they passed her, the dark stranger smiled almost imperceptibly, and touched his hat. Then he turned back to the door and walked off. The other man looked back at her, then he too turned to the door and strode away.

In her silence she thought, why am I so uncomfortable around that man? She shivered—and for some reason the shiver felt good. She was embarrassed. She rose from the bench, turned to the stairs, and returned to her room. She threw her shawl into a drawer in the chest and crossed to the window. She opened the casement as far as it would go.

Her window looked down onto an alley and, as she was leaning out, she again saw the dark stranger talking to two other men. Comforted by the wall between them, she allowed herself a smile. Safely behind the curtain, she could see the man's silhouette in the alley below.

He looked catlike and dangerous. His arms were sinewy and long. His shirt clung revealingly to his muscular chest. She noticed that his right hand always remained menacingly near his holster as he talked with two strangers. Watching him, she suddenly became aware of feelings she had never experienced before. Although this frightened her, it also excited her in a way she had never imagined possible. She felt a drop of perspiration run between her breasts. She reached to wipe it off—and became aware of the stimulating touch her hand had given.

She turned back to the window. He was gone.

A welcome breeze blew in through the open window caressing her. Before she could finish her thoughts, she fell on the bed and was asleep.

* * *

"Why aren't you interested in my background, Mr. Moriarity?" Lucas asked. "You intend to pay me a good wage and yet you care nothing about where I come from or what I am."

Nick Moriarity threw his head back and laughed.

"Why should I care what you are or anything else for that matter? If you can do what I'm paying you for—that's all I need to know." He looked into Lucas's eyes and continued.

"You'll be working for *me*, taking orders from *me*. If I ain't ever questioned you, then I expect you ain't never gonna question me or any of my orders." Lifting his hat he ran a hand carelessly through his thinning grey hair and set the hat back on his head.

"In other words, Lucas Sanger, if you ever question any of my orders then you can get the hell off my place," chuckling, "if you can."

"That sounds just fine with me, just the way I like to do business." Lucas looked down at Moriarity, his thumbs resting in his gunbelt. "And I'll go you one better. If I don't like any of the orders you're dishing out, then I may just change them"

Nick jerked his head up and looked directly into the other man's eyes. His hands closed into tight fists. He spoke through clenched teeth. "You just be at my ranch at sunup tomorrow." His hands slowly relaxed as he turned and stomped off.

Lucas joined his waiting friend and they walked together and talked.

"Ya know something Lucas, someday your mouth is gonna get us into more trouble than we can get out of."

He turned down the alley way, pivoted at the end and yelled back. "Ya wanna go have a shot of whiskey and maybe see what Josie's got to offer tonight?" He pushed his hat back on his head and sneered at Lucas. "O' course, I plumb forgot, Josie is all hot for you, ain't she?" He laughed, turned the corner and strode toward Josie's.

"Ha," Lucas sneered through his teeth, "Your jealousy don't bother me none, ole friend. I mean, after all, Josie knows a good thing when she sees it." He joined his friend and they disappeared into the saloon.

Josie Minter was a fun-loving, short, middle-aged gal who had hungry eyes for Lucas. She had been a friend to him many times in the last few years, always coming through when he needed help. She dyed her hair black and against her pale skin it made her look older and a little harder. But her heart was as big as she was and the men who knew her couldn't say anything bad about Josie. She had been married once, but when her husband beat her up, she skipped out on him and found her way to Durango. With the little money she possessed she knew she had to do something fast and the fastest way to make any money was with her body.

Before long she had a large following. One day another gal named Mandy offered to go into partnership with her and open their own place. They did well for a few years until Lucas came into their lives.

Mandy was a hot-blooded, fighting gal. She latched onto Lucas with such tenacity that he told Josie he wouldn't be coming back. Since Josie was very fond of Lucas and was fast losing patience with Mandy, she bought out Mandy's half of the business and went on her own.

In retaliation, Mandy opened up her own place across the street. It became a town joke to see these two walking on opposite sides of the street, pretending to ignore each other, yet each going out of her way to make the other notice her. It became a common thing for a fellow the threaten to "go across the street" if he didn't get the kind of treatment he felt he deserved from one of the gals. The minute this threat came from his mouth, Mandy or Josie, depending on the house, would rush to him and promise to make amends. Before long, the entire male population of Durango used this ploy whether they were satisfied or not.

Disappearing through the doors at Josie's, Lucas and

Chico walked to the bar and ordered a drink.

"Well, if my eyes don't deceive me and if I ain't too plied with whiskey to see straight, I could swear I see the face of Lucas Sanger and his erstwhile companion, Chico Santiani." Walking toward the two men with a smile as big as her heart, she put out her hand to Lucas.

"Josie, I never get tired of seeing that lovely face," he replied, taking her hand in his and lightly touching his lips to the back of it.

"What brings you two to Durango again?" Taking her hand from his and wrapping it through his arm she looked over her shoulder. "Joe, bring three whiskeys over to the corner table."

Lucas pulled out a chair. Josie sat down and put her hands together, resting them on the table. Lucas seated himself and Chico waited until the drinks were served. Then he sat down.

"Are you on the run again, boy?" she asked, sipping her drink.

"Well, you might say that, Josie," Lucas replied, looking at her over the rim of his glass.

"This man's honest streak got us in trouble again," Chico interrupted, "It ain't often he gets high and mighty, but when he does the whole goddamn thing usually blows up in our face." He smiled, "And what pisses me off is, I always seem to be around the jackass when he does it!"

"Tell me, Josie," Lucas questioned, "What do you know about Nick Moriarity?"

Josie looked up, tapping her fingers against her face.

"Well I know he ain't one to be messed with. He shot a man recently for stealing from his ranch. Told the sheriff the guy pulled a gun and he had to defend himself. Course, the sheriff had to take the word of Nick's men and they all backed Nick. Fear and money, I suppose, is a big power to fight against."

"I know he hates Ned Tyler with such a vengeance that some say someday his bottled hate will kill him." She twisted a ring on her finger and took a deep breath.

"His hate goes back a long ways. Supposedly Ned got in a shootout with Nick's brother after winning his ranch in a poker game and Ned killed him. O' course, it weren't near so big a ranch as it is now. Tyler built it up until today it's close to being the biggest ranch in Colorado." She reached into her cleavage and brought out a perfumed hankie and dabbed at her face. "Goddamn, it's so hot I swear the devil would complain." She returned the hankie and continued. "By the time Nick got out here from California, Tyler had moved onto the ranch. When Nick found out he went to him and swore he would get him one way or the other. He told him he had no right to take the ranch from his family and especially from a bereaved widow. Ned tried to explain that he won the ranch fair and square in a poker game and even paid money to the widow to help her out. Nick was too riled to listen by that time. He just kept saying that he would get Tyler and make him return the ranch to the rightful owner—that being him, o' course." She gulped down the last bit of liquid in her glass. "So, ever since then, Nick has had a sort of personal vendetta against Ned but so far ain't done much."

She stood up and smoothed her long skirt. "When they're both in town, as they are now, everyone keeps their distance. I guess they're fearing for their lives if one sees 'em talking to the other. Since Ned hires a lot of men and pays a good wage, they don't none of 'em want to offend him in any way." She bent over the table, exposing large, pendulous breasts to the two men. She placed her arms on the table and looked directly into Lucas's eyes. "If you ain't busy later you know where my room is. Chico, we have a new little senorita that just might be a salve to your ill humor tonight." She winked at him and he gave her a playful sneer.

"Oh, yeah, well now, maybe that's just what I need, a playful romp with a new little gal." He stretched his long legs and placed his hands behind his head. "What room is this little senorita in?"

Josie straightened and turned to walk to the bar. She looked over her shoulder. "I should make you find her but if you opened the wrong doors it could sure make tempers fly." Then she smiled and said, "First door on the left." With that she walked back to the bar, spoke to the bartender, and disappeared into the back room.

"Well, my friend, we shall have to watch very carefully this Mr. Nick Moriarity, won't we?" Chico stood, looked up the stairs in the direction of the room he was going to visit and straightened his hat. "I wonder what this little job you hired on for is going to be." He shrugged and turned toward the stairs. With a gleam in his eye he climbed them.

Lucas turned to the bar and raised his hand. "Bring me another drink, Joe." He stretched his legs under the table and relaxing into the chair, he tilted his hat down over his eyes and threw a coin on the table. His thoughts went back to the Dakotas. Funny how a man can stand up for something he feels is right, but if it's against the wrong people all hell can break loose. He couldn't stand the officer anyhow. Can't say he's sorry he killed the bastard. He had known for a long time the guy was stealing supplies that were meant for the Indians. Government supplies, meager though they were, would help the starving Nez Perce tribes. He probably wouldn't have noticed anything if he hadn't seen some guys walk away from the supply shack, mount their horses, and ride off. He checked the supply room door. It was shut but not locked. Strange, it was always locked and there was always a guard posted at the door. No guard this night and no lock. Suspicion crept into his mind like fog into a gully. The next three weeks he watched everyone and everything that went on. When he wasn't watching, Chico watched.

Being half Apache, Lucas understood only too well the starvation that constantly threatened the Indians.

When he had enough proof—after seeing the same men come on the same day each week, always after a big shipment from Kansas and when he noticed that the guard on this night was always detained or drunk or simply gone—then he decided to confront the major with his suspicions. Only the major wasn't about to let anyone ruin his plans for making quick money. Who gives a damn about Indians anyhow? They argued violently. When the major drew a gun, Lucas's instincts took over. He carried his gun but thought better of it. The noise would bring troops like Comanches to a wagon.

The major's downfall was shifting his eyes for a second

to check a noise at the window. Good old Chico. In that instant Lucas kicked the major's arm, sending his gun across the room. It went off just as Lucas threw his knife. The knife pierced the major's throat and his hands climbed to the knife. He gurgled, his eyes large and terrified as he dropped forward onto the floor. Lucas walked to him, removed the knife from the man's throat and wiped it on the major's sleeve. The door burst open and several men rushed in, some still pulling on their pants. Questions were thrown at him and he was arrested and thrown in the stockade. Only the guards at the stockade door had not figured on Chico. Chico knocked both guards out and released Lucas. The two guards were tied and in the stockade before Lucas could button his shirt.

After several days of traveling, they ended up in Durango. They knew they could hide out here for a while until they figured out what to do. Lucas couldn't go back to his ranch in New Mexico. The law would look for him there first. He had to bide time until he could locate the other two men involved in the scheme. He knew if he could find the men that drove the wagon loaded with the stolen goods, he could get them to talk.

That's when John Stade, a government agent, came into the picture. He had been looking for someone to infiltrate Nick Moriarity's gang, someone who could be trusted, someone who wouldn't be afraid of Moriarity.

Stade had been given Sanger's dossier several months before. After deciding to seek him out he left for the fort in the Dakotas. He walked into a hornet's nest. After questioning the commanding officer and several other men he learned what he wanted to know. Sanger was his man. Having been a guide for over five years he could handle a gun and himself. After contacting his superior in Washington he set out for Durango. He found Lucas in the saloon and approached him confidently.

"If you're telling the truth, Sanger, I'll bring the major's accomplices to trail. You'll be cleared of any involvement but . . . I guess you could call me a sonofabitch," Stade pushed his hat back, "I won't scratch your back if you won't scratch mine."

He bent forward, his eyes narrowing, "Understand?"

Lucas nodded. He didn't like this man having something to hold over him but this time he had no choice. And there was something about Stade that Lucas couldn't put a finger on, but something he trusted. He decided to bide time and keep his mouth shut and his ears and eyes open.

*   *   *

"Lucas," a hand was shaking his shoulder. "God, man, what do I have to do to get your attention. It sure ain't very flattering to have to shake the shit out of you to get you to notice me."

He stood and stretched, wrapping his arm around Josie's waist as he led her toward the stairs. "You know better than that, Joise. Why you're my favorite attention getter." A smile played at his lips as he looked into her face.

"Come on and I'll show you some real attention." They disappeared into a room behind the stairs, the sound of Josie's chuckles diminishing as the door slammed shut.

Chapter 2

"Ya know, Nick, maybe this plan of yours ain't so hot after all!"

A tall man with his hat pushed back stood in front of Nick, his arms akimbo, sweat droplets coursing down his face. "I mean, shit, going against Tyler ain't always been a good way to stay alive."

"Look, Blackmore, it you ain't got no balls then say so and we'll forget our deal now!" Nick had both arms resting on his gunbelt, his eyes cold as he answered. "I ain't gone this far to stop because of some chickenshit bastard with a yellow streak as wide as he is!"

Nick bent forward, his face suffused with anger. "I hired the guide. He's a halfbreed. Now we can travel through Indian territory without worrying. If you want outa this deal say so now. Otherwise, keep your big mouth shut!" Both men tensed, their faces grim and set as they eyed each other. After several seconds, Blackmore's muscles relaxed slightly and his arms dropped to his sides.

"All right, Nick, but if it don't work, don't forget what I said." And with this warning he turned and walked away.

The hate surging through the veins of Nick Moriarity had long ago driven thoughts of everything but revenge from his mind. He spent every spare minute of his time scheming to restore the Lazy Hat Ranch to the Moriarity clan. The plot came to him one summer two years before, when he saw Lindsay and her uncle walking arm in arm down the Durango streets. He knew then the answer to getting the ranch back was to trade Lindsay for it. Now all his time was spent on an elaborate plan to abduct Lindsay and reclaim his land. The old images burning in his memory fueled his revenge. All the images were there.

He constantly thought of the day he rode up to the door of the ranch house and shouted for Ned to come out and the look on Ned's face as he ordered him off his property. Turning and riding off his property . . . not Tyler's, but his. These thoughts were branded into his brain and he spent each night lying in bed trying to picture the look on Ned's face when he found out Lindsay was his captive. He would reclaim his property if he died trying.

Nothing would stop him . . .

Nick's bitterness was a source of constant squabbling in his bunkhouse. His foreman, Marty Benson, spent many hours trying to keep the men from fighting over some remark made about Nick. His men's loyalties were divided. Half were loyal to him—the other half to making money.

One night, after a particularly busy day, a man with long unkempt hair and chipped yellow teeth said, "Ya know, fellas, Nick acts as though he has a bee stuck up his ass. If I didn't need the money so bad, I'd tell him to shove it and start walking."

Rafferty got up from his bunk and, rolling up his sleeves, came toward Manny. "If you don't like the way Nick is treating you, Manny, maybe you should shove off." At this, Manny lunged to grab Rafferty's neck and they both fell, swearing, to the floor.

Marty jumped down from his upper bunk, grabbed Rafferty by the collar and stood between them. "Goddamnit, knock it off!" He shoved Rafferty behind him. "This goddamn fighting has to stop!" He stretched his free arm toward Manny. "If you assholes don't stop this fighting, I'm gonna fire the whole lot of you." Rafferty's eyes glared into Manny's as he slowly relaxed. He released himself from Marty's hold, turned, and walked out the door. Soon the other men returned to whatever they had been doing. But the peace was a tense one.

"Nick, I don't know what's gotten into the men, but they're as jumpy as frogs on a hot sand bar." Marty wiped his brow with his kerchief and continued. "You're gonna have to say something about what you're planning, boss, or the men are gonna kill each other and we're gonna have to hire a whole new crew. That ain't gonna be easy with so little time left."

Nick stood with his arms folded across his chest looking out the window. He turned slowly, and looked Marty in the eye. Through a crooked smile he replied, "The plan is almost ready to put into effect. Only a few more days and we'll see Tyler crumble and fall into my hands." His smile broadened. "So you keep them sonsabitches outa my hair and quiet until they're needed, ya hear me, Marty?" He was shaking and hard pressed to control his anger. Soon these men would make more money than they had ever made and all they could do is fight. Marty turned to the door, set his hat on his head, and walked out.

"Only a few more days and I'm gonna see a payoff," Nick said to himself as he turned to the stairs and slowly ascended them.

Chapter 3

Lindsay sat in the carriage looking out the window, her hands folded in her lap. The setting sun burned the mountains and the myriad colors were so beautiful she was mesmerized.

"Lindsay," Ned spoke quietly, "You look very beautiful."

She wore a white crepe ballgown with flounces of white satin looped up with pink tuberoses. Her shawl of white had silver threads running through it. Her hair was caught up in back in a white ribbon and ringlets hung loosely at the sides. White satin slippers and her favorite emerald earrings completed her attire.

"Is there something bothering you, honey?"

The carriage rocked and thumped along as the driver snapped the whip over the horses' backs and swore.

"I . . . I guess I'm just not in the mood for a party, Uncle Ned," she replied, looking at her hands. "I really would rather have stayed home and read." She smiled, her eyes glancing at his face, then resting again on her folded hands.

Ned plucked a piece of lint from his sleeve and without looking at her replied. "Well, girl, don't speak too soon, maybe you'll have a rousing good time."

The carriage pulled onto a large drive and soon the lights from many lanterns could be seen. The sun had disappeared from sight and the red sky and scudding black clouds gave a serene look to the house. The porch of the Starn home was lit with what looked to Lindsay like a thousand fireflies. It was enchanting. The carriage halted in front of the house and Ned climbed down and turned to assist Lindsay.

As they stepped into the entrance of the house, Julie ran

to her and hugged her lightly. "Why, Lindsay Tyler, you do look lovely." She giggled, turned to Ned and kissed him lightly on the cheek. "I was beginning to think Lindsay didn't own a ball gown." She turned around a couple of times, holding the sides of her dress. "How do you all like this creation?" Stopping, she turned to Lindsay. "I sent for it from my ma's catalog and it got here last week. I was beginning to worry it wouldn't get here and I did so want to wear it tonight. It came all the way from Denver. Isn't that exciting, Lindsay?"

Lindsay smiled warmly at her friend as she studied the dress. The burgundy silk complimented Julie's white skin, but the large bell shaped skirt held the material away from Julie's body, adding weight to her somewhat chubby frame. Rows of shirring covered the bodice with a ribbon of burgundy tied in a large bow at the back, the ends cascading to the floor. The filmy sleeves licked at her elbow and barely touched her shoulders. Her breasts swelled over the top of the dress and she wore a necklace of rubies and matching earrings. Her blond hair was pulled on top of her head with curls falling around her shoulders. She had ribbons of burgundy satin entwined through her hair. Burgundy slippers completed her ensemble.

"You look very lovely, Julie." Lindsay smiled. "I hope I have a dance tonight and don't spend all my time hugging the wall while you steal all the beaus." She turned to her uncle, her fingers grasping his arm.

"Julie, if I were a few years younger, your dances would all be taken by me but, alas, I'm afraid I'm getting too old." He placed Lindsay's hand in the crook of his arm and together they followed Julie into the parlor.

"Excuse me, Mr. Tyler, but I must see to some of my other guests." Lowering her voice she spoke to Lindsay, "I'll be back shortly . . . I have something I want to tell you."

The parlor opened onto a large ballroom. Jess Starn had the ballroom built so his daughters could hold many dances as they grew up. When they weren't using the room, two large ornately carved doors closed it off. But tonight candles adorned the ballroom and fresh flowers drenched the house with their perfume. A large frosted punchbowl, plates teeming with food, and fresh confections sat on large, cloth-covered tables. Lindsay looked around the parlor at the many faces. There were many familiar faces and many she didn't recognize.

"Honey, I see someone over there I haven't seen for a long time." He kissed her nose. "I'll claim my dance later." Ned strolled off, stopping to take a drink from a tray offered by a young waiter. He frowned . . . Lindsay certainly wasn't herself lately. Why, there was a time you couldn't have kept her from a dance if she were sick and abed. Something wasn't quite right with his beloved niece. He would have to talk to her.

Jess Starn was a wealthy rancher who started cattle ranching after a gold claim fizzled out. He had some money saved and on a trip through Durango heard about some land for sale down south. He liked what he saw, and purchased several hundred acres. Through the years he added on land and cattle. Although Ned and he were in the same business and each competitive with the other, they had helped each other in times of need and over the years became close friends. Jess's wife, Anne, was a tall, graceful woman who was very quiet. She and Jess had five daughters, Julie being the oldest.

"Well, I declare, if it ain't Miss Lindsay." Lindsay turned to face the voice and looked into the eyes of Tony Perez. "I aim to ask for a dance later, ma'am," he drawled, shifting his weight to better see her cleavage. "After all, you wouldn't want to upset any of your uncle's hands by refusing—now would you?"

Lindsay's face reddened slightly. "Why, Mr. Perez, whatever makes you think I wouldn't dance with you?" She dropped her lashes coyly. "I just can barely wait," she drawled sarcastically. She turned and walked to the other end of the ballroom. She could feel Tony's eyes burning into her back. Tony had tried to court her but each time she had refused him. She didn't feel comfortable with him . . . didn't trust him. He took the rejections angrily. He was very attracted to Lindsay and he knew other women found him attractive, most women, that is, except the one he wanted.

Lindsay Tyler! She wouldn't have anything to do with him. Well, tonight . . . tonight he'd charm her.

As the evening wore on Lindsay was becoming weary from her toes being stepped on and the leering stares at her neckline. She told her uncle she was going to the garden for a breath of fresh air.

"Don't be gone too long, honey," he whispered.

She smiled, turned to the open doors, and walked onto the veranda. The night was warm, a breeze played at the curls on her face, and the music was subdued in the background. She stepped down from the veranda and walked slowly into the garden. Jasmine and lilac permeated the air and she stopped to pick a flower. She sniffed its fragrance and lifted her eyes to the stars. Then she moved toward a swing at the end of the garden.

Jess had built a gazebo in the garden for Anne many years ago. Anne loved to sit out here and sew. Her daughters and Lindsay spent many hours here also. Lindsay seated herself on the swing and, humming softly, started it in motion. It was so beautiful. Anne spends so many hours working in this garden, Lindsay thought. It showed. It was the prettiest garden she had ever seen. The flowers grew in abundance and a pond topped with floating lilies completed the setting. Lindsay closed her eyes. With the warm night air, the perfume from the flowers, and the subdued music, she fell asleep.

Her eyes opened suddenly and without moving a muscle she listened. She couldn't hear anything except the hushed music and the laughter of the guests. Why had she awakened so startled? Nothing was different, no one was around and yet something had disturbed her sleep. She smoothed her skirt, brushed back the unruly wisps of hair and stood. Something caught her eye and she turned quickly. She could see a figure standing against the rough bark of a tree, but she couldn't make out who it was. She started to walk toward the house, her heart beating rapidly, fright beginning to nibble at her. The figure moved toward her. She turned to see if she could recognize him and her heart jumped.

"How long have you been standing there?" she asked insistently.

There was a pause. "Long enough to sear your beauty into my mind," came the reply. "Why are you leaving?" he asked. "It's much nicer out here than in the house with all that noise and cigar smoke."

"I really must return. My uncle will be worried." Lindsay turned back toward the house and took a step. An arm shot out, grabbed her arm, and pulled her against a hard, muscled chest.

"What do you think you're doing?" Lindsay brought her hand up to slap his face, but her wrist was caught in an iron grip.

"I had to see if those eyes were real." He looked down into her face and she glimpsed dark blue eyes with black lashes in a dark, handsome face.

"Well, now that you know, would you be so kind as to release me before my uncle sees you?" She struggled to be free and his hand released her wrist only to move to the back of her neck, caressing her hot skin as he pulled her face upwards toward his. His lips were almost touching hers, his breath warming her trembling lips. She struggled with all her strength but she was no match for him. His lips came down on hers, hard, searching, forcing her lips apart as his tongue raped her mouth. He crushed her to him and she thought he would surely squeeze the life from her. She must escape! She must be free of this man! And then . . . her body betrayed her! She was responding. She was kissing him back. Her arms slid around his neck and her lips began moving with his. He kissed her hungrily. Then, just as abruptly as he had grabbed her, he released her. She stumbled back gasping, her cheeks flaming as she straightened her skirts. She touched the back of her hand to her mouth and glared at him with dark green eyes.

He stood, arms akimbo, looking into her face.

"Well, ma'am, for someone who didn't want to be kissed, you sure fooled me." He rocked forward, looking steadily into her eyes. "Yes, you sure fooled me." He turned and walked toward the house. Then he stopped and faced her again. "I'll claim my dance later."

Lindsay stared at his disappearing back. Never had she been treated like that . . . never had she been degraded in such a manner. Well, she would show Mr.—and then she realized she didn't even know his name. Well, no matter, he was indecorous, uncivil, ill-mannered and she most certainly would not dance with him tonight—or ever. But she knew she lied.

She walked to the pond and scooped up water in her shaking hands and splashed it on her bruised lips. She stood straight, ran her fingers through her hair, and patted her cheeks. Turning toward the house, she straightened her shoulders and walked in.

"Wherever have you been?" Ned grabbed her arm. There was worry in his voice. "I was just getting ready to gather a few men and come search for you."

"I fell asleep on the swing out by the pond, Uncle Ned. I'm sorry if I worried you, but it was so beautiful. Before I knew it I was dreaming!"

She smiled and patted her uncle's arm. "If you'll excuse me I'm going to get some refreshments and talk to Julie." She turned and walked to the refreshment table. She placed a few cookies on her plate, filled a glass with cold punch, and turned to look for Julie.

She saw her across the room talking with Ginger Spurling. She walked through the throng of people to Julie's side and sat in a chair against the wall. She placed her plate on her lap and looked up to get Julie's attention. Only she looked directly into the handsome face of the stranger from the garden. He was standing with her uncle, staring directly at her. A crooked smile touched his face as he listened intently to her uncle. She blushed, turned to look at Julie, and took a sip of the cool punch. Don't let him see you're flustered, she told herself. I mustn't let him think he can ruffle me. But why should she care what he thinks anyway? But somewhere, in the deep recesses of her mind, she knew she did care.

"Julie, come sit with me awhile. I haven't seen you all night. You must be terribly tired of dancing with so many different young men." Lindsay giggled as Julie blushed and sat next to her.

"I am breathless with all the attention, Lindsay," she gasped. "I daresay I've met the most handsome man I've ever seen. His name is Lucas Sanger and I understand he has a rather intriguing background. Why, I even heard someone say he has Indian blood in him." She took a fan from around her wrist and began to fan herself. "I'll point him out to you. Yes, there he is now, talking with your uncle and my pa." Lindsay looked in the direction of her friend's gaze and directly into the eyes of Lucas Sanger, the stranger who had so crudely accosted her tonight.

"Oh dear, Lindsay," Julie blushed. "He's looking this way now!" She quickly looked at Lindsay and fanning herself rapidly she quipped, "I just know he's interested in me and I'm gonna do everything to keep his attention centered on little ole me." She glanced in Lucas's direction again only to see him talking to a tall, blond girl who had walked to him and urged her arm through his.

"Oh, if that Sheila Monroe isn't the most outrageous flirt in all of Colorado. If a handsome man is around, I swear, she can put her nose in the air and practically smell him." At this remark, both girls laughed and their conversation changed to an incident that happened to Julie during the day.

The music resumed and before long many couples were dancing the waltz, the ladies' dresses a kaleidoscope of colors and the laughter reverberating off the walls. Julie had been asked to dance and was walking onto the dancefloor with her escort when Lindsay caught a movement of someone coming toward her from the corner of her eye. She quickly stood up but before she could walk away her arm was grasped from behind. She whirled around and looked into the face of Lucas. A cynical smile played at his lips as he spoke. "I believe, ma'am, this is my dance. You did promise me one and I'll bet you do love to waltz." Lindsay was paralyzed with anger and embarrassment. "I know you are very selective about your dancing partners, ma'am, but you did promise, now didn't you?"

"I remember no such promise, Mr. Sanger," she spurted, looking down at his hand grasping her arm. "Now, if you will be so kind as to release me I must find my uncle."

"Ma'am, if I have to carry you onto the dancefloor, you can be guaranteed I'll do just that. So if you don't want to make a spectacle, I suggest you come willingly."

Lindsay's muscles tensed and she exhaled through clenched teeth. Slowly she turned to the dance floor and, with his hand holding tightly onto her arm, they made their way through the crowd. Stopping close to the corner of the dance floor, she turned toward him. He placed an arm possessively around her waist and took her other hand. His eyes caressed her face as she looked at the buttons on his shirt. She smelled leather and a man's cologne and she could feel a hard muscle in his back with her left hand. He was well dressed for an illbred bore, Lindsay thought. He wore black pants and a white shirt, open at the neck revealing a thatch of curly black hair. His black hair waved back terminating in shaggy curls around his neck. His long sideburns almost touched a short, trimmed moustache. His face was very dark, as were his chest and hands. But his eyes! Lindsay had never seen such eyes . . . they were the darkest blue. They reminded her of the sky before a storm. They narrowed when he smiled sending shivers down Lindsay's spine. She risked a look into his face and then quickly looked away. He was grinning and looking down at her. She blushed and when she spoke her voice quivered.

"Why do you insist on pestering me? With all the lovely girls here I would think you would pick on someone who enjoyed you advances."

"Why, Miss Tyler, are you trying to tell me you don't enjoy my company? After our adventure in the garden, I thought you were taking a liking to me." He continued looking into her eyes. "If I were a sensitive soul, I might be crushed beyond repair by your words."

Lindsay stiffened and avoided his eyes. She started to speak when the music stopped. Julie appeared at her side, giggling as she spoke. "Mr. Sanger, didn't you promise this next dance to me?"

Lindsay turned, feeling relieved, to see Julie's face. She walked off the dance floor but not before she heard Lucas's voice. "Why certainly, Miss Starn. You do look lovely tonight." Julie took his arm and they melted into the throng of dancers.

* * *

"Did you enjoy yourself tonight, honey?" Ned watched Lindsay's face intently, smiling as she attempted to feign an air of indifference.

"I had a marvelous time, Uncle Ned, but I really am very tired and will be most happy to fall into bed tonight." With no need to say any more, Lindsay rested her head against the back of the carriage and fell asleep.

Chapter 4

"Well, Uncle Ned, I really thought the man to be a bore and I feel sorry for the girl he settles his attentions on." Lindsay was eating her breakfast as she spoke.

"Ah, Honey, the man is used to getting his way with women and doesn't have to play as many silly games as a lot of young bucks do." He buttered a slice of hot bread. "I think he seems gentlemanly." He looked out the window. "I wouldn't offer any resistence to his calling on you."

Lindsay shot her uncle an angry look and continued eating. "Well, I would have to be mighty bored and mighty hardpressed for a man's attention before I'd go anywhere with that man!"

The next two days went by quickly. Lindsay rode every day, helped with the ranch chores, spent time reading some new books Uncle Ned bought for her, and even helped Zuni make bread.

* * *

It was a hot, muggy Tuesday afternoon. Lindsay lay by the river, her chin resting on the cool grass as her fingers played in the water. She shifted her weight as she noticed a cloud of dust in the distance. She sat up and shielded her eyes from the sun as she watched the dust cloud settle and reveal two men on horses approach the house.

"Looks like we have guests, Regalo." She stood up and brushed the clinging dust and grass from her pants. She led the horse to the outcropping of rock and climbed on the mount's shiny back. With Angel barking and jumping at Regalo's hooves, Lindsay started toward the ranch. She hadn't ridden far when she pulled Regalo up. Her eyes darkened as she recognized the riders. Turning Regalo sharply, more sharply than she intended, she kicked him into a gallop and raced back for the river, hoping Lucas had not seen her.

After reaching the river she led Regalo behind some large rocks and hid in the cool, tall grass.

"Now, if we're lucky, Angel, Mr. Sanger will leave the house shortly and we can go home. But . . . as long as he's there, I'll not leave here."

She rolled onto her stomach and splashed her fingers in the water, her heart beating rapidly as her thoughts centered on the stranger she had kissed at Julie's party. So deeply engrossed in thought she was oblivious to sound, and didn't hear anything until a voice drawled.

"Well, ma'am, fancy finding you here."

Turning quickly, she sat up and looked into the smiling face of Lucas. His eyes swept her body boldly as he climbed down from his horse. Lindsay started to jump to her feet as he sat beside her on the damp grass, but his arm shot out and grabbed her arm.

"Where do you think you're going now, little lady?" His lips curled in a mocking smile, "I think maybe you need to learn some manners."

Incensed at his words she turned her head sharply and spoke through clenched teeth. "What in hell would you know about manners, Mr. Sanger? You're about as gentlemanly as a rattlesnake!"

His hand held her arm tightly, his hat shaded his face. "Where did a lady learn language like that?"

Lindsay was attempting to pry his fingers from her arm

and stopped at his words. "You're hurting me, Mr. Sanger. If you don't let go of me immediately, I'll scream."

"Are you threatening me, little lady? Damn, I believe you are!" He pushed his hat back with his free hand. "Well, Lindsay, I didn't come here to fight with you."

Releasing her arm he continued, "I'm coming back tomorrow for a tour of the ranch. Your uncle said you'd be happy to guide me around. I'll pick you up in the morning." He stood, stretched, and looked out over the valley as he pushed his hat low over his eyes. His muscles rippled under the sweat damp shirt. He climbed on his horse, turned to Lindsay and smiled, his eyes raking her form, his eyes dark. Touching his fingertips to his hat he turned the horse and slowly rode off.

Seething with anger Lindsay rubbed her arm and spat at his receding back. "In a pig's eye I'll guide you around . . . you can go to hell!"

She watched Lucas as he traversed the hill, heading for the men waiting at the house. He rode a horse like he had been born in the saddle. She couldn't help admiring the way he sat on his stallion's back and the easy way he commanded his horse. The graceful pair they made as they wound their way down the grassy slope. Both strong . . . both handsome . . . She shook her head. Dear God! What was wrong with her? Admiring this man whom she found not at all to her liking. She splashed her face with cool water and mounted Regalo, riding slowly back toward the house.

But she couldn't put the sight of Lucas from her mind. His blue eyes gazed insolently at her. His strong dark arms held her close as he had that night. This is ridiculous, she sighed to herself. The man is a beast and here I am thinking constantly of him.

"Regalo, let's chase the wind, I need a good run," and nudging the horse into a fast gallop she disappeared into a cloud of dust.

From his mount Lucas watched Lindsay as she galloped through the fields, her hair flying behind her, the sun bouncing off the red curls. She crouched low on the animal's back and the big stallion's muscles bulged as he felt Lindsay release her grip on the reins and let him have his lead. Lucas watched them until they were out of sight, then turned back to speak to Ned. The half smile on Ned's lips did not reach his tear-filled eyes. He nodded quickly to Lucas, turned, and walked into the house.

* * *

The next morning dawned with the threat of rain. The sky vacillated between glorious sun and tumbling, dark clouds. Lindsay stretched slowly and smiled as Angel's wet nose nudged her hand. The smell of fresh coffee and frying bacon made her mouth water as she let the little dog out. She dressed hurriedly and raced to the dining room to eat. Her dress of white muslin with lilac flowers and lilac crossgrain ribbon tied under her breasts made her feel very feminine. She took an extra few minutes brushing her hair, deciding against tying it back. Thus, when she bent over her uncle at the dining table and caressed his cheek with her lips, her hair fell around her shoulders and brushed his face. He looked up into her bright eyes, then down at her decolletage. Her dress was cut very low, giving an almost unrestricted view of her milky breasts. The skirt hugged her slim legs, swaying when she moved revealing small white slippers on her feet.

Ned coughed slightly then returned his attention to his meal, a slight smile tugging at his lips.

"I'm so hungry I could eat a bear." She placed eggs, bacon, and hot bread with strawberry jam on her plate. When she finished eating she poured a mug of coffee and sipped slowly as she studied her uncle.

"Uncle Ned, did you tell Mr. Sanger I would give him a tour of the ranch today?"

Ned looked up from his plate and replied. "Yes, Lindsay, I did. He asked several questions about the workings of the ranch and I told him the best way to answer his questions was to show him everything first hand. He is leaving town tomorrow and since I wouldn't be able to show him around today, I told him you would." He took a bit of hot bread and continued. "Lindsay, I think the man has merit and I don't think you're giving him a fair chance. I've watched you whenever he's been around. You can't take your eyes from him . . . yet you can't speak civilly to him. Spending the day with him, showing him around our home might be a good way for you both to get to know each other. Since he is leaving tomorrow, it would be nice if you could spend the day being pleasant to him. Who knows, when he comes back to town maybe he'll court you and maybe you'll want him to." Ned perched his elbows on the table and studied Lindsay. "I have to meet with my banker today to go over some papers, but even if I didn't have prior commitments, I wouldn't show Mr. Sanger around." His voice trailed off and his eyes misted as he continued. "I'd let him have the honor of your presence for the day."

Lindsay watched her uncle's expression change from one of interest to one of sadness. He almost looked like he was going to cry. No . . . she must be imagining this sudden change. She was confused at her uncle's sudden interest in her social life too.

"Uncle Ned, how could you do this to me? You know I loathe the man. Can't you tell by the way we treat each other there is no love lost between us. Any time spent in his presence is agony for me!"

"I have told Mr. Sanger you will be free today, and by God, girl," his voice raised slightly, "you will be free and show him our ranch." He looked down at her decolletage and back up at her face and hair. "You wouldn't embarrass me by refusing, would you, Lindsay? No, I'm sure you wouldn't do that to your old uncle." He lifted his cup of coffee and took a long swallow. "Besides which, you certainly didn't dress like that for me, did you?" He smiled warmly but something in his attitude puzzled Lindsay.

After several seconds of silence Lindsay relaxed slightly and smiled. "Well, Uncle Ned, if anybody could talk the devil into giving up his pitchfork, you could do it. I'll show Mr. Sanger around but I guarantee you this . . . we will not come back friends and perhaps even stronger enemies." She stood up, smiled brightly at her uncle and walked out the door.

Ned turned to the window and watched her walk to the barn. "I hope I haven't made a terrible mistake. Dear God,

I hope I'm doing the right thing."

Lindsay walked into the barn and sat on a bale of hay. Deep in thought, she was not aware of the man standing in the doorway until he spoke.

"Good morning, ma'am. Are you ready for the grand tour?"

Lindsay jumped and tensed when she recognized Lucas's voice. Taking a deep breath, she drawled, "I'm as ready as I'll ever be."

Lucas walked to her and helped her up, his eyes boldly sweeping her body. A lazy smile appeared on his face as he surveyed her amply displayed cleavage.

"Must you always make a girl feel undressed, Mr. Sanger?" Lindsay stood rigid, watching him feast on her beauty.

"Only when the girl is already partially undressed," he replied laughing deeply as her face turned a rosy hue. She turned to the door and walked out, anger seething from every pore as Lucas's deep laughter bounced around her.

I promised Uncle Ned I'd show this man around and I will. But this is the last time I'll ever speak to Lucas Sanger, she thought to herself angrily as she stomped toward the buckboard.

"I suggest you take a shawl, Lindsay. We may be in for a storm." Lucas's voice drawled behind her. She jumped. She hadn't heard him walk up.

"Why are we going in that?" She pointed to the buckboard, then smiled shyly at Jonas who stood holding the pawing horse. "I thought we'd be riding."

"Now, ma'am, how did you expect to ride in that outfit?" He nodded his head at her. "Besides, this way I can sit closer to you." He smiled broadly again as Lindsay blushed profusely, her cheeks the color of burnished copper.

Damn! Why do I keep blushing in front of him? He only needs to look at me wrong and I turn crimson! Her thoughts whirled around in her head as she stood looking at the little wagon. The brown gelding nervously pawed the ground and lifted his head to sniff the approaching storm. He seemed to be telling them to hurry up . . . get a move on . . . I want to be back in my stall before it rains.

Ricco came out from the house with a shawl tossed across his shoulder. He smiled at Lindsay as he wrapped it tenderly around her. "Thank you, Ricco" she breathed, but she was perplexed at all this sudden attention. Jonas stood holding the horse's head, watching Lindsay intently, a touch of sadness in his eyes. Uncle Ned stood on the porch, his hands shoved deep in his pockets, his face waxen, his eyes shifting from Lucas to Lindsay.

Shrugging, Lindsay climbed into the wagon with the help of Lucas and turned to look at her uncle again. Maybe I've upset them by being so obstinate about showing Lucas around. No! Surely, they wouldn't show so much concern over a small thing like that. She shook her head as though to clear a clinging cobweb. Something is wrong! She looked back at her uncle. He hadn't moved. Ricco stood beside him but neither man spoke. They continued to stare at her. Jonas shifted slightly and Lindsay turned her attention on him. He moved back, partially hidden behind the horse. Lindsay thought she saw him wipe his eyes with his free hand.

Just then Zuni ran breathlessly out of the house carrying a large basket covered with a white cloth. She handed the bulging basket to Lucas and turned to Lindsay, smiling sadly. A tear slid from the corner of her eye as she turned and hurriedly entered the house. Ned frowned at Zuni as she passed him. Then, he quickly looked back at Lindsay and smiled warmly.

Lucas climbed onto the seat beside Lindsay, took the reins and slapped them against the horse's flanks. The horse leaped forward. Jonas moved back. As the little wagon lurched forward Lindsay looked back over her shoulder and blew a kiss to her uncle. "See you at dinner," she called.

"Yes, honey, see you at dinner." But Ned's voice was strained and as he turned to enter the house, Lindsay saw a tear slide down his cheek. She looked up at Lucas who was intently watching the horizon, a muscle in his cheek flexing. She turned and looked back at the house. Ned, Jonas, Ricco, and Zuni were all standing on the proch watching her departure. She waved happily and they all waved back. She looked again at the road in front of her and frowned. What was going on? She ran her fingers through her hair and sighed deeply. It must be her imagination. No . . . those were tears on her uncle's face.

She looked out over the green meadows and the cattle contendly grazing on the sweet grass. She could see Regalo throwing his head around, the wind blowing his glorious mane. He always acted up when a storm approached. She smiled as she watched him turn toward the barn and gallop off. One would almost think he was a chicken. She giggled at this thought.

Lucas looked at her. The wind blew her hair around her face and her cheeks were pink and slightly windburned. She looked very beautiful and desirable and he found himself hard-pressed to keep from taking her in his arms right then and making love to her.

"What are you giggling at, *niña*?" His voice brought Lindsay from her reverie and she clasped her hands together in her lap as she answered, "Nothing." She raised her face to the wind and breathed in the fresh air. They rode in silence after that. For several minutes Lindsay thought seriously about jumping down and running back to her uncle. She had a premonition that something was wrong.

Well, I'll talk to him after dinner . . . I'll talk to all of them after dinner, she thought.

Chapter 5

"Lindsay, I asked, which way do we go?"

Lucas reached his hand out and touched her cheek. She jumped and stammered, "Huh, oh, uh, that way, I think." She pointed a pink-tipped finger to the left and Lucas smiled as he slapped the reins on the horse. The buckboard lurched forward and Lindsay lost her balance and fell against the side of the buckboard. Lucas reached out, grabbed her arm, and pulled her against his chest.

"Damnit, Lindsay, what are you trying to do—get yourself killed? Pay attention and for Christ's sake, hold on!" Lindsay stiffened at his words and pulled away from his grasp. She wiped her hands on her dress, pulled the shawl from her shoulders, and wiped the clinging sweat and dust from her face. She felt as though she were several pieces of a puzzle and the center piece was missing. She felt out of place. Wrong! She couldn't continue to dwell on this feeling. She must shake whatever had hold of her and show Mr. Sanger around the ranch. After all, hadn't she promised her uncle she would?

A field blazing with wild daisies caught her attention and she asked Lucas to stop. "I want to pick some for the dinner table." She jumped down from the wagon and ran into the field, holding her skirts up. Lucas watched her as she ran through the field gathering the bright flowers and holding them to her breast.

Dark clouds heaped in the sky, pushing the sun behind them as they covered the sky. The two people below them were oblivious to everything but their own thoughts. Lindsay's thoughts were on gathering a large bouquet of flowers for her uncle . . . Lucas's thoughts were on the girl picking the flowers. How beautiful she was and yet so unaware of her beauty. He frowned. This was going to be no easy job. Protecting her would mean he couldn't let his guard down for one second at any time. If he did, it could mean her life as well as his.

A rumble of thunder made them both look up. Their thoughts returned to the present as Lindsay ran for the wagon and Lucas reached down to help her up. She held the batch of flowers close to her breast and sniffed their lovely fragrance as Lucas wrapped her shawl around her shoulders. She buried her face in the flowers to hide her blushing face from Lucas's view. Every time he touched her, she seemed to blush.

He, however, was more intent on the impending storm than on her and, as the horse trotted off, Lucas spoke.

"I think I know a place where we can shelter from the weather." He looked to the sky. "I have a feeling this is gonna be one hell of a storm."

The wagon bounced along the dirt path as thunder rolled and lightning seared the sky. The first drops of rain fell as they rounded a bend and Lindsay saw the shelter Lucas was talking about. An old dilapidated, abandoned miner's shack beckoned to them from under the shelter of lofty pines. Its shutters hung crookedly, the windows were shattered, and the chimney was missing several stones—but the roof seemed sturdy and at least it would keep them dry. Lindsay remembered playing here many times and wondered how Lucas knew about this place. Then the sky opened up and it poured with rain.

Lindsay jumped from the wagon. With her shawl over her head and the flowers securely in her hand, she ran into the shack. Lucas untied the horse from the buckboard and tied him behind the shack where he would have some shelter from the wind and grass to graze on. Then he grabbed the basket Zuni had given them and joined Lindsay inside.

The dirt floor of the shack had once been covered with wooden planks but the years of neglect had caused them to rot. The rotting wood and dirt mixed together gave the shack a musty, dank smell. The wind whistled through the shattered windows and filled the shack with an eerie sound. Lindsay shivered. Lucas shook his hat then ran his hands through his wet hair, which was plastered to his head. An old table, the legs long ago rotted off with age, leaned against a wall. Two chairs lay against the table, their wood peeling off. Lucas broke up the chairs and laid them in the fireplace. He kicked the table with the heel of his boot and it crumbled into several pieces. He laid these on top of the wood in the fireplace and struck a match to the wood.

"Rotten wood doesn't burn real good but at least it'll give us some warmth."

Lindsay watched him as he hunkered down by the fireplace, blowing and forcing flames to engulf the wood. His wet shirt clung to his skin and the muscles underneath bulged and danced in the firelight. After being satisfied the fire was burning he turned and reached a hand to Lindsay. She walked to him and stood watching the flames as Lucas briskly rubbed her shoulders and arms with her shawl.

"Are you going to hold those flowers all day?"

She looked down and realized she was gripping the bouquet tightly to her breast as though sheltering her bare skin from his gaze. He laughed deeply as he turned to the basket sitting by the door. He picked up the basket and walked back to the fire. A blanket hung across his arm and he spread it out before the fire. He set the basket down and beckoned for Lindsay to join him. She did so asking, "Where did you get the blanket?"

"It was in the buckboard. Your uncle thought of everything." Again that portent of something being amiss tugged at Lindsay. She shivered and she laid the flowers beside her. Lucas reached over and pulled the shawl closer around her shoulders. "Can't have you catching a cold. Your uncle would never let me use you as a tour guide agan."

Lindsay looked up at him sharply. "I assure you, Mr. Sanger, this is the last tour you will have by me. Perhaps the next time you wish a tour, Zuni can guide you."

Lucas laughed heartily at her remark. But preferring not to argue with her now, he said nothing further and proceeded to place the food Zuni had packed for them on the blanket between them. After eating ham sandwiches, fresh fruit, and chocolate cake, Lucas poured each of them a glass of white wine. Lindsay sipped her wine and soon the effects of the warm fire, the food, and the wine took hold. She laid her head down on the blanket.

"How did you know about this place?"

"I don't remember. I guess I spotted it one day while riding by here." His eyes rested on her breasts which swelled enticingly above the décolletage.

The rain spattered on the roof and the window sills, entered through the broken windows, and pounded furiously on the floor. Lightning streaked the sky and thunder echoed through the valley.

With the warmth of the fire, the monotonous sound of the rain, and the effects of the wine Lindsay found it difficult to stay awake. But when she looked up at Lucas, he too seemed to be having the same problem. His arms rested on his knees and his head hung down. Feeling no need to apologize for napping, she wrapped the shawl around her and slept.

Lucas slowly opened his eyes and peered at her. He waited until he was sure she was asleep, then gathered up the remaining food and put it back in the basket. He checked the rest of the contents and smiled. He went out, untied the horse, turned him toward the ranch and slapped his soundly on his flanks. As the horse galloped off, the sound of approaching horses could be heard. Lucas looked in their direction and returned to Lindsay. She slept soundly. Her shawl had fallen open and her breasts rose and fell with each breath. Her hair fell around her face and shoulders and one hand lay next to her face, curled in a tight little fist while the other hand clutched a flower. Lucas bent down to her, picked a curl off her breast, and touched his lips to it. He reached for the basket and turned to the door. Then he stopped, returned to Lindsay, picked a flower from her bouquet and tossed it under the cloth covering the basket. Then he walked to the open door and handed the basket to a man.

Lindsay woke with a start and blinked her eyes several times. She wondered what had woken her so abruptly. She sat up clutching the shawl around her shoulders as she realized the storm continued to rage outside and she was quite cold. She looked at the fireplace. A few dying embers sparked and popped but there was no warmth left. She turned to look outside when she saw the door open. She began to get up. She hollered for Lucas but only a strangled sound came out as she fell forward. Her head slammed on the floor as she realized someone had hit her.

Then blackness laced with pain descended upon her and removed her senses.

* * *

Lindsay opened her eyes, blinked once, then closed them again. She moaned, then raised her hand to her head. Someone grabbed her by the arms and forced them behind her and tied her wrists tightly. She winced with pain and through a hazy film heard a voice.

"Damnit, she ain't big enough to do much. You don't have to be so goddamn rough!"

Lucas! That was Lucas's voice! She opened her mouth to call him but someone tied a gag over her lips, choking off sound and again hurting her. A sob came to her lips but because of the gag it came out a whispered choke. A hand touched her cheek softly, then brushed the hair back from her face. "You're all right, Lindsay?"

A man yelled and Lucas answered him.

"Yeah, she's ready. Let's get the hell outa here."

The sound of men yelling, horses whinnying, and whips cracking rang through the air as Lindsay suddenly realized she was in a covered wagon. She tried to move but each movement brought pain so she lie still . . . waiting. Then soft lips touched her ear and ever so softly came the words. "Trust me, Lindsay." A tender kiss on her earlobe brought a strangled sound to her throat. Then Lucas was gone and she could hear his horse gallop off.

* * *

Lindsay opened her eyes and the sun burned through her senses and blinded her momentarily. Suddenly strong arms encircled her, lifted her into a sitting position against a wooden box, and removed the gag. She was given a cool drink of water and her face was wiped with a cool cloth. Her head had stopped its violent spinning and she was beginning to think more clearly. She looked into Lucas's concerned face as he continued to stroke her face with a cloth. Her arms were numb from being tied so long and tears of pain and frustration clung to her eyelashes.

"Please, Lucas, please," she whispered through swollen lips. "Please, don't do this."

A flask was held to her lips and her head was forced back as the fiery liquid burned a path down her throat and into her belly. She was forced to take another swallow, then Lucas lifted her, and laid her on a bedroll. He sat beside her, smoothing her hair back from her face, stroking her cheeks and watching her. She stared up at him. She couldn't believe he was doing this to her. And what *was* he doing to her? Her mind was racing in so many directions. As she stared at him, everything began to spin. His face became two, then one, then three. Closer, then farther away. She felt as though she was falling . . . falling down a long dark tunnel. She could hear Lucas's voice a long, long way off.

"She'll sleep for several hours now. Let's get going and put some distance between us and her uncle."

* * *

From a long way off a voice was urging her to open her eyes. "Come on, *Niña,* wake up." A wet cloth briskly rubbed her face and the voice continued, "Come on, niña, I have some food for you."

Slowly, very slowly, her senses came back. The pain in her arms returned and now was almost unbearable. Her head ached and her lips and mouth were dry. Her eyes felt like two boulders were holding them closed. "Come on, niña, open your eyes, you can do it." Slowly her lids opened and her eyes focused on the man above her. Lucas!

She tried to speak but only strangled sounds came out. Lucas lifted her in his arms and stood her on her feet. Her legs crumbled and she fell into his waiting arms. "Come on, niña, try to stand. Try to wake up." She rested against his chest and her breathing was uneven as Lucas rubbed her back. Then he drew a knife from the inside of his boot and cut her bonds. He laid her on the bedroll and rubbed her wrists, working the feeling back into them. When the blood rushed back to her stiff arms she groaned with pain and, unable to take any more, began to cry. Sobs shook her small frame. Lucas held her close and said nothing until her tears were spent. Then, when she couldn't cry another tear and her senses had returned somewhat, he fed her. The hot stew tasted good but she was not hungry. She turned her head away. Lucas gently but forcefully made her eat more. She gagged and pushed at his hands but to no avail. He continued to force the hot liquid between her bruised lips. "One more bite, niña." Finally, after Lindsay thought he would choke her with the stew, he laid her back on the bedroll and stayed by her side, caressing her face, stroking her sore arms until she slept.

* * *

How long she slept she had no idea, only that she had been in and out of awareness, climbing to an awake state only to plunge down to unconsciousness. Why she kept vacillating between sleep and wakefulness she didn't know until she heard someone say she didn't need to be drugged any more. Lucas! That's what he kept forcing her to drink. Drugged wine! No wonder she felt so terrible. Oh, God! What was happening?

As her senses came back and her mind cleared, she began to feel more frightened than she had been since that fateful day so long ago when her parents were killed. She was sure of only one thing . . . Lucas was responsible for whatever was happening to her. She lay on her bedroll and looked down at her clothes. Her pretty white dress was ruined. For some reason, she didn't understand, this made her angry and in her anger she found strength. She peered through the laced canvas to catch a glimpse of the driver of her wagon but only a sliver of dreary light came through. The wagon rolled and lurched along and she tried to stand. But weakness and motion kept her from standing so she crawled to the back of the wagon. The opening was uncovered and she was determined to look out and see where she was. She was pulling herself up to the opening when two men riding alongside drew the canvas closed and laced it. She heard laughter and a bawdy remark, but anger kept her from caring what they said.

"If I live through this, I'll see Lucas Sanger hang. Uncle Ned will believe me." She closed her eyes as she thought of her uncle. He would be frantic with worry and grief. He would probably search until he either found her or dropped in his tracks. Lindsay could withstand almost any tribulation, but hurting her uncle left her beaten. She bowed her head as the tears fell freely onto her dirty dress. She cried. Finally exhausted and weakened by the drugs, she slept.

Hands shook her awake. Alarmed, Lindsay opened her eyes and focused on Lucas.

"I'm glad to see you're feeling better, niña, I was beginning to worry." He stood and reached down to pull her to her feet. She staggered, her legs still weak, but when Lucas reached out to hold her, she pushed him away and leaned against the canvas side.

"Don't ever touch me again," she whispered between swollen lips. The tone with which she spoke was so filled with hatred that Lucas winced. He knew what she thought. But to be safe, then she must continue thinking just that way. It was a little sacrifice. Her hatred for him versus her life! After this was over . . . well . . . then he would tell her the truth.

He grabbed her arm and pulled her to the back of the wagon. He jumped down, then reached up for her. She backed away from him but not before he snatched a handful of her dress and pulled her forward, throwing her off balance. She fell forward and Lucas caught her. He lifted her down and set her on her feet. She stood for several seconds, weaving, drunk with weakness and fatigue. He watched her, his arms ready to catch her if she fell, but determination won out and she walked slowly backward, away from Lucas.

"Come on, Lindsay, you can't escape my touching you so why try?" He took hold of her hand and pulled her along, away from the wagon and toward a campfire. She shook her head. This dizziness was making her sick. How long before she'd regain her strength, she wondered?

A pot of some bubbling concoction perched in the fire and the odor emanating from inside made Lindsay's mouth water. She was hungry . . . so hungry she felt sick. Maybe eating would help to clear her mind. A man stood over the pot and every few minutes he would stir the interior with a long-handled spoon. She looked around her. They were in a small clearing, surrounded by pine trees, and thick with musty smelling ground cover. Lucas's horse was tethered off to the side of the camp and, other than the man tending the cooking pot, she could see no one else.

The sky was clear. The sun hung low over the horizon and the air was refreshingly cool. She moved to the fire and sat on the hard ground. A hand touched her and she jumped. Lucas held a bowl of bubbling stew under her nose and the delicious smell made Lindsay's stomach growl hungrily.

She ate heartily and looked up once to see Lucas sitting under a tree watching her. With the setting sun and the trees shadowing the camp, Lindsay couldn't see the cook's face clearly. She suspected he was older as he walked with a limp and moved haltingly. Neither Lucas nor the cook had bothered to speak to her since feeding her.

After eating another helping of the stew, she was offered a cup of coffee and took it eagerly. She leaned against a tree and sipped the strong brew slowly, staring into the cup and wondering what to do about this desperate situation she was in. Her head had cleared considerably. The dizziness was diminishing and the pain in her arms was slowly lessening.

"Would you like to take a walk?" Lucas stood over her, his legs apart, his hands resting on his hips. Lindsay looked up at him. She clenched her teeth and turned her gaze away. "No . . . I mean, no, thank you." She sipped her coffee.

"I think you need a walk, niña." He reached down and pulled her to her feet. She spilled her coffee and turned on him with the vengeance of a cornered bear with cubs.

"Now look what you've done, you, you, woman stealer. You've kidnapped me, tied me, hurt me, ruined my clothes, probably killed my Uncle Ned . . . Oh, I wish you were dead. Yes, I wish you were *dead*." Her eyes were bright with unshed tears and her hands were clenched in tight fists, aching to pummel his face, scratch his eyes out. She threw the empty cup at him, turned angrily toward the wagon and stomped off. Lucas chuckled. He was glad to see the old Lindsay returning. "Fire and Ice." She was sure she could take care of herself in any situation, including one like this. He smiled at her receding back and then with a shrug, followed her.

"Would you like a bath, niña?"

Lindsay stopped dead. Had she heard right? Was this mad man proposing she bathe out here in the middle of God knows where and with strange men all around. She whirled on him and with her fingers spread, she attacked him, reaching for his face . . . trying to scratch his eyes out, hurt him, draw blood, as he had done to her. But her wrists were grasped and drawn behind her and held tightly. A deep laugh escaped Lucas's throat as he looked down into her face. He held her tightly against his chest, her arms pinned behind her. When she tried to kick him betwen the legs, he held her leg between his with his thighs.

The contact of their bodies had an effect Lindsay was not prepared for. She felt as though an electric shock coursed through her body. She weakened and Lucas felt her body go lax. But he did not release her. He held her closer and with his free hand, he raised her face to his. Her face was dirty and bruised. Her lips were swollen but her eyes were magnificently bright and clear. The few stars beginning to peep through the lazy clouds were dim in comparison to her eyes.

"Would you like me to escort you to the river to bathe, niña?"

The teasing note in his voice incensed Lindsay, but for some reason she could not react. Held close to him like this she felt weak . . . so weak. Yet it was a strong weakness. One she enjoyed—not hated.

After a tremendous effort she pushed herself free of Lucas. She staggered backward, her hand at her throat, her breath coming in jagged gasps. But Lucas slowly approached her, stalking her. That's what he reminded her of . . . a stalking cat. She backed slowly, carefully away from him until the wagon stopped her progress. She watched him warily, unsure of what he was going to do. He smiled at her . . . a devilish grin . . . and his eyes twinkled in the diminishing light. She wasn't sure what she was going to do, but one thing she knew for sure. She mustn't let him touch her. As long as he didn't touch her she could think straight. But as soon as he touched her, she weakened. She became jelly. For some reason, his touch caused feelings in her she had never before known. She watched warily, waiting for her chance to escape. He was within arms length now. If she kicked him between the legs she could duck his grasp and escape. She waited for the right moment. Barely breathing, the moment came when he leaned forward to place his hand on either side of her, imprisoning her between his arms. She kicked out but Lucas was prepared. He jumped to the side and Lindsay's foot touched air. Before she could regain her balance Lucas leaned against her, holding her tightly against the wagon. After she wore herself out struggling, he spoke,

"Do you really think you can fight me, niña? I outweigh you twice over. Now, really, why continue this constant struggling? Relax. Enjoy. I guarantee it'll be easier on you."

"Oh . . . you . . . damn . . ." but the sentence disappeared as his lips came down on hers, softly searching. He nibbled on her bottom lip, then kissed her again. Hard. His tongue forced its way into her mouth and Lindsay began to kiss him back. A flicker of desire grew and burst into a flame as she relaxed in his arms. He brought out feelings in her she had never known possible. She didn't want him to stop.

Then, like a dash of cold water, she remembered her uncle, wiping a tear from his cheek. She jumped to awareness and began to push at Lucas. But that was like pushing against a brick wall. She went limp and fell to the ground. Lucas wasn't expecting this and jumped back. That gave her the advantage and she leaped to her feet and ran to the back of the wagon, climbing in with all her strength and cowering in the far corner, away from view.

Lucas smiled at her clever ploy. "One day, niña, I'm gonna tame you." And he turned to walk to the fire.

Lindsay cowered in the corner of the wagon. Her heart beat so furiously she was sure Lucas could hear it. She sat stock still for several seconds waiting, listening for his approach. When she heard no footfalls, she mentally shook herself and stood up. She had never been so affected, so weakened by a man's touch. He only need look at her with his dark, searching eyes and she became weak. *I'm unable to fight against the feelings he causes in me. I mustn't let him touch me. As long as I'm not in his arms, I can think clearly.* But, oh God! How those arms affected her! His lips could bring her cold emotions to the surface, boiling with response and then bubbling over with desire. Why? Why this man?

Her mind filled with tortuous thoughts of her uncle. How long before someone found her and then . . . then . . . a fight. And knowing Lucas, it would be to the death. But whose death? She shook her head. *I can't allow myself to think of that. I won't think of that.* Somewhere down deep in the dark recesses of her mind she knew that if there was a fight to the death, somehow Lucas would be the victor. And for some reason, very puzzling to her, she didn't want to see Lucas or her uncle fight. She did not understand her reasoning. She hated Lucas. Why not death? That would surely solve this problem.

She walked to the back of the wagon and cautiously peered out. The sun had disappeared but its final rays of golden light fell over the trees, giving them halos. It was quiet. The only sound was the campfire crackling and popping. Feeling braver, she stuck her head out and peered around the corner of the wagon.

"Well, niña, are you ready for a bath?" Lucas was leaning against the side of the wagon and grinned when he saw the startled expression on Lindsay's face. She pulled her head back and grasped the canvas, pulling it closed and holding it tight. Her shaking fingers were no match for Lucas's strong hands, as he pulled open the canvas and stood looking up at her. Quickly, Lindsay backed into the dark interior of the wagon, clumsily attempting to hide herself. Lucas pulled himself up and after allowing a few seconds for his eyes to adjust to the darkness, he approached her. Her outstretched arm stiffened as she backed up slowly, one hand behind her, feeling and groping for obstacles. Lucas laughed as he sat on a box and wiped his arm across his brow.

"Lindsay, I didn't come here to torment you. I know you're confused and hurt. But, niña, trust me . . . everything will be explained soon. Now, look at you! Have you taken a good look? Niña, you're really a sight. There's a spot close by where you can bathe . . . in privacy . . . and I'll give you something to put on that at least will be clean."

Lindsay stood against the wagon wall, her arm still outstretched, her eyes watching him warily. I mustn't let him touch me. Please don't touch me, Lucas. Her mind was jumbled with thoughts of his lips crushing her, his arms holding her tight. How could a person hate someone with so much vengeance and yet . . . yet . . . be so attracted to him? Her eyes were large and her heart beat rapidly as she answered. "I . . . I . . . as long as I can bathe in private

". . . I would like that." Her arm slowly lowered but she kept her eyes on his face. "Just show me the way and I'll only be a few minutes."

Lucas pushed his hat back and stood up. "Sorry, niña, privacy you'll have from everyone but me. My job is to guard you and that means all the time." There was no playfulness in his voice.

He bent to the basket Zuni had packed for them that fateful day. The sight of it brought memories rushing to the surface and spilling over her mind.

"Lucas, how long have I been here or gone from my home? Everything is so fuzzy." She looked down at her skirt and gently touched a rip. "Where are we?"

Lucas bent over the basket searching its contents, "We have been traveling for four days." He found what he had been looking for and turned to her. "Don't ask any more questions, niña." Lindsay's face was a kaleidoscope of emotions, fear, anger, worry. Lucas smiled at her, wanting very much to comfort her. Holding out his hand to her he continued, "Come on." She made no move to leave her corner. Finally Lucas walked to her, grabbed her hand and pulled her to the entrance. He leaped to the ground effortlessly. Then, after throwing the package he held on the ground, he reached up to lift her down. She stood still, as if in a daze, staring down at Lucas as he reached up and lifted her to the ground. He bent to pick up the package, then holding her hand securely he led her away.

For the past four days Lindsay had been drugged, unable to decipher reality from imagination. Her body ached, her head hurt and she was puzzled and very, very frightened. But for some reason, as Lucas pulled her along to wherever he was taking her, her mind snapped and she realized she had to save herself. She must regain her senses and form a plan. A plan of escape! Yes, that's what she had to do . . . escape. The word tasted good in her mind. Sweet as she rolled it over and over in her thoughts. She had been raised to take care of herself. She could ride and shoot a gun and probably a lot more if she had to. She rubbed her hands together mentally as a small smile touched her lips. With this renewed strength she also found her tongue. She stopped abruptly, startling Lucas, and attempted to push his hand from her wrist. His iron grip held her tight and, although he did not hurt her, she could not break his grip. She looked up at him and spat, "Get your hands off me! I can walk without your assistance!" Lucas shrugged his shoulders, turned back in the direction of the river and continued to pull her along. She tried again to break loose but it was no use.

They walked through trees so thick the lower branches hung limply from lack of sun. Dead branches would grab at Lindsay's bruised legs but Lucas pulled her on. After a breathless trek, Lucas stopped abruptly and released her wrist. She began to rub her arm, then stopped as she spied the river.

The river moved heavily, its surface reflecting gems of dying sunlight against its deep green current. Its shorelines were strewn with huge boulders, the most brilliant red she had ever seen. Squealing with anticipation she ran forward and splashed into the cold water. She threw handfuls of water over her shoulders and hair, flapping her arms, and throwing her head back and laughing.

Lucas watched her. As the water soaked her dress, making it cling revealingly to her every curve, he began to feel desire grow, desire such as he had never known before. He sat on a rock and began to remove his boots and shirt. Lindsay was too enthralled with her game to pay any attention to her captor. The cool water cleared out the final cobwebs in her brain and gave her added strength. She splashed handfuls of water of her face. The water dripped down between her breasts and her skin glowed with moisture in the fading sunlight. Lucas's desire would have been evident to Lindsay had she paid any attention to him. But she was too engrossed in her play. She laid back and floated, her hair fanned out behind her and sparkled like liquid gold as it undulated. She closed her eyes and relaxed in the water. A splash startled her and she clumsily turned over to see what Lucas was doing. She had forgotten about him.

He stood on the shore laughing, his chest bare and droplets of moisture clung to his brown skin. His hands were on his hips as he stood watching her. Her eyes studied him with admiration in them. The muscles in his arms flexed and relaxed as he began to remove his belt. His chest rose and fell with each breath and Lindsay's fingers opened and closed as she wondered what it would feel like to caress those muscles.

"There's some soap, niña." He pointed to a small bar floating beside her. She reached for it and laid her head back in the water, too lazy to do anything but luxuriate in this feeling. She was so engrossed in her thoughts she heard nothing until another splash disturbed her reverie.

She began to lift her head when something caught her around the waist and pulled her down . . . down . . . under the dark, cool water. Unprepared and shocked, she gulped in a mouthful of water and began to choke. Lucas's strong arms lifted her above the water and she gulped in air, coughing and sputtering. After she stopped coughing, Lucas lowered her into the water and held her close. His hands caressed her back, her arms, and her wet clinging hair. He took her face between his hands and tilted it up. The world stopped . . . all movement ceased, as these two wet people stared into each other's eyes. Lucas's eyes hungrily searched the depths of Lindsay's as though trying to read her innermost thoughts. Lindsay reached her hands up and covered Lucas's strong fingers with her small ones.

Lucas's breathing was heavy, uneven as he continued to peer down at the wet woman in his arms. Lindsay's breath came in short, jagged gasps as she tried to decide between getting away from him and staying in his embrace. Then, unexpectedly, Lucas released her, turned sharply and dove into the water. Lindsay stood for a few seconds, her legs rubber, her thoughts confused as she watched for him to surface. When he broke water several yards downstream, she turned slowly and spied the bar of soap floating nearby. She grabbed it and walked slowly to the shore. She soaped her face and arms and scrubbed them until they glowed. Then, entering the water again she soaped her hair. After being uncombed for so long, she had to shampoo it four times to remove all the dirt. But when she had finished, her hair shined in cleanliness and she left the river. She looked around for something to dry with but saw only the tied package Lucas had brought. She picked it up and after a struggle to untie it she rolled back the brown paper and gasped when she saw the contents. Her hands went to her mouth and she felt weak and bewildered. The package contained her clothes!

There was a dress, a pair of jeans, a shirt, and a chemise. A pair of old, worn boots lay underneath and a brush and comb. She reached out a shaking finger and lightly touched the clothing. She must be dreaming! Where did these come from? Who packed them?

Her body was convulsed with trembling when Lucas's arms went around her and pulled her back against his wet chest. He lowered his face to her head, kissing her hair. "Now you'll have something clean and dry to wear."

But Lindsay was in no mood for games. She pulled away abruptly and turned to face him, her hands akimbo, her mouth set in a grim line.

"Where in hell did these come from?" Her voice was low and Lucas knew she was on the verge of hysteria. He had to say something that sounded believable.

"I had your uncle pack these extra things in case we couldn't find shelter from the storm that day. I also thought we might do some hiking if we felt like it."

Lindsay stood listening. Her head tilted, her muscles taut with anger. Maybe he was telling the truth. He had to be telling the truth. If he wasn't . . . well, that meant someone —Zuni or Uncle Ned or someone she loved knew about her abduction. No, he was *not* lying. He probably did think they might climb the hills or ride or who knows what. For now she would give him the benefit of the doubt, but she still would not trust him. She would never trust him. Lucas breathed a sigh of relief as Lindsay relaxed.

She bent down to gather the jeans and shirt and turned to find shelter to change. Lucas folded his arms across his chest as he spoke.

"Why not change here? Your dress leaves little to my imagination and I'll be happy to help." She glared at him with half-closed eyes and then stomped off toward a clump of trees behind some rocks. Lucas's laughter reverberated in her ears as she walked into the shelter and quickly changed. The pants were large as she had lost a little weight. But they were clean and warm. Her shirt clung alluringly to her damp skin and its rust color accentuated Lindsay's cheek color.

As she walked back to Lucas she held the front of the pants together and wondered what she woud do to keep them from falling to her feet. Lucas looked up as she approached and realizing her problem, grabbed a piece of the rope that had bound the package. He beckoned for her to come closer but she stood her ground.

"Damnit, Lindsay, I'm getting tired of your stubbornness." He reached her in two long strides and holding the rope in one hand he grabbed her arm with the other. She stepped back and he yelled, "Hold still!"

She stood watching him, chewing on her bottom lip as he fed the rope through the belt loops, pulling it tight in front, then tied it in a knot.

"There, now you can use your hands for something other than holding up your pants." He handed her the boots, then walked to pick up her wet clothing she had left behind the rocks.

It was dark now and the moon was beginning to peep at them from the horizon. Lucas gathered up their belongings and reaching out he took hold of Lindsay's hand and again pulled her along.

Soon the campfire was visible through the trees and Lindsay gasped at the number of men sitting around it. She didn't recognize any of them. The firelight played on their faces and turned them into strange and eerie creatures. A shiver of fear ran down Lindsay's spine. Lucas, aware of her fear, squeezed her hand tightly as he led her to the fire.

As they approached the fire Lindsay recognized the two men who had laced up the back of her wagon and the cook, but the rest . . . well . . . she was glad she hadn't seen them before. They were a dreadful looking group and Lindsay's fear began to grow.

The men looked up as Lindsay and Lucas drew nearer.

"Well, well, will you look at that!"

"Yeah, I'm looking—I'm looking and maybe this job ain't gonna be so bad after all!"

Lindsay did not see the muscles of Lucas's face tense but she felt his grip tighten on her arm. She turned to him and whispered, "Does it give you pleasure to hurt me? Or are you trying to show off in front of your friends?" Lucas slackened his grip and after a few seconds he dropped her arm, walked to the coffee pot and poured a mug of steaming coffee. He watched her over the rim of his cup for a few seconds, then turned, strode to the shadows, and leaned against a tree.

Lindsay looked at her captors. After a few minutes of silence, feeling like a slave on an auction block, she asked, "Is someone going to tell me what is going on? I hope you all realize my uncle will see you hang for this!" Her voice raised slightly as she played with the rope around her waist to still her shaking hands.

"Come on over here, little gal, and let me tell you what's going on. Better yet, let me show you." The man chuckled and Lindsay shivered. But not from the cool breeze. Angered and embarassed she turned to walk to the wagon. She had just begun to enter when someone grabbed her and picked her up off the ground. She screamed and kicked but her captor only laughed. Whoever had her in his clutches was carrying her to the underbrush. A sickness permeated her. She saw no movement but the next thing she knew she was lying on the ground and beside her lay the man who had carried her off.

"Our job is to escort the lady to Mexico, Blackmore, not use her. She'll be of no use if she's hurt. You lay another hand on her and I'll kill you!" Lucas stood over them, his hands on his gunbelt, the firelight reflecting from the icy blueness of his eyes. Breathing had seemed to stop as all eyes were centered on Lucas and Blackmore. After several seconds, Blackmore relaxed and moved to get up. A foot on his chest prevented him from moving. He looked up at Lucas who was smiling down at him. "I mean what I say, Blackmore. I'll kill you if you touch her again." Lucas frightened the man and he slowly nodded his head.

Lucas turned to the other men and spoke, "That goes for all of you. If any one of you lays a hand on her, you'll reckon with me. We're to escort her—not use her for pleasure." He turned and held out his hand to Lindsay. She reached up and he pulled her to her feet but he kept his eyes on Blackmore. He placed Lindsay in front of him and, turning to the wagon, escorted her from the frightening scene. He lifted her into the dark interior and she could hear his footsteps fade.

She sat on the bedroll and before she knew why, tears were coursing down her cheeks making rivulets onto her breasts. Suddenly she heard a noise and afraid it was Blackmore, she hugged the side of the wagon trying to hide from his view.

She saw movement through the slit in the canvas. She straightened slightly and peered into the darkness, squinting hard. Lucas was smoothing a place on the ground to sleep. He cleared away some rocks and placed his saddle near the rear wagon wheel. He laid down and rested his head on his saddle. He couldn't see into the wagon but he knew she was watching him. He smiled and whispered to her, "Someone has to make sure you don't sneak away during the night." He rolled over and soon Lindsay could hear his breathing, deep in sleep. She knew he wasn't worried about her escaping as much as he was worried about the other men coming to her. But she was puzzled. Why should he care about her? After all, if it hadn't been for him, she wouldn't be here in the first place. Sighing, she laid her head down and covered herself with a blanket. She could feel the warmth of the wool around her. The fire crackled lightly. She felt strangely secure and drifted to sleep.

Chapter 6

The sun sprinkled through the opening at the back of the wagon and played on Lindsay's face. Slowly, her senses returned as the smell of coffee and cooking ham drifted from the campfire. She rolled over and relished the warm sun on her face. Then it dawned on her where she was. She sat up and rubbed the sleep from her eyes. Maybe today I'll find out what's going on.

Lucas opened the canvas just then and handed in a tin plate filled with bacon, beans, and muffins. She reached for the plate and a cup of steaming coffee and ate ravenously. Lucas watched her for a moment, then turned and walked off.

She stared at her empty plate. She needed to take a walk but she was afraid to ask Lucas. She was too embarrassed to tell him the real reason and yet, necessity was a powerful antidote to shyness. She leaned out and looked around the corner of the wagon for Lucas. He was talking to man by the fire. Seeing her from the corner of his eye he turned to face her and a smile came to his lips. He walked to her and lifted her to the ground.

"Would you like to take a walk?" Her face turned scarlet as she gulped, "Yes, alone if you don't mind!" He walked to the edge of a clump of trees holding her wrist securely. Then releasing her and turning his back, he whistled "Buffalo Jars" while Lindsay groped through the underbrush and trees.

He returned her to the wagon after her walk, and although she was weary with nothing to do, she knew it was safer in the wagon than in the open with the men. She sat on the floor deeply engrossed in her thoughts when the wagon lurched forward and she fell back. She was frightened, more frightened than she even wanted to admit. She had no idea what was going on, only that she heard Lucas tell Blackmore they were escorting her to Mexico. As the wagon began another days travel from her home, she began to feel real terror. She had believed yesterday that there would be an end to this nightmare. But this morning, as the wagon began making its jerky, creaking motions, she felt an overwhelming wave of futility touch her. The back of the wagon was again laced closed, blocking out the view. She laid on the floor, and placing her hands over her face, she wept.

After traveling what seemed to be an eternity to Lindsay, the wagon came to a creaking halt. Voices surrounded the wagon and soon the canvas was drawn back revealing a sinking sun. She sat up and stared at the opening. She could hear Lucas's deep voice talking in low tones to someone. She did not recognize the other voice, but, when he laughed, she was sure she had heard that laugh before.

Soon she could see Lucas's dark head bending over the entrance. He sprung lightly into the wagon and avoided looking at her. Another man followed. She gasped. "Nick Moriarity! What are you doing here?" She jumped up. "I don't think you understand what has happened to me!"

He sat on the side shelf and looked into her face. Lindsay shrank from the hate directed at her.

"I know just what's happening to you Miss Tyler." He spoke her name with a sneer. He put his hands on his knees and bent closer to her.

"I once told your uncle I would do anything . . . anything to get my ranch back. But I wasn't sure what lever I would use. Then, one day, after seeing you on the arm of your uncle, I knew." He shifted his weight and stretched his legs in front of him. Then he placed his hands behind his head and leered at her.

Lindsay clenched her hands, digging her fingernails into her palms. She mustn't lose her temper. She must remain calm and use her head. Now she knew why she was here. She was to be returned to her uncle in exchange for the ranch. She shivered as she spoke. "My uncle will never sell you the ranch!"

Nick laughed, throwing his head back. Then he narrowed his eyes and glared ar her, "Who the hell said anything about selling? He'll give it back to me, lock, stock, and barrel in return for you. If he wants you back alive, he'll do as I want or he ain't ever gonna see you again!"

Lindsay stood and rubbed her hands together, "Mr. Moriarity, I think you may have delusions clouding your thinking. My uncle will not deed you the Lazy Hat Ranch in return for me. He won't give up a lifetime of work and dedication to appease a madman's demented plan."

Before she finished, Moriarity stood and slapped her

across the face with a resounding crack. Lindsay fell back against the canvas and then onto the floor. She quickly regained her composure. Touching the growing welt on her cheek, she bit her lip, fighting back the tears that threatened to spill. She must never let these men see her cry. Slowly, she stood, glaring at Nick. Her eyes glistened as she parted her lips and moistened them with her tongue. She faced Nick with a wildly thumping heart. Rubbing her cheek, she spoke through clenched teeth, "If you ever do that again, Mr. Moriarity, I will somehow, find a way to kill you!" Her eyes were glacial as she watched him.

Lucas's hands were clenched at his sides, watching every movement made by Nick. He must not interfere. He couldn't let them think his prime concern was for Lindsay. To Nick, he must appear as though he is following his orders. He must act passive toward Lindsay. As passive as any man can be to a beautiful woman. If any suspicions were aroused his cards would all be out on the table and Lindsay might be left to the mercy of these men. She may be a hellcat, a spitfire, but she was no match for these bastards. No, he must play their game until it was time to show his hand.

Moriarity was watching Lindsay, his arms akimbo, his protuberant stomach heaving with each breath. He smiled and grabbed a handful of her hair and pulled her close to his face. His breath, hot and malodorous, touched her senses. She struggled to be free but he pulled her hair fiercely, seeming to enjoy her struggles. After a few moments he tired of watching her. Grabbing her face with his free hand, he squeezed her cheeks until tears came to her eyes.

"Now, little girl, you'll do as I say. If you want to stay alive you'll follow orders. If you should try to escape, let me warn you . . . escape would be an assinine thing to try. You wouldn't be successful, I guarantee. If, by some small chance, you should manage to slip through our fingers, I'll return to your ranch and kill your uncle. I ain't planned this venture only to have a simple-minded wench destroy it. So, my dear, I suggest you be a good girl, follow Sanger's orders and stay out of the way of my men. If you become, ah, burdensome, we'll hog-tie you to the back side of this wagon."

He released her and she gasped as she stumbled back. She rubbed her fingers over her cheek and with a caustic smile replied, "It must make you feel like a big man to be able to push me around. I'm sure you command great respect from your friends."

Moriarity turned to the entrance of the wagon and pushed back the canvas. He looked back at her and with a cruel grin spat, "Where you're going, little gal, the men respect me no matter what I do."

He jumped down and disappeared from view.

Lindsay watched him retreat, her eyes large and fear-filled. She collapsed on her bedroll, her face a mask of anguish, her body trembling. She had forgotten Lucas's presence and flinched when he placed his hand on her shoulder. She shrunk away from him as he bent down to look into her face. The welt on her cheek was dark red and impressions of fingermarks unevenly covered her face.

"I don't know what I've done to you or him to deserve this, but I hope you're both enjoying it." She spoke between sobs. Lucas stood, a muscle twitched in his cheek. His eyes were dark, unreadable as he gazed at her. Then, very lightly, he touched her hair, turned and jumped from the wagon.

Lindsay covered her face with a corner of the blanket and sobbed, long, heartbreaking sobs.

Lucas listened for several minutes fighting the urge to go back to her and take her in his arms. He wanted to explain everything. He gulped in the hot desert air, slowly exhaling, then turned to the campfire. Not until the right moment could he tell her the truth.

*　　*　　*

The next five days went by without incident. A traveling routine had settled in. They covered many miles each day and at night they would set up a camp, eat, and sleep. Lindsay left the wagon only to bathe and for personal reasons. Lucas brought her her meals and usually left without a word. Sometimes he would stand for a few moments looking at her, but she would turn her back and he would leave. He constantly slept behind her wagon and he was at her side whenever she left its shelter.

She looked forward, desperately, to the times when she could bathe. When she couldn't she felt angry, bitter. But she kept her mouth shut about her feelings. It wouldn't do any good anyway she rationalized. Lucas always turned his back while she bathed. He knew she wouldn't bathe if he watched. Although he would grit his teeth and repeat over and over to himself that he had no right to watch her, these forays to the bathing holes were becoming harder and harder on him. If he watched her she would stomp back to camp, glaring at him, and he didn't want to ruin her one pleasure.

Lindsay began watching him from the safety of the water and admired his muscles rippling under his damp shirt. He was so powerful, so sinewy. Her thoughts raced back to the night he kissed her and she would wonder if she would ever feel the same bubbles bursting in her body with another man.

Moriarity would ride out of camp, be gone for several days and return, usually at night. She didn't know where he went and was satisfied at not seeing him when he was around.

She didn't know where she was, only that she was traveling to Mexico. She rode all day in confining quarters. When evening came and the canvas was drawn back, she relished being able to see the sky and earth.

One evening, after she had eaten and was sitting on the ground at the back of the wagon, she heard a voice raised in anger.

"The hell he will, the sonofabitch. He ain't her protector. We were given our orders and not sampling her charms weren't one of them!" The man was bellowing, his common sense having been subdued with liquor. He stood and reeled toward the wagon. Lindsay heard the footsteps coming closer. She jumped up and looked for a place to hide. She had turned to run when an arm reached out and grabbed a handful of hair. She squealed and bounced back against her captor.

"Well now, honey, let me look at you." He grabbed a handful of her shirt and pulled it open, baring her white breasts to his leering eyes. She grabbed her shirt and tried to cover herself but the man shoved her down and she sprawled painfully onto the ground. Her heart beat furiously as she looked for something to hit him with. Where's Lucas? He's always so eager to protect me and yet when I really need him he isn't here. She looked up at her attacker as he began removing his clothes. He was watching her with a lecherous look and she knew she had to move now or his strength would be upon her.

Every muscle in her body was taut. Her eyes stared at the man standing over her and she braced herself to flee. When he stooped down to her she would shove him and run. With his chest heaving he said, "I aim to take you tonight, little gal. If that halfbreed don't like it, he can go rot with his redskin mother!" His fingers fumbled with the buttons on his shirt and his eyes hungrily feasted on Lindsay's taut nipples, now open to view as her shirt had fallen open again.

"Sonofabitch, these goddamn buttons . . ." as the sound of rending material hit the air, "I'll be with you soon, little gal," he blubbered impatiently. "After all, anything worth having is worth . . ." the sentence was never completed as he fell to the ground. He hit with a thud and his breath came from between his teeth with a swooshing sound.

Lindsay's eyes were round and frightened as she looked up to see Lucas standing above the man, his legs spread, his hands inches from his gun.

"I told you once, Blackmore, I'd kill you if you touched her again. I meant it. Stand up and go for it." Lucas stood perfectly still. He reminded Lindsay of a powerful animal waiting to spring on his unwary prey.

Blackmore attempted to get up and rolling onto his knees his hand went into the dirt. Lucas, seeing the movement, swung his leg at the man's arm. With a grunt of pain, Blackmore let go of the handful of dirt that he had intended to throw in Lucas's face.

"Get up very slowly." Lucas's voice was deadly calm and his eyes were glued to Blackmore's face.

Blackmore felt a shiver run through his body as he very slowly rose to his feet. He put his gunbelt on as fear began to nibble at his mind. He had seen Sanger draw. He knew he was fast. He too was fast. But a sense of doubt gnawed at him. He had to draw against Sanger. He had no choice. To refuse would be admitting defeat and he would be labeled a coward. But . . . if he won, he could taste the body of the girl. And what a body!

Ever since she had been taken captive he had ached to touch her flesh and caress those milky breasts. He had never seen a woman like her. She was the main topic of conversation among the men each night. They spoke of their dreams of tasting her, bragging to each other how she would respond to their lovemaking. Goddamn, he thought, I'll kill him. Nothin' is gonna stop me tastin' her body.

Angrily he whirled to face his adversary, his hand clamping over his gun. His mistake was evident to him immediately. His coordination had been affected by his anger. As he drew he knew it was too late. Lucas fired before Blackmore's gun had cleared his holster. The bullet hit Blackmore in the chest driving him backwards. Lindsay screamed. Lucas grabbed her arm, pulled her to her feet, and held her shaking form close. Blackmore reached for his throat as a bloody spittle came to his lips . . . he died before his hands got there.

Lindsay was too frightened to cry. She stood in Lucas's embrace, shivering. After several moments he guided her to the wagon, helped her up, and closed the canvas behind her. He turned to the men and spoke with deadly calm. "I told you I'd kill if I had to. Blackmore pushed me. Don't you!" He turned, then stopped and spoke again. "Someone had better bury him." Then he disappeared into the wagon.

Lindsay's fright had given vent to tears and she sobbed into the blanket she held. Lucas stood watching her. He let her cry for a few minutes, then crossed to her and placed a finger under her chin and tilted her face up. "I want you to stay in this wagon all the time unless I'm with you. You don't leave here again unless I say you can."

Lindsay reacted as he suspected she would. She jerked her head from his grasp and turned away from him. He turned to leave the wagon, then said, "Don't disobey me Lindsay. I'm a patient man only so far as my temper isn't aroused." He left and Lindsay shuddered. The smell of sulphur was still with her, and the sight of the man being thrown back by the impact of the bullet made her shiver . . . the bullet that had saved her from rape. Lucas's bullet. And Lucas who had gotten her into this terrible nightmare. Oh, God, she thought, how I hate being grateful to that man. How I hate him for all this. Thank God, though, he was here. And she fell into a troubled sleep.

The group headed deeper into the frontier of New Mexico. They always knew their exact location for they skirted certain areas of danger and drove headlong into other areas where Indians watched their travel.

Lindsay stayed in the wagon as Lucas had ordered and left only when accompanied by him. She would listen through the canvas at night and catch snatches of the conversation at the campfire.

This is how she learned Lucas was part Apache and how they were able to cross over Indian land with no trouble. Some land they had to skirt. Evidently some Indians were not sympathetic to the little group for after angry bartering, Lucas would return and tell the men to turn back. Lindsay hated not being able to see anything. The canvas was kept tightly laced all the time now unless Lucas opened it. But she could listen. They couldn't shut out sound.

Lindsay lost track of time and wondered what her uncle was doing. Was he still searching for her? Or had he given her up for dead? In a way she hoped he thought her dead. At least he could put her from his mind and rebuild his life. Whenever she thought of her home, tears splashed onto her lashes and down her cheeks. She missed her family terribly. She could imagine how Uncle Ned felt insisting she show Lucas around the ranch that day. But, she mustn't dwell on painful memories now. She must keep her mind clear and watch and listen. Her planned-for escape was to become reality. She watched the stars when she was sitting outside with Lucas. She was trying to remember how to guide herself by the stars. She would study her surroundings and hope she would remember each place when she escaped.

Her mind was filled with thoughts of escape and she rarely noticed Lucas watching her. She mustn't let anyone suspect what she was going to do, especially Lucas! She had to be extra careful around him. And she knew that she had to make her escape soon. She knew they weren't far from the Mexican border.

When she was safely back home she would make sure everyone knew about Lucas Sanger. She would certainly attend his hanging and she might even blow a kiss to him as the noose was placed around his neck. . . .

Chapter 7

The terrain now was sagebrush, mesquite and yucca cactus —no trees or rivers. They stopped at every water hole, creek, and mudhole they saw, even traveling miles out of their way for water.

The sunsets were spectacular. Lindsay's bright spot in the day was watching the sky burst forth in a display of color so vivid and resplendent it took her breath away. The variegated colors playing on the sand floor and bouncing off the red hills captured her imagination and she found herself hypnotized with the beauty of the desert.

Her confinement to the wagon began to rub her nerves raw and she slept fitfully and ate poorly. Her face began to look sallow and dark circles appeared under her eyes. Lucas noticed the change and his temper became shorter as he watched her suffer with confinement. The only solace Lindsay could find was watching the purple sunsets. As much as she hated going to bed, she couldn't wait for the sun to begin its descent in the sky.

Nick Moriarity hadn't ridden into camp for several days and she relaxed slightly. Tears would threaten to spill when she thought of her uncle having to give up his ranch because of her. Then she would push those thoughts to the back of her mind and think only of her escape. Escape! Tonight was the night! She knew where the men slept and where the guards were posted. She also knew the direction she had to take to return home. Only she didn't know how to look for water. But a plan had formed in her mind. She would learn what she needed to know from Lucas. He would never suspect her reasons. Lucas usually went to sleep after everyone else had bedded down. Tonight she would make her move after he was sleeping.

Their camp was at the base of a group of flat-topped hills. If she were to flee in the direction they had traveled from she would be seen by her captors. There was no shelter that way. But, if she went in the same direction they were traveling, toward Mexico, she could hide in the hills and the men would never suspect she would go that way. She scanned the hills looming over their camp and sighed, I'll be running to you tonight, please hide me well.

On one of her forays for water with Lucas, she had found a discarded arrowhead. It was white, crystalline, easily seen against the red sand by the watering hole. She slipped it into her pocket while Lucas filled the canteens. This was how she would cut a hole in the worn canvas and untie the laces . . . and flee. She had tested it on a small section, cutting herself a small peephole. This is where she sat for hours watching their progression toward Mexico.

She would hide in the rocks until the men gave up looking for her. Then she would start back toward Colorado and home. Home. It has such a sweet sound. She gathered her few meager belongings and prepared for her escape. She braided her hair with shaky fingers and tied the braids together low over her neck. She tied the bandana Lucas had given her loosely around her neck and decided, after much thought, to take her dress. It has been so long since she had worn a dress. She didn't think she would ever yearn to wear a dress, but having it with her gave her a strange feeling of comfort. She took her shawl and spread it out on the floor, placing some confiscated jerky, cornbread, and a piece of fruit in the center. She placed her brush, comb, bar of soap and towel on top of the food. Then she wrapped the contents into a tight ball and tied the ends of the shawl around a stick. Now she could carry her meager supplies over her shoulder. She stopped as she spied the dress laying across a box. She tenderly folded the garment and opened her shawl, placing the tightly folded dress on top of the towel. Then looking around her prison she hid the shawl under an empty trunk, crawled to the peephole and looked out. The setting sun again filled the sky with a myriad of fiery colors. Lindsay kneeled, and with her eyes glued to the spectacular display, she watched the sunset show its fading hues of orange and blue.

Lucas brought her dinner as usual and as he was unlacing the canvas Lindsay smiled at the thought that this would be the last time she would watch him do this. He handed her the plate of steaming beans and hardtack and left. Lindsay ate the food greedily, knowing this would be her last meal for a long time.

Lucas returned a little later and asked, "Are you ready to stretch your legs?" He reached up to assist her down and she eagerly came to him. She even smiled as he lifted her down. He took her hand and led her toward the hills. Her heart skipped a beat as she realized he was unknowingly aiding her escape. A giggle broke from her lips and she walked faster.

For several days she had been subdued, bursting forth with temper tantrums when Lucas gave her an order. He was tired of her vitriolic mouth. She was a spitfire, no one could deny that. Taming her under different circumstances would be a very interesting prospect. But, he couldn't let his emotions cloud his vision or affect his nerves. And, if given the chance, she would certainly do both. Even disheveled, dirty, and in man's clothing, she was the most beautiful woman he had ever seen. So often he had had to turn and walk away from her or he would have thrown her to the ground and made love to her. He was a little befuddled that this slip of a girl had wiggled into his life and chipped away at his heart. His thoughts were always filled with her. He must shake free of her hold . . . he couldn't let her affect him this way. It could mean her life. His thoughts were interrupted as Lindsay ran ahead and tried to climb on a rock. Lucas bounded after her and grabbing her around the waist asked, "What do you think you're doing?"

"I want to look around. I want to climb high so I can see." She pushed at Lucas's arms and tried to climb on the slippery rock. Lucas laughed and lifted her onto the rock. She shoved her hands into her pockets and turned slowly, drinking in the countryside. She looked at the sky and the desert, peering intently around her, trying to figure out where she was, which way was home. Lucas leaned against the rock and watched her. After a few minutes he pointed his hand southward, "That way's forest if you go far enough. Over that way . . ." he pointed northward "toward Colorado, is desert. Nothing but desert for miles and miles." He looked at her, contemplating her for several seconds. "This country is like a woman. She has as many types of scenery as a woman has moods." He folded his arms across his chest, "She can be purring and soft one minute and clawing and screeching the next. This is God's country, Lindsay, God's country. Every day he mixes a new color and splashes it on his canvas. It's almost like he can't make up his mind which color to use so he keeps trying new ones. I hope he never settles on one color." His eyes were scanning the horizon as he spoke in hushed tones. And anyone listening could have guessed there was an intense love affair between the desert and Lucas Sanger.

Lindsay was surprised at his words but her escape was uppermost in her mind and she pushed thoughts of Lucas out of her mind.

"Lucas, if a person were lost in this country, how could he live?" She began to climb down from her perch and Lucas reached up and lifted her to the ground. He peered into her face as he answered, "If a person knows this country he can live forever."

Her liquid green eyes hypnotized him as he looked down at her. He shook his head as he realized this was neither the time nor the place to make love to her.

"Lucas, what's wrong?" Lucas's mind cleared as he felt her struggle to be free from his grasp. "What's wrong, what are you thinking about?" She watched him but she didn't really care where his thoughts were centered right now.

"Huh, oh . . . nothing's wrong. I was just thinking."

"Well, answer me, then, how could a person live out here? Where would he find food and water? She walked backwards, away from him as his arms released her. Lucas walked a few steps, bent over and picked something up and walked back to her.

Tossing a small rock in his hand he replied, "These hills are a veritable garden, Lindsay. You can look anywhere around you and see food and water. Water is stored in the cactus, in certain plants it lies in pocketlike areas. Edible roots grow all around, berries are thick in many spots, and the fruit of the Saguaro cactus is found everywhere." He swept his arms in a circle emphasizing his point. Then looked back at her and continued, "But why are you so interested in this land, niña? You have no need to know how to survive. Your care is entirely in my hands and I have no intention of letting you starve." He reached his hand to her, "Now, let's return to camp before someone comes looking."

Lindsay took a deep breath and licked her lips. Her nerves were taut with anticipation.

Lucas lifted her into the wagon and as he laced up the canvas he softly said, "Goodnight, niña. Oh, there's a full moon tonight." He walked away quickly. Lindsay's head snapped back! What did he mean by that? Surely he didn't suspect. No! Maybe he knows how I sit and watch the sky. That's it. He told me so I would have something to watch tonight. Well, I'll have plenty to watch tonight.

She heard the men preparing to bed down. Her heart beat rapidly as she realized the time for her escape was very near. The campfire was glowing embers, the blackened coffee pot sitting crookedly in the coals. She heard Lucas approach the wagon, spread out his bedroll, and lie down. She waited, listening carefully for Lucas to breathe deep in sleep. After what seemed an eternity to Lindsay, Lucas slept.

The full moon hung low over the horizon, poised for its journey across the sky. Everything was so quiet! The fire crackled and spit once in awhile but no other sound came from the camp. The men slept spread out—a caution against ambush. If they snored tonight, Lindsay couldn't hear them. Her heartbeats drowned out the sound. She gulped down several breaths and stretched her tight muscles. Maybe this would help relax her nerves. She took the arrowhead and placed it in the slit she had cut several days earlier. Slowly, she began to enlarge the hole. A noise! She sat motionless, listening. Sweat glistened on her upper lip. The noise again! She breathed a sigh of relief. It was a horse. She had forgotten about them. They were never silent. She would love to steal a horse for her escape. But she would be an easy target on horseback. And they were not always quiet when you needed dead silence. She smiled.

She would walk back home. Somebody was bound to come along and offer help. Surely a wagon train, a rancher, someone.

Her hands moved slowly again, cutting away the weakened canvas. Thank God, this wagon had seen better days, and the canvas was worn and old. Slowly the canvas was rending, slowly the opening was getting larger. She whispered to herself, trying to calm her raw nerves but nothing seemed to help. Her life was dependent on her escape! She knew if she didn't get away Moriarity would kill her. When, she didn't know, but she knew she would never be returned to her uncle.

She wanted to rip fast but she knew the sound would awaken Lucas. He could hear the slightest noise and be on his feet before the camp was even awake. Sometimes, Lindsay wondered if he were human. Sometimes she wondered if he even slept. But he did. She checked.

The moon's rays glistened around the camp. The moonlight gave an incandescent look to the rocks. Her escape would be well lit. She wasn't afraid of the dark but this was strange country. She needed all the help she could get.

The opening was now large enough to reach her arm and head through. She turned back into the dark interior of the wagon and felt on the floor for her shawl. Finding it, she dragged it to her side, then turned back to the opening and stuck her head through it. She waited while her eyes adjusted. She couldn't see the men but she knew approximately where they usually slept in a circle around the wagon —an uneven circle.

Lucas had his back to her but she could see his back rise and fall in sleep. She could barely make out the path she would take away from camp and she felt a shiver of excitement run through her veins. Slowly she put her arm through the opening and reached for the resricting laces. She untied the first one. It was difficult leaning out, untying with one hand and pushing her body with the other. But it was the only way to escape. If she cut a hole big enough to climb through the men would see it right away, thus narrowing her chance for escape. She didn't want anything to look tampered with. A small hole in the back of the wagon would go unnoticed for awhile. She untied the second lace, then the third. On the fourth she grunted, and afraid she might have awakened Lucas, she sat perfectly still for several seconds listening, waiting. But Lucas slept like a baby, she mused. She untied two more laces. How many of these damned things are there? I should have counted them. She released two more and then a slight breeze blew through the camp and caressed her face. The released laces slapped against the canvas and Lindsay blanched. Oh, no, they'll slap against the canvas and wake Lucas. She looked up at the sky, pleadingly. Silently she prayed and as though it understood the breeze died. She relaxed her clenched fists and noticed she had drawn blood with her fingernails. She returned to the laces and untied the last two. The canvas slowly unfurled, stretching outward, as though it, too, relished freedom, then fell limply against the wagon. Lindsay sat momentarily looking around and then grabbing her shawl, she descended to the ground. She lowered herself slowly, bearing her weight on her arms. Her arms quivered with the weight of her body and she took a deep breath as her toe touched solid ground. She stood for a few seconds and took several deep breaths. She laced one lace of the open canvas, then turned carefully and backed away from Lucas, keeping her eyes on his sleeping form. When she was a safe distance from Lucas, she turned toward the hills and ran.

Lucas's eyes opened as he listened to her retreating footfalls. He smiled. When he could no longer hear her, he quietly rose and climbed into the wagon, checked its interior and then climbed out. He laced up the canvas, turned to the darkened hills and blew her a kiss. Then he returned to his bedroll . . . and slept.

* * *

The sun came up with such ferocity one would have thought it was angry. One minute the sky was a pearly pink, the next blood red. Lindsay stretched and rolled onto her side, snuggling deeper into the warm sand. Her eyes flew open. They must be looking for me by now! She jumped to her feet, threw her shawl over her shoulder and walked off. She had walked many hours last night. It was cool and the breeze on her face refreshed her. Nothing could have ruined her exhuberance. She had escaped! She was going home! She only stopped after her legs began to cramp from walking. She heard little animals scamper away at her sudden intrusion on their home. She smiled, "I know how you feel, I'd run too." Finally, after her legs couldn't carry her another inch she crawled under an outcropping, dug out a hollow and slept. She dreamt of her uncle running down the lane, his arms extended to her. She was the happiest she had been in a long time and no amount of hardship could dispel her happiness. She walked deeper into the hills, scanning the horizon behind her for any movement. She knew the men would search for her but she had the advantage. They would surely look for her in the other direction.

Chapter 8

Lucas finished rolling his bedroll and after tending to his horse he walked to the fire. The smell of coffee attacked his nostrils. As he scanned the hills, he wondered how Lindsay was. He filled a plate with eggs and bacon, turned, and walked to the wagon. He unlaced the middle lace, placed the plate on the floor, and laced it up again. There was nothing he could do about the hole Lindsay had cut in the canvas. He hoped it wouldn't be noticed for awhile. He returned to the fire, filled a plate for himself and ate slowly.

The camp was packed up and the fire extinguished. Everyone was ready to move out when Lucas announced he was going to do some scouting. A renegade band of Indians had been spotted close by and he wanted to check it out.

"There's a river not far from here. Make camp there and I'll join you later. If I'm not back by nightfall, don't fret. I assure you, I'll return." He jumped on his horse and rode off.

"Well, now ain't that a shame. Might not be back by nightfall. Well, with that little piece of fluff all alone . . ." the man's eyes glistened as he licked his lips and rubbed his hands together. "Yeah, ain't that a shame." He looked longingly at the wagon and thought about the treat he would have tonight if that goddamn halfbreed didn't return. "Maybe we'll have us a party tonight, Marty, maybe we'll have us a party!" And turning his horse, the man rode on ahead, a smile playing at his lips, a glint of desire in his eyes.

*   *   *

Lindsay walked along humming and laughing out loud once in awhile. She felt free. Even being dirty and hungry couldn't ruin her feeling of elation. "I wonder what they're thinking," she spoke to herself, then giggled when she realized she spoke out loud. I wonder what Lucas is doing right now. I wonder if he feels stupid. I hope so. But she didn't have to wonder about him ever again. She didn't have to put up with his temper or his ordering her around . . . or his arms holding her tight . . . or his lips, his soft lips caressing her throat . . . his eyes burning into her soul. She stopped! She heard a sound. She listened. She knew she had heard something! Her head was cocked, waiting to hear it again. She scanned the horizon. There! There! She spoke aloud. "A horse!" The sound of a horse neighing drifted to her again. Somebody has picked up my trail. Surely they would have thought I would go the other way. Why? Why did they come this way? She began to panic. I covered my trail, I thought. I tried to hide any obvious signs. She began to cry. Tears fell down her cheeks.

"Oh, damn it, Lindsay, don't act like a baby now! Hide! I've got to find someplace to hide!" And then she stopped. Maybe it was a stranger! Maybe it was a traveler and he would help her! Her spirits began to rise as she searched the horizon. There was only one rider. If Lucas were searching for her she thought he would be accompanied by at least one of the other men. But as the rider approached she recognized him. Lucas! Damn! She ran forward, stumbled, and twisted her ankle. Panic nibbled at her brain. She looked around, frightened, more frightened than she had ever been in her life. If she were caught she would probably be killed! With fear pushing her she stood and ran clumsily. She stopped and looked around. Nothing to conceal her! She rounded a bend in the trail and saw it. An old rotten tree lying across a small wash. She looked back but she couldn't see Lucas. She limped forward. Her ankle pained her a great deal now and she could barely put weight on it. She crawled into the musty interior of the tree. She squeezed back as far as she could and brushed the ground to cover her tracks. She mounded dirt and mulch close to her body, hoping to mask herself.

She remained perfectly still, breathing as quietly as she could. The only sounds she could hear were the birds whistling and a family of squirrels cursing her for disturbing them. Now began one of the longest waits in Lindsay's life.

She closed her eyes and remembered another time she had hidden in an old log. Only that time she could make all the noise she wanted. The attacking Indians would never have heard her over their screaming and war chants. But she was quiet then too. She barely breathed as she saw her parents falling to the ground, the arrows sticking grotesquely from their bodies. She saw the Indians jumping down from their horses, grabbing her parents by their hair. Tears began to spill down her cheeks. She sniffed and swore under her breath for being such a baby.

Chapter 9

They both had to escape and things seemed to be working out just fine. He smiled to himself as he remembered her questions about living in the desert.

Their escape couldn't arouse suspicion. If the men suspected anything, Lindsay would have been killed. Now it would be hours before they figured out what happened and by then he would have Lindsay far, far away. He remembered back to the night they walked to a creek for water and he dropped the shiny arrowhead. Then she had the means to cut her way out of the wagon.

Following the tracks with his eyes he murmured, "She's limping." He rounded the bend and his eyes fell on the fallen tree. She might as well put signs up pointing out her direction. She sure doesn't know how to cover her tracks. But then, she's never had to cover her tracks. He leaned forward in the saddle and in a husky voice called, "Lindsay, you can come out now!"

Every fiber in her body froze. She squeezed her eyes shut as if in that action he would not be able to tell where she was. Her heart thumped crazily, sweat ran down her neck, coursed over her breasts and plopped to the ground. She held her breath and waited. Maybe he doesn't know where I am. The musty smell surrounding her made her nose itch. The heat was stifling as the world outside stopped for Lindsay.

"Lindsay, come out now!" His voice had an irritated edge to it. "If you don't come out *now*, I'll drag you from that log, turn you over my knee, and wallop you good!" He moved impatiently in the saddle and quickly looked behind him. Her stubbornness could give any searchers time to catch up.

Lindsay's spirits sank to rock bottom when she heard him mention the log. Her plans for escape had failed and she would probably die now. A heavy feeling, such as she had never known, descended upon her. She lay quietly hoping something would either come down from the sky and whisk her away or a great hole would open up beneath her and she would be swallowed. A feeling of impending doom swirled around her and she had no desire to ever move again.

Suddenly the dirt and mulch she had piled in front of her was being swept away. She watched Lucas's hands as though she were outside her body. She was dead. She felt nothing but a great sense of loss. Lucas's hands grabbed her by the shoulders and pulled her from the log. She blinked in the bright sunlight. Lucas lifted her to her feet and held her by the shoulders. She breathed deeply, savoring the fresh air. Her arms were scratched and covered with a film of dust. Mulch stuck to her hair, changing its redness to dull gold. Her face was streaked with dirt and he could see the tracks her tears had made on her cheeks. Her pants and shirt were filthy with dust and mulch and her boots were nearly worn through. Sweat beads clung to her upper lip and as she stood silently in front of him he thought she looked very beautiful.

"You know you're going in the wrong direction. Colorado is behind us." His grip slackened on her shoulders as he continued, "But then, I guess you aimed to throw us off by going this way, right?" He looked up, then toward the horizon. "You're a smart little gal, Lindsay, but remember, I'm smarter. You cannot escape from me. Don't try it again." The smile on his lips did not reach his eyes and his words barely penetrated Lindsay's unresponsive mind. She stood looking at him, her face a mask. She was drained of emotion.

Lucas turned to his horse and walked to the waiting animal. Lindsay stood watching his receding back. She took a step forward and fell. Her ankle would not hold her weight. The pain was too great. A grunt of pain escaped her and Lucas whirled. Seeing her huddled on the ground he walked quickly to her side. Her pride slipping, her hopes for escape dashed with defeat, she buried her face in her hands and wept. Long, hard sobs came from her small frame and shook her body.

Lucas had never seen a woman cry so dejectedly before. As the sobs wracked her little body he couldn't talk any more. He bent down and picked her up, holding her close. He walked to his horse, set her on the saddle, and climbed on behind her. He wrapped his arms around her, pulled her back against him, and held her close as he turned the horse and they walked off. She cried for a long time.

After awhile, the sobs stopped and changed to hiccups. He looked down at her. Her eyes were swollen and she clutched fiercely to the shawl. Her breathing came in uneven gasps.

She had the longest eyelashes he had ever seen. They lay against her tear-streaked skin and curled ever so slightly. Her creamy skin, even when covered with a film of dirt, was soft and meant to be kissed. He smiled as he thought about her eyes. If emeralds could be fashioned after her eyes, women would never wear diamonds again. Lucas found it difficult to concentrate when she was looking at him. He felt he could be swallowed up by her liquid eyes. She stirred against his chest and he softly asked, "There's a place ahead where we can stop and you can wash off the dirt, okay?" She didn't answer but he knew she agreed. A ragged breath escaped her swollen lips.

They continued traveling and no further words were spoken. Soon water could be heard as it cascaded over rocks and splashed against boulders. Lucas stopped and carried her to the river. He sat her down on the cool sand and she opened her eyes.

They had traveled farther into the hills but the scenery was the same. Desert. This river was a pleasant surprise though. She thought how easily she could have escaped Lucas had she known about this river. He would never have been able to track her in water. But it was too late now. She was on her way back . . . to death probably.

Lindsay leaned forward and splashed the cool water on her face. Soon she forgot the pain in her ankle and sat on the river edge spalshing water over her hot and tired body. She removed her bandana and dipped it in the water and wiped it across her neck and down her throat. Lucas splashed water on his face and across his shoulders. Then he put his hat back on his head and climbed a tree. From his vantage point he scanned the horizon, watching for any movement. But he saw none and looked down at Lindsay. She had thought Lucas to be out of sight since she couldn't see him and had removed her shirt. She washed her arms and repeatedly dipped the bandana in the river and dripped it across her shoulders and breasts. She closed her eyes and held the bandana against her face.

Lucas's breath caught in his throat as he watched her. He couldn't have dragged his eyes from the scene below him if Nick Moriarity himself had appeared on the horizon. Her breasts were so firm, so soft, so alluring. Her rosy nipples thrust impudently forward. His desire for her rose as beads of sweat popped out on his forehead. Only after she dressed could he tear his eyes from her and search the horizon again. Satisfied, he climbed down and walked to Lindsay. She sat with her arms wrapped around her knees staring into the water and he studied her for a few moments before disturbing her thoughts.

"Lindsay", he held his hand out to her, "we better be going." He carried her to the horse and they rode off.

* * *

They rode for several hours. The sun beat relentlessly down on them. She leaned against him for support but kept her face forward and would not talk. After all, he would be responsible for her death. Why should she make it easier for him by badgering him.

Suddenly Lindsay sat up! She turned questioning eyes to Lucas. They were going toward Colorado. He wasn't taking her back to Moriarity! Lucas laughed at her startled expression.

"I wondered how long it would be before you noticed." He placed a finger on her sun pinkened nose and continued, "You haven't been paying attention. You'll not be returning to the wagon." And he lifted his eyes to the horizon and scanned it carefully. They rode on and on. It was obvious she wasn't going to get any more information for awhile. But her spirits lifted as she thought about being out in the air and not kept prisoner in a stuffy wagon.

She slept on and off as they traveled. The sun was scorching and her clothes were damp with sweat and clung to her. Lucas didn't seem bothered by the heat. She was thirsty, hungry, tired, and her ankle hurt terribly but Lucas kept pushing the horse further and further into the desert. Then, when she didn't think she could ride another step, he stopped. He lifted her down and she fell into the hot sand. It felt so good to stretch. Lucas tied the horse in the shade of some large rocks and attached an oat bag over the hungry animal's face. When he was content the mount was taken care of he returned to Lindsay and smiled as she rolled and stretched in the sand. He bent down to her and handed her a canteen of water. She drank greedily. "Slow down." He grabbed the canteen from her hands and scolded, "You'll get sick drinking that fast. Only a few sips at a time. Roll it around in your mouth and then swallow. We don't have enough water to be gulping it down and I don't have the time to search for more." He turned and walked to the saddle that lay in the shade by the horse. He took a blanket roll and a package from the saddle bag and laid them in the shade of the rocks. Lindsay watched him as he stretched out on the blanket and bit off a piece of jerkey.

"If you're hungry you'd better get over here and eat." Her eyes feasted hungrily on the jerky. She had always hated jerky but she hadn't eaten since last night and she was starved. She stood up but on her first step fell to her knees with a squeal of pain. She took a couple of deep breaths, tears of pain clung to her lashes. She leaned forward on her arms and hung her head down, waiting for the pain to subside. Lucas was at her side and had her in his arms before she realized what was happening. He sat her on the blanket and she leaned against the cool rocks. Breathing a sigh, she closed her eyes.

"I'm gonna have to examine this ankle, niña. It's gonna hurt." He picked her foot up gently. "Bite your lip and hold tight." He turned her ankle from one side to the other as beads of sweat popped out on her face. She bit her lower lip until blood droplets appeared. She thought he was being unnecessarily rough but she would not utter a sound. She would show him she was no ninny.

"Why don't you take the boot off?" she asked.

"Cause your ankle is probably swollen up bad and the boot is giving it some support. I don't think it's broken but you sure as hell have a dandy sprain."

He picked up the shawl she had clutched closely for so long and undid the knots and emptied its contents on the blanket. He looked at the dress and a sneer touched his lips. She quickly grabbed the dress and hid it behind her. "What do you think you're doing? That's my shawl and you have no right to take it!"

He ripped a long narrow piece of the shawl and threw the remainder to her. He lifted her ankle and wrapped the material around the top of the boot and in a figure eight around and under the heel of the boot. After he was satisfied it was tight enough he tore the ends in pieces and tied them together. "There, that should give you some support." He stretched out on the blanket and pulling his hat over his eyes, he yawned. "You might as well sleep for awhile. We won't leave until the sun goes down. Oh, why did you take that dress? Seems to me you would rather have burned it."

Lindsay glared at him and then retrieved her spilled contents. She replaced them in the shawl, tying it as best she could. She ignored his remark. It's my dress, she thought huffily.

She ate a piece of jerky and leaned back against the cool rocks and peered at the sleeping man beside her. His hat hid his face but she looked down his lean body and up again. His shirt was open to his waist and black curly hair covered his chest. His belly was rock hard. His thighs looked as though he would rip his pants apart if he flexed them. He was solid iron. Lindsay wondered what it would be like to make love to such a man. She had heard her friends talk about such things. She knew it was supposed to be a woman's duty to satisfy her husband. But, someone had told her once, that it was also very nice . . . having a man hold you naked and kiss you all over. She blushed at the thought. If she ever married she hoped her husband had a body similar to Lucas. Strong. Big.

She was sure she had just fallen asleep when Lucas was shaking her awake. The sun had sunk below the horizon and the deep purple sky darkened with each passing minute.

"Come on, Lindsay, it's time to go." He turned to his horse and finished saddling him. She stood up and surprisingly, her ankle did not give out on her. Lucas's bandage worked, but then didn't everything he do work? He helped her to mount and settling in behind her they rode off.

Chapter 10

The next few days dragged slowly by. They slept during the day and rode all night. They ate only jerky and water for their meals and Lindsay felt if she had to eat another piece of jerky she would scream. The cornbread she had wrapped in the shawl so long ago had hardened to the consistency of rock. She threw it down and swore under her breath. Lucas smiled at her then returned his attention to the horse, a chuckle escaping from his lips. She whirled at him and spat, "Go to hell," then stomped off.

Her ankle must be much better Lucas mused, too bad her temperament hasn't improved.

Early one evening, after a particularly hot and restless day, Lucas asked, "Would you like to bathe this evening, Lindsay?" She jerked her head up and looked at him suspiciously. The anticipation of a bath sparkled in her eyes. He continued, "There's a stream up ahead. We'll stop and bathe."

She peered into the countryside, looking for a sign of water. All she saw was sand, sand, and sand-covered hills. How Lucas knew this country so well she would never understand. Soon she could hear the water bubbling and she squirmed in excitement. She licked her lips and rubbed her hands together as the river came into view. Lucas reined in the horse and slowly climbed down. Rather than lifting her to the ground as he usually did, he walked the horse to the river and while she sat impatiently, the animal drank. Lucas watched the horse drink and paid no attention to Lindsay. Finally, in anger she yelled, "Well, what am I supposed to do, sit up here all night?"

"Oh, I am sorry, niña. I completely forgot about you." He reached up to help her down and laughed deeply at the anger in her eyes. He was teasing her again and she was in no mood for his play.

She ran into the water and then turned slowly to Lucas. She had forgotten to remove her boots. For some reason, this made her feel very sheepish. She looked down at her feet. The water trickled around and over the leather and she could feel the insides filing with water. She stood for several seconds watching the water suck at her boots. Then, with a red face she looked at Lucas. He stood by his horse, watching her intently, a half smile on his lips. Then flipping her head back she stomped to a rock and sat down. Her boots weren't going to come off easy now that they were wet. She struggled and worked and was huffing with the effort when Lucas hunkered down and began pulling them off. He wadded the bandage and threw it down, then examined her sprained ankle. "It looks pretty good. It's still bruised but you should be able to walk on it now."

He moved aside as she stood and limped back to the water. She began to walk into the cool river when he spoke again. "Aren't you going to take your clothes off? You've ruined your boots, why ruin your clothes?" Lindsay ignored him and continued walking into the water.

"Lindsay, I mean it! What are you going to do for clothes? It gets cold out here at night," he chuckled deeply, "especially when you're naked."

Lindsay whirled on him, her fists clenched tightly against her thighs.

"Lucas," her voice was strained with anger, "why don't you leave me alone? Whether I remove my clothes or not is none of your affair." She turned and dove into the cool, clear water, disappearing into its blueness.

Lucas shrugged and began stripping. "Well, niña, I have no false modestly. I damn well don't intend to ruin my clothes either." He dove into the water and Lindsay could hear his splashing.

She turned in time to see him surface and turn on his back and float. My God! He doesn't even have the decency to wait until dark to strip!

She watched him curiously as he leisurely floated on top of the shimmering surface, beads of water glimmering on his brown skin like diamonds. She watched his muscles flexing as he moved closer to her. She had never seen a naked man in her life. She supposed she should feel something like . . . embarrassment or shame or discomfort . . . something other than what she felt.

His broad chest and narrow hips. His stomach rippling with muscle and his . . . his . . . manhood. My God! Lindsay, you're disgraceful, she chastised herself . . . staring at his nakedness with no guilt.

"What's the matter, niña, do I embarass you?" He floated easily on the water but he was watching Lindsay. The sound of his voice startled her from her reverie and she stammered, "I . . . I . . . no . . . no . . . of course not." She turned her head, averting her eyes from his body. Her face felt hot and she touched her cheeks with wet fingers.

The coolness felt good. She reached down with cupped hands and splashed more water on her hot skin. She raised her eyes slowly, cautiously to see where Lucas was and looked directly into his smiling face. He stood in front of her, unashamed of his nakedness. He reached out a finger and placed it under her chin, tilting her face up. "I think it's time we dried off and rode on, niña. You're gonna have to ride in wet clothes. Your modesty ruined a good pair of pants." And laughing at his remark he turned and walked ashore. She watched him, her eyes taking in every inch of his back and legs as he sauntered to shore.

Lucas grabbed his pants and began dressing. He looked up and smiled, "Close your mouth, Lindsay, you'll sunburn your tongue." Mortified, Lindsay whirled away from him, dove under the water for one last quick dip and an attempt to cool her raging emotions. Then she slowly walked toward the shore. She had never before felt such humiliation. She wouldn't be able to look him in the eye again.

But why should she care what he thought? She hated him. He was a savage. He even admitted he lived with Indians. Why should she care what he said or did or thought . . . why should she care that when he held her close she felt so secure? Or that his lips tasted sweeter than water after a week without any? Or that his blue eyes made her flush and uneasy, as though she wanted to slowly undress for him, tease him, run her fingers through his shaggy hair and press her naked breasts to his chest . . . she shook her head. What is wrong with me? She frowned. Her mind wandered on such absurd thoughts these days. She thought at times she was going mad. Pull yourself together, Lindsay. Keep your mind sharp. You don't know where Lucas is taking you. You don't really know anything about him, except that he's responsible for this predicament. Watch out, girl, you need your wits about you now more than ever. She sat on the hot sand and ran her fingers through her hair.

An object plopped in the sand beside her and she jumped before she realized Lucas had thrown her the brush. She whispered thanks and then began brushing her hair. Lucas had finished dressing and was leaning against his horse watching her. Glints of gold reflected from her wet hair and tight, unruly curls framed her face. She reminded him of a small child—a vulnerable, frightened child. Funny how appearances can be deceiving. Lindsay was certainly not a child. Even in man's clothing she was the most beautiful woman he had ever seen. She certainly was not easily frightened. Perhaps she hid it well, but through this whole ordeal he had only caught fleeting glimpses of fright in her eyes and that was quickly replaced with anger. His mind was filled with thoughts of her running like a carefree child through a field, picking wild flowers, sitting on a garden swing, the moonlight touching her white skin and gleaming in her eyes. He thought of her moist, soft lips. How many times he had wanted to kiss them . . .

"Lucas . . . Lucas, I'm ready." Lindsay stood in front of him, her hair flowing down her back, her wet clothes clinging to her body. Her nipples pushed through the material of her shirt and desire began to show in Lucas's eyes and physically as well. He turned abruptly toward the horse and spoke harshly, more harshly than he intended, "How the hell are you going to ride in those wet clothes? In an hour, you'll freeze your pretty little fanny."

Lindsay straightened her shoulders and stood as tall as she could. "Well, it's my ah . . . fanny . . . as you put it, and why should you care about my comfort. You sure haven't cared before."

Lucas shrugged and mounted the horse. After helping Lindsay on, he jerked the horse around and they rode off. Lindsay frowned at his mood. I wonder what's bothering him now? But she was tired and before long her head bobbed forward as she fell asleep. Lucas pulled her back against him and turned her head against his shoulder. He looked at her as she slept in the crook of his arm, then bent down and kissed the tip of her nose.

* * *

The next two days seemed endless. The heat and sand and sun all combined to make Lindsay irritable and Lucas began to tire of her temper.

They slept in the cool hours of the morning and rode

during the hottest part of the day and late into the night, stopping again at dawn and sleeping. Lindsay rubbed her buttocks frequently, afraid if she didn't the constant riding would forever render her numb. Whenever Lucas chuckled at her antics, she would walk off huffily, raising her nose in the air.

Lucas knew the constant traveling was hard on her but it wasn't easy on him either. And she certainly didn't make it any easier on either of them by her griping and bitching.

One morning as they were preparing to ride on, Lindsay sat down, crossed her arms on her knees and huffily remarked she wasn't riding any more. She had had enough of the constant traveling. She hated the desert, she hated the horse, and most of all she hated Lucas.

Lucas strode to her angrily, grabbed her by the shoulders, and lifted her up. Her feet barely touched the ground as he glared down into her shocked face.

"Damn it, Lindsay, I've had enough of your mouth. If you don't stop bitching, I'm gonna gag you!" He released her abruptly and she tumbled back, landing on her backside. Nothing was hurt but her pride but she'd never let him know that!

"Why. . . you . . . you halfbreed. Don't you ever touch me like that again!" Her throat constricted in anger and her words were mixed with gasps. "I'll kill you if you ever do that again!"

Lucas snatched his bandana from around his neck angrily and holding it in front of him strode back to her. She watched him approach her and for the first time she felt she had pushed him too far. He was very angry and if she didn't back down he was definitely going to gag her. She reached out her arm in a supplicating manner and spoke softly. "I . . . I'm sorry . . . I won't say anything more, I promise . . ."

Lucas stood over her staring down at her, his eyes cold, his hands twisting the bandana back and forth. Then, without another word, he threw the bandana at her, turned, and stomped off. She had never seen him that mad at her before. She couldn't remember him being that mad when he killed the man that attacked her, but that night she was so upset she couldn't remember much.

She stood and picked up the red bandana. She wrapped it around her hand several times, then walked to the horse. Her eyes were downcast as she stood waiting for Lucas to finish saddling the animal. Without any words between them, they mounted and rode away.

Damn, I shouldn't let her get to me that way, Lucas thought. I'll have to control myself. He had never let a woman affect his thinking before. Women could cause you to lose control . . . do things you normally wouldn't do. He looked down at her head, the sun had bleached her hair and streaks of light gold mixed with the darker red. But, he had to admit, Lindsay did cloud his thinking. He found himself thinking and doing things he had never done before. If he wasn't careful, this wisp of a girl could get under his skin.

* * *

Lindsay began to notice a change in the scenery, trees loomed up now and then, the red sand gave way in some spots to a mossy green color. More greenery was evident on the horizon and the stifling heat of the desert gave way to a cooling breeze.

Lindsay was convinced Lucas was taking her home, but she couldn't figure out why. Questions tumbled in her mind as she tried to piece the puzzle together. He had kidnapped her, now he was aiding her escape back to Colorado. She could tell by the stars they were traveling north toward the Lazy Hat Ranch! But when she questioned Lucas about their travels he only shrugged. If she persisted, he would glare at her and after that last time Lindsay felt it better not to push him. Maybe he would tell her after awhile. Well, it really didn't matter. It was obvious they were traveling toward Colorado. If he didn't plan on taking her home, she would wait until she had some idea of her location and then escape! As close as they were to Colorado, she would surely be able to find her way home or find someone to help her. Her spirits rose considerably and at times Lucas could hear her humming as they rode along.

One evening, after they made camp, Lucas went off on

foot. He returned a while later carrying a brace of rabbits over his shoulder. Lindsay wrinkled her nose at the sight of the bloody animals, but after Lucas skinned them and they were cooking over the fire her mouth watered in anticipation of eating meat again.

"Lucas," she looked at him over the fire, "why are we camping at night?"

"I'm sure our tracks could never be followed now, niña. It's more difficult to track at night—so we traveled at night. Now, we can travel during the day." Her brow furrowed as she tried to figure out what he meant but with the smell of roasting rabbit and the knowledge that she was close to her home, she really didn't care any more.

The rabbit tasted delicious, more delicious than Lindsay had ever imagined. She laid her head back and rested it on her arms. She looked up at the star-filled sky. I wonder how long it would take to count the stars she thought. A shooting star raced through the sky and Lindsay giggled. Lucas looked at her and then up at the sky.

"Did you make a wish, niña?"

"Yes, but it's a silly one."

"No wish is silly if you really want it. Tell me what you want."

Lindsay giggled as she spoke, "I wished I could lie right here until I had counted all the stars in the sky. Isn't that stupid?"

"I can make it come true."

Lindsay sat up and looked at him. "Don't be ridiculous. I told you it was only a silly statement."

Lucas shrugged, "We could stay here until your wish is complete if you want."

He turned back to the fire and poked it with a stick. A pair of owls hooted and Lindsay jumped. She felt so uneasy, as though something were going to happen. She reached down and pulled off her boots. The cool ground felt good on her toes and she dug them into the sand and wiggled them. She wrapped her arms around her legs and rested her chin on her knees. The sound of silence hypnotized her. She listened for noise but heard only a few leaves rustled in the breeze. She felt drunk with contentment. This country was beginning to get to her. She had never felt such peace in the outdoors. She could understand Lucas's love of the desert.

Her mind was so deep in thought she didn't hear Lucas approach. He stood quietly and watched her. Then he touched her shoulder. She started at the intrusion, then softly whispered, "Isn't it beautiful? If I were to describe heaven, it would be this place." He sat next to her and leaned back on his elbow and smiled.

"This country will get in your blood and devour your soul. After this beauty touches your eyes you'll never be satisfied with second best."

He placed a dark finger under her chin and slowly turned her face to his. Her eyes were soft and luminous as he gazed into them. "I could be swallowed by your eyes, niña. I could fall into them and never need to come up for air." His voice was soft and husky, touched with desire. As his face moved closer she could feel his breath, warm, moist against her lips. Her heart beat rapidly as her lips parted with a sigh. His lips brushed hers lightly and then he kissed the corner of her mouth, the tip of her nose, and then her eyes. She swallowed slowly as he looked into her face and smiled, "You are so lovely, Lindsay." His lips came down over hers and he crushed her to him as he slowly laid her on the ground. His tongue forced her lips apart and he probed her mouth deeply. Her breath caught in her throat. She had to stop this. It wasn't right to let a man kiss you like this! But her body was responding to his kisses and she didn't want him to stop. He kissed the corner of her eye and nibbled her ear. He placed warm gentle kisses on her throat and shoulders. He kissed the pulse in her throat and she arched her back. Her breathing was uneven and perspiration beads glistened between her breasts. His lips took hers again, hard, exploring, burning, and she felt lightheaded. He had one arm around her shoulders, caressing her arm and his other hand went to her shirt. Slowly, he began to unbutton the front, his hot fingers brushing her skin. He cupped a breast in his hand and tenderly explored the creamy flesh. His fingers brushed her nipple and a shiver of delight ran through her body. His lips moved from hers to her throat and then to her breasts. He nibbled the creamy flesh and pressed his lips to her pink nipples. She moaned as his mouth moved over every inch of her breasts, teasing, gently tugging, kissing. His lips took hers again possessively and Lindsay's head began to spin with dizziness. His lips nibbled her throat as his hand untied the rope at her waist. Slowly, he removed her pants as his lips burned a path down her throat across her breasts and down her stomach. He nibbled the soft skin on her belly as she wriggled in pleasure. But when his hand moved lower and touched her between the legs she gasped and began to fight him. "Don't fight me, niña," he whispered hoarsely.

"No . . . no . . . please . . . you can't, we mustn't . . ." His lips silenced her pleas as his hand continued to caress and probe her softness.

He threw his leg across her thighs to stop her fighting and looked into her face. "Relax, honey, I won't hurt you." He murmured against her throat, "You were made for love, niña."

His hand was exploring her intimately and Lindsay arched her body, moving sensuously as her hands caressed his back. She felt his muscles rippling and ran her fingers down his back and across his buttocks. She reached for his belt buckle but her hands were so shaky she couldn't undo it. He smiled as he undid it and shrugged out of his pants. He laid on top of her and she could feel his manhood, hard, warm, pulsing with desire. She ran her fingers around his belly and down the curly hair of his stomach and down lower . . . lower . . . and when she touched him he moaned with pleasure.

She felt him spread her thighs with his knees and she became aware of what she was doing. "No . . . Lucas . . . no . . ." but his kisses stopped her protests and holding her hands above her head he slowly entered her. He stopped momentarily, looked into her face, kissed her closed eyes and murmured softly. Then he began to thrust, deeper and deeper, slowly at first, then a little faster. Her eyes flew open and she arched her body upward. Tears dangled on her lashes as pain burst in her belly and then slowly lessened. Lucas kissed the tears on her cheeks, murmuring softly as he slowly moved up and down . . . up and down. She stopped struggling as the pain disappeared and when he released her arms she wrapped them around his body, clinging to him tightly, caressing his hot skin. She began to move with him and their movements quickened. He thrust deeper and faster and she clung to him with every ounce of strength she could find. Her body moved instinctively to this strange, incredible feeling. Drums pounded in their heads as they both soared to dizzy heights and Lindsay had never known such ecstacy existed.

Afterwards they lay entwined in each others arms, their breathing thick and uneven. Lucas ran a finger down her cheek, around each pink-tipped breast and down her belly to the mat of gold curls. She lay with her head on his shoulder, snuggled close against his side, a feeling of intense satisfaction on her face. Later, Lucas carried Lindsay to their bedrolls and after crawling under the covers he held her possessively.

"Why haven't you married, Lucas?"

His hand gently played with her hair as he slowly answered. "I have never been in love. I don't like being tied down." He closed his eyes and Lindsay snuggled closer against him. The night air was fresh and sweet and quiet. The only sound was a mournful hooting of a single owl. A touch of sadness tugged at Lindsay's heart.

Chapter 11

The next morning Lucas cooked them each a piece of meat left from the night before as Lindsay sat and braided her hair. She looked up and studied this strange man she had become intimate with a few hours ago. She had given him the most prized possession she could give a man and yet she barely knew him. He was gentle with her last night, so loving. He seem so familiar with her body. He is so handsome, a man any woman would welcome to her bed. Why, she didn't even know his age!

He handed her a plate of food and smiled.

"Hurry, chica, we must leave soon."

They rode on, the sun becoming warmer as it moved higher in the sky. The air looked clearer to Lindsay, the trees larger and the grass greener. She smiled to herself.

They stopped at a river and slowly Lindsay stripped. She knew Lucas watched her, his eyes greedily scanning her body. She held her hands over her breasts, not yet secure enough to stand naked and proud in front of him. She could feel the heat when he walked up to her, his eyes feasting on her white skin. She hesitated momentarily at his touch, then dove into the water, gasping as she surfaced and then swam away.

She heard the splash of Lucas's dive and she heard him swimming to her. She playfully swam harder trying to elude him. He laughed as he easily caught her and grabbed her leg. He pulled her under the surface with him and she felt a hand touch her softly. They surfaced and Lucas pulled her to shore, her body floating on the shimmering water, gold and wet. He picked her up and carried her to a sandy area. He laid her down in the warm sand and pushed her hair from her face. He gave her a long, passion-filled kiss. His hands roamed her body and soon she was begging him to take her.

They made love with the sun caressing their entwined bodies. The sun was slowly moving to the horizon when they began riding on. Lindsay laid her head on Lucas's chest and closed her eyes. She had never felt this way before. She couldn't understand how any woman could feel making love was only a duty. She wondered what sex was like with someone you loved. . . .

* * *

They traveled another two days when Lindsay spotted wisps of smoke over the tops of trees. The sun filtered through the trees and touched their bodies with warm fingers. The smell of burning wood assailed their nostrils.

Lindsay was certain they were close to Durango. The thought of returning home didn't bring the great joy she had thought it would. A sad feeling tugged at her heart when she thought about her long journey with Lucas ending.

They rode down an embankment and followed a dried-up river bed. Then they went up a hilly slope and through some trees. A camp stood under the shelter of huge pines. The smell of fried venison made Lindsay's mouth water. Four horses tethered in a meadow, grazed greedily on sweet grass. A man at the fire stood and pushed his hat back and grinned at them. Two other men appeared from the brush.

"*Amigo*, I was beginning to wonder if you would ever show." He came forward, grinning broadly and helped Lindsay from the horse. Lucas smiled and nodded at the man.

"How did you manage?" The big man nodded his head toward Lindsay as Lucas shook the man's hand. They both walked to the fire and after pouring a mug of coffee, Lucas sat beside his friend and they talked.

Lindsay looked around. She recognized the big man, having seen him in Durango with Lucas. The other two men joined Lucas at the fire. She watched them and listened to them but she could only hear laughter and gruff expletives. After awhile Lucas brought her to the fire and handed her a plate of food. Soon she was engrossed in filling the void in her stomach. The big man said something in Spanish to Lucas and both men looked at her and laughed. She blushed, lowered her face and poked at her food while a nervous smile forced its way to her lips.

Lindsay finished her meal and waited for Lucas's friend to walk away from him. She moved to Lucas's side when Chico walked off and asked softly, "How far are we from my uncle's ranch, Lucas? How long before we'll be there?"

Lucas looked down at her, exploring her face and fighting the impulse to kiss her. Then he looked away.

"What makes you think you're going home?"

Lindsay's startled expression said more than any words.

"Niña, I'm sorry if you thought that. You are not going home. At least not yet. But you will be comfortable."

He watched her eyes fill with tears and his fists clenched

as he turned sharply away. Her crying affected him more than he liked to admit. She continued to stare at Lucas and he changed position, uncomfortable under her scrutiny. When he looked back at her, tears were coursing down her cheeks, silver droplets dangled from her lashes, but she did not look away. Then after several moments she spoke, her voice filled with sadness.

"I should have seen through you. I foolishly thought you were honorable after all. You protected me, kept me from getting hurt back there," she tossed her head in the direction they had come from and continued, "I was beginning to let my guard down. God, did I make a mistake this time! Uncle Ned always told me I was too trusting. I never believed him. I do now . . ." She wiped at the tears with the back of her hand. "I'll tell you the same thing I told Mr. Moriarity. My uncle will not give up a lifetime of work to appease a madman. You won't get the ranch any easier than Nick would have." She turned and walked away, her shoulders slumped, her soft sobs echoing through the trees.

She walked into the woods, she had no idea where she was, but she wouldn't stay another minute by Lucas Sanger. She began to run, blindly. She had to escape! Her sobs shook her body as she veered through the trees. How could I have been so stupid? Not only did I begin to believe him, but . . . but . . . I gave him my body! She stopped running momentarily, startled by a noise! She cocked her head to listen and wiped at her eyes with her sleeve. The tears continued to fall but her sobs had stopped. Then she heard it again! A low growl! She whirled! She stood stock still as she peered intently around her. Fear took hold of her and she felt heavy, as though she were being sucked down into the ground. The growl was louder and closer! She whirled to her left and looked up. Perched in a tree, watching her, readying to leap at her, was a mountain lion! Lindsay turned deadly white as she stared at the animal. His paw lashed at the air several times and he growled at her. Then from behind her came the crack of a gun and the lion peered behind Lindsay, jumped down, and ran off. Lindsay breathed. She hadn't realized she'd been holding her breath and she was slightly dizzy.

She whirled and saw Lucas approach, his rifle smoking, an angry glint in his eyes. She didn't stop to wonder about any further danger, only whirled and continued running. She would never stay with him! If she died . . . well that would be better than submitting to Lucas.

"Lindsay, come back here!" his voice was hard and cold. "Right now!" She didn't stop to listen.

"Lindsay, don't make me do anything we both may regret."

Ha! What could he do that he would regret? Hasn't he already done more than he can ever imagine. She continued running, her heart beating wildly. Then something circled her body and she was momentarily lifted off the ground, then fell hard into the dirt. The wind came from her lungs with a forceful gasp as she realized Lucas approached her winding the end of a rope around his elbow, another end wrapped around her. She fought the bonds with all her strength, but he pulled his end tighter and the rope burned into her sleeves and pinched her arms. She watched him approach and kicked out when he bent down to her. Lucas was prepared. He grabbed her leg and flipped her onto her belly. She began to scream and Lucas put his hand over her mouth. "Sssh, niña, you'll wake the animals." The teasing note in his voice and the half smile on his lips belied the anger in his eyes.

But Lindsay was on the verge of hysteria and paid no attention to his mood. She only knew she had to free herself from this man and escape him.

He removed his hand from her mouth and she screamed again. This time when he reached down to quiet her she bit him and he pulled his hand back and swore. "You shouldn't start something you can't finish, Lindsay." He pulled the bandana from around her neck and wrapped it tightly around her face, pulling it between her lips and she gagged and grunted, but she could not speak . . . or scream.

He slowly removed the rope from around her chest but as soon as Lindsay could feel her bonds loosen, she lashed out at his face. She felt the skin on his cheek give way as she raked her nails down his face. He grunted in pain and then pinned her to the ground with his knee. She thought he would break her back as he held her immobile. He grabbed her wrists and tied them behind her tightly, then tied her ankles together. When he was finished he stood and rubbed his bleeding cheek as he looked down at her. "I told you once before you could never escape from me. I meant it, Lindsay. Don't push me."

She couldn't see his face but she could tell from the sound of his voice that he was very angry. But she didn't care about him. She didn't care if he hated her and beat her. She hated him! She hated him for lying to her. She hated him for kidnapping her. But most of all she hated him for humiliating her, for making love to her, and she hated herself because she loved what he did to her. If she lived through this she would never let another man touch her . . . she would never allow herself to be that weak again.

Lucas threw her over his shoulder and stomped back to camp. His shoulder dug into her ribs and each step he took made her breath rush out and she groaned with pain. He tossed her roughly onto a blanket and stood looking down at her. Her tears had mingled with the dirt and her face was covered with mud and grime. Her eyes were large and icy as they stared back at him. Her hair tumbled in disarray around her face and throat. Lucas shook his head, then turned and strode off. *My God! I want to make love to her. She drives me wild with desire one minute and so damn mad the next, I lose control. What the hell has she done to me?* He poured himself a mug of coffee and watched Lindsay fight her bonds.

Chico approached and Lucas smiled sheepishly. "She has a bad temper."

"*Si*, a spitfire, eh?" Chico chuckled as he averted his eyes from the scratches on Lucas's cheek. He finished his coffee and walked to his horse. "The men are waiting to go, *Amigo*." Chico watched Lucas toss the mug to the ground and mount his horse. Lindsay could hear the horses prance and neigh and then the sound of hoof beats disappeared.

* * *

The silence became ominous. She lifted her head to look

around. No one was in the camp. Damn! If she was free she could run again. With Lucas gone, she would probably escape this time. Damn! Damn! She fought her bonds furiously, rubbing her wrists back and forth, trying to loosen the rope. But the only thing she succeeded in doing was to rub the skin from her wrists. As sweat dripped down her arms and onto the raw skin, she gasped with pain. Surely, Lucas wouldn't leave her here like this! Surely, someone must be around to watch or protect her! What if the mountain lion came back? If something happened she couldn't even scream to warn someone. But with no one around what good would that do? Oh, God! Was this what Lucas had planned for her? Leave her out here trussed up, unprotected, with no water or food! No! Surely he wouldn't do that. But he was part Indian! Maybe Indians killed this way. She remembered hearing the men on the ranch talk about a band of renegade Indians who had captured some women from a wagon train. They had been found weeks later by two trappers, each tied to stakes in the ground, naked, their skin burned raw from the sun. The skin that was left . . . most of it had been eaten by God knows what. Lindsay shuddered. She remembered thinking then how cruel men could be. What reason would anyone have to inflict such suffering and pain on a helpless woman? Well, if she was to die the same way she hoped God gave her strength. Strength not to beg. She would never beg for anything from Lucas Sanger again.

A woodpecker swooped low over the campsite. She watched him glide to a tree and latch onto the bark. The sound of his tapping echoed through the forest. As she watched the little bird, her eyelids became heavy, the sound of his tapping was hypnotic. Tap . . . tap . . . tap. . . .

* * *

The smell of beans and bacon made her mouth water. She opened her eyes. The sky was black and laced with thousands of stars. The fire crackled loudly as Chico threw more wood on it. She turned her head and looked for Lucas. He stood by his horse doing something with his saddlebag. Her body ached with stiffness. If she weren't released soon she'd die with the pain. Her arms and wrists throbbed and her mouth was dry and she could taste blood from the dry cracks on her lips. Thank God, she'd slept for so long. At least while she was asleep she couldn't feel pain. She closed her eyes and tried to think about her home. She wondered how Regalo was. Was he getting exercise?

Her eyes flew open as Lucas touched her. He smiled as he lifted her and leaned her against a tree. Slowly he removed the bonds from her ankles and wrists. He rubbed her ankles briskly, then her wrists, stopping when he saw the blood ooze from the raw spots on her wrists. He poured some water from his canteen on his bandana and gently wiped the crusted and fresh blood away. Then he untied the gag and again wiped at the crusted blood on her lips. She ran her tongue around her lips and turned her head away from him. He jerked her head back to him and held her chin in his fingers as he continued dabbing cool water on her swollen face. Damn! Why did he lose his temper so easily with her? He hadn't meant to hurt her. He tied her because he knew she woud run away while he and Chico were gone. He was afraid she would get lost if she left the camp. It was better to leave her tied and gagged and hating him than running free in the wilderness and in danger. She was certainly not able to protect herself against the elements. She may think she's strong, but until she's seen what some Indians could do . . . well, she would learn how very weak she was. Then, there was always the danger of wild animals. She had had one encounter and luckily he had followed her right away. He shuddered to think what might have happened had he not been close behind her. Another minute and that lion would have leaped on Lindsay. One powerful swipe of his paw and he would have removed half her face.

Lucas finished wiping the blood and dirt from her face as she glared at him icily. He felt awkward under her icy stare, and turning to the fire he walked away.

"Come here, Lindsay," he called over his shoulder. "Come and eat."

Lindsay wanted so to turn her back on him and ignore him but her stomach growled with hunger. She looked at

Chico slowly eating his food and decided she would only be hurting herself if she didn't eat. She stood slowly, the pain in her ankles severe as the blood rushed back into her dead feet. She gasped with the pain and bent forward to rub her legs. Lucas was at her side and had her in his arms before she could blink. He carried her to the fire and sat her next to Chico. She was handed a plate of beans and bacon and a mug of coffee. She began eating slowly, feigning indifference to the food, but it tasted so good she forgot her pride and dove in. She sipped her coffee and watched the fire when she finished eating. The pain in her arms and legs was diminishing and her mouth felt much better. She paid no attention to Lucas and Chico who talked around her.

After several minutes Lucas rose and pulled Lindsay to her feet. He held her wrist in an iron grip as he led her away from the campsite. She tried to pry his fingers from her wrist but she couldn't budge them. Her ankle twisted and she yelled in pain as she fell. Lucas picked her up and carrying her close to his chest he walked on. Lindsay heard the sound of water as Lucas carried her farther from camp. Then, when she could see the tumbling river, he stopped and placed her on the ground. She rose clumsily to her feet and started to walk back toward the camp. Lucas grabbed her around the shoulders and pulled her back against him.

"Let me go! I hate you, Lucas Sanger. Leave me alone."

His eyes narrowed as he stared down at her. He crushed her to his chest and spoke slowly. "I didn't bring you here to fight. I brought you here to bathe. Now, I'm only going to warn you one more time. Either you stop trying to escape from me and keep your mouth shut or I'll handle you my own way!" He squeezed her tighter and she gasped. "I would rather reach an agreement or truce with you, but either way, I'll be the winner. And, you won't like losing, Lindsay. My alternative methods are far from comfortable. So . . . I want your promise now. No more attempts at escape and no more spitting at me like a cornered cat." He gazed down at her, his arms holding her tightly against him. She began to feel desire nibble at her entrails like a hot poker.

"I . . . I don't know what you're talking about. Escape!

Where would I go out here in the middle of—I don't even have the slightest idea where we are!" Her voice raised slightly as she tried to remain calm. She had to break loose from his hold. As always, her body was betraying her. She wanted to make love to him right now! Right here! Shame crept into her thoughts and she spoke coldly, "Now, if you'll please let me go, I'm tired and I would like to go back to camp."

Lucas chuckled. "Oh, come on, Lindsay. Do you think me a fool? You know damn well where we are and I know you think you can reach help and get back to your uncle if you can get away from me. It's your choice, Lindsay. I want your answer now."

"I have no intention of reaching a truce with a . . . a halfbreed. Now, let go of me or I'll scream so loud everyone for miles around will hear and then you'll be the captive . . . not the captor."

His hand began unbuttoning her shirt and as realization of his intention dawned on her she began to struggle. He continued to hold her close to him with one arm as he spread her shirt and fondled her breasts. She gasped as his fingers tugged gently on her nipples, the fire in her belly spreading upward and bursting like a thousand rockets in her brain. She started to protest, to yell but her words were blocked by his lips as his mouth covered hers. He forced her back until she thought her neck would break. His hand slid down, unfastened her pants, and moved down lower, between her legs. She shivered with delight and went limp in Lucas's arms. A chuckle escaped his throat as he pushed her pants down and laid her on the cool ground. His fingers continued to probe gently between her legs as his lips nibbled on her breasts, tugging and sucking on a nipple. She felt as if a huge weight were holding her arms and legs down while her body floated higher. She couldn't stop him now if she wanted to . . . and she didn't want to.

When he touched her, her will became his. Apart they were Lucas Sanger and Lindsay Tyler. Apart they were two separate beings with two separate lives. But when they made love, when they were together, embracing, holding . . . they became one. They floated above the clouds, each clinging to the other, each intense on the other, the only two people in the world.

After they finished making love and they clung to each other, Lucas spoke softly, his lips against her damp hair. "Niña, you are so beautiful. I would rather die than never be able to make love to you again."

And Lindsay silently agreed. She would exist without his caresses, but she would not be living.

The moon blanketed the earth with its golden light when Lucas carried Lindsay to the river's edge. He walked into the cold water and laid her on the surface, his arm supporting her. She gasped as he dribbled the cool water over her body. The moonlight reflected off her gold body and Lucas couldn't tear his eyes from her. She had acquired a tan from all the riding and her hair was getting lighter and lighter from the sun. She reminded him of a golden statue. A small, gold, perfect statue.

She splashed him and he smiled. She wanted to play, huh? He pulled his arm out and she sank into the water, gasping and choking as she went under. They played in the water until both were exhausted. Then they dressed and returned to camp. Lucas held her hand as he led her to their bed. She sat on the bedroll, wrapped her arms around her knees, and watched the firelight reflect off Lucas's muscles.

"Lindsay, I need your answer."

She looked up at him feigning innocence. "What answer, Lucas? What are you talking about?"

"Oh, come now, chica, don't play dumb. It won't work." He spoke lightly, but Lindsay knew he wasn't teasing.

"What if I can't give you my word. What if I can't reach a . . . truce . . . with you?"

He hunkered down in front of her and rolled back on his heels. He reached out and took her hands in his.

"Then I would have no choice, niña. I would tether you to my side."

The thought of being tied to his side was not as loathsome as she wanted him to think. But, if the chance for escape did come and she were tied . . . well . . . somehow she had to run away while she was close to her home. She had no knowledge where Lucas was taking her so she had to be ready to run while she was in this country.

"You don't need to tie me. I won't try anything."

He bent to her and kissed the tip of her nose. "Good, I don't like to see anything beautiful tethered." He threw back the blankets and stood. "Good night, niña." He walked to the fire and joined Chico.

Lindsay lay back and wrapped the blanket around her.

* * *

The sun peeked through dark clouds and the smell of coffee wafted through the camp when Lindsay opened her eyes. Her back hurt. She stretched and groaned as she sat up. God what she wouldn't give for a night's sleep in a bed!

After eating a light breakfast of biscuits and coffee they rode deeper into the hills. Lindsay rode the extra horse brought for her and she enjoyed the feel of the animal beneath her. She had no sense of time. The land they traveled through looked the same hour after hour.

As the sun was setting, the men made camp under some trees. There was no river to bathe in tonight. Lindsay could feel the sticky layer of sweat and fine dust from the day's ride. She had to settle for washing from the canteen. She unbraided her hair and combed it. Her hair smelled of horses and sagebrush. She was beginning to love the smell. She looked up at the dark sky, ran the comb idly through a curl, and then froze. They were now traveling east. They were moving away from the area of her home. Lindsay began to tremble. As long as she was close to Colorado she felt safe. She knew she could run at the first chance and find Uncle Ned. But they were traveling east! A direction she was a stranger to. How far were they going? She studied the sky again. East! She looked around her. They were in a grove of thick pines. If they traveled a few more days in country like this, Lindsay could escape and easily hide. She had to be prepared now. She had to see her home, Uncle Ned, Zuni . . .

When Lucas finally went to their bed, Lindsay was sleeping. Her breath came in slow, long sighs and her mouth was slightly parted. Her hair fell in disarray around her face. She was so changeable—one minute, soft and purring, the next spewing wrath. He reached out and touched a curl.

"Niña, I know what you're thinking, but you won't get away from me. I may never let you go." He spoke softly and bending over he kissed her cheek lightly, then lay beside her and slept.

Morning came and they rode on. Lindsay always rode at Lucas's side and Chico rode in front. The other two men had departed several days ago and Lindsay wondered where they had gone. A suspicion nagged in the back of her mind that they may return to Moriarity to tell him where she was. This thought reinforced her plan to escape as soon as possible. But she couldn't believe Lucas had helped her escape Nick only to give her back to him. No! He planned to keep her for some other reason and she would do everything in her power to destroy his plans.

They had stopped at a creek to water the horses and fill their canteens. Lucas offered Lindsay a piece of jerky and they continued their journey.

That evening when they made camp, Lucas told Lindsay they were going to have rain soon. "A storm is brewing and out here they can be more violent than anything you've ever seen, niña."

Lindsay looked up at the sky and shrugged. She could see no signs of an approaching storm. But she hoped he was right. A storm would aid her escape. The next morning dark clouds bubbled on the horizon. The air rent with silence as every creature prepared for the impending storm. They rode on until Chico motioned to a hillside and pointed.

A small dark cave would give them protection from the impending onslaught. The trees bent back and forth with the wind and Lucas said he wouldn't be surprised to see many of them blown down by the time they left.

They put their supplies in a corner of the cave and Chico built a small fire to keep the interior warm, Lucas carried several armloads of wood to the cave and smiled as Lindsay helped Chico arrange the stack out of the way.

Their bedrolls were spread out and a pot of coffee bubbled from the fire. The wind had picked up intensity and it howled around the mouth of the cave. The rumble of thunder could be heard in the distance and Lindsay wondered if trying to escape tonight was wise after all. She glanced at Lucas. He stood at the entrance and surveyed the sky. His lips were in a grim line as he turned back into the cave. He looked down at Lindsay and smiled. "Don't worry niña, the worst part of the storm won't hit for awhile. By then, you'll be used to the noise."

She smiled uneasily. If Lucas felt this was going to be a bad storm, then she probably would be wise to wait until it was over. But his next words made her decision for her. "Soon it will be nothing more than rain and then we'll start out again." How soon, she wondered. They were getting farther away from familiar country. No, she must escape tonight! She had to be successful this time or she would never have another chance. And, if her suspicions were correct, if those other two men had gone back for Moriarity . . . well . . . chances are she wouldn't have much time left anyway.

With her mind made up Lindsay took a deep sigh and settled back to wait for the right moment. Lucas threw some wood on the fire and then he and Chico talked a few minutes before retiring.

Lucas slept between Lindsay and the entrance. She would have to crawl around him and that wasn't going to be easy. Chico slept on the other side of the fire. If she could get out of this cave without either of those men hearing her . . . well . . . she could do anything. The horses had been led around the side of the mountain, behind some rocks and tethered. They were protected as much as possible and Lindsay knew she would be wasting precious time in trying to locate them. She would walk! Surely she would come across help soon.

Lindsay could hear the first drops of rain pelt the earth. Lightning coursed through the sky rending the inky blackness and bouncing eerily around the cave interior. Thunder pounded the earth, shaking the trees. She smiled. The noise of the storm would help to conceal the noise of her escape. She turned to watch Lucas. His back rose and fell with each breath. He was alseep.

She crept to the edge of the bedroll and looked for her boots. They weren't where she had left them. Damn! Somebody moved them! Well, she couldn't spend half the night looking for them, she would go without them.

She pushed her body slowly to the wall of the cave, watching the sleeping men intently. With the sound of the storm they would have a rough time hearing her. When she felt the wall of the cave against her back, she slowly moved to the entrance. She was hunched down and guiding herself by the flashes of lightning and the dying embers from the fire. When she reached the entrance she looked around quickly for her boots. They were nowhere! She couldn't imagine what had happened to them. She hadn't seen Chico hide them because Lucas felt that without her boots she wouldn't be so apt to try escaping.

A bolt of lightning and a crack of thunder caused her to jump. She grabbed her throat and hugged the wall with her body. She watched the men. They hadn't moved. She would have to be more careful. She almost screamed at that last flash of lightning it startled her so. She looked outside. Rain pelted the ground and the wind blew harshly. A streak of lightning lit up the sky momentarily and she could see the tall trees swaying and jerking in the wind. She looked back into the warm, secure cave, and for a fleeting moment wondered if she was being foolish. But, the thought of Nick Moriarity and fear of what was going to happen to her drove her on and she ran headlong into the rain and wind, gasping as the first cold drops hit her body. She ran to a tree and stood for a moment, squinting her eyes against the wind. She wasn't sure which way to go with no stars to follow, but if she got far enough away from Lucas she could hole up somewhere until the storm passed and she could tell directions again.

The rain pelted her body and her clothes clung to her skin. Her hair hung in wet strands and she brushed it out of her face. Another streak of lightning lit up the sky and she took advantage of the instant light and ran into the trees. She ran wildly, darting in and out of trees, running into fallen logs with her bare feet and falling on the slippery ground. She stopped for a minute of rest and leaned against a tree. Her feet were numb with cold and she could feel the warm blood from the many scratches and cuts. She was freezing cold and shivering with fright, but she had made this decision and damned if she wasn't going to follow through. She started walking again. She had to find some place to rest and get out of the rain. She would catch pneumonia at this rate and die for sure. The mud began sucking at her feet and each step became agony for her tired and raw feet. She knew she hadn't gone very far from the cave but the rain would erase her tracks. She really didn't need to go too far in this weather. Maybe this storm is a good omen after all, she thought. Another jagged streak of lightning rent the sky and Lindsay spied a cluster of rocks and ran toward them. She crawled into an opening. With the reprieve from the rain and the feeling of freedom she soon fell into a restless sleep.

Lucas rolled over and sighed. He reached over to pull Lindsay close to him. He reached farther when his arms touched air and his eyes flew open. He jumped to his feet and yelled to Chico. Chico pointed to a ledge and Lucas saw Lindsay's boots sitting back in the shadows. She had left barefooted! He had underestimated her! Nobody with any sense would walk through this country without shoes. He should have realized Lindsay didn't always think clearly. She felt rather than did. She reacted and much of the time in anger. Well, this would be the last time he would trust her. A shiver ran through his body. As his eyes met Chico's, the fear in them was evident.

Chico nodded. "*Amigo*, we'll find her. She can't have gone far tonight."

Lucas began searching on foot while Chico went for the horses. His eyes weaved back and forth, up and down. At least she wasn't in any danger of running into any other human on a night like this, but animals, snakes and the greatest danger of all was flooding. If she crawled into a wash for shelter, she'd never get to high ground if a flash flood occurred.

"Goddamn her! He pulled his serape closer and searched the ground. He could hear Chico approach and he yelled. "Over here." He grabbed the reins of his horse and spoke.

"You search over that way, holler if you see anything. I'll take this direction." He shook his hat and water splashed on his legs. "I doubt if she'd have gone any other direction. She would probably go north and then west." He pulled his hat low over his face and growled, "Sorry, friend, to make you go out on a night like this. It won't happen again."

Chico nodded and turned his horse in the other direction. Poor chica. She'll regret this for many days to come. His eyes searched the ground for any signs of humans, preferably a small, beautiful redhaired human. I think maybe Lucas is in love with this girl. I have never seen him act so unpredictable. I have never seen him so frightened about anyone's safety. Chico smiled. Poor chica.

Lucas's blood pounded in his temples. He was angry to the point of losing control. He shook his head. Calm down he thought, you won't gain anything by losing control. He bent low over the horse's neck and surveyed the wet ground. She had given her word and he had made the mistake of believing her. Well, she won't have another chance to break her word. She won't be trusted again.

A flash of lightning lit the sky and Lucas spotted a footprint. Her foot had sunk so deep in the mud, the rain had not yet obliterated it, only filled it with water. He looked up and scanned the horizon. Trees and more trees. She had gone further than he thought she would. He continued riding slowly, his eyes scanning the ground, waiting for lightning to enable him to see. He spotted another muddy print and then another. He swore at her for this stupidity. His anger increased again and magnified until the heat from his fury matched the heat from the lightning. He stopped. His eyes fell on another print. She had changed direction. He scanned the horizon again and his breath came out in a low groan. A group of rocks stood against the hillside. He climbed from the horse and walked to the rocks. Another flash of lightning tore through the sky and Lucas saw her hair streaming out from under a rock. He approached slowly and hunkered down by her head. He pushed his hat back and smiled crookedly. She was shivering, her body drenched, her hair plastered to her head. The outline of her nipples showed through the wet material and Lucas felt a desire begin to rise in him.

A bolt of lightning rent the sky and the thunder that followed deafened Lucas with an ear-splitting crash. Lindsay sat up abruptly. Her sleep had been fraught with nightmares and fear. The sudden explosion of noise became a real and threatening gunshot. She began screaming as the lightning outlined a man bending over her but a hand clamped down over her mouth and she began to fall . . . down . . . through a long, wet, cold tunnel . . .

Lucas carried her to his horse and after wrapping his serape around them both, he turned and returned to the cave. He yelled to his friend who returned the yell and soon he could hear Chico behind him. Lindsay's limp body trembled with the cold and Lucas needed to get her warm and dry before she got sick. Lucas carried her unconscious body into the warm shelter as Chico led the horses back to their shelter.

Lucas laid her on the bedroll and stripped off her wet clothes. He began rubbing her body briskly with a blanket when she opened her eyes. She blinked several times and then looked up into Lucas's face. She started to sit up but he held her down and continued drying her off. She laid her hand against her forehead and closed her eyes. The cold and fear was nothing to the embarrassment of laying here and letting him dry her body. He took what seemed to Lindsay extra time on her breasts and inner thighs. Then he rolled her over and dried her back, rubbing briskly, almost painfully as he brought blood to the surface. When he was satisfied she was dry and warm, he wrapped several blankets around her and turned as Chico handed him the whiskey flask. He held it to Lindsay's lips and forced her to take a swallow. The hot liquid burned down into her belly and she coughed and gagged as tears came to her eyes. After several seconds she stopped coughing and Lucas forced her to take another drink. She turned her head, trying to avoid the nasty stuff but he held her by the hair and forced the flask between her lips. Soon the whiskey began to warm her and she stopped her violent trembling as it saturated her blood, relaxing her limbs and making her feel lightheaded. Lucas took a long draught from the flask and handed it to

Chico who did likewise. Lindsay closed her eyes and wondered if Chico had been present when she lay naked on the blankets.

But I guess it really doesn't matter . . . nothing matters any more.

Chico threw more wood on the fire and the dry wood crackled and popped and Lindsay lay watching the shadows dance on the walls. She heard Chico crawl under his blanket and she turned to see where Lucas was. He was laying her clothes by the fire. When he turned back to her, their eyes met and held, the fire reflecting blue and green as they stared.

The storm was gaining in fury and the wind whipped rain into the cave which plopped into the dust. Lucas walked to her side. He stood looking down at her and she felt the heat rise and color her cheeks. She hugged the blanket tightly, pulling it higher around her face and exposed her feet. He took note of the cuts and scratches and swollen skin and finally spoke. "You know you did the most stupid goddamn thing I've ever seen."

He turned to his saddle bag and after rummaging through it returned with a jar in his hand. He kneeled down and picked up one foot in his hand. Lindsay raised herself up on her elbows to watch him but he yelled for her to lay back down and she did so. He rubbed her feet with the strange smelling ointment. After the initial stinging, the pain subsided and she relaxed. After he had rubbed both her feet with the ointment he ripped a corner of the blanket and wrapped each foot. Then, smiling coldly, he tied her feet together. "Since you can't seem to be trusted and your word ain't worth a damn, well, this should keep you around." Then he grabbed her arms and forced them behind her and tied them together. The blankets fell from her body and her skin shone in the reflected light.

Lucas threw his hat down and began removing his clothes. Lindsay watched him and knew what his intentions were. She closed her eyes as a tear slid between her lid and down her cheek. Lucas reached out his finger and touched the silky tear. Then, without speaking, he laid next to her, held her close against him and wrapped the blankets around them. Lindsay's eyelids began to get heavy as she listened to the rain and soon she slept. She hadn't said one word tonight. She didn't argue or curse. If there was one thing you could count on from Lindsay, it was not knowing what she would do next. Well, he would finish reprimanding her in the morning. Now he wanted to hold her warm body and relax. He took a deep breath. Thank God, he had found her.

She woke in the morning to the sound of rain and the smell of coffee and beans. Her mouth watered and she started to sit up. She fell backward and swore as she realized her arms and legs were still tied. The blanket slipped down and her breasts were exposed to view. Lucas approached her and casually pulled the blanket up.

"You'd better be still, niña, or you'll expose your body to Chico. And although I don't think he'd mind, I know you would." Chico smiled and shrugged as he looked at her and she blushed profusely, her skin flaming with embarrassment. She opened her mouth to speak when Lucas's hand came down over it. "Don't say one word. I'm in no mood to listen to your lies and threats." The ice in his eyes startled Lindsay and she closed her mouth. She snuggled down into the blankets and watched him. What's wrong with him, she thought? He walked to Chico and returned carrying a plate of steaming beans and salt pork. He lifted her into a sitting position and after draping the blankets around her he began to feed her. She started to protest but he glared at her and she thought better of pressing him now.

Thunder rolled through the sky and the ground shook. She glanced outside and Lucas spoke. "The storm has worsened. If I hadn't found you, you would probably have drowned." She shivered and when she looked back at him, the look in his eyes made her tremble more violently. He carried the empty plates to Chico and then returned to her, bending close to her face, his eyes hard as he spoke.

"Lindsay, you gave your word. I believed you. Because of your stupidity, you endangered Chico, me, and you. I cannot tolerate your behavior any longer." She looked away, avoiding the look on his face, but he grabbed her face and yanked it back, holding her securely as he continued talking. "I haven't the time or the patience to continually search for you. From now on, you will be tied up. And if you argue or scream, you'll be gagged." He left her then and walked to Chico who sat by the fire. Chico handed Lucas a mug of steaming coffee. They sat and and talked in muffled tones.

Lindsay watched them. When his words sunk into her brain she began to get mad. He had no right to keep her here. What did he want with her? If they were waiting for Moriarity, what did he expect her to do. Sit by and wait for her death sentence. He's mad at me because I endangered him and Chico. Well, what the hell does he think he's done to me? He's the one who took me from my home! He's the one who gave me to Moriarity.

"You . . . you bastard." The words came out sneeringly, filled with hatred as Lucas looked up at her. "I endangered you . . . what the hell have you done to me? I was led to believe all you wanted was a tour of the ranch. Some tour! You're the one who lied, Lucas Sanger. You're the one who can't be trusted. I pray to God I'm around when they hang you. I want to see the look on your face when the noose tightens and your eyes bulge. I hope your death is slow and painful. I hope you suffer the same fears I've suffered all these weeks . . . you lousy, rotten bast . . ."

Lucas's hands gripped her arms as he yanked her to her feet. The blankets fell from her body and she stood naked. Chico turned away. Lucas's hands bit into Lindsay's flesh. He held her in front of him, her toes brushed the ground. A muscle twitched in his cheek and his eyes glared coldly at her. Her face was white with anger and her nostrils flared out with each breath she took. The pain from his hands digging into her flesh momentarily stopped her thoughts but she soon felt nothing except animal hatred. "You're crazy! You're a madman, Lucas Sanger."

As though a taut rope snapped, Lucas began shaking her. He shook her until she thought her head would snap off. Finally when the tears fell down her cheeks and a sob escaped her throat, Lucas stopped. He stared down at her momentarily, then pushed her backward onto the bedroll, and threw a blanket over her naked, shaking body. He turned and stomped out of the cave, into the raging storm.

The fury of the storm matched the fury within Lucas as he disappeared from view. Lindsay lay on the blanket sobbing softly. Her arms hurt terribly where Lucas had gripped them and her body ached with fear and fright.

Chico watched his friend stomp off and shifted his gaze to the sobbing girl. He wondered if Lucas knew. He wondered if Lindsay knew. He wondered how long it would be before they admitted their love to each other.

Lucas stood in the raging storm, the rain pelting his face and body. He looked up into the dark sky and watched a streak of lightning touch the horizon. Why did he let her get to him like that? Why didn't he ignore her barbs and close his ears to her? He looked down at his hands. They were trembling and he wrung them together. Never, in all of his life had he lost control of his emotions like he did with her! What the hell had she done to him? He leaned against a tree and relaxed his taut body. A smile touched his lips as the words came from his mouth.

I love her. He groaned as he ran his fingers through his wet hair. My God, I think I've loved her from the first moment I laid eyes on her. Jesus Christ! What do I do now? She hates me with every breath she takes. And I can't say as I blame her. I wonder how long I have before Tyler sends for her. I wonder if I'll be able to let her go. Goddamn! Why in the hell did I ever take on this job? I should have told Stade to shove it and left for Solano. Now, no matter what happens, I'll lose. She'll never believe me. Even if Tyler tells her the truth, she'll be with him and probably have forgotten I ever existed. His thoughts wandered to Lindsay's words, "I hope your death is slow and painful. I hope you suffer the same fears I've suffered all these weeks . . . ." He cringed as he remembered the hatred in her eyes. His eyes softened as he thought of her lips, her warm, sensuous body, so ripe for love, so easy to arouse. He stood straight and shook the clinging water from his hair. He turned to the cave and spoke under this breath, "Well, one thing's for damned sure. No matter how hard she fights, I'm not gonna stop making love to her."

He stopped as he reached the entrance and heard her soft sobs. His stomach tightened and the blood pounded in his temples as he finished, "I would rather she fought me and screamed her hatred at my touch than not to touch her at all. I am not that strong."

He entered the warm, dark cave. Chico looked up, his eyes soft, his lips set in a grim line. He poured a mug of hot coffee and held it to Lucas. Lucas took the proffered cup and stood watching Lindsay. Her hair lay spread out and hid her face but her body shook with each sob. The blanket covered her back and upper legs and her tethered feet, wrapped in the makeshift bandage, jerked with each sob. He looked down at Chico and reddened as he met his friend's gaze. Chico smiled crookedly and lowered his eyes. Lucas walked to the back of the cave and sat, leaning back against the cool rocks and closed his eyes. He didn't feel like talking to Chico.

Several hours went by before anyone moved inside the little cave. The storm raged on without a sign of letting up and Lindsay slept.

Lucas moved beside her and sat watching her. Her face was streaked with tears and dirt and her eyes were swollen from crying. He gritted his teeth when she rolled and the blankets fell, exposing her bruised arms. Long red welts marred the skin and purple bruises began to surround the welts. Chico slept against the far wall and after waking left to check the horses.

Lindsay's sleep was fraught with nightmares. She saw herself balanced on the back of a giant horse. The horse's legs were as tall as fir trees. Its back was flat and slick and Lindsay was fighting frantically to stay on. Then she felt her balance fail and felt weightless. The air rushed past her skin as she fell faster and faster toward the black abyss below. The nightmare ended with a start. And then she slept peacefully.

The day dragged by slowly and the rain continued to pour down. Lindsay woke in the late afternoon and hunger gnawed at her. Lucas fed her a plate of beans and jerky and gave her sips of hot coffee. He did not attempt to release her bonds and she stretched and moved as the ache from being tied made her want to scream. But, she dared not say a word. She was afraid of what he would do to her. She lay on her side and watched the rain pelt the ground when she heard Lucas approach. He hunkered down and pushed her gently onto her back. She shivered and blinked in fear as he reached for her feet. Her actions angered him and he grabbed her tied feet and cut the bonds, more harshly than he meant to. He was angry with himself. He was mad because he had caused her to fear him. Every time he reached for her now she winced. And her wincing angered him more so he was rougher. But he couldn't tell her he wouldn't hurt her. She wouldn't believe him and until she was safely at his ranch perhaps it was best she feared him. Then maybe she wouldn't do anything foolish again. He removed the dressings from her feet and swore under his breath at the swollen, infected flesh. He reached for the jar of ointment as he spoke, "Goddamnit, Lindsay, look at your feet! They're so goddam infected you probably won't be able to walk!" Lindsay cringed as she listened to the anger in his voice. She was too frightened to hear the concern.

Chico walked over and looked at her feet. Shaking his head he walked to his saddlebag and looked through the worn bag. Finding what he looked for he walked back to Lucas and handed him a pair of thick, wool stockings, and a piece of cloth. "Here, wrap her feet in this and put the socks over them." Lucas nodded thanks and began rubbing her feet with ointment. The pain brought tears to her eyes but she bit her lip and remained silent. Lucas looked up at her and his gaze softened as he saw the tears dangling from her lashes. He rubbed more gently and wrapped her feet in the cloth Chico handed him. Then he pulled the thick socks over the dressings and spoke. "You have lots of splinters stuck in your feet, but I'll wait to remove them until the swellings gone down some."

Darkness descended and the lightning continued to light up the area. The wind blew with such intensity Lindsay thought the horses would surely blow away. The pounding rain hit the ground with such force that it sounded like spikes being driven into wood. She stretched her legs and flexed her sore feet and wondered how long Lucas would let her stay untied. She had rolled onto her stomach, the blanket had fallen away, and she began to shiver with the cold when Lucas laid beside her and pulled her into his embrace. He wrapped the blanket securely around her shivering body and held her close. She stared at the pulse in his throat and wondered why this sudden show of concern but with the warmth of his body next to hers, she fell asleep.

When morning dawned, the sky continued to seep its contents onto the earth but the wind had died and Lucas announced they would again journey on. Chico fixed a pot of coffee, threw the remainder of the bacon in the pan, and then went to get the horses. Lindsay watched the men gather their supplies and pack them into the saddlebags.

She ate the food Lucas fed her. When everything was ready for their departure Lucas looked at her and asked if she would like to take a walk. She reddened as she realized what he meant and after acknowledging him, she kept her eyes averted. Lucas picked her up and carried her into the rain. She gasped as the cold water hit her face but she was wrapped in a warm blanket and Lucas held her close. He sat her on a log, then turned his back, and walked a few yards away. When she stood, the pain from her feet caused her to gasp. Lucas whirled and raced to her, picking her up and holding her close. They returned to the cave and Lucas laid her down and then gathered her clothes from the rocks and dressed her. She blushed and felt the heat rise as his fingers brushed her breasts as he buttoned her shirt. When he pulled the pants on her and reached down to button them, his fingers brushed her inner thigh. She gasped. It was as though an electric shock flowed between them and Lucas mentally shook his head. He sure as hell couldn't make love to her now. With Chico waiting for them and the hatred she felt, to rape her now would only add to her angry feelings.

The sleeves of her shirt hung at her sides and Lucas smiled down at her as he tied them together. Then reaching into his boot the brought out a knife and picked up a blanket. He folded the blanket in half and then in half again, the cut visible diagonally across the folds. He opened the blanket and with a nod of approval moved to Lindsay and pushed the blanket over her head. It fell around her shoulders and about her body like a serape. She remembered her remark to Julie so long ago, "Wear long pants and a serape and be accepted . . ." She giggled. Lucas looked at her. Had he heard what he thought? He shrugged and tied the serape around her waist with a piece of rope. Then he carried her to his horse and lifted her into the saddle. The rain fell on the blanket and soon it shimmered with silver droplets making rivulets to the bottom of the blanket and then plopping to her feet. Lucas jumped behind her and wrapped another blanket around her body, immersing her in darkness. He pulled her back against his chest and they rode off. She relaxed against him and sighed. I'm not going to think about what's going to happen to me. She was too tired and hurt too much to care. She would quit fighting.

They rode on and the rain continued. They stopped at a river and Lucas lifted Lindsay down and set her against a tree. The rain had slowed and a fine mist played at the trees, making them look ghostly. Lindsay sat and watched Chico prepare their food. Even though everything was wet, a fire soon burned and a pot of coffee bubbled from the innards of the flame. Soon Lucas approached her with two plates of beans and jerky. After feeding her, he ate. Lucas looked at the sky and frowned. "Looks like more rain coming. We'd better get started. The longer we sit around, the longer we ride through water."

They continued their journey. Lindsay wrapped warmly in front of Lucas while Chico led her horse. The horses struggled through the quagmire. With each step they took, the mud sucked at their legs, fighting with the horse for possession. It became a struggle just to travel a few feet and Lucas swore. Rain began to fall again and Lindsay could hear the drops touch the leaves of the trees and splash to the ground. They finally stopped, unsaddled the exhausted horses, and tethered them under a tree. There was grass for them to graze on but Chico attached an oat bag to their heads and walked off. A crude shelter was constructed from sticks and blankets. As Lindsay sat under the uneven blanket and looked around, she perceived slight changes in the landscape. The hills were smaller and the trees had thinned considerably. The rain finally stopped but the sky was dark and forebidding. Chico lit a fire under the shelter and soon the warmth from the fire caressed her face and she slept.

She woke with a start and realized it was the middle of the night. The men had packed everything and Lucas wrapped Lindsay in a blanket and lifted her to the horse's back. They rode . . . on and on and on.

When they stopped for a few minutes, Lindsay laid on the ground savoring the opportunity to stretch out. The moon hung low on the horizon, giving off an eerie, orange light that touched everything. The remnants of the storm tumbled through the sky and Lucas stood and watched the stars shining down.

Soon they were riding again and Lindsay thought she would scream with the constant traveling. Her arms ached terribly from being tied and her feet hurt even though Lucas changed the dressings and reapplied the ointment every time they stopped. She slept restlessly, her dreams filled with blue eyes and probing lips. She saw her uncle run to her and wrap his arms around her. Suddenly she felt lips on hers, hard, passionate. Her eyes flew open to scream at her uncle, only to be looking at Lucas. She tossed and fought to put the blue eyes from her mind but to no avail. They would pop out at her from everywhere. Finally, she gave up. She listened, she watched, and she grew weary, but she kept her eyes open.

And then one night she heard the sound of a guitar! She shook her head. But the sound grew louder and she strained to hear it better. Lucas tightened his hold on her and she wriggled to sit up and hear. But she knew unless Lucas wanted her to, she would not know where the sound came from. She relaxed against his chest. What's the use of fighting or hoping . . . nothing, nobody would be able to save her.

They stopped and she heard Lucas talk in hushed tones to Chico. Then, she felt Lucas wrap his arms around her and lift her down. She heard a door open and close behind them. Laughter and music wafted to her ears. She felt Lucas carrying her up some stairs. Clearly, there were people here—but she couldn't reach them, still in Lucas's bond. A door opened and then closed behind them. She was tossed unceremoniously onto a bed and lying there she wondered what would happen now. She heard a lock click, then felt Lucas's hands as he removed the blanket shroud from her body. She looked around and saw that she was in a small, sparsely furnished room. It contained only a bed, a chair, and a table with a bowl and pitcher. Towels hung from a hook above the table and a dingy bar of soap lay next to the pitcher. There was a small window, but shutters had been drawn across them and were obviously locked tight. The bed had clean sheets and an old, worn but clean quilt folded at the foot.

She looked at Lucas. "Where are we?" He walked to the chair and hung his serape and hat on the back. "Santa Fe" he said. Slowly, he walked to her and placed an arm on each side of her, imprisoning her. He bent close to her face and she could feel his breath on her lips. "But don't get any foolish ideas. We're leaving here shortly and you won't be out of my sight for one blasted second."

She listened to him, then spoke, her voice soft and pleading, "Please, please let me go. Please. I promise I won't tell anybody about you. Please, Lucas . . ." The last words came out in a sob as tears fell down her cheeks and onto the bed. His teeth clenched and the muscle twitched in his cheek as he listened to her. He abruptly stood and walked away. He couldn't stand to hear her plead. He had to say something to stop her from crying and begging or he might give in to her. He walked to the bowl and pitcher and poured some water into the bowl. "Lindsay, you're wasting your time and mine by begging. I'm tired of listening to you. Now shut up".

She felt dumbstruck. She was so shocked at his words and tone she stopped crying and watched him. He walked back to her carrying the bowl of water and some towels slung over his arm. He set the bowl on the floor and sat on the edge of the bed. He reached over and pulled her to his side. He soaped a cloth and holding her face he rubbed it furiously with the soapy cloth. She sputtered and tried to bite his hand but he held tight and rubbed her skin harder and seemed to enjoy watching her spit soap from her mouth. He scrubbed her face until she thought he would rub the skin from her and then he dried her face with a fluffy towel.

"Well, there *is* a woman under all that dirt. I was beginning to wonder." He chuckled as he stood up and she glared at him. He turned her over and untied her wrists and rubbed them for several seconds. They had not been tied tight but lack of movement had stiffened them and Lucas rubbed them furiously. Lindsay lay stiff, gritting her teeth. She ached all over—her feet, her arms, her back, her head. She wondered if she would ever feel good again or if she would ever be given the opportunity.

He rolled her back facing him and began to remove her clothes. He threw the blanket serape on the floor and began unbottoning her shirt. With her hands free, she began fighting him. She reached up to claw his face and he chuckled as he grabbed her wrists. After removing her shirt, he retied her arms in front of her and began to remove her pants. His fingers brushed her skin. As he pulled her pants off, he deliberately touched between her legs and she gasped. He smiled lazily as he reached for the cloth and soap and began washing her body. Lindsay closed her eyes and bit her lip. She knew it would do no good to fight him and getting mad was a waste of time, but she could feign indifference to him. She could pretend his touch didn't affect her. He gently soaped her breasts and down her belly to her inner thighs. He washed between her legs with a deliberateness that infuriated her, but try as she might she could not remain indifferent . . . she was weakening. Desire began to bubble up from the depths of her belly and she broke out in a cold sweat.

He laughed deeply as he watched her fight with the desire she felt. "If you think I'm sleeping with a wench who hasn't bathed in a while, you'd better think again, chica." He washed her legs and rolled her over and washed her back. When he was finished he dried her, rubbing her briskly with a big towel. Then he removed the socks and dressings on her feet. The swelling had gone down and the ointment was working. The many infected cuts were beginning to heal. He washed her feet with soap and removed some splinters, then reapplied the ointment and dressings.

When he had finished ministering to her she asked him softly, "Why all the time and attention? Seems such a waste of time if I'm going to die in the end. You are so good at making people suffer." Lucas spun around and bent over her, his face a mask of anger. "You have a way of making me lose my temper, niña, don't push me too far. You won't like the consequences." He stomped across the room and ran his fingers through his hair before he opened the door. Then as though he had forgotten to say something he whirled to look at her. She lay quietly watching him. Her naked body moved sensuously on the bed as she tried to hide under the covers. Her hair fell around her shoulders and across a cheek. Her eyes were large and questioning. He turned around to open the door and stomped out angrily.

She heard him lock the door and remove the key and she lay there for a few minutes wondering what he was going to do next. Looking around the room, she thought about going to the window and pounding on it with her tied fists, but it would do no good. He must hate me terribly, she thought. And for some reason that thought bothered her. She reached down and pulled the quilt over her. The bed felt so good and being clean felt good. She fell asleep and for the first time in several nights she was not troubled by nightmares.

She came awake slowly, climbing to awareness, her eyes lead weights, her entire being felt heavy. And then her muscles tensed and her heart began beating rapidly. She could feel the hot, whiskey-laden breath of Lucas on her neck. He moved and she felt him nibble on her earlobe. His lips burned a path down her throat and when he kissed her, she tasted whiskey. He kissed every inch of her face and throat and when his lips moved to her breasts she was breathless with desire. She wanted to run her fingers through his hair and knead the muscles of his back, but she couldn't. She knew she would be wasting her breath if she asked him to release her, so she remained quiet. But she couldn't hold still. His lips and hands worked on her body and brain and she began moaning softly and writhing. He raised his body over hers and lifted her legs. "You are very easy to handle, niña. All I have to do is begin making love to you and you'll do anything I ask. Such passion is hard to find." She heard his words but she didn't blink at their meaning. He was right.

His hands gripped her knees, spreading her legs. His lips nibbled on the flesh of her inner thighs. She opened her eyes and gasped. What was he doing? She tried to wriggle free but he murmured something inaudible and his mouth came down over her womanhood. His tongue probed and Lindsay arched her back and moaned. He released her legs and she wrapped them around his neck. She thought the top of her head would explode with desire. When she climaxed she threw her head back and the veins in her neck bulged. Lucas continued to probe with his tongue and when she was gasping and heaving with each breath, he moved over her, fondled a breast and kissed her passionately. When she began to writhe and squirm again he entered her, slowly at first, then faster and faster. Their passions again united in ectasy. As the fever of their desire slowly diminished, Lindsay slept in the protective circle of his arms. Her cheeks blushed with color and her body glowed from their lovemaking.

* * *

A whack on the buttocks awakened her and she opened her eyes, then snuggled back into the quilt and closed her eyes. She was dragged from the bed half asleep. She stood weakly against Lucas and struggled to open her eyes. He pulled her pants over her bundled feet and up around her waist. He wrapped her shirt around her, buttoned it and then pulled the serape over her head. Through the shuttered windows she could see it was pitch black. What was he doing dressing her in the middle of the night? She yawned and closed her eyes as Lucas gathered her into his arms and walked from the room. He kicked the door shut behind him, walked down the stairs, and out into the night. Chico sat on his horse holding the reins of the other two animals. After Lucas lifted Lindsay into the saddle he mounted behind her and again wrapped her in the thick blanket. As they rode into the night Lindsay laid her head against Lucas and slept. She dreamt she was in a bed with crisp white sheets and a down quilt covering her naked skin.

Not much farther, eh, Chico? Did you talk to Milly?" Chico shook his head. "*Si*, most of the girls were busy and

Milly was trying to figure out what you had in your arms. Milly's business has grown. There was a birthday party in the parlor for the sheriff," Chico laughed. "It was a good thing I joined them and you joined Milly." He laughed again. "Milly was furious when she found out you brought a girl to her house. She said her job was to supply men with girls, they don't have to bring their own."

Lucas laughed. "Yeah, she was a little angry until I went to her room. I talked her out of being mad. Did you find out how many men had been asking about me?"

Three. They all wanted to know where you live but no one knows where your *hacienda* is." Chico smiled, then turned to look at Lucas. "I don't like it, Lucas. Someone is bound to find out where she is," he nodded at Lindsay, "and knowing Moriarity . . . well, he's crazy, *amigo*. A crazy man acts without regard for anybody's life including his own. I think we will double the guards around the ranch, no?"

Lucas nodded in agreement as they rode into the mountains. Neither man said any more as they rode along. Lucas's thoughts centered on Lindsay and how he was going to keep her safe until she was back with Tyler. He frowned. He didn't want to think of the day when she would leave and return to her home. He wanted her with him, by his side, safe and protected by him from now on. He couldn't give her up.

* * *

The day dawned hot and clear. Lindsay yawned. She licked her lips and struggled to get comfortable. Her body ached. She wondered how Lucas and Chico could ride so long. They didn't seem bothered by the constant traveling. She groaned and Lucas smiled down at her. "Soon niña, soon we'll stop."

The sun was straight up when they stopped and Lucas lifted Lindsay from the horse and sat her on the ground. He pulled the blanket from her head and smiled at her. She fell back on the ground, luxuriating in the cool sand against her hot skin. She stretched and groaned with pleasure and Lucas laughed at her antics. She ignored him as she continued to writhe on the ground. She took in the surrounding area and marveled at its beauty. The sky was azure blue, the rugged hills blazing red in the midday sun. Soon they had consumed a potful of beans and mugs of hot coffee.

Lucas lifted Lindsay to the horse and this time he left the blanket off her. The day grew hotter and under the serape, Lindsay's skin itched and sweat ran down her throat and between her breasts. She was sticky and dirty and she felt like screaming. She swore to herself that once they got to their destination she would never ride a horse again, at least not for a long time.

They rode through prairie land now. Undulating grass looked like waves washing over the sand as far as the eye could see. She watched the grass blow and lifted her face to the breeze, cool against her hot skin.

They made camp in the open that night. Lindsay lay on her blanket and thought she had never seen so many stars. They were thicker in the sky than freckles on Julie's sister's face. She giggled. Such an idea.

Lucas walked to her. She looked at him and with an impish grin said, "You know your eyes are as bright and distant as the stars, Lucas."

He bent down to her and replied, "And you, niña, you defy understanding." He lovingly touched a curl on her breast, then walked away.

The next day brought more painful riding to what had become an exhausting ordeal. They stopped only briefly in the early evening to rest the weary horses. Lindsay slept for a short time and when she opened her eyes the sun hung low and black clouds tumbled past the orange ball. They continued riding and as they circled a rock escarpment Lindsay saw a pinprick of light. Her heart thumped a little faster. She felt both anxious anticipation and reluctant fear at the same time. Light meant people. And people meant help, maybe.

The beacon of light grew larger as they rounded a bend and then the outline of a building loomed up. They rode through a gate and several men ran to them. Lucas jumped down and after much handshaking and words of greeting, he lifted Lindsay to the ground. She stumbled and he picked her up and carried her through an open door.

They entered a large, airy room with quarry stone floor. Three archways opened off this room and Lucas continued walking straight ahead and down a hall. He stopped in front of an ornately carved door and kicked it open. Lindsay's eyes widened in surprise at the large, white stucco bedroom. A bed stood in the middle with a bedspread of brightly colored squares. French doors opened onto an enclosed patio. A large, intricately carved dresser and mirror stood along another wall. There was an exquisitely carved bench covered with brightly colored pillows. The red tile floor was enhanced with several throw rugs. Large urns with plants stood around the room and a pair of tall, brass candle holders guarded the bench. The smell of jasmine and gardenia came through the open doors and filled the room with their fragrance. Lindsay's eyes surveyed the room and her lips parted as she looked around. Lucas watched her for a few seconds and, laughing, he tossed her on the bed. She bounced and wiggled upright and leaned against the headboard. Lucas threw his hat on the dresser, sat beside her, and pulled her to him. He reached down and untied the bonds from her wrists and tossed them on the dresser. "I may need them again so I'll keep them around," he teasingly smiled. Lindsay stepped on the floor and turned slowly looking around her, astounded at the beauty that surrounded her.

"Where are we, Lucas?"

"My *rancho*." He answered. She spun and looked at him. "Yours? But how does a highway man like you come to own such a house?" she teased, "Good year ransoming innocent women?"

Lucas ignored the barb. "Do you think that I don't enjoy beautiful things, Lindsay?" He was watching her intently. It was a serious question.

"I didn't mean it that way, Lucas, but you don't give one the impression of enjoying anything but that which appeases your baser instincts."

Smiling, he stood up, undid his gunbelt and put it on the dresser. Turning back to her he spoke in a hushed, derisive tone. "Your bonds have been removed because there is no possible escape from here. When I'm not around, guards will watch you at all times. You'll be comfortable here and need nothing. If foolishness overrides your common sense and you should try to escape, there is another room for guests below us. You so much as look at a horizon too long and I'll lock you down there to sing with the cockroaches." Holding his arms out to her, he finished, "But I'm sure you've learned your lesson, right, niña?"

Tossing her head and lifting her nose in the air, she turned to the patio and walked outside. Stars twinkled down from the inky black sky. Two lanterns swung from hooks on the wall, their flames leaping in the glass, leaving black marks and diminishing the light. A light-crazed moth flew in wide orbits around one of them. A stone fountain standing in the corner splashed water from its innards onto the patio tiles. A large pot was filled with fresh gardenias and their fragrance permeated the night air. The combination of the warm breeze and lovely perfume made Lindsay feel a little besotted and she relaxed when Lucas came up from behind and wrapped his arms around her.

"Lucas," she breathed, "this is so beautiful. I never imagined anything could be so lovely."

"I have only seen one thing lovelier," he replied, "and I'm holding her in my arms."

He turned her face to his and his kiss was long and soft. He carried her to the bed. With the fountain making its light tune, the scent of flowers suspended in the air, and the amber glow of the lantern, the two lovers made their own music.

Chapter 12

The sun was peeping over the wall of the patio and a fly buzzed irritatingly at her ear when Lindsay opened her eyes. She swatted at the fly, missed, and sighed. She rolled over and looked into ice blue eyes. A lazy smile touched his lips as he gently grasped a pink-tipped breast in his fingers and whispered, "Morning, niña. Did you sleep well?" Her heart skipped a beat as his hand lowered to her belly and with a finger he traced little designs on her skin.

"Ummm." She snuggled down under the quilt and then, with a giggle, she threw the quilt over his head and rolled away from him. He grabbed the quilt, tossed it to the floor, and gazed at her naked body hungrily, his eyes roving over her body. She blushed, her cheeks crimson as she turned to rise from the bed. Lucas pulled her back to him. She fell against the pillow and opened her mouth to speak when his lips came down on hers. His hands explored her soft, willing body and the words that finally escaped from her lips were barely audible. But Lucas heard them and he grinned as he bent to nibble her earlobe. "Take me, Lucas, take me now."

The sun was high over the wall of the patio when they rose from the bed. Lucas dressed and went to the door.

"I'll have bath water brought in and clothing, niña. After you're dressed, come to the dining room for breakfast."

Momentarily, a compact, jovial man with twinkling eyes brought in a round wood tub and put it down. He turned, clapped his hands, and two small boys with black hair and dark eyes entered, each carrying two buckets of water. They poured the water into the tub, giggling the entire time, then turned and scampered from the room. Lindsay sat on the bed with the quilt wrapped around her as the little man lowered his eyes and said, "I'll return with clothing, señorita." He stepped from the room and moments later returned carrying a large box. "I'm sure you'll find what you need in there." Then he left the room and closed the door after him.

Lindsay looked longingly at the steaming tub. It had been so long since she had bathed in warm water. She was almost afraid if she sat down in the tub she would wake up and find she was dreaming again.

The water felt silky against her skin as she lowered herself in the bath and leaned back closing her eyes, enjoying this moment, savoring it as though it were her last. She bathed slowly and when she finished she washed her hair. She had forgotten how marvelous it felt to have clean hair. After she finished, she wrapped a towel around her hair. She stepped to the dresser, found a small bottle of cologne, and splashed some over her body. She turned the little bottle over in her hand and wondered where Lucas got it and why a man like him would keep perfume.

Turning her attention to the box on the bed she emptied its contents. Her eyes widened on seeing the texture and rich colors of beautiful *camisas*, skirts, and riding clothes. She giggled as she held a skirt up to her and danced around the room. It had been weeks since she had worn a dress or skirt and she was enjoying the feeling of being able to dress like a woman again. I wonder where he got these clothes, she mused, but she really didn't care.

There were several skirts and *camisas*, two long plain, richly textured, muslin dresses, a chemise, and ribbons. She picked out a brightly patterned skirt and a low-cut cream-hued *camisa*. After dressing she sat on the patio and brushed her hair until it dried. Then she tied it back with a yellow ribbon. She walked to the dark oak dresser and beheld her image. She was startled. Her skin was dark gold. She was thinner. Her hair shone in lustrous highlights and the ribbon contrasted boldly with the auburn tones. She felt beautiful, a feeling she had forgotten she could have.

The dining room wasn't difficult to find. She heard loud banter and laughter and knew it came from there. The occupants looked at her as she turned into the dining room.

Lucas walked to her and led her to a chair next to his. She heard a gaggle of "howdy, ma'ams" and "nice day" as she smiled shyly. A plate of Spanish eggs, strawberries and avocados was set before her. She ate ravenously, trying to feign a ladylike indifference to the feast. The men were lighthearted and chatty as they ate, talking in a mixture of Spanish and English so Lindsay was unable to understand them completely.

She marveled at the pristine elegance of this room. They were sitting at a long, ornately carved table in a room with white walls and dark wood beams running across the ceiling and down two walls to the floor. The end wall had French doors that opened to a large tiled patio dominated by a large fountain and scattered with comfortable looking chairs. The walls of the patio were covered in a maze of twisted and intertwined vines that burst forth in a riot of color. The doors were ajar letting a slight breeze enter the dining room. A large, beautiful sideboard stood against a wall and Lindsay admired the hand-carved design. The quarry tile floor was covered with a hand woven rug in muted shades of beige and white. To the right a small archway led to the kitchen. A short man entered, carrying a tray with cups which he set on the table. Lindsay recognized him as the man who had brought her bath tub. He smiled at her shyly and quickly made his exit.

Lucas smiled answering her unspoken question, "That's Manuel, my cook, and there's no better in the territory. He also manages my house."

A muffled laugh erupted from the table and somebody spoke in a hushed tone, "But God help ya if ya don't like something he fixes." With that the men broke into loud guffaws as Lindsay smiled and poured a cup of coffee.

After eating, Lucas spoke to the gathering. "It's time our guest was introduced to this ill-bred group of women-chasing, tequila-gulping range bandits." He smiled again and Lindsay chuckled. She was beginning to feel welcome.

Lucas pointed to the man sitting to her left. She looked into the face of a man who she was sure had never tasted fear. His face was grizzled with the hard living he had seen. A black beard and moustache covered most of his face. He had unruly black hair and she wondered if he ever combed it. His eyes looked unflinchingly into hers and she lowered her eyes under his scrutiny. His black, liquid eyes narrowed as he studied her.

"This is Vic, Lindsay. He's the foreman and if I'm not here and Chico is gone, he's the boss." He smiled at the dark man. "His name is Victorio, but *no one* ever calls him that."

He continued introducing the men and Lindsay smiled politely at each one. She had never seen such a feral, menacing group of men and she shivered at the thought of being on their wrong side. They all appeared to be Mexican except one who she thought was Indian. She caught a few names, Diego, Alfredo, Sam, Pecos, but she paid little attention to their duties. Surely Lucas had no intention of leaving her in the care of these men? She shuddered as Chico smiled at her warmly.

Vic stood up, placed his flat-crowned hat on his head. He touched it as he nodded slightly, smiled at Lindsay and walked out of the room. She watched him leave. He walked with grace and strength; he was a big man, as tall as Lucas but with more muscle on his body. Lucas was big and lithe; this man was big and burly.

Lucas bent close to her speaking softly. "He's a very loyal friend. I've known Vic for many years. He's to be your bodyguard. When I'm not here, he'll be within shouting distance to you."

Lindsay spun to Lucas and glared at him, "If you think I'm going to have that man around me, you just think again, Lucas. I don't need a bodyguard since I have no intention of trying to escape. I don't have the slightest idea where I am and I have no thought of subjecting myself to your bizarre form of punishment again." She stood, "Now, if you'll excuse me, I'm going to look around my . . . ah . . . prison." She tossed her head and walked out.

Lucas watched her with a half smile. Then he turned his attention to the group of men who were watching him.

"The señorita is headstrong, no?" said Alfredo. The men laughed heartily and Lucas answered over the rim of his coffee cup, "*Si*, the señorita is headstrong." And his eyes glowed.

* * *

Lindsay walked through the pattern of sunlight that was now filling the casement window. She leaned against the wall, her hands clasped behind her, surveying this main room. She saw the huge fireplace at the end, bordered by tall shelves filled with tattered books. The hearth reached out like a wide apron, and below it rested a thick Navajo prayer rug, its natural colors spilling across each other in exquisite patterns. A large shaggy dog lazed contentedly on the rug. Lindsay thought of Angel and a sadness filled her for a second, but then passed.

There was a wide, white wool couch facing the hearth, guarded on each side by tall clay urns filled with bright flowers. The remaining furniture, tables, chairs, a large armoire were all shining ebony, their surfaces filled with elaborate carving of men on the hunt, with pheasants, dogs, and intricate clouds. She walked back to the dining room. The men were gone except for Manuel who was cleaning up the dishes. He smiled at her at a shy angle. She picked up some dishes and followed the confused Manuel to the kitchen. She liked this little man.

She pushed the door to the kitchen open and entered a room rich with the smell of spices. A fireplace dominated this room but a large cook stove seemed to be the hub of activity. The two small boys she had seen earlier were at the stove, each stirring a bubbling concoction and giggling. They became silent when she approached them. "What are you cooking?" she asked. They giggled some more and looked away.

"They speak no English," Manuel said, "And they are embarrassed to see the señorita in the kitchen."

"Oh," she replied, "can I help Manuel? Please?" He nodded and she began to wash the dishes. The kitchen was small but adequately supplied with the necessities for cooking and meal planning. There were cupboards against the walls filled with neatly stacked dishes and a large pantry with food stored for an army. Pans hung from brass hooks over the stove. There was a washing area against another wall. She noted that this outside door did not open onto a patio. The floor was tile and the absence of bright rugs seemed strange.

She enjoyed washing and drying the dishes and watching the boys giggle and jealously guard their bubbling pans from each other. Manuel busied himself cleaning up and started mixing a strange batter. Lindsay watched him as he worked. "Tortillas. They are for the evening meal."

She liked being with Manuel. He was friendly, asked no questions, and accepted her offered help graciously.

After she finished helping Manuel she decided to take a walk, to see the whole *rancho*. She looked at her bare feet. She had no shoes other than her boots. She shrugged and walked out the door. Boots would look ridiculous with the skirt and she enjoyed being barefooted anyway.

She stopped outside the door. The house sat in a small valley, surrounded by austere mountains. They seemed to have sparse foliage and were oddly shaped. In some spots it looked as though an accordian had been set down and covered with sand. They were so unlike the mountains that she had ever seen that she had a strong desire to hike into them to see if they would crumble beneath her feet. Desert sagebrush surrounded the house. Lucas's love for the desert was reflected in his home. The few trees surrounding the house swayed in the hot breeze and lent what little shade they could to the earth. The house itself was terra cotta. Lindsay had never seen this substance before and ran her hands over the exterior. Vines tangled and tumbled over the walls with many desert flowers. There were more pots of brightly colored flowers everywhere—by the doors, on balconies, and at each corner. Lindsay found it difficult to imagine that Lucas had a side to him that nourished such a house. He seemed so unsettled, opposite to the kind of man who would have a home like this, and yet, now that he was here he seemed to be a part of it.

"Where are your shoes, niña?" Lucas stood next to her, his thumbs hooked in his belt, a thin Mexican cigar hanging from his lips.

She looked at her feet and then at his face. "I don't have

any. Besides it feels good to be out of my boots. If I had comfortable shoes, I'd wear them."

"We'll have to remedy that situation," and taking her by the elbow he led her into the house.

"Let me go, Lucas, I want to look around."

He continued to guide her through the entry and down a hallway. He stopped in front of a door, opened it and pushed Lindsay inside, closing the door behind them. They were in a study done in very dark, rich wood—a very masculine room and extremely comfortable. Several books lay on a desk, some open to a page, others marked with pieces of paper. He released Lindsay's arm and walked to a closet. He rummaged through it and presently returned carrying a pair of *huaraches*. He handed them to her. "Keep these on your feet all the time, niña. We have scorpions and other such critters around that would love, I'm sure, to take a bite of your lovely feet." Her eyes widened as she put them on. She blushed as she thanked him.

She left the house and walked toward the barn. It was small but well taken care of. A fenced corral attached to the side was filled with several new colts and fillies, hugging their mothers' side and watching her approach carefully. She walked to the fence and climbed up for a better view. The mothers viewed her momentarily, snorted their indifference, and returned to their oats. The babies moved closer to the protection of their mothers, warily watching this stranger. Lindsay delighted in seeing such well-bred animals. She felt the sense of quiet security that beautiful horses had always given her. She climbed down and turned to walk toward the bunkhouse. She knew the men would be here so she stayed her distance but her curiosity drove her to see what lay beyond it. The bunkhouse was terra cotta and large enough to comfortably house the men Lucas had working for him. In the distance there was a stable with more horses, and beyond this a small creek bordering a pasture filled with fat, grazing cattle. Strange to see pasture with all this desert, she thought. She walked around the stable and admired the horses. A few of the men nodded a greeting. They watched her with manly appreciation and a little jealousy as she passed.

The next few days flew by quickly. Lindsay helped Manuel in the kitchen after each meal and learned the names of the boys, Pedro and Luis. She learned they were orphans brought to Lucas by the Indians. They no longer giggled in her presence and even spoke to her in broken English.

Lucas was busy during the day so she rarely saw him, but at night, she looked forward to his coming to their bed.

One afternoon, while helping Manuel with the kitchen duties, she asked him how long he had worked for Lucas.

"I have been at this *rancho* thirty-four years, señorita."

"Thirty-four years. Why Lucas wasn't even born yet, was he? Who owned this house at that time?" She leaned against the counter watching Manuel as he kneaded an obstinate roll of dough.

"Senor Sanger's mother and stepfather lived here then. His stepfather built this house for his bride, Lucas's mother, right after they were married. They lived in a small, wooden house until he had finished this one. Señora Sanger designed and furnished thees place and Lucas has not changed anything except to add a piece here or there and buy more land." He stopped, plopped dough into a pan, put it in the oven and turned back to her. "Would the señorita like a cup of tea?"

"Yes, Manuel, I would, and then will you tell me more, please?"

He fixed the tea and they talked. He seemed to talk about Lucas's past with a touch of regret.

"Señora Sanger married without her parents' permission. Her father, Don Emanuel Gaspar de Sosa, was a descendent of the first *alcalde* of Monterrey and later the first governor. He died in a duel. Estrella's father became an *estadista*. They lived in a large and beautiful *hacienda* in Monterrey. John Sanger was traveling through Monterrey with several other men. They were cattle men and had heard that a rancher in Monterrey had a new breed of cattle so they made a trip to talk to thees man. They were invited to Gaspar's *hacienda* for a party and, of course, John saw and fell in love with Estrella. But foolishly, they had an affair and when Gaspar found out he ordered John out of Mexico or he would kill him. Estrella followed him and they married. He brought her to this land. But he lived in a wood house and Estrella wanted so much to have a *hacienda* like her parents. It took many years but John built what she wanted and bought her anything she wanted to furnish it. After a few years of marriage, Estrella missed her family terribly and after many weeks of begging and crying, she talked John into letting her make a trip back to her home to see her parents and try to convince her father to accept them both. She left with several of John's men as guards. They were only fifty miles from here when a band of Indians attacked and killed every one of the men. As a brave raised his hatchet to kill Estrella, another came up and stopped him. Estrella was very beautiful. She had long black hair and dark eyes and white skin. Very beautiful." Manuel stopped talking and stared into his cup for a few seconds. Then sighing, he continued.

"She was taken captive and for many weeks John searched for her. He became a driven man. It was as though a *demonio* took over his mind and no one would go near him. He raved that Estrella's father had planned the attack and taken Estrella back home to punish him. He accused the men on the ranch of selling her to the Indians. He said terrible things."

"Then one morning a rider appeared in the hills. John went to investigate. It was his Estrella. He fell on the ground weeping at her feet and the men had to carry him back to the house. Many weeks he watched her, touching her constantly. He even cried when she smiled at him. We thought maybe he had gone *loco*. But things got better and he slowly improved."

"Then one day, as he was watching Estrella he began to scream and hit her and it took several of us to pull him away. She was pregnant and he knew it was not his baby. After Estrella returned she would not sleep with John. She had conceived by the Indian that saved her life and she intended to have his baby and raise it. But John would not have this child in his house and told Estrella he would kill it.

She feared for its life, knowing John would harm it if he had the chance. She gave birth and as soon as the boy was strong enough to travel, she bundled him up and crept out one night with no escort. She rode into the mountains. She took the boy to his father and asked that he raise him and when he was old enough to explain why she had given up her child."

"She returned to John and neither ever spoke another word about the boy. John started to drink heavily and his temper would explode at any time. Estrella lived in constant fear of him. His hatred and drink killed him sixteen years later and he was still warm in his grave when Estrella saddled up and rode into the hills. Lucas returned with Estrella but he lived with his father. His visits here became more frequent as he got older. She loved him more than anything in this world and would sit at the window waiting for him to appear at the top of the rise and ride down to her, whooping and carrying on. Each time he came to the *rancho*, she scolded him for staying away so long. He was very loving toward his mother and I used to watch them walk together, his arm around her waist."

"Four years after John's death Estrella took sick and after several days with a high fever, she died. Lucas never left her. He slept on the floor next to her bed, he fed her, talked to her. Before she died, she opened her eyes, looked up and smiled. She spoke very softly and Lucas bent close to hear her. When he stood up she was dead and he turned to me, tears on his cheeks and said, "She asked me to tell my father, Grey Wolf, that she loved him and would watch over him from her post in heaven."

"Lucas took her body. He was gone for many weeks and when he returned he took over management of the *rancho* and never spoke of Estrella again. From what I could piece together, she was buried Apache style. John is buried in the hills and Lucas had a grave marker made for him."

Manuel stopped talking, staring at his hands bent around the cup.

After several seconds Lindsay asked, "Manuel, his mother was Spanish, his father an Apache, both dark eyes. Where did he get those blue eyes?"

Manuel looked up at Lindsay and smiled, his eyes shimmering, almost moist. "Don Emanuel married an English girl. She had light brown hair and the most beautiful blue eyes you have ever seen. Lucas has those blue eyes. Gaspar, too, married without his parents' consent and he spent many years trying to restore himself and his wife in his parents' favor. He understood how love could mar a sensible mind, but when his daughter reacted the same way, he disowned her. I left him and came to Mexico to work for Estrella. I couldn't stay with Gaspar." Manuel got up from the table and walked away and as he turned to the kitchen door, Lindsay caught a glimpse of a tear rolling down his cheek.

She sat staring into her cup, absorbing this knowledge. She didn't hear Lucas approach. He walked up behind her and ran his fingers through her hair. He laughed as she jumped. "Niña, it's me. Surely you're used to my touch by now. Or," his eyes took on a glint as he teased, "are you so repulsed by my touch you have to steel yourself against it?"

She continued to stare and then asked, "Lucas, what are you going to do with me? Why have you taken me captive? Do I ever get to go home?"

Lucas dropped his hands, a muscle twitched in his cheek. "Lindsay, I can't answer you yet. I told you, you'll be comfortable. I don't know when I'll send you home. Don't ask me again. I'm tired of your mewling and crying."

If she had looked at him she would have seen the hurt in his eyes, but she continued to stare in her cup. She said nothing more and after a few seconds, Lucas walked out.

She laid her head on her arms and wept. Lucas, standing outside the door heard the cry. He walked to the stable door. With anger and hurt, he mounted his horse and raced off toward the hills. Chico watched him and said nothing. He knew Lucas would be gone for several days.

He was right.

Chapter 13

Lucas did not to return that night and Lindsay lay in their bed restlessly. His name came to her lips many times as she reached over to touch his pillow. But he didn't come to their bed for several nights and Lindsay lost her appetite and dark shadows appeared under her eyes. Manuel began to worry that the señorita would make herself ill if she didn't eat and sleep.

Six days later Lucas returned. He walked into his bedroom and saw Lindsay lying across the bed crying softly. He watched her for a few seconds. Now that it was time for her to leave he wasn't sure he would be strong enough. He wasn't sure he could let her go.

Women had always been a pleasant enjoyment. An interlude between travels but certainly nothing to get serious about. At least not yet. He had never had trouble finding a willing woman. His trouble had been in getting rid of them. And now, the shoe was on the other foot. He had found a woman who wanted to get rid of him, only this one, he loved. A few more weeks and maybe he could have wooed her into falling in love with him. Maybe there would have been a chance. But now it was too late. It was time for her to leave him and with the memories she had, she could surely feel nothing but hatred for him. He really couldn't blame her.

He approached the bed and touched her hair softly and whispered, "niña." Lindsay thought she was dreaming. She lifted her head and saw him standing beside her. She leaped into his arms, crying his name. She kissed his face and head and throat and tears fell from her cheeks onto her breasts. Lucas laughed and after she had calmed down he lay beside her.

"For someone who says they hate me, you have a lovely way of showing it."

She lay in the protection of his arms, running her fingers down his throat and playing with the mat of hair on his chest.

"Oh, Lucas, I've been so worried. You said nothing about leaving and when you were gone so long I just knew something had happened to you and if something happened to you, I never would see my home again."

His lips tightened, the muscle twitched in his cheek as he spoke, "Niña, you *will* be going home. I made the preparations to send you back to your uncle and soon you'll be riding through his fields again." He rose to his feet and turned to the door. "In a few days you'll leave."

She stared at the closing door and realized she had been holding her breath. She was going home. Home. She had prayed for this for so long and now it was going to happen. Only shouldn't she feel bubbling happiness and anticipation? Shouldn't she be tingling with excitement and expectancy? She laid her head on the bed and the only sensation she could feel was an emptiness. She lay awake for awhile staring at the ceiling as a dawning came over her like the rising water of a river. She sat up slightly, her skin white, her eyes narrowed as she spoke aloud to herself.

"You idiot, you stupid, pigheaded imbecile. You love him." She sat up for this realization gave her confidence in what she would do. She would tell him and refuse to return to her uncle's ranch. She would *make* him fall in love with her. She ran her fingers over his pillow as she remembered the many nights they had shared this bed. She remembered being kissed by other men and feeling nothing except dread at having to repeat the kiss. But with Lucas, he made her weak. She smiled as she remembered her false efforts at fighting him, how she had tried to make him think she didn't like his touch. But all he had to do was smile and she melted. She was a ball of soft wax, pliable. He could mold her into anything he wanted with his long, dark fingers. Now she would let him know she enjoyed his touch, his love making. No more phony efforts at putting him off. She would respond to his every touch as though she was his wife. Wife. She smiled. If things went right she would own that title.

She hummed a love song as she washed her face and pinched her cheeks to get a little color into them. She ran a brush through her hair and tied it back with a white ribbon. Then she went to find Lucas, to tell him of her love. She felt light as a feather, warm and, oh, so very happy. Near the dining room she heard Lucas talking to Chico in a low voice. She stopped, backed up against the wall and although she knew she shouldn't, she listened.

"Have the men ready to leave day after tomorrow. Everything is ready. Tyler's men will be waiting at the designated spot." He stopped talking and Lindsay wondered what he was doing. Holding her breath in fear of being discovered, she waited. He spoke again.

"Be sure and tell Vic to watch her closely. She has no fear and little common sense. She may get herself into Lord knows what kind of a predicament. Be sure to remind him that she is to be kept hidden from everyone except our men. Vic will know how to handle it. It's just that I want nothing to happen . . . Damn, Chico, why in hell did I take this job? She's been a thorn in my side from the beginning. I should have known when I saw her that day in Durango, she was different. Why didn't I listen to you? Goddamnit, Chico, I'll be glad to be rid of her. She demands more of my time and attention than I'm willing to give." Chico nodded his head as Lucas spoke.

"Well, *amigo*, the pay hasn't been good, but the side benefits, haven't they been worth it?"

Lucas glared at his friend, then stomped from the room slamming the door behind him. Lindsay heard the dishes rattle. Chico glared at the closed door. *Amigo*, he thought, don't be a fool. Tell the girl your feelings. Don't let pride ruin your chances for happiness. He jumped as he heard a door close.

Lindsay! She must have heard. He wanted to go to her and explain everything. He wanted to ease the ache in her heart, the embarrassment she must be filled with after hearing their discussion. But he could not get involved. He must let Lucas handle his own life. He must stop trying to protect him. Somehow, someday, they would both let down their wall of stubbornness and realize what they were missing by not confessing their feelings.

Lindsay could not believe what she had heard. She felt as though a knife had been plunged into her heart. "They pay had been bad but the benefits good." She was the benefit. She had been used to compensate for lack of money. She was confused and hurt and hadn't meant to slam the door. She knew Chico was still sitting in the house. Her head was spinning wildly and her stomach heaved with nausea. Tears blinded her as she made her way to be bedroom. She barely made it to the door before a sob escaped her. She fell to the floor, sobbing uncontrollably.

An hour passed before she managed to stop crying. Finally, she walked to the dresser mirror and looked at her face. Her eyes were swollen and red-rimmed. Her mouth was puffy with purplish tinge. How could she have fallen in love with him? How could she have allowed him to humiliate her so? How could she . . .? She walked to the patio doors, threw them open and lifted her face to the sun. Tears began to fall again and she felt herself begin to retch. She thought she would never be able to stop. Finally, she lay down on the tiles. They felt cool to her skin and then she felt the sickness come again. She pulled herself up to wash, and fell exhausted and miserable on the bed. She cried until she was too weak to do anything but sleep.

When she woke the sun was low on the horizon. She watched it go down and tried to remember some of the things Lucas had said to her after their love making. She couldn't believe a man could express such tender thoughts, caress her so lovingly and protect her so if he didn't care. Yet, he didn't. She was a benefit to be enjoyed until the job was finished. She remembered hearing those words, and tears began to fall again. A soft knock on the door startled her.

"Señorita, I have your dinner." Manuel spoke so softly he could barely be heard.

"Take it away, Manuel. I'm not hungry." She spoke as strong as she could.

"But you will get sick if you do not eat," he answered.

"Take it away," she yelled. "Don't you understand? I'm not hungry. Now leave me alone."

She felt bad the minute the words were out of her mouth, but it didn't matter. It was too late . . . nothing mattered now.

She lay quietly for a long time, deep in thought. She did not hear Lucas ride off and did not notice the sun disappearing and the sky grow dark. She was deeply engrossed in a plan that had begun to form in her mind, a plan that would return her to her Uncle Ned. She wanted to get away, *now*. She couldn't stay here another minute and be near Lucas. She couldn't watch him breaking a horse or laughing with his men. She couldn't stay here and know the words he spoke to her when they made love were just that. Words. No meaning behind them. She couldn't stay here and listen as he played his guitar and listen in the evening after dinner when several ranch hands play sad love songs or lively dance music. Music so beautiful came from these men and she couldn't bear to her it again. She could never stay, even though she knew if Lucas asked, she would push her pride back and do just that. No, she would return home and without any help from Lucas. She would get out of his life now and try to forget him. She would build a new life of her own. She had to get away from here now. Away from these painful memories, away from Lucas.

* * *

She slept for a few hours and when she woke she had a purpose and a plan that helped her to pull herself out of her pain. She got up, searched the drawers of the dresser, and found her old clothes. Her shawl lay beside them. It had been washed. Her dress was gone. Likely, Manuel had thrown it away—it looked like a rag. She lifted the pants and shirt she had worn for so many days, put them on, then pulled on her boots. She brushed her hair and pulled it severely back from her face and pinned it into a tight bun on her neck. She found one of Lucas's flat-crowned hats and placed it on her head. She turned and stared sadly at the bed that held so many fond memories. Then she slowly crept from the room. She closed the door quietly and looked at Manuel's room. No light peeked from under his door. She continued down the hall and instead of leaving by the front door she turned and went through the kitchen. Slowly she opened the kitchen door and peered into the inky blackness, waiting for her eyes to adjust to the night. She looked in the direction of the bunkhouse. It was quiet. She wasn't sure if Lucas had posted guards, but she knew if she was quiet and stayed in the shadows, she would not be seen. She ran in the shadows to the stables. She knew she couldn't risk taking time to saddle a horse, but if she could take a bridle, she didn't need anything else. She walked along the shadow of the stable wall and felt for the doorway. It was open. It wasn't closed since the horses were quartered in separate stalls. She heard one of them whinny, so she moved in carefully and stepped in the first stall. She reached in and felt around blindly. The horse came up and sniffed her hand. She spoke to it softly. Then her arm hit something that made a clang. She stopped, her breath in her throat. It was a bridle. She breathed a sigh of relief as she removed it from its hook and laid it over her shoulder. She carefully opened the stall door. She bridled the horse easily. He was well trained. She led him from the stable, across the small creek and toward the hills. She walked the horse slowly since she didn't want the sound of his hooves churning up the soil, making noise. She reached the hills, jumped up, and galloped off.

Lindsay followed the stars, north by west. This time she wouldn't stop to rest until daylight. She felt safe at night and she knew the ranch hands would be out searching for her in the morning. She didn't know where Lucas was. She hadn't seen him since he had talked with Chico. She didn't want to see him. She wanted to put as much distance as possible between her and the *hacienda*.

The hills gave way to desert and then to mountains. She could feel the cool mountain breeze caress her face and smiled as the sun began to peek around the clouds, resting on the horizon. She had ridden far and hard. She knew she had a long way to go but she had come a long way and it would be difficult for Lucas and his men to catch up with her. Maybe Lucas wouldn't come after her this time and the thought made her despondent.

She stopped when the sun was directly overhead and rested. She drank some water from a small sandy stream, watered her horse, and then resumed the ride. The day wore on and soon the stars were playing in the sky again. There was no moon, but she didn't care. She had learned to trust this sure-footed little bay. She was beginning not to care if she made it home. She felt empty and knew that she could never forget Lucas. She would never be able to build a life without him. Oh, Lucas, she breathed it could have been good between us. I could have made you happy. I know I could.

She rode on trying to push Lucas to the back of her mind, but when she looked at the sky and the stars twinkling down at her, she was reminded of icy blue eyes and she wiped at the tears that fell down her face and across her mouth.

Her head felt heavy and she was exhausted as she pushed on. The hills loomed up around her and the trees blocked the stars. She heard the rush of water somewhere in the distance. A pair of owls hooted at her from the night.

She rounded a bend and a noise startled her. She jerked her horse to a stop and looked at strange eyes gleaming in the darkness. Then she saw a red explosion and something knocked her from her horse. She fell slowly like a dust mote to the ground. It happened so quickly that there was no time for thought, words, or pain, only the sensation of falling into a dark abyss. She lay for a moment, then looked up hearing strange mutterings over her. She looked into dark eyes and dark faces. It was so difficult to see with no moon. She closed her eyes a minute, hoping to regain her lost breath. These creatures smelled sour and foul. She opened her eyes for a moment and looked into the fierce faces of Apaches. But something was pulling her down, down . . . a heavy weight. A weight so big, so immense she lost control to it. Then she blacked out.

Chapter 14

Lindsay opened her eyes. Her father stood over her. "Daddy, daddy, where have you been? You promised to take me to buy a ribbon and now it's too late." She began to cry as a hand unbuttoned her shirt.

"No, no, it's all I have. If you take it from me I won't have any clothes." She pushed at the hands and then into her Uncle Ned's face. "Oh, Uncle Ned, I want a puppy. I want to see Regalo, I want to see Angel. Take me home, Uncle Ned." She tried to get up but strong arms held her down.

"Lindsay, hold still." The voice was stern and harsh.

"Please don't yell at me, Daddy, I'll be good, I promise."

She could feel her shirt being taken off. She screamed, "No, no, the arrows hurt. Don't kill them. Please don't kill them. Oh, my God, you put an arrow in her chest and she's crying. Stop. Stop." She screamed and a voice from above her spoke, "Niña, niña, don't fight me. I have to remove the bullet. Now, for once, be still."

"I'll be good, Uncle Ned, don't scold me. I'll be good. Only please don't put an arrow in me. Mama cried when they put an arrow in her. She held her arms to me and cried. I'll be good, I promise."

Then hands grasped her arms drawing them over her head, holding them in a steel grip. And something was holding her legs and hips.

"I'll be good," she screamed at the top of her lungs as she fiercely fought her bonds. "I'll be good, don't punish me for hiding when they didn't. Please don't put an arrow in me." She tried to move her head from side to side but something held her so she couldn't look in her daddy's face.

"Daddy, they won't let me look at you. I want to see you. I want to touch you." Something cool was running over her chest, getting her wet. "No, no, don't get my clothes wet. They're all I have to wear. Lucas, please don't throw water on me."

Lucas spoke to the men holding Lindsay. "She's going to scream and pitch wildly. She'll be hard to hold because she is out of her head. I have to remove that bullet. She'll soon black out."

"Mama, will I be as pretty as you when I grow up? Will I marry and have children like you did? Will I have a little girl and die and leave her like you did? Why did you die, Mama? Wasn't I a good girl? Why did you make me hide, why couldn't I have stayed with you? Why are you crying, Mama? Why are you lying on the ground with an arrow in your chest? Why aren't you holding me on your lap and singing? Why are there tears on your cheeks? Mama, Mama, don't die. I'll be good, don't die."

She screamed and another scream was torn from her throat and still another before she mercifully blacked out.

She relaxed under the men's hands but they continued to hold her tightly. Lucas held up the bullet. Sweat ran down his face and plopped onto Lindsay's breasts. He threw the bullet on the ground and a man put a red-hot knife in his outstretched hand. He pushed it in the wound and the smell of burnt flesh assailed his nostrils. He bandaged the wound and when he finished he picked her up and carried her to his tepee.

When she opened her eyes she was sitting with Lucas at his table eating. "Why, Lucas, I thought I was a thorn in your side. Why are you here?" Lucas cringed at her words.

She thrashed around as the heat became unbearable and she had to get away from it. Something cool touched her back and she opened her eyes and smiled. "How did you know I wanted to swim, Lucas?" She started to get up. "Come on, I'll race you to the other side of the river."

Gently, hands laid her back, holding her down.

"Take your hands off me. You don't love me. Don't touch me if you don't love me."

"Niña, you're wrong. Again, you're wrong," but Lucas's words fell on an unconscious Lindsay.

Something cool was held to her lips. 'But, Mama, I don't like it. I don't want to drink." She drank and it tasted good. "Make it for me again, Mama. It's good."

A voice in the distance spoke, "How is the woman today?"

"I can't get her fever to break," Lucas answered.

He continued to force her to drink and she slapped at him defiantly. "Go away, I don't want anymore. Daddy, don't let Lucas hurt me anymore. Please, Daddy, I don't want to be hurt anymore.

Lucas set the drink down and touched her cheek. "I never meant to hurt you, Niña. I never meant for you to suffer like this." But Lindsay's mind was riddled with pain and fever and she heard nothing Lucas said. She fought against everything he did and her flailing and tossing opened her wound and she began to bleed profusely.

Lucas clenched his teeth and sighed in exasperation as he attempted to stop the bleeding. A voice startled him and he whirled around. He relaxed when he recognized Little Bird.

"You must tie her arms to her sides. She will then be unable to open her wound." Little Bird approached Lindsay and stared down at the girl. "You need rest, Lucas. I will tend the girl." Lucas shook his head, "No, I will not leave her."

"Then sleep beside her but you must rest. I will help you." Little Bird turned to Lucas and handed him two lengths of rope. "Tie her hands. She will not know what you are doing. She is too delirious. She will die unless her fever drops and her wound stops bleeding. I will gather some herbs and make a poultice to stop the infection. Then I will bring you food." She turned and left the tepee.

Lucas tied her arms to her waist and breathed a sigh of relief when Lindsay continued to sleep. Little Bird was right. Lindsay was not aware of what was happening.

Little Bird returned with food for Lucas and a pouch of strange smelling herbs. She began to mix them and after she was satisfied with their consistency, she turned to Lindsay and carefully removed the bandage. The wound still bled profusely and blood dripped onto the floor. Little Bird washed the wound thoroughly and placed a handful of the concoction directly into the wound and the surrounding skin. Lindsay thrashed around as the medicine began to sting. She screamed and Lucas bent over her and talked softly, holding her head as Little Bird continued her ministrations. Lindsay was unable to raise her arms and Lucas knew she suffered great pain when he saw her dig her fingernails into the palms and droplets of blood appeared on her white palms. Tears fell down her cheeks as Little Bird rewrapped her wound and she opened her fever-bright eyes and whispered, "Why, Lucas, why are you doing this to me? I thought you cared, a little, I did."

She blacked out and Lucas kissed her softly on the forehead. Her skin felt hot and dry to his lips. He picked up a wet rag and gently wiped her face and neck.

"She will sleep for several hours. When she wakes I will bring her something for the pain. You eat now." Little Bird left the tepee and Lucas turned his attention to the food. But he had no appetite. He lay on the floor beside Lindsay and slept.

Little Bird changed the bandage twice a day for five days and each day the wound looked better. Lindsay slept almost the entire time. Little Bird gave her sips of a liquid that had a potent drug in it. The pain gave way to a healing sleep and soon the fever broke and Lindsay began to recover. Lucas rarely left her side and then only for a few minutes at a time. As Lindsay healed, Lucas slept better and his appetite increased.

* * *

The sun was low in the sky when Lindsay opened her eyes. She ached all over and her mouth was dry. She tried to sit up. Her arms were tied to her waist and a bandage covered her chest. A searing gut-wrenching pain crossed her stomach and she laid back down.

Lucas looked down into her face, his eyes filled with concern. "Niña, can you hear me?" She nodded as a tear slid down her cheek falling to the bed. Lucas held a cup to her lips and she sipped the cool water. The pain in her chest reared again and she moaned and gagged. Lucas turned her head to the side and after a few seconds she took a shallow breath and shuddered. "Lucas," she whispered, "what happened?"

He leaned close to her face and touched her cheek gently, "You've been shot, niña, but you're going to be all right."

"Why am I tied?" she moved her hands.

He began to untie her. "It seems to be the only way I can handle you, Lindsay. You thrashed around so violently you kept opening the wound. I had to tie you to give the wound a chance to heal."

"How long have I been here?" she closed her eyes.

"This is the seventh day, niña." He brushed her hair from her face and reached for the cloth. He wiped the sweat that glistened on her brow. She had fallen asleep. He pulled the blanket over her body, then sat and watched her. He watched her chest rise and fall. Her face reflected her pain. I wish I could take her in my arms and erase all the hurt, he thought.

The next morning when the sun hung lazily in the morning sky, she opened her eyes again. She lifted her arm to scratch her face and the pain that little movement produced made her groan. Lucas was immediately at her side.

"What is it, niña? What do you want?"

She lie still for a moment, letting the pain subside. Then she spoke. "Lucas, I want to go home."

Lucas touched her face softly, replying, "As soon as you're well, niña, you'll go home to your uncle." He walked outside and Lindsay did not see the hurt in his eyes.

"Lucas," she called softly. But he did not hear her. She turned her head to the side and whispered as the tears spilled down her cheeks, "Not to Uncle Ned's home, Lucas, to yours."

The fever had weakened her so much and she had lost so much weight that her recovery was very slow. As the days went by she attempted to sit up and take care of herself. At first any movement at all made her cringe with pain, but gradually she was able to move her arm and one day sit with her feet touching the floor. The first day she sat up she struggled and groaned and gasped but when she finally made it she looked at Lucas and with sweat glistening on her forehead and a proud but weak smile, she breathed, "I'm stronger than I look, huh, Lucas?" Then she passed out, falling into his arms.

"Yes, niña, you're stronger than you look," he smiled sadly and laid her gently on the little cot.

Each day she grew stronger. Each day she attempted to do a little more and Lucas was constantly at her side.

Two weeks after she sat up she took her first walk around the little settlement. Lucas had explained a little about Apache life so she wasn't startled at her strange surroundings.

Several tripods stood around the camp with chunks of skewered meat hanging over the fire by leather strips. Lucas explained how the women kept the rawhide strips wet so they wouldn't burn while the meat cooked. She watched a woman pulverize jerky on a metate and mix ground berries with it. "Pemmican," Lucas said. "Very nutritious. When we hunt, we always carry a parfleche filled with pemmican."

The smell of the cooking stews and soups made Lindsay's mouth water. After a short walk Lucas made her return to the tepee and rest. "Don't overdo it, niña. You have lots of time to see everything."

Little Bird brought them each a bowl of stew and Lindsay ate ravenously. Her appetite increased daily and Little Bird stopped bringing her the liquid that relieved the pain. Lucas told her Little Bird had given her pulverized mescal buttons mixed with water. It had a strange taste but it relieved her pain and helped her sleep. Lindsay was grateful to this quiet woman for all she had done but when she tried to express her gratitude Little Bird turned and walked out of the tepee.

"You've embarrassed her, niña. She wants no thanks for what she has done. Her husband was the brave that shot you."

Lindsay gazed at the disappearing figure of the Indian woman and her mind filled with thoughts of their lives. She wondered if she could ever be wife to an Apache brave. Lucas. Would she be able to live like these people? The food and exercise made Lindsay sleepy and she lay back on the cot. She looked up as Lucas stood beside her. She smiled warmly and held her hand to him. He kissed her fingers, then placed a kiss on her brow. Lindsay closed her eyes. Lucas stood there caressing her sleeping face with his eyes.

One evening after they had eaten a bowl of soup, Lindsay decided she wanted a bath. An entire bath. She was tired of sponging her body from a bowl of water. She wanted to luxuriate in a river. Lucas consented and led her to a nearby river. On the way they talked.

"How did I get shot, Lucas?"

"You were in War Eagle's land. War Eagle and Yellow Cat were listening to your approach. When you came in view you looked like a man, dressed like one, especially with my hat on. They have learned to shoot first and ask questions later. They went to you after you had fallen from your horse and your hat had come off. Your hair fell loose around your face so they brought you here. I saw you in War Eagle's arms as they rode into camp. I was greatly relieved when War Eagle told me you were still alive . . . barely. I don't know how you managed to escape from my ranch, but that's behind us now."

Lindsay wanted to ask why he had left the ranch that last day. Why he hadn't said goodbye, why he left without a word to her. But she knew his answer. She knew he didn't love her so why should he explain his actions to her. Rather than hear his excuses, rather than hear the words that would slice into her heart, she would ask no questions.

They reached the sparkling water and Lindsay started undressing.

"You're not embarrassed anymore to strip in front of me, niña?

"I spent many days lying naked on your bed. I had begun to feel like a married woman, familiar and bold. I feel no shame now."

He smiled and sat down to watch her bathe. She stepped into the cold water gasping with shock. She walked deeper into the water and Lucas yelled, "Be careful, niña, not too far. You're still weak and that water is swift."

Soon she was splashing and enjoying herself thoroughly. She washed her hair, then stood to leave the water. The setting sun on her gold body, her wet hair hanging down around her shoulders, the smile on her face, and her green eyes dancing with light made Lucas shudder with desire. He clenched his teeth. Not now, he thought, I can't make love to her yet. She's still not fully recovered and if I rape her she'll only have more reason to hate me. He turned his head and looked at the countryside absent-mindedly, but his gaze went back to Lindsay.

She sat beside Lucas and dried her hair in the fading sunlight. She left it hanging down her back and her face was framed in unruly flyaway wisps of curl. Lucas took her hand as they walked back to the tepee. She couldn't speak of her feelings of betrayed love yet. She couldn't spoil this moment. She would have to speak her mind sometime, but not yet.

The camp was quiet now. Several women were grinding corn and making pemmican. Children were playing their favorite games, imitating their fathers and holding mock battles. Many of the men had ridden on the hunt, a few remained to guard the camp. Lucas and Lindsay sat in front of the tepee and watched the children.

"Tell me about your father, Lucas."

"My father is Grey Wolf. He is the chief of this tribe. We are members of the Rio Colorados Apache. My father rode with Mangas Colorados for many years. Then he put down the war against the white man. He took his people and settled here where they remain at peace. There is talk the white man will one day come and run us off. So Grey Wolf waits."

"But, Lucas, you're also a white man."

"No, niña, I am not. I was raised Apache. I believe in their way of life and I will die Apache."

"But your ranch, Lucas, you haven't given that up." She reached out a hand and rested it on his arm. Her skin was gold against his dark arm. He looked down at her tiny hand and started to touch her fingers but stopped

—"The ranch will run with or without me," he lowered his hand slowly, his fingers curled in a tight ball. Her hand continued to grasp his arm and her touch was like a branding iron, hot and almost painful. "My men will take care of it and it will always be there when I decide to return." He stood and held his hand to assist her. He couldn't sit any longer with her touching him. It took more will power than he had not to take her in his arms and smother her with kisses. "Come on, niña, you've been up long enough. Time to rest. You'll soon be strong enough to travel."

She let him help her to her feet and with her eyes cast downward, she entered the tepee.

* * *

The last day she was in camp, she met Lucas's father, Grey Wolf. Lucas had asked if she would like to meet him and he felt proud when she responded enthusiastically.

He took her arm and led her to the tepee where his father lived. The door flap was closed and, as is custom, Lucas announced his presence and waited for his father's reply. Soon they heard his response and Lucas pushed aside the flap and gestured for Lindsay to enter. Lucas motioned for her to move to the left and sit. She did, then he moved to the right and sat cross-legged.

Lindsay watched the man sitting in front of her from the cover of her lashes. He was big, bigger than she had him pictured. He had long, black hair and a thin strip of rawhide was wound around his forehead. He wore a white deerskin shirt with fringe at the sleeves and deerskin pants and moccasins. Lindsay marveled at the beauty of the string of beads he wore around his neck. His head was down, his eyes closed and his hair hung around his face. He seemed to be muttering something but she knew he was aware of their presence. She glanced at Lucas and he nodded quickly as though to tell her to wait.

After several minutes Grey Wolf raised his head and looked directly at Lindsay. His eyes were so startling, she unconsciously moved back slightly. He stared at her for several seconds, showing no expression. Lindsay regained her composure and took this opportunity to study him as he was studying her. His eyes were the most distinct feature about him—they were black, so black they made the whites look blue. He had long, thick black lashes. His face was wrinkled and very bronze. His nose was long and prominent. There was a small hump on the bridge of it. His lips were set in a grim line. He had not moved or taken his eyes from her face and she began to feel uncomfortable, but she would not look away. She kept her eyes on his face and finally he turned to his son.

"She is everything you have told me." His voice was deep, throaty, and scratchy.

"Yes, father," Lucas replied quietly.

Grey Wolf looked back into Lindsay's face. "Are you well?"

"Yes, I am well."

"My son tells me you will soon be returned to your uncle. Is this your wish also?"

She glanced at Lucas but he looked straight ahead at his father. No expression crossed his face. She looked back at Grey Wolf and her eyes misted ever so slightly.

"Yes," she lied and Grey Wolf knew she lied. But she would not ask Lucas to keep her. Her pride was too great. He would have to ask her and obviously he was never going to do that. No, she would return home to her uncle and try to pick up the pieces of her life after she was away from Lucas.

Grey Wolf nodded his head and lowered his eyes. Lucas stood and Lindsay realized they had been dismissed. They walked into the bright sunlight and Lucas held her hand as they walked to his tepee.

They entered and sat on a blanket facing each other.

"Arrangements have been made for your trip. You will leave at sun-up. Two guides will lead you to the Rio Brazos where your uncle will be waiting." He stopped talking and stood. "I hope you will be happy, niña." He walked out into the bright sunlight and Lindsay could hear his footfalls diminish as her tears began to fall. She lay on the blanket, her mind filled with thoughts of Lucas. Strange how empty she felt. She loved her uncle, the ranch, everyone there, but they would never be able to give her what Lucas could give her. But she had just been a surplus benefit while they traveled and now that his job was finished, she would be forgotten.

She fell asleep, tossing and turning as she dreamt of Lucas. She could feel his arms around her, taste his lips. She could see his smile, mocking or warm, and his eyes, so blue at times they almost appeared black and so icy when he was enraged. Her sleep was so troubled that when a hand touched a curl on her pillow her eyes flew open. Lucas was hunkered down, the curl between his fingers. She wanted to tell him she loved him. But the words choked her. They stuck in her throat. She couldn't bear to have him laugh at her. She would rather die than be the brunt of his ridicule. Maybe someday she would be able to forget those blue eyes. His lips brushed her throat and she shuddered with desire.

He held her close after they made love. Her heart beat rapidly as he ran his fingers down her throat and across her shoulders.

"Niña, the trip back will be long and hard. War Eagle and Yellow Cat will be your guides. Do as they tell you and stay close to them. Don't wander away and, please, promise me you won't try to escape from them." He laughed but his laugh was tinged with concern.

She ran her fingers down his chest. "No, I won't escape again. I promise." A tear made its way down her cheek and she quickly brushed at it so Lucas wouldn't see. He held her close and they slept. The moon was high overhead and the only sounds entering the Apache camp were those of the forest.

Lindsay woke and lie quietly, looking into Lucas's face. Her eyes traveled from his eyes to his nose and down to his mouth. How she loved every line, every mark on his face. A dark curl fell onto his forehead and she wanted to touch it but she knew that would wake him. His moustache and beard had been trimmed and a sprinkle of silver ran through his beard. She slowly left the blanket and walked to the tepee entrance. She raised the flap and breathed in the cool night air as she sat on the ground. She looked into the sky and gazed at the blinking stars. She looked at the village and pondered the harsh life these people lived. She had seen the side of Indian nature she never knew existed. She looked toward the tepee of War Eagle and Little Bird. She liked Little Bird.

She had helped Lucas gather the herbs and grind the medicines for her gunshot wound. She had fixed the meals for them and had made sure Lucas ate when Lindsay was delirious. Little Bird was short, dark, and slightly plump but her smile was warm and gracious and her eyes twinkled when she laughed. Lindsay remembered the day Little Bird told her about Apache women. The work they did was unbelievable to Lindsay but Little Bird assured her they were proud of their lives and their braves and their children. Although these two women had little in common, a bond of friendship grew between them and Lucas had heard them giggling together many times. Little Bird told Lindsay that starvation was their ever-present enemy.

Lindsay also learned that many of the unwed girls in the camp had hoped to be the one Lucas chose for a wife. One by the name of Spotted Fawn had treated Lindsay coldly since her arrival, glaring at her whenever their eyes met. Little Bird explained that Spotted Fawn had grown up with the idea she would become the wife of Lucas. Although Lucas had never led her to believe this, she spent much of her time endeavoring to win his hand in marriage. Lindsay was a serious threat to Spotted Fawn. The beautiful redhead was constantly under his watchful eye and when a brave approached her, Lucas turned on him with such a glare that he soon backed away. It was obvious to Spotted Fawn that Lucas was interested in more than just the health of this woman. Spotted Fawn resented Lindsay with all the ferocity of a catamount. Lindsay wondered how Spotted Fawn would feel now that she was leaving. Would she again attempt to get Lucas to marry her? A violent stab of jealousy tore through her as she brushed at the tears on her cheeks.

She felt a hand on her shoulder and jumped. "Why are you crying, niña?"

She looked down at her folded hand. "I, I don't know. I guess I'll miss your home here and the people. I've grown to love them, Lucas. I've been gone so long from my Uncle Ned and I guess I'm frightened. I really don't know why

I'm crying." She looked up and smiled as Lucas bent and lifted her to her feet. He held her close and spoke.

"Niña, it has been many, many weeks since you have seen your home. Now you are returning. Your feelings are mixed but you must return. You must see your uncle. He's been worried and his health has been weakened. I had hoped you would have been returned to him by now. But since you were injured, there was no way to send you back until you were stronger. Now you are ready. Soon your uncle will have his Lindsay back again." He smiled at her.

Lindsay looked up urgently. "Lucas, what do you mean Uncle Ned's health has been weakened? What's happened to him? Why are you telling me this? How do you know? Lucas sighed, led her to the cot and sat down, pulling her down beside him.

"Lindsay, there are many questions you will have answered when you return home. Many of these questions your uncle can answer. I can't answer them now. I want him to be the one to tell you everything. I can tell you, your uncle is impatiently waiting your arrival and he is feeling well. You are the answer to his ailment. Now, please, niña, no more questions. Let your uncle be the one to answer them." He put his finger under her chin and tilted her head back. Her eyes were moist with unshed tears.

She started to speak but Lucas quieted her with his lips. He laid her back on the blanket and soon her thoughts were only of their lovemaking.

* * *

A hand shook Lindsay to awareness and she stretched. The sky was grey, the horizon pink with the rising sun. "Come, niña, it's time." Lucas stood over her. She blinked the sleep from her eyes and snuggled deeper into the warm blanket. "It's too early."

Lucas laughed and pulled her from the bed. He stood her in front of him and shook her body. "Come on, niña, time to wake up. Open your eyes."

She jerked her head back, angry at his rough treatment. "Who do you think you're jerking around, you, you . . .

just because you won't ever see me again doesn't give you the right to manhandle me now."

"Oh, niña, our final moments and they're spent fighting." He pulled her body into his embrace, holding her close to his chest. She looked at him and smiled. A dimple peeped out from the corner of her mouth and he bent and kissed it lightly. He buried his face in her hair, inhaling her light fragrance and ran his hands up and down her back. She snuggled closer to him and murmured, "Ummm, this is a much nicer way to wake up."

She threw her head back and studied him momentarily before speaking. "Maybe I should hire you. You could come home with me and your main duty, your only duty, would be to wake me every morning by any method you deemed necessary, such as . . . well, let me think." She giggled as Lucas bent down and nibbled a pink nipple.

"Don't tempt me, Lindsay." He ran his tongue over her breast caressing the soft flesh and Lindsay moaned with desire.

Abruptly Lucas straightened and stepped back. "But I doubt you could afford to pay my price for waking young ladies from their night of rest. My prices have increased drastically since I met you." He turned and left the tepee, his laughter floating back to her long after his footsteps had diminished.

Lindsay stood facing the direction of his departure, savoring the memory of his lips. After several seconds, she shook her head and began to dress. She packed the few items she had acquired since her arrival in the camp. As she began to place her hair ribbon and an ivory clip in her satchel, she stopped. She held the items tenderly, turning them over and staring at them. Lucas had given her the clip several days ago. One day while she was swimming in the river, Lucas swam up behind her, gathered her hair on top of her head and clipped it. She remembered reaching up, removing the clip, and fingering it lovingly. It was very beautiful, a large, ivory clip with carved flowers on each end.

She finished dressing and after tying her hair back with a piece of rawhide, she walked outside. The sun glowed brightly and the still air was a portent of the hot day to come. Lindsay blinked several times and then went in search of Little Bird. She found her crouched down digging up Indian potatoes. Lindsay stood behind her, watching her work. She used a sharp stick and, with seemingly little effort, would poke the ground a few times, twist the stick and dig up the potato. It never ceased to amaze Lindsay the ingenious ways these people found food in so barren a land. One of her favorite foods was a peeled, sweet thistle stalk. The first time she saw Little Bird eating one she almost gagged. But it was delicious. It reminded her of a banana. Little Bird had a basket almost filled with the Indian potatoes. She threw another one in, stood up and rubbed her back.

"Little Bird," Lindsay spoke softly.

Little Bird turned to Lindsay. "You are learning our ways well. I did not hear your approach. You will soon be an Apache sister." Lindsay smiled.

"Thank you, Little Bird, that is truly a compliment." Lindsay sat on the warm ground and motioned for Little Bird to sit beside her.

"The time has come?" Little Bird asked.

"Yes, I am ready."

Little Bird gazed up at the sky. "I do not believe it will be many moons before you will return." She looked at Lindsay. "I feel in my heart," she touched her breast, "you will return to us."

Lindsay gazed at her hands. The white ribbon hung from her palm. The other hand gripped the hair clip. A lump formed in her throat and she coughed in an attempt to gain composure.

"Little Bird, you remember when I laid on Lucas's bed hovering between life and death? I didn't know what was happening to me nor did I care. As the days dragged by and my pain subsided, I realized if it hadn't been for you and Lucas I would have died." She took a deep breath and continued, "Perhaps at the time it wouldn't have mattered. I was sick. I was frightened. I remember thinking just before I got shot that I didn't care what happened to me. I wanted to die. I wanted to wander the desert, feel more pain physically than I felt in my heart. But then as I began to heal, I began to fight. I wanted to live. I had to live and although I am not sure why you did it, I do know you are responsible for my living. I'm an outsider here. I have interrupted the lives of people who cannot trust the white man. And yet you have welcomed and nursed me. I will always be grateful to you, Little Bird." She raised her hand. "Wait, let me finish, please. But most of all, I will always be grateful for your friendship." She placed the ribbon and clip in Little Bird's hand. "I want you to have these. Not because I want you to remember me, although most certainly I do. I want you to have these because they are beautiful. I want them to belong to someone beautiful." Lindsay stood and brushed at the tears on her cheeks. She gazed at Little Bird's sad face. And when a tear slid down her dark skin, Lindsay bent and kissed her on the cheek, then slowly walked away.

Spotted Fawn sat in front of her tepee scraping a hide. She looked up as she heard Lindsay approach. Spotted Fawn saw her wet cheeks and smiled. As Lindsay walked by, Spotted Fawn's smile turned to laughter, taunting, bitter, malicious laughter.

Lucas was talking to Yellow Cat and War Eagle. When he saw Lindsay approaching he turned and waited for her. Lindsay took a deep breath, wiped the tears with the back of her hand and smiled at Lucas. She could see everything was ready. The horses pawed the ground and snorted, anxious to run. She would be riding bareback and she was pleased. She would not have to suffer riding in a saddle. War Eagle held her horse for her. A rope was hitched around the animal's lower jaw—that was the bridle—and the only method of control Lindsay would have. Yellow Cat would lead the pack horse. Lindsay entered the tepee, picked up her satchel, and looked around one last time. Then, straightening her shoulders she walked outside, into the bright new day and mounted her horse with help from War Eagle. She took the bridle and turned to speak to Lucas. He was gone. The sound of hooves echoed above her and she looked up. Lucas rode at breakneck speed up the incline and into the trees. He was barely visible in the dust clouds. Lindsay shuddered. It took all her will power to keep from riding after him, screaming at him to take her with him. She turned her horse and trotted through the trees. War Eagle and Yellow Cat followed. They stayed behind her. They left her alone. As soon as she left the thick forest, she spurred her horse and galloped off. Her hair blew back, rippling in the wind and her shirt filled with air, ballooning out as she rode faster and faster, her face streaked with tears and dust.

From the top of a hill Lucas sat on his horse watching the beautiful girl riding into the wind, away from his home, away from him. The ache in his heart made it difficult to breathe.

Chapter 15

They had been traveling for several days. Although War Eagle and Yellow Cat were kind and undemanding, Lindsay wanted to be alone. She wanted to throw her head back and scream. She wanted to run until her lungs were close to bursting. She wanted to cry until her tears were spent. She could do none of these things with her guides. So she retreated into a protective shell. She spoke only when spoken to. Dark circles deepened under her eyes and her skin lost its rosy tinge. She was tired but she couldn't sleep. War Eagle and Yellow Cat became concerned, but no matter how hard they tried to force her to eat and sleep she shook her head and withdrew into her shell.

The nights were beginning to get cooler. After the evening meal, the Indians would sit around a small fire talking softly. Lindsay sat apart from them, enjoying the cool night air. As the air got colder, she enjoyed it more, as though the pain of shivering would help erase the painful memories of Lucas.

War Eagle tried unsuccessfully to get Lindsay to eat. Each night she refused the food and rarely slept. She had to eat. She had to sleep.

One night after making camp, War Eagle prepared a hot drink. It was made with herbs and sweetened with berry juice.

The sky was covered with clouds and a full moon played in and out of them. The Indians had prepared a stew and the smell wafted through the camp and into the hills. But Lindsay could not be enticed to eat. She shook her head and walked away.

War Eagle approached her after they had eaten and held a steaming cup to her. She shook her head.

"Lindsay, drink this. I will not force you to eat. I will not force you to sleep. But I will force you to drink this." She looked up at him. He stood straight, holding the cup to her.

"Why?" She looked away.

"You must have nourishment. If not food, liquid. Now drink."

Set it down there," she nodded, "I'll drink it later."

"No. You will drink it now. If you do not, I will hold you down and Yellow Cat will force it down your throat."

Lindsay was shocked. He had never spoken to her like that. It startled her. But, rather than force him to follow through with his threat and rather than argue—she was too tired to fight—she would drink it. She took the cup and began to sip the contents. It was delicious. She drank it all and when she finished she handed the cup back.

"Thank you, War Eagle, that was very good."

He nodded, a smug look of satisfaction on his face as he walked away. He sat beside Yellow Cat, the fire blocking his face from Lindsay's view but he could see her. After a few minutes her head began to bob forward. She sat on the rock but she could not hold her head up. Yellow Cat walked to her bedroll and held the blankets up while War Eagle carried her to the bed. After they had covered her and they had settled in for the night, Yellow Cat spoke, "Your woman has wise visions. I will ask her how she knew Lindsay would need drugs to sleep."

And in the darkness War Eagle smiled at Lindsay's deep breathing.

*   *   *

One early afternoon, they crested a hill and below them, camped on the Rio Brazos, was her uncle. Lindsay had not felt well that day and Yellow Cat had given her his blanket to wrap around her shivering shoulders. They dismounted and stood looking down. Lindsay's heart jumped at the thought of seeing her family again. But even that long-awaited dream wasn't enough to snap her out of the stupor she had settled into. The last two mornings she had suffered with violent nausea. War Eagle scolded her for the damage she was inflicting on her body. "No sleep, no food. Lindsay, you cannot continue to do this."

But his words fell on deaf ears. She had no intention of listening to his badgering. And now that she was genuinely sick, the thought of food only made her sicker. She was sure that she had gone so long without eating that now she couldn't eat if she wanted to.

War Eagle and Yellow Cat each gave her a parting gift. War Eagle gave her a pair of white moccasins that came almost to her knees and were decorated with intricate beadwork and laced up the sides. She had never seen moccasins so beautiful. And because War Eagle had made them, they meant even more. Yellow Cat gave her a saddle bag made from rawhide. It also had been handmade and her initials were carved in the side. She hadn't expected this and was astounded and speechless. She raised her hands in a supplicating manner and finally in a thick voice said, "I, I have never seen anything so beautiful." She looked from one face to the other. "I am ashamed. I have been nothing but trouble this whole trip and you have been so patient," she laughed softly, "My gosh, help me, don't let me stand here like an idiot wallowing in self-pity. Say something." She sniffed loudly and both Indians smiled.

"We ask only one thing in return," War Eagle said.

Lindsay shifted her weight. "Anything, War Eagle, I'll do anything you ask."

"You must take care of yourself. Eat right and sleep. You will see soon why it is so very important." War Eagle turned to pack the horse and opened his saddle bag. He took out several articles and turned back to Lindsay.

"Promise me, little one, you will do as I ask."

She nodded her head smiled, "Yes, I promise. I'll take care of myself." She looked across the river at the wagons below them. "I guess I can't very well take care of my uncle if I'm sicker than he is." She looked at War Eagle.

"I know thank you sounds so, so insignificant for everything you both have done for me. But I mean it from the depths of my heart. Thank you."

War Eagle handed her two parfleche's filled with pemmican, berry bag, and a tobacco pouch for her uncle. "The pemmican will help you regain your strength. Eat some every day. The berries are good. You will like it. The tobacco is for your uncle from Lucas." War Eagle turned and mounted his horse. Yellow Cat lifted Lindsay on hers and then she watched him mount his pinto.

"I'm going now. If I don't, I'll cry and I don't want to cry." She turned her horse and slowly moved down the hill. She stopped and looked back after walking only a few feet. The Indians were watching her. They smiled and waved and then disappeared over the crest of the hill. Lindsay watched them with tear-filled eyes and then she turned toward her uncle. She pulled the blanket tightly around her shoulders as a wave of nausea washed over her again. After it subsided she sipped some water from her canteen and continued walking.

Four horses were winding their way toward her and she recognized Justin Devor, Pete Sheldon, Michel Langriose, and Tony Perez. She arched her back, lifted her head up, and closed her eyes as a sob escaped her. She clenched her hands and bit her lip as she continued walking closer to her uncle, closer to her home.

And farther from the man she loved.

Chapter 16

Her reunion with her uncle was quiet. He was not well. But he had insisted on coming to meet her. She kneeled over his propped body and softly brushed his hair from his forehead. The illness had been severe and she was shocked at the way her uncle looked. His face was grey, his eyes ringed in purple, and his lips were white and drawn. When she touched his face, he opened his eyes and a smile filled his face. He whispered something and she bent close to his face. "My little Lindsay." A tear fell from his eye and rested on his cheekbone. She touched it. Several more fell on his face and she realized her tears were mingling with his. He fell asleep in her arms and she sat by him, holding his hand and caressing his face.

Several ranch hands had accompanied him. Only Jonas, Ricco, and Zuni were not there. The men had fixed a comfortable bed in the light wagon for Ned. Lindsay learned from Justin that after she had been abducted it had rained for several days, but her uncle insisted on continuing the search for her. He searched, soaked to the skin, and then one night he began to cough. Within a few hours he was out of his head with fever. He was returned to the ranch where he lay near death for many days. Zuni nursed him the best she could but he called for Lindsay constantly. The doctor said he could treat the fever and cough but only Lindsay could mend his broken heart. He began to improve slightly and one day a couple of riders appeared and asked to see Ned. Zuni would not hear of it but at the mention of Lindsay's name, they were led to his bedside.

The men were Mexican and spoke broken English but Zuni soon had a conversation going with them. They told her of Lindsay's whereabouts and arrangements were made for her return to the ranch. They produced her dress, the one she had taken with her when she had escaped from the wagon. Lindsay smiled. She remembered carrying the dress with her, wrapping it in her shawl. And when she had noticed it was gone she shrugged, thinking she had left it somewhere in the desert or that Manuel had disposed of it. The dress was ruined so she didn't care. It never dawned on her that Lucas had taken it.

When her uncle saw the dress, the white dress with violet flowers and how ripped and dirty it was, he began to cry. The doctor had to give him something to calm him down. He was sure Lindsay had suffered terribly.

* * *

The group spent the night at Rio Brazos and early the next morning they started out for the Lazy Hat Ranch. Lindsay rode in the wagon holding her uncle's hand, talking to him. She fed him, washed his face, and scolded him for not taking better care of himself. "After all," she said, "What reason would I have had to return home if you had not been here?" He smiled and squeezed her hand.

Soon Lindsay began to recognize the countryside. She recognized the rolling hills, green mountains, tall pines. The familiar landscape made her shiver with anticipation but a nagging sadness tugged at her heart and everyone noticed that the bright smile that was once a part of Lindsay was no longer present. Her laughter had lost its tinkling quality. Ned swore to reap vengeance on all who were responsible for this. Somehow, someday he would see her sadness replaced with happiness. He would see the men suffer that had hurt his Lindsay.

They crested a hill and the ranch lay below them. Smoke curled from the chimney. Angel was lying on the porch, Regalo was in the pasture next to the house. Invisible waves rolled across the tall gold wheat field beyond the house. Zuni was rocking on the front porch working on her sampler. Ricco and Jonas emerged from the barn. When they got closer Lindsay jumped from the wagon and began running down the lane, to her house, to Zuni, to Angel, to her family, to her home.

Ricco and Jonas came toward her, tears streaming down their cheeks. Angel barked and jumped madly at her feet and even Devil came from the barn to see the commotion. After much hugging and kissing and tears, Ned was put to bed. Lindsay climbed the staris, bone tired, to take a hot bath. The bath was prepared and Zuni clucked about like a mother hen, but when she saw Lindsay's head nod off to sleep she quietly walked out.

Lindsay woke late the next day. The sun streamed in through the window and for a minute she forgot where she was. She lay in the bed and looked around her room. Everything was the same. Angel was lying at the foot of her bed the way she always did and Lindsay felt content.

Suddenly she felt a wave of nausea sweep over her. She swallowed a couple of times, blinked back a few tears, then flew out of bed to the bowl on the dresser and retched. She wet a cloth, lay back on the bed and placed the wet cloth on her forehead. All the traveling and excitement and strange food must have upset me, she thought. She lay quietly for awhile and soon the nausea left. She rose and went to the closet to look for something to wear. Picking out a dark blue muslin dress, she threw it on the bed. She stared at the dress for a few seconds. Funny, she thought, I picked the darkest color dress I own. Almost as though I'm mourning. She pondered . . . I am mourning. I've lost the man I love. She turned to the dresser and peered at the clothing she had worn for so many weeks. It was threadbare and even though she had washed it as often as she could, it was badly stained. She picked up the shirt and held it to her breast. She closed her eyes and remembered the time Lucas had given it to her. A soft knock interrupted her thoughts. "Lindsay, are you awake?"

"I'll be down in a few minutes, Zuni." She folded the shirt and pants, placed them in a drawer and turned to dress.

When she walked into the kitchen Zuni looked at her and a frown creased her brow. "Are you all right Lindsay? You look ill." Lindsay nodded and told her she felt fine but she didn't want anything to eat right now, only a cup of tea. She took the tea over Zuni's protest that she really should eat something and went to her uncle's room. She knocked lightly.

"Come in." Ned was sitting up in bed, eating from his tray. He beamed at her. "Good morning, honey. How does it feel to be home?"

She sat on the edge of his bed and pulled his hand to her cheek. He stroked her face with a palsied hand.

"I've missed you so much, Uncle Ned. I don't ever want to leave you again."

"My little Lindsay has grown up." He paused, "Would you set the tray over there, honey?" He pulled himself up against the pillows and held her hand. He looked into her face, "Lindsay, was it rough?"

"At first it was, Uncle Ned. At first I was very frightened. But, soon I learned how to handle myself well enough. Now, no more talk about that, at least not for awhile. I want to know what's been happening here and how you are feeling."

He looked at her for a few seconds and then he told her about the new cattle he had purchased, a new colt that promised to be a great sire, the new outriders he hired. As he talked, Lindsay's mind wandered back to New Mexico and to Lucas. She wondered what he was doing. Was he with another woman. Did he miss her? Did he even remember her? She remembered his lips on hers, his hands caressing and probing. Droplets of sweat popped out on her brow and she wiped at them absentmindedly. Suddenly another wave of nausea washed over her. Perspiration showed on her upper lip and chin and she grabbed her stomach, stood, and started for the door.

"Lindsay, what's the matter?" She heard her uncle yell but she couldn't answer. She opened her door quickly and ran to her room, where again she emptied her stomach. She wiped her face with the cloth and fell on the bed. She decided to stay in bed for awhile. Maybe her ordeal had tired her more than she realized.

Zuni came in. Seeing how flushed Lindsay was, she went right out, promising to return with a bowl of soup and a cup of tea laced with brandy. Lindsay rolled over in bed. She wiped her brow and licked her lips. Her head was spinning and there was a lump in her throat. She lie still, hoping the nausea would soon pass.

Zuni returned carrying a tray with hot soup and tea. She laid the tray beside the bed and bending over Lindsay she felt her brow. Her cool hand felt good and Lindsay smiled.

"You have no fever, Lindsay. Let me help you sit up, then you drink this tea and soup."

Lindsay groaned her disapproval at the prospect of eating but Zuni would not be put off. She propped some pillows behind Lindsay, held the cup of tea to her lips, and forced her to take a swallow. The hot liquid burned Lindsay's throat and the brandy made her feel warm all over and she drank it all. Soon a little color tinted her pale face. She laid back against the pillows and a wan smile touched her lips. "You're right, Zuni. The tea has made me feel a little better." Zuni instructed her to sip the soup and rest. She promised to return later with more tea and then she left Lindsay alone.

Lindsay snuggled deeper into the pillows sighing as the feeling of nausea left her. She closed her eyes but opened them again as the sight of blue eyes danced in front of her. Every time she closed her eyes he came into view. She sighed deeply. I suppose I'll have to go through life with my eyes open. Everytime I close them, I see him.

She wiped her face with a corner of the sheet. "I must get hold of myself. I can't go on like this. Damn! Damn! Damn! She looked around. The sun shone through the window and bounced off the ceiling, reflecting thousands of tiny diamonds. I have to pull myself together. How long will it be before I forget him? How long before he's not in my every thought? She sat up. Sleeping was impossible. She couldn't think of anything but Lucas so maybe a walk would help her get him out of her mind. She rubbed her bare toes across the rug. As she looked at her feet she thought of the time Lucas had rubbed them with ointment and wrapped them in socks. She shook her head. This is ridiculous. She walked to the window and gazed out across the wide expanse of land. Thick white clouds raced through the sky. The wind was blowing and the leaves were beginning to change. It seemed so long ago that she went down and joined Lucas in the wagon for a tour. Tour. She laughed at the memory of how angry she was. She had told her uncle that she would never forgive him for making her show Lucas around. Yes, she would never forgive her uncle. But now for an entirely different reason.

She walked into the kitchen where the smell of freshly baked bread assailed her and the smell of spices made her mouth water. She gulped and took a deep breath. Every time she smelled food she got sick. Maybe, as War Eagle had said, she had done some damage to her body by not eating. Maybe now she wouldn't be able to eat without gagging.

"Are you feeling better, carino?" Zuni was lifting the hot bread onto the breadboard.

"Yes, a little better, I guess." She leaned against the table and folded her arms across her chest. "Zuni, how long has Uncle Ned been sick?"

Zuni wiped her hands on her apron, reached into a cupboard and brought out a bowl.

"After you disappeared he spent every minute searching for you. He had his men search in shifts but he searched constantly. He searched in the rain and wind. He searched at night. He even searched in his sleep. We could not get him to stop. Then he got the cough and fever. He got so weak he had to stop looking for you and go to bed. He was so upset and so sick. I didn't think he would live, Lindsay." She placed the bowl in the oven and turned back to Lindsay. "He was vowed to kill Nick Moriarity. But no one has seen him since you disappeared. Extra guards have been placed around the ranch and they have been told to shoot Mr. Moriarity on sight." She removed the warm bowl from the oven and placed a dollop of butter in it. Lindsay walked over and watched the butter slowly melting.

"Does Uncle Ned know what Nick's plans were? Does he know Nick planned to use me to get the ranch?"

"Yes, carino. Your uncle knows everything." Zuni looked at Lindsay and smiled warmly. "Why don't you ask him, Lindsay? He'll tell you everything." Zuni moved to Lindsay and touched her cheek. The puzzled look on Lindsay's face prompted her to say more.

"Go, carino, go talk with your uncle. He knows how you were to be protected by Lucas Sanger. He knows all. He will tell you and put your mind at rest." She turned back to her bowl of melted butter and Lindsay knew she would say no more.

* * *

Her knock was answered by a muffled "Come in." She entered her uncle's room slowly and crossed to the chair by the window. She smoothed her skirt and ran her fingers through her hair before she sat. Ned watched her attempts at calming her nerves and finally asked, "Lindsay, what's the matter, are you sick?"

She looked at her uncle's face. The illness had left lines of fatigue and pain. His eyes were sunken in his grey face and the weight he lost made his skin look too big for his bones.

He beckoned for her to sit next to him. She laid her head against her uncle's shoulder and with trembling lips spoke softly, "Uncle Ned, I love Lucas Sanger. I think I loved him from the beginning but I was too stubborn to admit it. And now, it's too late. I'm back home with you and he is many miles away. He will soon forget me. It is too far for us to see each other often and I don't know if I can bear to be apart from him." Ned rubbed her shoulder lovingly and looked out the window at the increasing wind.

"Lindsay, many months ago I decided to take you into Durango for a few days. I felt you needed the change. You were growing up, becoming a woman. A woman needs a man, or I should say some women need a man, not all do. But, I knew you did. I knew placing you in a situation whereby you could meet a man would also be jeopardizing my life. You are my life. If you were to fall in love, I would lose you. But as time went by I knew I had to give you up some day. I couldn't keep you to myself. I may be selfish, but I'm not that selfish. And who knows, maybe if you married someone with a big spread I may live with you and help run the place."

"At any rate, while we were in Durango and Jonas and I were having a whiskey, a man came up to me and asked to talk to me in private." Ned shifted his weight and moved Lindsay into the crook of his arm. "Well, this man had a very interesting story to tell me. I made him repeat it to Jonas. He had proof to back his story and his friend, a man named Chico, verified the story." Lindsay peered at her uncle and her breath came in short gasps as he continued.

"I certainly felt this man could be your match. But his story upset me and I swore if he was lying to me I'd hunt him down and kill him with my bare hands. He finally brought a Mr. Stade in the room and introduced him as a government agent. Mr. Stade had an interesting story to tell and, well, before the night was over a plan that would change your life and mine had taken root in that small room."

Beads of perspiration popped out on Lindsay's brow as she listened intently to her uncle. Her hands were clenched in tight fists and to Lindsay, the world stopped as she listened to this story unfold.

"Lucas told Jonas and me about Moriarity's plan to abduct you and why. He told me how he had been hired to infiltrate Moriarity's gang to get information for Stade. But when he learned of Moriarity's plan he knew he had to tell me. Saving your life became much more important than the information Stade needed. And, of course, Stade agreed. I wanted to kill Moriarity right then. I wanted to feel his neck under my hands. I wanted to hurt him." Ned's eyes stared out the window and Lindsay touched his cheek, bringing him back to awareness. He sighed, then continued.

"Sanger and Stade explained how I had to go along with their plans if your life was to be saved. If you weren't taken by Moriarity it was certain somehow, someday, he would have gotten to you and chances are no one would have been there to protect you. Sanger promised me you wouldn't be hurt. He said he wouldn't leave your side for one minute." Lindsay smiled. She brushed at a curl on her face and sighed, and he didn't, she thought. "Sanger also said when it was safe you would be returned to me. He said it might be a long time, but you would come back . . . he didn't lie."

Ned turned back to the window. His eyes reflected the anguish he had suffered.

"And then, after you were gone, after the arrangements had been made for your abduction, and after we settled down around here, we waited. We waited a few days and then I began to search for you. Sanger told me Nick had planned to take you to Canada. Only, after you were taken, he changed his mind and took you south. We weren't supposed to look for you. Sanger and Stade were afraid if we were seen by any of Moriarity's men you would be killed. But I couldn't just sit here and wait. I had to look for you. I had to see if there wasn't some way to ambush the group and bring you home. Only, I looked in the wrong direction. I began to panic. I knew I had been duped. You were in real danger and not just from Moriarity but from Sanger too. I felt desolate, sick, and mad." He squeezed her close to him and held her for several seconds, reveling in her presence.

"Oh, honey, you have no idea the guilt I carried. I knew I had sentenced you to death. I, your uncle, had killed you. I wanted to die. When I got sick, I gave up fighting. I couldn't live with the knowledge of my deed eating my insides away. I had betrayed my daugh . . . ah . . . niece. I had betrayed the only person I lived for."

"And then one day, a couple men rode up with your dress in their possession. They had a note from Sanger explaining what had happened, where you were, and that he would let me know when you would be returned. He told me he wanted to keep you at his ranch for a couple of days until he was sure Moriarity and his men were hunting in the area of Silver City. He didn't want to run into them and jeopardize your safety. He warned me to watch for strange men around the ranch. Nick would probably have someone watch this place for any signs of you and Sanger. Only Sanger had made sure that you were seen in Silver City. He threw Nick off your trail by getting him to travel there in search of you. I don't know who he found to parade as you but whoever it was couldn't possibly be as lovely." He smiled and kissed the tip of her nose. "Anyway, I'll spend the rest of my days hoping for the chance to kill Nick Moriarity. I want to pay him back for my misery . . . I want to make him suffer as I suffered all these weeks."

"Uncle Ned, why didn't you tell me? Why couldn't I have known about this plan before I was taken. It would certainly have saved me a lot of fright and anger."

"Honey, your life depended on this plan being carried through exactly as Nick called the shots. If you had not shown fear, or had lost your temper and said something wrong, you would have been killed. I know you, Lindsay. I know how you can lose your temper and spit at people. You say things you don't mean. If you'd said something to Nick that aroused his suspicious, well, it would have been the end, Lindsay. God knows, I wanted you to know. I wanted to be sure you wouldn't be scared out of your wits. I wanted you to know you had a friend with you. But even though Lucas thought it would be safe to tell you, I didn't. Saving your life was the only thing I cared about. Moriarity could have had the ranch and every damn thing on it for all I care, but you, you had to be safe. And, if you remember, I did try to get you to know Sanger before your abduction. I tried to make you see what kind of man he was. I was hoping you would trust him before this happened. But you were too stubborn. You wouldn't listen." He laughed lightly as he hugged her again.

Lindsay sighed deeply. "I remember how you kept telling me I had to show him around the ranch, forcing me to be with him. I never thought anything about it. I only knew I was mad because you insisted I be with someone I didn't like. I remember thinking it strange that you took such an interest in my social life all of a sudden. But I had been so moody that I pushed it out of my mind. I thought you were trying to get me out of the mood I was in. Anyway, Uncle Ned, it's over. We're alive and together. Only what do I do now? How do I find Lucas? How do I make him love me and how do I live without him, Uncle Ned?" She sat up and dangled her legs over the side of the large bed.

"Well, this is a problem I'll have to think on for a few days, Linday. But, girl, we'll find your man. It may take some time, but we'll find this er . . . marked man," he chuckled. "But now this old man needs some rest. If I'm to find my niece's future husband, I'll need to regain my strength. I can't do that if I'm not allowed to rest. He patted her on the back and she stood and gazed down at him. Her eyes were misty as she bent and kissed him on the cheek. Then without another word, she crossed the room and opened the door. She looked back at her uncle who was watching her.

"Oh, Uncle Ned, when arrangements were first made for me to leave Lucas's ranch and meet you, I ran away. And then after I healed from my wound, you met me. How did you know when to meet me the second time? And how long did you wait for me the first time? I don't understand how you knew."

"Lindsay, honey, Lucas has several men working for him. I was kept informed of everything. After you had been shot, several of us wanted to go to you. Mr. Stade was afraid we would put Moriarity on your track. He told us you were in good hands and if we foolishly rode out of here to where you were, we would probably cause the death of many innocent people. Lucas, Stade, and Chico kept me well informed of your whereabouts."

Lindsay shuddered as she thought of Nick and his men riding into the Apache camp killing those people, Little Bird . . . War Eagle.

"Uncle Ned, has anyone ever told you you're a con artist?" She walked out into a sun-dappled hallway, into her cluttered bedroom. After flinging herself on the bed, she fell into a relieved sleep.

Chapter 17

"But, Lucas, I thought you loved me. I thought you cared and we would be married."

"Spotted Fawn, I have never said I would marry you. I

love you, Spotted Fawn, but not as a husband loves a wife." Lucas touched her arm softly as he spoke, then looked at the horizon, in the direction of Colorado.

"You are in love with the white woman. It is written on your face. I guess I knew it as soon as I saw you with her. You never left her side." She looked at him, her eyes flashing. "She is a white woman. She is not Apache. You are Apache. You will hurt your father if you marry a white woman. Grey Wolf loves me and I will tell him you are disloyal to your people. Grey Wolf will force you to marry me. I will fix the white woman." She whirled and stomped away and Lucas sighed as he watched her disappear. He knew Spotted Fawn expected him to follow her but he had no desire to do so. She questioned his every move and threatened him constantly. He walked to his tepee and entered.

A faint scent touched his senses. Lindsay. He knew now, after being apart, he couldn't live without Lindsay. She had dug deeper into his heart than even he thought anyone ever could. Although he realized long ago that he loved her, he didn't realize how much until now. She had ripped his heart from his chest and carried it with her to Colorado. He would have to go after her to retrieve it. He chuckled at the thought. Well, he thought, if Nick's ever gonna find me it sure as hell ain't gonna be here. I'll go back to my ranch. Maybe Chico has heard something. Then, I'm gonna take me a jaunt to the Lazy Hat Ranch and look up a certain little redhead I know.

The next morning as the sun came up and the cool breeze rippled through the trees, Lucas went to talk with his father. When he returned to his tepee Spotted Fawn was waiting for him.

"Are you leaving?"

"Yes."

"Will you return soon?"

"No."

Spotted Fawn's face turned pale. She turned her face up and let the cool breeze touch her skin. Then, she turned back to Lucas.

"Lucas, what must I do to make you love me? What

do you wish me to do? I love you, I'll do anything to get your. . . ."

Lucas turned to her and stopped packing his things in his saddle bags. "Fawn, please, don't make this harder than it is already. I told you, I love you as a sister, not as a man would love his wife. There is nothing you can do or say to change that."

"You will be sorry, Lucas Sanger. You have made Spotted Fawn a fool. I told many we would one day marry. Many of the women who dream of you have been warned to stay away from you. You were mine. I felt in my heart," she placed a shaking hand across her chest, "that we would be man and wife someday. Now, you make me a liar. I will pay you back for this. I will make you sorry you ever lied to Spotted Fawn. I will make you hurt too." She ran from the tepee and Lucas could hear her sobs.

He walked out of the tepee and looked for her. She was nowhere to be seen. He bowed his head and shrugged. Maybe it would be best to leave her alone. He could only make things worse by trying to talk to her. He walked back and finished his packing. When he had mounted his horse and traveled several yards down the mountain he stopped and looked back. Spotted Fawn was not visible. He turned back and slowly descended the mountain. But a chill swept over him and he looked up at the sky. The orange sun glowed down on the surrounding country, warming the earth. A cold breeze caressed his skin. He shrugged and pulled his hat down low over his face. Maybe Spotted Fawn was a witch. He laughed at the thought. But a nagging doubt tugged at him. Spotted Fawn would bear watching. Only he wasn't sure why.

* * *

The ranch hands were happy to see Lucas and they announced that Moriarity hadn't been seen or heard from. Lucas walked into the house and after speaking to Manuel went to his bedroom to get some sleep. He threw his hat on the dresser and whirled as he saw Lindsay's *camisa* lying across the back of the chair. He fingered it and rubbed it across his face, caressing it, inhaling the fragrance that spoke of Lindsay. He crossed to the patio doors and stood looking out. The sun hung low on the horizon and Lucas recalled how much Lindsay loved to watch the sunsets. He chuckled as he remembered the first time she told him she was busy watching the nightfire.

He turned to the bed and, after removing his boots, he laid back. His senses were filled with Lindsay. Her fragrance lingered in this room, on this bed, in his mind. He saw her creamy skin shimmering with moisture, how after they made love, she glowed with a film of wetness. He groaned. Damn! How can such a little gal be so powerful, so everywhere, so beautiful . . . his thoughts were filled with visions, of moist, parted lips, soft and yielding emerald eyes, eyes that filled a room. When she looked at you, nothing else was evident. He got up and walked to the bowl of clean water Manuel kept on the washstand. He splashed some water on his face and neck and returned to the bed. He was bone weary and desperately needed some sleep. But each time he closed his eyes, red hair would caress his face, soft, perfumed hair, and then her arms would wrap around his neck and press him close to her soft body. When he reached out to hold her she would bound back into the shadows. Finally, he got up, swearing under his breath, and walked out of the room. *That damn room is filled with Lindsay. I'll sleep on the couch.*

He walked into the dark parlor and after lighting a candle he poured himself a glass of brandy.

"I thought you were sleeping, *amigo*."

Lucas spun to face the voice. "What are you doing in here, Chico?"

"I have been sleeping in here since you returned to your people. I want to be close if Moriarity shows up."

Lucas took a long swallow of his brandy and offered the bottle to Chico. After swallowing the contents of his glass he sat next to Chico and fingered the glass, twirling it absentmindedly in his hand.

"Everyone seems to be on edge, waiting and wondering. I'm glad Lindsay is safe. Nick is probably crazed with anger and the only solace he'll find now is in her death."

Chico stood and stretched his long arms above his head and walked to the door. He peered at the darkening sky. "I'm gonna take a walk. Helps clear the cobwebs from my brain. Helps ease the longing for Lita." He disappeared into the darkness and Lucas watched him.

Chico rarely mentioned Lita. He wondered why he did now. Was he suggesting a walk would help him too? No. Nothing would help him sleep. Nothing except Lindsay lying next to him. He leaned back, lifted his legs and rested them on the hearth, and closed his eyes. His thoughts traveled back to a day so many years ago . . .

He had been traveling to San Antonio. A friend of his had been unjustly tried and found guilty of murder. Lucas would either get him off or break him out of jail. But he wasn't prepared for what he ran into. He watched from the top of a mountain for several minutes. Then, after he loaded his rifle and checked his gun, he rode into the clouds of dust below him. The attacking men had riled up so much dust that a person could barely see across the street. There were only eight men but there might just as well have been eight hundred. The town was unprepared for attack and being so small they had only a few people to help fight. And those who could were killed on the spot. He probably wouldn't have gotten involved except he saw a woman holding a small child by the hand gunned down. Well, he was certainly no bloody hero, but he had lived with people that had lost many women and children because of crazy gunmen. He rode into the midst of the fighting, hiding behind his horse and shot at every man that shot at him. He had killed six and finally the last two rode off. But not before Lucas got a look at them. He seared their faces into his mind. Soon the dust cleared and the smell of blood and gun powder hung in the air. A couple of town people shyly approached him smiling and offering their thanks. Many dead and injured people lay in the doorways, on wood railings and in the dirt. Their blood mingled with the dust. He pushed his hat back and leaned against a wobbly store railing. The cries of women and children began to get louder and louder and Lucas turned to his horse. Then, suddenly, from out of nowhere came a man, riding hard, his horse lathered and struggling to keep running. The man rode to the woman and child lying in the dirt and leaped from his horse. He approached the woman, pushed his hat back and lifted her head gently. She struggled to open her eyes and a tiny movement of her lips brought the man closer to her face. Lucas approached the man. When the Mexican looked up at Lucas, his eyes filled with pain. Lucas lowered his head. He helped carry the young woman into the store and the storekeeper's wife hastened to put her in a bed. Lucas went back outside . . . the little boy was dead. He wrapped the tiny body in a blanket and handed him to the priest who began speaking the last rights.

Lucas walked into the room and stood against the doorjamb, listening to the man talking to his wife.

"Lita," he said softly, "Lita, you must fight. You must not leave Antonio and me. You must not . . ." his voice broke and he lowered his head, touching his lips to the woman's white cheek. After a few minutes the priest came in, bowed his head over the two people and prayed. A few people had gathered in the store and he could hear their hushed voices.

The woman on the bed lay very still, her hands chalky and limp in the hands of her husband. Her long dark hair fell around her and across the white pillow. She was so pale, so fragile looking. Her lips were drawn tight and her suffering was evident. The bullet had struck her in the lower back and blown away part of her left shoulder.

The priest touched the man, calling him by name. Chico looked at his wife's face. No pain showed now, only a quiet peace. Chico hugged her lifeless body to him, crying as he kissed her throat, her lips, her cheeks. It took Lucas, the priest and two others to pull Chico away from his wife's body. Lucas took him to the saloon and made him drink a stiff shot of whiskey. Chico looked down at his blood-soaked clothes. "The boy was only three years old and Lita was only nineteen." Then he cried.

Lucas stayed with him that night and the next. They have been together ever since. The two men who escaped had never been found but their faces were still there and someday Lucas would see them. Only this time, Chico would be the one to avenge his wife's death.

The next morning Manuel quietly picked up the glass that had slipped from Lucas's hand. Lucas slept through breakfast. After Manuel had finished the morning dishes he fixed a plate and took it to Lucas. He opened his eyes and stretched. He felt as though he had been drugged. His head pounded and his mouth had a taste like sour milk.

Chapter 18

The leaves fell on the ground in piles. The wind would pick them up and blow them around. They would settle again, only to be scattered by the cold wind. Frost covered the windows and the sun bounced off the glass, shining brightly and slowly melting the white coating. Zuni's garden looked artificial covered with ice. The corn stalks hung limply, their brown arms coated with frost. Lindsay sat at her window and stared at the garden. Everything looked so strange, so lonely, she thought. The vines and flowers flopped back and forth in the wind. She curled up in the chair and laid her head back. The wind howled past her window making eeire sounds under the eaves. She had been awakened in the night by the constant nausea and rather than try to sleep, she had curled up in the chair and watched the dawn. Suddenly the nausea struck her again. She leaped from the chair and after retching for the third time, she sat back in the chair and wiped her brow with a wet cloth. She closed her eyes. This constant sickness was beginning to worry her. She remembered War Eagle's words about damaging her body. No, she couldn't have done this much damage, could she? She tried to think back to the first time she had noticed the sickness. It was soon after she left the Apache Camp and Lucas, and . . . Oh, my God! She sat up straight. It can't be! But, of course! How could I have been so stupid?

She jumped to her feet and ran to her dresser. She tilted the mirror downward and raised her nightgown above her waist. She stood sideways and peered intently at her reflection. Nothing. Her figure had not changed. She bent closer to the mirror and ran her fingers over her belly. She looked the same. She smiled. I thought missing my time was because of my traveling and wound and . . . but, but . . . She threw her robe around her and bounded down the stairs, almost stumbling once, then rounded the corner into the kitchen breathless and flushed.

Zuni turned, a startled expression on her face and asked quickly, "Lindsay, what is wrong? Are you ill again?" She turned to the stove and placed a pan of water on top of the coals to boil. "I'll fix you a cup of tea." She poured a healthy draught of brandy on top and handed the cup to Lindsay. After Lindsay had sipped some and a warm glow replaced the nausea, she relaxed.

"Zuni," she smiled up at the big Mexican lady's worried face, "I'm pregnant."

Zuni looked at Lindsay a few seconds, wiped her hands on her apron and sat down. Immediately, she stood, walked to the stove and fixed another cup of tea, lacing the top with brandy, and returned to Lindsay. She sipped the tea and watched Lindsay.

It's all right, Zuni. I'm not upset." Lindsay stood and walked to the window. Sun melted the frost and Lindsay watched the drops of moisture. "If anything, I'm elated. I am carrying Lucas Sanger's baby." She turned back to Zuni. "Only, please, Zuni, don't say anything to anybody yet. I'll tell them. I should have known this was the problem." She turned back to the window. "I didn't come sick for three months, I should have realized then . . . I should have known."

"What are you going to do, Lindsay. Oh, your uncle will be, well, he'll be so upset. What will you do?" Zuni wrung her hands together and gulped down the last of her tea.

Lindsay smiled. She touched the cool glass and traced a bit of melting ice with her finger. "I'll have a baby. Maybe a boy with icy blue eyes. Or a girl with sorrel-colored skin." Her hand went to her belly. "I'm going to have a baby. I can't lose Lucas now, he's part of me. He has to know. Somehow, we have to get word to him. Somebody has to tell him. No, *I* have to tell him." There's so much to do. I have to regain my health. Uncle Ned has to be told. Lucas has to be told. Zuni, I need your help."

Zuni wrapped her arms around Lindsay. "I'll stay by you, child. Zuni is here."

Chapter 19

The first snows were falling gently, cloaking the countryside in a mantle of white. The wind blew softly, gusting occasionally, picking up clouds of the white stuff and hurling it around, then slowly it would settle again. Lindsay sat in the parlor, her nose pressed to the window, waiting and watching. Her uncle came around the house and the snow mingled with his white hair and settled on his beard. His cheeks were ruddy and the breath came from his mouth in great bursts of mist.

A fire crackled in the fireplace, leaping up the giant chimney. Lindsay kept wiping the foggy windows with her sleeve. Ned opened the door and entered, accompanied by a gust of cold wind and snow. He removed his jacket and shook it gently, releasing the clinging snow. Then he hung it on the clothes rack.

Lindsay listened for his approach, her heart beating rapidly. She wasn't sure how he would take this news. She wasn't sure how she would tell him. But she knew she had to tell him now. She had put it off long enough. Her clothes were getting tight and he had commented only last week that she seemed to be putting on weight. Ned coughed as he walked into the parlor. "Well, Lindsay, winter has arrived."

He walked to the sideboard, poured himself a generous glass of whiskey and walked to the couch and sat beside her. Unconsciously, Lindsay moved away from him, her hands clasped together in her lap. She smiled nervously then looked up at her uncle.

"Uncle Ned, I have something to tell you." She stood and walked to the fireplace, wringing her hands and peering into the flames. "I've wanted to tell you for quite awhile, but, well, I couldn't." She turned back to her uncle and he looked down at her hands, then back to her face. I can't put this off any longer. She took a deep breath, straightened her shoulders, and gripped her dress with clenched fists. "I am . . . I'm . . . I . . . Uncle Ned, I'm going to have a baby." The words tumbled out and Lindsay's shoulders slumped. Then as though she were a puppet on a string, she became rigid and backed up a step.

Ned looked at her, his face did not change expression. After several seconds, he sighed and looked down at the glass in his hand.

Encouraged by his silence, she went on. "It's Lucas's baby. I'm due sometime in June." She walked to him and stood looking down at his bent head.

"Oh, Uncle Ned, I never meant for this to happen. I never meant to disgrace you or make you unhappy. I don't have any excuses for myself."

She turned away from her uncle. Now his silence embarrassed her, made her feel guilty. "Only we were together so long. I was so dependent on him," and she turned back to face him. "I know how this affects you, Uncle Ned, but believe me, please, I never meant to hurt you. I wouldn't hurt you for anything in the world. I love you so, I just, well, I don't know why. I know it was wrong. I know it's against everything I've been taught by you and the church. I don't know why, Uncle Ned. Please believe me. I'm sorry."

She knelt at his feet and laid her head on his knee. He touched her head and she closed her eyes as tears fell. He raised her head with a finger under her chin and wiped the tears with his hankie.

"Honey, what did you think I was going to do? Strangle

you? Disown you? Lindsay, certainly I would rather this hadn't happened, but we'll make the best of it." He stood and walked to the sideboard to replenish his empty glass. He stood silently staring at the contents. His brow wrinkled, his face pale. He looked so old, so sad. Lindsay went to him and wrapped her arms around his waist, laying her head on his chest. He returned the embrace. "A grandson." Lindsay hugged him.

"Honey, I love you. I loved you from the moment I saw you step off the stage that day in Durango. You were so frightened, so alone, so small. You were trying so hard to be brave." He guided her to the couch and they sat, holding on to each other. "That's one of your strongest qualities, Lindsay, bravery. But sometimes you flaunt it. It's as though you're telling everyone, 'go ahead, hurt me, I'm brave. I can take it.' And honey, although you are strong and brave, you are also a little girl in many ways. You have been fiercely protected by me, Jonas, and Ricco. You haven't had a chance to see what the world is really like. Now, now you're going to have a baby. Lindsay, I'm disappointed in you. Didn't you trust me? Didn't you think I would stand behind you? Oh, I know, you didn't want to hurt me, but don't you think not telling me and letting me find out this way hurts me more. Don't you think your not trusting me hurts more than finding out you're pregnant? Lindsay, you are my daug . . . uh, my niece, my flesh, my life. I will protect you and help you always. I would die for you. You did me a great injustice by not telling me sooner. But, now that you know how I feel, how do you feel? What do you want to do? And honey, please, don't ever be afraid to tell me anything again. Remember, I love you."

He looked down into Lindsay's face and gently kissed the tip of her nose. Tears made rivulets down her cheeks as she buried her face against his shoulder. They were sitting, holding each other when Zuni entered the room, wringing her hands together. Ned looked up at her and smiled. Zuni breathed deeply. "Would you like to eat now?"

"Damn, you know I am hungry, hungry as a bear. How about you honey?" He lifted Lindsay's face and smiled as he wiped her tears away with his hankie. "My hankie is soaked, Lindsay. If you're gonna keep crying, I'll have to get another one."

Lindsay laughed and brushed her hair back as she stood. Ned wrapped his arm around her waist and they followed Zuni into the dining room.

* * *

The weeks went by slowly and Lindsay's nausea began to lessen. Color began to reappear in her face and her appetite increased. Christmas was only a few days away and the house was buzzing with preparations for the holiday. Zuni was busy fixing the holiday bird and baking cookies, bread, and pies. Lindsay helped as much as she could but food still made her somewhat nauseous so she avoided the kitchen if she felt the slightest bit queasy.

Ned was feeling good and had even put on some weight. But he still coughed. Although the doctor had pronounced him recovered, he was left with a persistent cough that would rack his body in spasms. There was nothing much that he could do except drink brandy and honey in hot water (which he did at Zuni's insistence), and use steam and hot packs on his chest. Ned scoffed at Zuni's attempts to rid him of this cough but at times he was frightened at its intensity. He was left weak and breathless after an attack and was thankful that Zuni stayed with him.

Although the house was bustling with activity and several brightly wrapped packages found their way onto the table in the parlor, Lindsay was not happy. She moped around the house and rarely laughed or joined in the lively after dinner conversation. Time after time Ned or Jonas or Ricco would attempt to draw her out, get her to laugh, but to no avail. She would only smile and make her excuses to go to her room. Ned was becoming increasingly worried about her.

"Maybe the doc should examine her, Jonas. Maybe there's something wrong." And so, at everyone's urging, Lindsay was given a thorough examination by the doctor. When the doctor finished and started down the stairs he smiled at the people waiting at the landing. Ned, Ricco, Jonas, Zuni, and even Angel stood waiting for a verdict.

"Well, doc, what's the problem? Is she all right?"

Doc Fleming smiled and nodded his gray head.

"Yeah, Ned, she's just fine. Healthy as a horse as a matter of fact." He put his faded hat on and turned back to the gathering. "In fact, I think she's better off than all of you. At least she's not worried about her health." He laughed and walked into the kitchen with Zuni to have a cup of hot chocolate. The men followed, still concerned about Lindsay.

* * *

Lindsay sat in her chair, staring out the window. She pulled the blanket closer around her body and laid her head back and closed her eyes. How could she tell them what she felt was not physical? How could she tell her uncle not to worry, that she was not sick from illnes, but from not being with Lucas? How could she explain the reason she woke during the night, her gown damp with sweat, was because of Lucas? Every breath she took, every thought she thought was centered on him. She was aware that her absence at the dinner table upset them. She knew her withdrawal bothered them. But she wanted to be alone. She wanted to sit and look out the window. She wanted to be with Lucas. Tentative plans had been made for her to leave for Lucas's ranch in the spring. She would travel with several of the men from the ranch. She wanted to leave now, but Zuni had a fit when she mentioned traveling in the winter in her condition. Even Uncle Ned got mad when she brought up the subject. No, she would have to wait until spring and hope Lucas would welcome her and the baby. She frowned as she thought of Spotted Fawn and her hatred toward her.

She smiled. Watch out, Lucas Sanger. I'm carrying your child and our lives will be changed for it.

And soon.

Chapter 20

Christmas passed. For all the joyous frivolity and gift giving and festive food, no one could bring Lindsay out of her despondency. Jonas and Ricco tried to make her laugh—to bring back the old Lindsay. But all was lost. She was vacant and listless. She kissed them perfunctorily, then excused herself to go to her room. They were all concerned about her but there seemed to be nothing they could do.

Justin Devro came to the house Christmas day and gave Lindsay a leather-bound book of poetry. She thanked him, but it only gathered dust until finally Zuni took it up to her room. Pete Sheldon came to have a holiday drink with the family and he too brought Lindsay a gift—a pale yellow silk scarf. Michel couldn't even get a smile from her and finally excused himself and returned to his quarters.

It was the consensus of the ranch that Lindsay was not well. Soon the men gave up trying to communicate with her.

* * *

It was the last week in January. Lindsay watched from her window as Angel played in the snow. Her clothes were tight on her now and Zuni had helped her alter several dresses to allow for growth. Her pregnancy was a secret from the ranch hands, except Jonas and Ricco.

She would take a walk.

She changed her clothes and struggled into a heavy cotton dress. She knew the time was close that her secret would be out. She wrapped a cloak around her shoulders, tied the hood, grabbed her gloves, and walked down the stairs and out into the cold air. She stopped on the porch and pulled on her boots and gloves. She looked out at the white landscape. The trees blended into the land with their cloaks of white. The fence posts looked funny with their hats of snow and crumbling brown exteriors. A few birds chirped happily as they ate the crumbs Zuni had thrown to them. A mare, heavy with foal, was snorting in the corral. Her breath streamed from her nose as she stomped and pawed the ground. The sky was a dusky blue gray, a portent of an impending storm and Lindsay looked to the west and saw the big snow-filled couds moving toward her.

She pulled the cloak closer, stepped from the porch, and called for Angel. She went to the gate, opened it, and walked into the wind, her cape billowing out before she grabbed it and wrapped it around her again. Angel ran ahead of her, stopping now and then, her pink tongue hanging, to wait for her mistress. Lindsay lifted her face to the wind. The cold air felt good against her hot skin. She listened to her feet crunching in the snow and remembered a similar sound when she had walked into the hills of New Mexico, away from a wagon and guards, away from the man she now knew she loved but was too stubborn to admit it. So long ago. *It's been so long since I've looked into his eyes. How much longer do I have to wait? How much longer* can *I wait?* She was deep in thought paying no attention to her direction.

The wind blew a little harder, causing her to shiver and she stopped. She turned around. "Angel, look the distance we've come. Oh, my gosh, I didn't realize we had come this far. We'd better head back before this storm breaks." She turned toward home, walking through the trees.

She hadn't gone far when she heard a noise. She stopped and listened. Angel barked once, then ran ahead. Lindsay continued following a snow path and coming around a bend she stopped. A man was bending over Angel, petting her, talking softly. Lindsay called her dog and strained to make out who the stranger could be. His face was partially covered by his hat and a scarf was wrapped around his throat and lower face. He straightened as Lindsay called Angel. A smile touched his eyes.

"Well, well, If it isn't Miss High-and-Mighty. Now what could a snobby little gal like you be doing out here on a day like this?"

It was Tony Perez.

"Come, Angel."

She started walking rapidly but as she passed him he reached out and grabbed her arm.

"Ya know, I've tried to be nice to you. I offered to take you riding, to picnics, to dances, but you always turned me down. Now, I want to know. Ain't I good enough for ya? Is there something about me ya don't like? Just what's a fella gotta do to get a little attention from you?" He stared down into her face.

"Would you kindly let go of my arm? I'm late for dinner and Uncle Ned will be worried." Lindsay struggled to be free of his hand but he would not release her.

"Mr. Perez, I don't intend to stand out here and argue with you. Either you let go of me or I'll scream." Her voice was cold and calm but underneath Lindsay felt a glimmer of fear.

Tony laughed and threw his head back. Then he looked down at her, his voice sneering, his eyes filled with anger.

"Well, ain't it a shame. The little bitch hasn't got anyone to help her carry out her threats but she still don't give up. You really think anyone can hear you out here? You gotta be crazy girl. You think anyone's gonna hear you scream? No, I don't think so. I think I finally got the upper hand and I intend to use it, honey. So now, why don't you just relax and enjoy what I'm gonna give you." He pulled Lindsay to him. She struggled but her strength was no match for his. He laughed at her attempts to get free as he bent close to her face. Through clenched teeth he said, "I've wanted to do this ever since I first met you." His lips came down hard on hers, his tongue forcing them apart, searching, probing. Lindsay fought to breathe, nausea surging from the pit of her stomach. She pushed and kicked but he only held her tighter, kissing her harder. She felt her strength leave her and she prayed that she wouldn't faint. He held her arms pinned to her sides, bending her head back so far, she felt sure it would snap. Finally, when she was sure she was going to black out, he stopped kissing her, abruptly picked her up and carried her into the woods. She struggled fiercely to regain her breath so she could scream, but in an instant they were on a horse, riding swiftly. He held her close to him. Then, he stopped in front of the same shack Lucas had taken her to that fateful day so many months ago. He jumped down, tied the horse, and grabbed Lindsay. He carried her into the crumbling shack. "No, Lindsay, this time you won't have a chance to refuse. I've waited too long for this. I'm gonna prove to you that I'm as good as the next guy." He dropped her roughly on the floor, stood over her and removed his jacket. She sat up, retreating slightly to the wall.

"Why are you doing this, Tony? What have I ever done to you?"

He threw his head back and laughed. "What have you ever done to me? Lindsay, it's not what you have ever done to me, it's what you haven't done. You and your high and mighty uncle. You think you're too goddamn good for me. Well, I aim to show you how good I am." He reached out, grabbed Lindsay's arm and pulled her roughly against him. She struggled but he laughed and held her tighter. He brought his lips down on hers hard. It was the kiss of a man filled with lust and vengeance, not tenderness.

Lindsay was paralyzed. Flashes of black and white filled her mind. A feeling of nausea crept from her stomach. His scent was sweet—she felt like gagging. Tony stopped kissing her and literally sneered, "Well, little girl, how does it feel to be kissed by a man?" He threw his head back and laughed but when she moved he brought his face close to hers again, "Forget it, Lindsay, I have you where I want you and I ain't letting you go until I've damned well finished with you." He pulled her toward the fireplace, gripping her wrist until she screamed. He had thrown a bedroll on the floor and shoved her onto it. She fell face down, putting her hands out to break the fall. She thought, he must have been here first, for kindling had been gathered and laid in the fireplace. He struck a match to his heel and touched it to the wood. Lindsay glared at him as he forced a fire, impatiently. When he was satisfied, he turned to her. She was pale with rage. "My uncle will kill you, Tony Perez."

He scoffed, "Take your clothes off."

Lindsay flinched imperceptibly and without changing expression replied, "I'll never take my clothes off for you. I'd rather die."

Tony laughed and moved a little closer. "That can be arranged, too. Take your clothes off."

Lindsay's heart beat faster and it was all she could do to keep from lashing out at his face but she knew that would only anger him more. She must try to remain as calm as possible and try to outwit him. Watch for a chance to get away from him and then leap at that chance. When she looked up he was unbuttoning his shirt.

"Take em off," he nodded at her clothing, "Or I'll rip the damn things to shreds."

She glanced at the door. "Forget it, bitch, you ain't leavin'. The shoe's on the other foot this time. Instead of Miss High-and-Mighty sneering at me, putting me down, her royal highness is gonna learn she doesn't always have the upper hand." He reached for her and she jumped as a scream of fright escaped her lips. He pinned her to the floor, impatiently tearing at the buttons on her dress. Then with a grunt of anger, he yanked and Lindsay coud feel her dress part down the back.

As though she realized the futility of fighting and the hopelessness of her situation, she went limp. Her hands went to her belly and her head fell back on Tony's arm. "Forgive me, Lucas, I can't fight anymore." She whispered the words but they hit Tony like a bucket of ice water.

"What the hell do you mean?" She watched the stubble of his beard move as he talked. He clutched her shoulders angrily, "Answer me. What the hell did you mean?"

He shook her violently, his face ashen with rage. He took hold of the collar of her dress and pulled hard. The dress fell open and he pulled it down until her breasts were visible through the silky chemise. His breath came in jagged gasps as he stared at her exposed body. He ripped her chemise down the front. When her hands stopped the tear he shoved them out of the way and ripped until she lay completely naked, her dress in a heap at her knees. Tony snickered as he peered into her face, then slowly his eyes traveled down her body taking in her soft, white breasts, her creamy skin, her . . . "Whaaa . . ." He moved back and her head fell on the blanket. She lay still watching him. He reached out a shaky hand and lightly touched her belly. Then without uttering a sound he stood and dressed, continuing to stare at Lindsay's unclad body. He spoke low as he put his jacket on, "You goddamn whore, Miss Pure-and-Innocent Lindsay Tyler. Shit, you ain't as good as the whores in Durango. At least they're honest. I wouldn't touch you if you were the last piece of ass in the state. So, Miss Tyler's been screwing with a dirty halfbreed. That's what you said, ain't it? It's Sanger's kid. A dirty halfbreed. Damn, wait'll the men hear this. Their dream angel, Lindsay Tyler, screwin' around with an Injun." He picked up his hat and dusted it with his sleeve. As he walked to the door he exclaimed under his breath, "Shit, the beautiful virgin, livin' it up behind everybody's back." He walked out the door.

Lindsay watched him through the open door as he put his hat on and untied his horse. Snow was falling and he squinted as he watched the sky. "I wanted to be the first man to make you a woman. I wanted to make love to you." He reached in his pocket and took out a cigar. He twirled it in his fingers then put it in his mouth and lit it.

Lindsay climbed to her feet and pulled her dress up, holding it together at her throat. She walked to the door.

"Tony, listen to me. Tony, in order to make love to a woman, a man must feel love. There's a big difference between lust and love. You have no love for me, Tony."

He climbed on his horse and turned to her. His eyes glared shards of ice and his lips twisted in a sneer.

"How would a whore know the difference between love and lust? How would she, whore?" Lindsay cringed at his words and he laughed sharply. "You and your coy, virtuous game, and all the time you've been bedding a halfbreed. How many others, Lindsay? Now you got caught and won't it be fun to see everybody's surprise when I tell 'em about the icy virgin queen?" He touched his hat and rode away, cigar smoke disappearing above his head.

Lindsay watched as he galloped off. Then she turned

back into the shack and closed the door behind her. The fire crackled but what little wood was left burning wouldn't last long. She would have to stay here and hope someone would come looking for her soon. She was not dressed for walking in a storm. She sat huddled in front of the diminishing fire. She pulled her cloak to her and draped it over her shoulders. Strange, she had practically been raped, brutally ravished, and yet she was dry-eyed. She who had cried continuously with Lucas.

She had no idea how long she had been sitting in the shack watching the dying embers, but a sound shook her from her reverie. She lifted her head and listened to the approaching horses. Then she heard Angel bark. She stood, wrapped her cloak securely around her, and opened the door. Jonas and Ricco had accompanied her uncle and relief flooded their faces when they saw her. Ned climbed down and walked to her side.

"Are you okay, honey?"

"Yes, Uncle Ned, I'm fine."

He reached out and took hold of her arms. The cloak fell apart slightly and he glimpsed her torn dress. At the realization of what had happened he reddened with anger. She touched his arm with a cold hand. "Please, Uncle Ned, take me home." Ned nodded but his eyes flashed with rage. They rode in complete silence.

At the house she climbed from the horse and turned to her uncle, "We'll talk later." She smiled wearily and her shoulders slumped as she entered the house.

"Tony Perez is responsible for this," Ned said as he turned to Jonas and Ricco. "I don't know what he did but I'll find out, so help me God I'll find out. And when I do . . .," his eyes fixed on the empty stairs.

"Ned, you better be able to prove it was Perez," replied Jonas.

Ned jerked his head up. "It was Perez. You said you saw him follow her and who else has been dogging her every since she grew up? Every time he sees her his tongue hangs out like a damn horny dog."

"Come on, Ned, you know damn well he ain't the only one that chases after Lindsay. She's got so many young colts after her, I'm surprised there aint' been more fights in the bunkhouse because of her."

Ricco shifted in the saddle. "Yeah, but most of them got some manners. Perez ain't. Did you see what he did to her dress. Did you see the way he ripped it. How many men you know would do that?"

Ned answered, "I saw her dress, she was practically naked. That sonofabitch is gonna pay for this. Didn't I tell you fellas he wasn't any good? Didn't I tell you he was a trouble maker?" He dismounted and walked slowly into the house as Jonas shook his head and sighed.

"I don't like it, Ricco. Ned ain't the shot Perez is and Perez would love to shoot Ned. He hates him." They walked toward the stable. "Well, Jonas," Ricco pushed his hat back, "I kinda think we've seen the last of Perez around here. But if he does show his face again, I'll shot off his balls."

* * *

Lindsay sat in the bathtub luxuriating in the hot water. She lay her arms across her belly and thought about Tony. Strange. I never really trusted him, but I didn't know why. I never gave him any reason to hate me, except perhaps I hurt his ego. He knew there could never be anything between us. He knew the first day I talked to him. Suddenly she sat up straight, her eyes glued to her stomach. The baby. Oh, Lucas, she sighed, your baby just moved. I wish you were here to share this with me. She stepped from the tub, wrapped a towel around her, and laid down on the bed.

Exhausted, she slept.

Chapter 21

Spring! The river hurried to rid itself of its abundant supply and in spots on the shore new growth was washed away by the angry water. The sky was filled with the cacophony of thousands of birds returning to their homes after their southern nesting. The cattle were calving faster than the men could handle them and the horses, too, were foaling with astonishing speed. Butterflies put in their appearance regularly and Zuni's treasured garden was beginning to stretch after sleeping so long.

Zuni helped Lindsay alter clothes but they were unable to hide her blossoming figure. She felt good. Her cheeks glowed a dewy pink and her eyes twinkled. But she felt cumbersome and swore under her breath at her inability to move as quickly as she once could. Ned and Zuni laughed at her impatience and pampered her more.

One warm afternoon as Lindsay sat on the porch reading, Julie rode up the lane. Lindsay threw down her book and lumbered down the steps to greet her friend.

"Lindsay Tyler, whatever do you mean by not letting me know all about your escapade? Why, I thought I was your dearest friend. And here you just let me go on without one little word about your exciting winter," Julie snickered. She embraced Lindsay, her perfume drifting to Lindsay's nose. "I just may quit being your best friend." She puckered her lips in a feigned pout and unable to hold her merriment in check any longer, laughed.

"Let me look at you, Lindsay Tyler, turn around. I just can't believe it." She bent close to her friend and whispered quietly, "Don't let anybody know this, but I envy you with all my heart." Lindsay laughed, happy to see her friend.

"Come and sit with me, Julie, we have a lot of catching up to do."

Julie's pink, lacy gown swayed as she climbed the stairs. The girls sat in the swing and Julie set it in motion as they looked at one another. Julie's curls bounced as the swing moved and the ribbon wound through the curls blew around her face finally forcing her to remove it.

The silence was broken by the squeaking of the swing as both girls stared at each other, remembering each face, each fantasy they had shared about their make-believe lovers. As though embarrassed by the silence, they both spoke simultaneously. "You go first, Lindsay."

"No, Julie, you."

"Well, all right, but Lindsay, please, if I offend you, say something. I'm more curious about what happened than a cat with a noisy tin can, but I don't want you to think you have to reveal something personal, something you really don't want me to know. She leaned forward slightly, "Is it true, Lindsay? Are you really going to New Mexico to marry Lucas Sanger?" Julie's breath came out in gasps as her excitement could no longer be contained.

"Do you realize that you'll be the envy of evey girl in Colorado? Lucas Sanger is the most handsome man in the world. Why, I just can't believe it. My best friend marrying him." Her voice drifted off momentarily.

"Ah, Lindsay, does he know you're coming? What does he think about the baby? What kind of wedding dress are you going to wear? Have you decided where you will get married?"

Lindsay's attention waned. She tried to picture Lucas when he beheld her well-rounded figure. She wondered if Julie ever breathed between her questions and she thought about Grey Wolf and what his reaction would be.

". . . and then, when Tony asked so many questions about you, well, I really got a little mad, Lindsay. I mean, after all, wouldn't you if your beau asked questions about me?" She giggled brightly and began chattering again, "but I told Tony if he was so interested in you he should come ask you, but he told me he was only being nos . . ."

"Julie, what's Tony's last name?" Lindsay bounced back

to reality at her friends talk about Tony.

"Why, Lindsay Tyler, you mean to tell me you didn't know I was dating Tony Perez?"

"No, Julie, I didn't. How long have you been seeing him?"

"Not long enough, if you know what I mean." She put her hand over her mouth to stifle a giggle.

Lindsay didn't smile and Julie shrugged and continued. "Well, I really don't think my story will be half as interesting as yours, but I've been seeing Tony for, let's see, about two or three months, I think. But actually, Lindsay I haven't seen him for two weeks now. We had planned to go on a picnic and I had a big basket of yummy food packed. I waited all afternoon but he never came for me. I haven't seen him since." A blush creeped up Julie's throat and across her cheeks. "I guess he got busy or maybe he found . . . well, anyway, I'm not sure I'll see him again even if he does come around." She leaned over and touched Lindsay's hand. "Oh, Lindsay, he was so handsome, so manly, if you know what I mean."

Lindsay smiled at her friend. "Would you like a glass of lemonade, Julie?" She reached for two glasses Zuni had set before them and handed one to Julie. They sipped silently for several seconds.

"I've always had a problem rambling from the mouth, Lindsay. My pa says I'm the only person he knows that can talk, eat, and laugh at the same time." Both girls laughed and Julie continued. "I was riding with Tony one day and I mentioned how I had overheard my pa and your uncle talking about your trip to New Mexico. I told him how romantic it all seemed and how you always had all the luck. But Tony got mad. He didn't think it was romantic at all and he even swore at me. We had a fight and it was two days before he apologized. But I couldn't stay mad at that handsome man. It puzzles me that Tony should be so upset about your business. Do you have any idea why he got so mad, Lindsay?"

Lindsay shook her head and smiled. "No, Julie, I really have no idea why he should care anything about me. We seldom saw one another."

"My pa sure was pleased about Tony. He said any man

working for Tyler had his stamp of approval. Well, I guess it doesn't make any difference anymore. Tony is probably with some other girl now. You know Lindsay, I think I was begining to care for him. It hurt more than I wanted to admit when he stopped coming around." She swallowed the remainder of her lemonade. "Is Tony around today? Where does he usually work?" Her eyes scanned the yard.

Lindsay looked down at her hands. "No, Julie, he left here several weeks ago. I don't know where he went."

"I see." She turned her head from Lindsay's gaze, embarrassed at her uneasiness.

The girls visited until late afternoon. Their laughter could be heard throughout the house. Lindsay told Julie as much of the kidnapping as she felt safe about and Julie absorbed it with wide eyes and breathless anticipation.

The sun was beginning its descent when Julie stood up, embraced her friend and said goodbye. Lindsay watched her until she was out of sight, picked up the glasses, and went in the house. The smell of freshly baked bread greeted her. She was hungry. She went to her room to clean up and change for dinner.

Ned was seated at the table talking with Ricco and Jonas when she came in. They looked up when she entered.

"How was your visit with Julie, honey?" Ned asked.

"Fine. Wonderful." She sat down, filled her plate with sliced beef, buttered carrots, and a slice of hot bread. She frowned as she thought about Julie and Tony.

"Lindsay," Ned's voice was raised slightly, "Where were you? I've been trying to get your attention and you were a thousand miles away." He leaned forward, "Are you all right?"

"Yes, yes, I'm fine. I just . . . Uncle Ned did you know that Julie was seeing Tony Perez?" She watched for his response. Ned took a bite of carrots in his mouth and chewed slowly before answering. "No, I didn't, honey. But I'll talk with Russ. Tony shouldn't be allowed to see any respectable girl. Is that what's bothering you? Are you worried about Tony and Julie?" He watched her.

Lindsay looked up, a chill swept her body and she shivered slightly. She wiped at a curl on her brow and tried to shake the feeling of doom that had settled on her ever since Julie's visit. "I guess I'm just jumpy. I don't like Tony leaving here and running to Julie. It doesn't make sense. He never had anything nice to say about her. He used to make fun of her. I have a feeling he's going to do something and he has been using Julie to gain information. Maybe I'm being foolish." She looked up and smiled. Ricco, Jonas, and Ned were all staring at her.

"Well, Lindsay, Perez ain't big enough to fight all of us and, believe me, gal, if he ever shows himself around here again, he'll have to do just that," Jonas stated. Ricco nodded in agreement and returned to his plate of steaming food. "I second that, Lindsay," Ricco replied.

"Well, that should relieve your mind, Lindsay. Two of the strongest, most stubborn gunmen in Colorado have just spoken." Ned leaned toward Lindsay, "And probably the oldest, but we won't tell them, so you see my dear, you have nothing to worry your pretty little head about now that you know you are protected by such, ah, dangerous fighters." Ned's laughter shook his whole body. After a few remarks by Jonas and Ricco in defense of their age, they laughed too.

Lindsay sighed. "Well, I suppose you're right. With you here I have nothing to worry about." Her eyes twinkled but she couldn't shake the feeling that something wasn't right.

"Honey, I'll ride to Starn's tomorrow and talk with Russ. I'll let you know what he says."

"Well, I'm surprised Mr. Starn didn't ask you anything about Tony before allowing him to court Julie. I mean simply because he worked here doesn't mean he isn't capable of double-dealing. Mr. Starn should have thought about that and checked into Tony's record with you." She looked at the men. They were surprised at her oblique anger. She smiled quickly and returned to her plate. She played with the food and after a few minutes excused herself and went to her room.

The men watched her and after they were sure she couldn't hear, Ricco said, "I think she's really worried about Julie and Tony. She's upset for a reason. I don't think she told us the whole truth." Jonas nodded in agreement and Ned peered out the window, his thoughts returning to the day he found Lindsay in the shack, her clothes ripped off, her eyes sad. He looked back at the men.

"Well, I know one thing for sure. When she leaves for New Mexico, I want to send the best men with her. We'll hire more outriders for this place because I want our best gunmen with her. And men," Ned leaned over the table to whisper, "when the final arrangements have been made, I'm gonna send someone to Sanger to tell him she's coming. I won't tell Lindsay because she wouldn't like it. But I want Sanger to know. I want him prepared. It wouldn't be fair to drop her in his lap if he were laying beside another. He kept us informed. He helped us more than Lindsay will ever know. I think we owe him this. I'm not worried that he won't want her. I know he loves her, but I don't want Lindsay traveling all that way, carrying a baby, only to walk into a situation that would not only embarrass her but also break her heart. If it hadn't been for Sanger, Lindsay would probably be dead. I want to make this as easy as possible for both of them. Don't say anything about this. And if you think of any one who might be good for the job, point him out." Ned poured himself a cup of coffee and Zuni brought them each a piece of apple pie dripping with melted cheese.

"My, oh, my, Zuni, if I didn't know better, I would think I was in heaven." Jonas took a bite of the hot pie and closed his eyes as he relished the taste. The men visited over their coffee and pie. After an hour, Ned left the dining room and went to Lindsay.

Lindsay anwered his knock and he opened the door and gazed in. A candle burned on the dresser and Lindsay sat in her chair, staring out the window. Her feet were curled under her and a quilt enveloped her shoulders. She looked up as Ned closed the door, then back out the window.

"You know, Uncle Ned, when I was growing up I used to watch the stars and wonder how many little ones were hidden. There's only so much room up there. The bigger ones pushed the smaller ones out of the way, blocking them from earth's view. But when I traveled through the desert, I decided the little ones weren't hidden after all. They had gone to New Mexico and shined on the desert. And, although they were smaller, they worked harder. They shinned brighter and longer." She touched her uncle's hand as it rested on her shoulder.

"Uncle Ned, we have to start making arrangements for my trip. My time is getting shorter and I want to be with Lucas when the time arrives." She looked at her uncle and saw the look of hurt that passed through his eyes.

"I hope you understand how I feel, Uncle Ned. I do so hope you understand."

Ned sat on her bed and rested his hands on his knees.

"Lindsay, I do know how you feel. I know how it feels to be in love, in love with someone you want to share your life with. I know you love me, but that isn't enough for you. I had my love, now it's your turn to share that feeling. And I know there is still plenty of room for me in your life." He smiled at her startled expression and put his hand up to silence her.

"Let me finish, honey. This isn't going to be easy and if I don't rush in and go straight through, I may not be able to finish." He ran his hand through his hair.

"Many years ago, long before you were born, I was a wanderer. I went from one end of this country to the other. I gambled when I needed money, I stole food when I was hungry, and I hired out as a gunfighter. I lived for the day, not for the future. I cared about no one except me and I even avoided my brother, your father. He worked hard, saved his money and let me know how he felt about me. But that's not important, he was a good man and it couldn't be helped if we were so different."

"I was on my way to California to see what was going on when I got into a poker game in Durgango. I won some land from John Moriarity and he turned the title over to me. Only that night he had second thoughts, and with whiskey giving him courage he told me he wanted the title back. Well, we fought. He drew and I killed him. I gave his widow some money and she left for the east."

Now that I had something that belonged to me I settled down a bit. I began to build a house and hired some men and bought some cattle. I even stopped gambling. It took many years of hard work and the loyalty of good men to build the Lazy Hat Ranch into what it stands for today. Jonas and Ricco were the first men that hired on with me. They were sorta like me, wandering and looking."

Then one day in Ignacio, I met Rosa Delgio. I couldn't take my eyes off her. I followed her around the town that day until I got up enough courage to introduce myself. She was a dressmaker and lived behind her shop. I had to get to know her. I think I fell in love with her on the spot. I began visiting her every day and two weeks after we met I asked her to marry me. She accepted. I wasted no time in making her my wife. We were married the next week and she took over as mistress of the ranch. We worked hard and together built the Lazy Hat up to what you see today. Rosa used to tell me that someday we would sit on the porch, sip tea, and just watch our children work, but until that day we must devote all of our time to building up the ranch."

Ned rubbed his hands on his pants. "We tried for years to have a child. Rosa was so patient. I wasn't. I couldn't understand why two healthy people couldn't have a baby. Rosa would smile at me and say 'In God's good time, Ned, in God's good time.' She was aching inside but she wouldn't let me know."

"Then one day, Rosa came running to the barn, breathless, crying, and carrying on like I had never seen her do. It scared me. I remember holding her and she was quivering all over. She couldn't talk for a few minutes so I just held her and comforted her as best I could, scared that something bad had happened. But her news was good. She was going to have a baby. She had just seen a doctor and he had given her this wonderful news."

We spent the next few months planning and preparing. Among many other things, Rosa made a bunting and embroidered both a blue and pink quilt. She was ready for either a boy or girl. I was, too. I fashioned a cradle from willows and listened for clues on Rosa's stomach. But I didn't know what color to paint that cradle."

"Two months before the baby was due, Rosa went into labor. They both died." He stopped talking and wiped his eyes with a crumpled hankie. "I was hollow, a shell with no feeling. I wanted to die. I wanted to be with her and our baby. Everywhere I looked I could see Rosa laughing, running, giggling. This place became a jail. I had to get away, sell, and move elsewhere. But Jonas and Ricco wouldn't let me. They kept me busy—made me go to Arizona to buy cattle, then to Texas and Kansas. I began to heal and instead of dreading my quiet rooms, I began to relish the peace. One by one I took Rosa's things from the attic and put them out. I hung her picture in the parlor, I used her quilts," he touched the quilt Lindsay had around her, "and I ate from her china."

Ned stood and looked out the window. "I finally began to live again and put all my energy into the ranch. I suppose if I had sold this place I would still be wandering around, looking for another Rosa. Jonas and Ricco stood fast, they knew I could never replace her. They made me relish every memory I have of her."

He folded his arms across his chest and looked up at the stars. "Then one day, I got a letter from a judge in Medicine Bow, Wyoming, explaining how my brother and his wife had been killed. He asked if I would consider raising you. I was the only living relative you had, but if I was unable to do this he would understand. They had a nice place in Cheyenne for homeless kids and you'd be sent there if I couldn't take you. It took me ten seconds to decide. You know the rest."

He returned and gazed at Lindsay. "In a way honey, you brought a touch of Rosa and the baby back. You gave me something that had been taken away, a feeling I had forgotten I could have. So, you see, I know what you're going through. I know how much Lucas means to you and I want only for your happiness." He reached out and carressed her cheek, "So you had better prepare to do some traveling. You should probably leave within the month if you're to be with your man before that baby, my grandson, arrives." He smiled and winked. Lindsay stood and stretching on her toes, kissed her uncle on his weather-hewn cheek. Ned pushed her gently back in the chair.

"Now, look, you stay here. I have something for you." He ran from the room. Lindsay looked around, puzzled. Ned returned carrying a tiny cradle. He was beaming. He held the cradle in front of her. "For your son, for my grandson."

Lindsay looked at the elegantly detailed cradle, her eyes moistening. She fought to hold back the tears. Her hand moved lovingly across the light blue sideboards.

"Oh, Uncle Ned," she said. "Oh, Uncle Ned, it is for your grandson."

Chapter 22

"Uncle Ned, as soon as the baby and I are able to travel, we'll be back. I promise you'll see your neph . . . ah, grandson, before he's old enough to sit up."

May had burst forth in a myriad of colors. Indian paintbrush, larkspur, and columbine fought with each other for possession of space. Scent-laden breezes caressed the lush prairie grasses and from a distance it looked like the sea undulating in the valley.

Lindsay stood with her arms around her uncle's waist as tears streamed down her pink cheeks. Everything was in readiness for her journey and Jonas made a hammock in the wagon for Lindsay. He wanted her as comfortable as possible. the handmade cradle was wrapped carefully, padded with blankets, and tied securely against the side of the wagon. Lindsay was heavy with child and it was hard for her to bend or sit for long periods. Zuni was incensed that Ned would let her travel in her condition but Ned knew he couldn't stop her. Rather than have her run away, he wanted her trip as safe as possible. Ten men would accompany her. She would be well protected.

Ned held her close, his breath came in jagged gasps as he fought to control his emotions. His coughing spasms had not cleared enough for him to travel with her. Jonas and

Ricco would stay with Ned but every other good man would accompany her.

"Now, I want to see that baby before he's too old to learn anything from me. As soon as doc says I can travel, I'll be there. But if I can't go until next year, well, you and Lucas had better bring that child here. He smiled down at his niece. The niece who had become his daughter. The daughter Rosa had carried for him. Ned didn't want to let her go. The ranch would be so lonely. Maybe he could talk Lucas in to returning and living here. He smiled to himself. Somehow he would bring Lindsay back to him.

He watched as she talked with Ricco and Jonas. She giggled. Her curls bounced and Ned looked away. God how he would miss her tinkling laughter. She would be so uncomfortable in that wagon, but he couldn't talk her out of going. He blew his nose and dabbed at his eyes. He didn't cry easily but lately it seemed a simple matter to shed tears. He watched as Lindsay walked back to him.

Her final goodbyes said to her friends, now she must face that dreaded moment. She didn't know how to handle this. She loved her uncle very deeply. She remembered the day she said her goodbye to Lucas, the memory was still crisp. And now she felt the same dread. She would rather suffer physical pain. She approached Ned slowly, then reached out and caressed his cheek. Her fingers were hot and she kept them on his cheek as she whispered. Jonas and Ricco watched them, trying to hear what she said. Then she turned and walked quickly to the wagon. Arms helped her up and she disappeared into the dark interior. The leader gave the order and the wagon lurched forward and moved slowly down the lane. Ned, Ricco, Jonas, and Zuni stood watching until she was out of sight. Zuni took Ned's arm and forcefully pulled him into the house. She sat him on the couch and fixed him a glass of whiskey. Ricco and Jonas joined him and they all sat staring at their glasses.

"What did she say, Ned?" Jonas asked.

Ned shook his glass, watching the swirling liquid and replied, "She said, 'I'll be back, Daddy. I'll be back. For you and Rosa.'"

Chapter 23

The group had traveled slowly all morning, finally stopping under a grove of tall aspen. Lindsay had never been so uncomfortable. Her back hurt and the ache went deeper into her muscles with each mile. *And this is only the beginning,* she thought.

"Miss Lindsay, I have a plate of food for you," a voice interrupted her thoughts. "Miss Lindsay, are you awake?"

"Yes, I'm coming." She stood, walked to the back and threw open the canvas flap. The sun was directly overhead and its golden rays touched Pete Sheldon's red hair and bounced off, creating a prism effect. Lindsay shielded her eyes and lifted her skirt to climb down. Pete offered his arm and she gratefully accepted. She liked Pete. He was affable and had an easy humor about him. He certainly had a way with words, although lately he had been somewhat withdrawn. He helped her to a blanket spread in the shade and she knelt clumsily. She was embarrassed and flushed.

"I can't wait'll you try to stand, Miss Lindsay."

She laughed. "I've never felt so clumsy in my life, Pete."

He took off his hat, holding it close, "Well, Miss Lindsay, it's a disease that has a cure." He was shuffling, uncomfortable and a little embarrassed.

"Sit down, Pete, it has been a long time since we talked." They chatted compatibly together, the old ease of their friendship returned. After a while Pete went to feed the horses. Good old Pete, she thought, maybe this trip won't be so bad after all. She watched the men working the team and the wagon. It reminded her of another time, another camp. . . . Nick Moriarity. She shuddered.

"Miss Lindsay, it's time to go." A voice disturbed her thoughts and she looked up as she realized Pete was trying to get her attention.

"Oh, I'm sorry, Pete. Guess I was far away again." She held out her hand. Pete helped her up and into the wagon. "Strange, I spent many miserable and unhappy days doing exactly this same thing. You would think I would have learned a lesson but, no. Here I am again doing the same dreadful thing." She moved into the wagon and stared out the back. Pete watched her for a few seconds, then pushed his hat back on his head and walked to his horse.

The trip was hard and Lindsay suffered with her discomfort. She became short-tempered and stayed to herself as much as possible. The men tried to make her as comfortable as they could but she griped and moaned and at times railed against them and against herself.

The scenery began to change as they traveled into the desert. The green lush carpet gave way to intermittent sand. The trees changed from towering pines to mesquite- and yucca-studded expanses. The wagon creaked ponderously through plateaus, deep canyons, colorful buttes, and mesas. As the desert became more evident Lindsay's temperament changed back to one of easygoing cheerfulness. The men marveled at her chameleon exterior. Only Lindsay understood the effect the desert was having on her soul. She felt at peace again. As Lucas had said, "This is God's country." And it was. She felt in awe of its beauty and was soothed by it. Lucas was right, this country gets under your skin and burrows its way into your heart.

The men relaxed as Lindsay seemed to be less antagonistic and their journey became more tolerable as she joined in their singing, laughing, and joking.

Chapter 24

"*Amigo*, why do you think he hasn't come?" Lucas and Chico were riding along slowly, the moon lighting their way as they talked.

"Damned if I know. I was sure he would have found my ranch by now. Somebody, somewhere would have told him. That's what worries me, it's been too quiet. That's not like Nick." Lucas looked up. "I know we better be ready every minute. When Nick shows, I guarantee it'll be to our backs. He doesn't face a man."

"*Amigo*, I have never known you not to be ready."

It had been many weeks since Lucas had left the Apache camp and returned to his ranch. Anticipation of Moriarity's next move was beginning to irritate him. He decided to go to Santa Fe for a change. He needed to get away for a few days and so did Chico. Just sitting and waiting was driving them crazy. Lucas looked up at the stars, twinkling, cold, beautiful, so like Lindsay's eyes—twinkling when she laughed, cold when angered, but always beautiful. God, how he ached to hold her body next to his, bury his face in her hair, inhale the fresh scent that spoke of her. He wondered what she was doing now. Probably the belle of the county—courting, flirting. He frowned. Jealousy was a strange sensation for him. But since he had met Lindsay, he felt he would kill any man that laid a hand on her. When Nick was out of the way, the path to the Lazy Hat Ranch would be open and he would go to her, this time more freely. Maybe after a time of gentle courting she would come around. Give him a chance. He knew now he would spend as much time as it took to win her hand in marriage. He couldn't face life without Lindsay at his side, as his wife.

They crested a hill and the lights of Santa Fe glittered in the black desert night. He knew Conchita would be happy to see him. He smiled as he thought of Millie and Conchita fighting over who got him first. He needed to relax, needed to have a woman. He needed Lindsay.

As they neared Santa Fe they didn't speak, each experiencing his own anticipation. Chico was anxious to feel Diana's soft body, Lucas was wondering what sport Conchita would offer him tonight.

They tied their horses to the hitching rail and entered Millie's cantina. Music came from the parlor and soft voices could be heard. They walked down the long musty hallway and stopped in front of the parlor. Several tables were scattered around, candles burned on a few. A woman played the piano and a drunk client stood over her, leering at her amply displayed cleavage. A few couples sat at the small, wobbly tables. The heavy red velvet drapes were closed and a faded painting of a nude woman hung crookedly over the piano, its gold frame chipped and dusty.

Chico whispered that he was going to find Diana and walked off. Lucas walked in and sat at an empty table in the back room. The candle burned with effort and wax dripped down the sides and spread in a pool on the patched table cloth. Several wall-mounted lanterns hung precariously, the object of a drunk's anger. A few were lit, their flames subdued, causing shadows on the walls. A spider crossed the dusty tile floor and Lucas watched as it skittered through the room. In the dim light it was difficult to make out faces. Milly preferred it this way. She said anonymity was the second most important thing a brothel could offer. The first, she had said, was obvious. Although most of her clients knew each other during the day in their business roles, here at Millie's they simply preferred to be strangers. Lucas poured himself a healthy shot from the bottle on the table. Milly kept a bottle of whiskey on each table and added the price on the final bill. It was cheaper to buy a drink at the bar, but this was nice, being able to sip or guzzle, whichever suited your mood.

Lucas put his hat on the table and stretched his legs. He

closed his eyes and was sipping his drink when he heard the couple approach the table next to his. The girl giggled and he heard the sound of liquid being poured into glasses.

"Look, baby, I said I would, now drop it for now, okay?"

"But, Tony, I only want to make sure I have that night open for you. I mean you aren't exactly the most reliable person I know. If you show up and I have other plans, you get mad. If you don't show and I've got nothing to do, Millie gets mad. Please try to understand my side.

"Look, I may have a job next week. If Moriarity decides to go after her, I'll ride with him. If not, then I'll be here. I can't tell you anymore. I don't know anymore."

Lucas tensed. Moriarity! He held up the square bottle and saw the man's reflection in it. Couldn't tell who he was.

"Job, my foot. When have you ever held a job more 'n a week? Why, Tony, I've known you for years and the only job you held for any length of time was on that ranch outside of Durango. You know, where you attacked the owner's niece and left in such a hurry." The girl's voice was filled with mockery.

"Shut up! How did you know about that?" Tony sat up and glared at the woman.

"Why Tony, you told me."

"The hell I did." His voice was low and angry.

"Yes, my love, you did. One night after filling your belly with whiskey. Don't you remember? I told you then you'd better be careful about drinking and talking since you always brag when you're drunk."

"Shut up, you bitch. I don't have to explain anything to you. What I do ain't none o' your business." He stared her down, then relaxed back in the chair, the whiskey taking effect now, numbing his senses and soothing his temper.

"Who was that woman, Tony? How can she ruffle your feathers so easy? She must be quite the lady. Did she tell you to go to hell? Did she snub your 'so-called' charms, Tony?"

Tony's grip tightened on his glass as he stared into its contents. He heard the girl's voice diminish as his mind wandered back to Lindsay. She was so beautiful, so ripe, so much a woman. And she had already been plucked from the vine of womanhood. God, how he had wanted her. He regretted not taking her that day. But when he found out she was pregnant his sexual desire died and all he could think of was destroying her. The icy virgin. Shit, she was no better than the girl that sat across from him now. She wasn't as good. Lindsay had lied and deceived. At least this doxy was truthful.

Tony's thought came back slowly, like murky water running over a dam. He looked at Loralee. She was watching him, a frown on her brow, her mouth puckered. He leaned toward her and spoke.

"She'll get hers. She ain't no lady and when she gets her dues, I aim to be there. I want to see her eyes. I want to laugh in her face." He leaned back and took a drink, emptying the glass. "The bitch. She thinks she's so damn good. Well, she ain't nothin but a whore. She's pregnant with that halfbreed's kid. Only the halfbreed don't know it. Moriarity aims to kill her and the kid and then," Tony snickered, "He's gonna send the kid's body to Sanger."

He poured more whiskey into his glass and continued, "God, what I wouldn't give to be there when Sanger sees his kid."

"Tony, you can't be serious. You ain't really gonna kill no innocent baby just to get even with some man. Tony, you can't do that." Loralee stared at Tony unbelievingly.

"Don't raise your voice to me." Tony reached across the table and grabbed her wrist. "Now, you listen to me. This ain't no ordinary man I'm talking about. He doublecrossed Nick and he's gotta be dealt with." He released her wrist, then grabbed her again.

"You know something, gal, I'm beginning to feel the need for something other than booze and talk." He stood and pulled Loralee behind him. Lucas heard them ascend the stairs.

He drained his glass and stood. A muscle twitched in his cheek. He left the parlor in search of Chico. As he started down the hallway a door opened and Conchita walked into the dim light. She looked up and saw him.

"*Querido*, what a nice surprise." She wrapped her arms

around his waist and laid her head on his chest. "Come, we will go to my room." She turned to the stairs and when he didn't speak, she turned back to him. She tilted her head and frowned.

Lucas was furious. His mind was staggering with what he had just heard. Anger and fear bubbled in his brain and Conchita was no longer important. Lucas continued walking which made Conchita mad.

"Bastard, where are you going?" She ran and stood in front of him, trying to stop him. He gently pushed her aside and continued walking. Conchita leaned against the wall, her heart thumping wildly, her brow glistening with sweat. This was the only man she had ever known that could make her feel a whole woman. Such a man, he couldn't be compared to any other. How dare he treat her like this? She wouldn't allow him to ignore her. She needed him. She ran to him and grabbed his arm. He stopped and looked at her.

"*Carino*, I had planned to stay with you tonight but something very important has come up and I've got to go." He pushed her gently aside. "Don't stand in my way, Conchita, please."

She watched him, puzzled, angry. He frightened her. No, she wouldn't say anything else. Common sense overrode her anger and hurt and she leaned against the wall as she saw him listening at the doors. After a few moments she said, "If it is Chico you are looking for, he is with Diana. Her room is upstairs."

Lucas nodded and scrambled to the stairs taking them two at a time. Conchita admired the muscles that bulged on his back and thighs. Somehow she would figure a way to keep him here tonight, a way to get him in her bed.

A few moments passed. Lucas came down with Chico following, strapping on his gunbelt. Lucas walked to Conchita and asked, "Chica, you have a girl here who was in the parlor with a guy named Tony."

"And why do you want to know, *querida*?" A smile crossed her lips as she attempted to delay him.

"Don't play games with me, Conchita. If you don't tell me, I'll go through this place room by room and I'm sure Milly wouldn't be happy."

Conchita shrugged and pointed upstairs. "It's the last room on the left."

"Now, *cariña*, you go back to the client you left a few minutes ago and stay there. Do not come out of that room not matter what you hear." He turned quietly and walked up the stairs. Chico waited until Conchita entered the room. When he heard the door close and the bolt click shut he followed Lucas. Lucas approached the closed door and listened for sound. Nothing. Chico stood at the side of the door and drew his gun. Lucas grasped the knob and turned slowly. He smiled. It wasn't locked. Cautiously he opened the door a crack and peered into the darkened room. The sound of heavy breathing came from the bed. He pushed the door open and entered. Chico followed and closed the door behind him. They approached the sleeping couple.

Lucas went to the side where Tony slept, and Chico to Loralee. When they reached the bed Lucas pulled his gun and placed it against Tony's temple. Chico placed his hand tightly over the mouth of the sleeping girl. Lucas grabbed a handful of Tony's hair and quickly pulled the sleeping man to a sitting position. A groan of protest escaped Tony's mouth. Lucas bent Tony's head back and cocked the hammer of his gun. This sound jolted Tony's dull reflexes and he opened his eyes. Tony's level of consciousness was obscured as he fought to comprehend what was happening. He wanted to shake the cobwebs from his foggy brain but something was holding his head. He slowly raised his eyes to the face of the man standing before him. His lips formed the name "Sanger." Quietly, breathlessly, he asked, "What, what do you want?"

Lucas stared unflinchingly into the face before him, "You."

The deadly calm in his voice made Tony shiver.

The girl had awakened and lay there with frightened eyes, watching her captor. She had not moved, aware of Chico's strength. As Chico leaned closer to her she closed her eyes tightly.

"Chica, we will be leaving soon. If you try to stop us I will kill you." His lips parted in a semblance of a smile and Loralee opened her eyes and stared at the gleaming white teeth. "Do you understand?" She nodded slightly and Chico removed his hand from her mouth but kept his gun aimed at her head.

Lucas had Tony at the foot of the bed putting his clothes on. No further words were spoken. When Tony finished dressing Lucas placed his gun against his back and walked him to the door. Chico opened it and Tony stopped momentarily to look at the girl. Her face was white and her eyes were filled with fear. Tony nodded at her and walked into the hallway. Chico took the lead. They left the house and went into the cool night air. They continued walking until they reached a large tree. Chico left them. Tony's fear had become tangible and he was sure Lucas could feel it. Beads of sweat popped out along his forehead and rolled down his cheeks. The salty fluid burned his eyes but he did nothing. Lucas had not taken his eyes from him since they had left the house and his silent staring unnerved Tony. Suddenly Chico appeared leading three horses. Lucas motioned to Tony to get up and after each had mounted they rode off, Tony's horse on a lead between Chico and Lucas. Two guns were pointed at him as they rode out of town into the Saguarro hills. They slowed up and Tony asked, "Where you takin' me?" He received no answer. He slumped in the saddle and rode in silence.

The three men had ridden a few miles when Lucas suddenly reined in his horse and jumped to the ground. He motioned for Tony to dismount and Chico took the reins of the horses and tethered them to a tree.

They were in a valley, high mountains stood like sentries. The wind blew through the trees and veered and dodged in the crevices of the hills. A half moon lay in the sky occasionally obscured by clouds tumbling past. The beauty of the night did not parallel Tony's somber mood. He was not an easily frightened man. He had looked death in the eyes before and walked away. But Lucas Sanger was not a man you walked away from. Tony looked into Lucas's eyes and a shiver of icy fear ran down his spine. He felt an overwhelming sense of dread. Whatever was about to happen, he had doubts he would come out on top.

Lucas had still not taken his eyes from Tony. As he

watched him now, coldly calculating his death, he wished this man could suffer longer. He could not believe he had heard him speak so casually of killing a baby—his baby. If it took him the rest of his life he would hunt down Nick Moriarity and kill him. But first, he had to discover Nick's plans from the bastard in front of him—and find them out he would. He motioned for Tony to sit. Lucas holstered his gun, pointed at Chico who was leaning against a tree with his gun aimed at Tony, and spoke.

"Where's Moriarity?" His voice was hard.

Tony glanced at Chico, then looked at Lucas. "I don't know who the hell you're talking about."

Lucas turned his back to Tony and walked a short distance, resting his foot on a rock, leaning his elbow on his knee. He scanned the horizon with dark, impenetrable eyes.

"You want to die hard, you two-bit bastard? Right now I want to pull your eyes out. Don't push me."

Tony stared at Lucas's back. His palms were sticky and he rubbed them on his shirt. He glanced at Chico, then back at Lucas. Fear bubbled up from his soul like bile. He didn't want to die. Maybe if he could catch Lucas off-guard, but no, this man was never off-guard. He would stall for time.

"Where's Moriarity?" The voice cut through Tony as tendrils of fear clung to his mind. He shrugged and then did something that surprised him. He laughed. Loud and deep. He was still laughing when the fist hit him. He grabbed his nose as blood spurted from a wide cut across the bridge. Abruptly he stood and with his hand covering his face, blood dripping over his fingers, he swore, "Goddamn you, Sanger. You goddamn halfbreed . . ." The words had barely escaped when his head snapped back. The sound of bone hitting bone resounded through the trees. This time Tony attempted to hit back. A grunt of pain could be heard through his swollen lips as he hit the dirt. Lucas grabbed his arm and twisted it up high across his back. Tony struggled to be free but Lucas twisted harder and Tony relaxed trying to ease the pain.

Lucas put a foot in the middle of Tony's back and holding his arm in a grotesque position calmly asked, "Where is Moriarity?"

pressure increase, he grunted, "I, I don't know." Then he screamed. "You're breaking my damned arm."

"I'll break the goddamn thing off if you don't answer me." Lucas was tiring of Tony's stubbornness and his impatience showed in his cruelty.

"Answer me." He twisted Tony's arm further up his back and Tony screamed in compliance. Lucas released the pressure slightly and waited while Tony spit a mouthful of blood-stained dirt. Lucas stood over him, holding Tony's arm above his back, waiting.

"Nick is hiding in the hills north of Los Alamos waiting for Lindsay. He had a group of men prepared to kidnap her. After her baby—your baby—is born he plans on killing them both and sending the bodies to you. He figures you'll search for him crazy-mad, then he'll get you, too. He ain't gonna stop at nothin'. He wants you to suffer."

Lucas merely stared at the man, expressionless, then went on, "What's she doing out there? Where's she going?"

"She's looking to find you, before the baby. She wants you with her when the kid comes."

"How do you know all this?"

"Her friend, Julie Starn." Tony spat a stream of blood-tinged spittle.

Lucas looked across at Chico, then back at Tony,

"How long before Lindsay will reach Los Alamos?"

"Four or five days. Nick has men following her. Plans the ambush in Chicoma Canyon. She'll never get out of there alive. She's heavy with your kid."

Lucas released the man's arm and turned sharply to the west. "Jesus Christ! Why in hell did Tyler let her do this? What's wrong with that woman. She needs her ass stomped on good for doing such a damn fool thing."

Tony sat up slowly and rubbed his arm. "I don't think her uncle had any say-so in the matter."

Lucas smiled. He was right. She was the most stubborn woman he had ever known. He tried to imagine her. He saw her face rounded and flushed with womanhood, her hands on her unborn child, smiling at him. He looked back at Tony Perez.

"Take your boots off."

"What?"

"I said, take your boots off." Perez looked at him for a moment, then sat down and pulled them off.

"Throw them over here."

Perez complied. Lucas picked them up, walked to the rim and hurled them into the chasm below. Returning he said, "I know what you tried with Lindsay, Perez. I want to throw you over that rim with your goddamn boots, but I won't. You listen to me good, though. If you ever touch me —or mine—again, I'll make you curse the day you drew breath. You *hear* me, Perez?"

Perez looked away from Sanger's stare and nodded.

Chico handed Sanger the reins. Lucas mounted and pulled Perez's tethered horse behind him.

They made their way through the rock terrain, heading west toward Chicoma Canyon. Perez stood quietly, trembling as he watched them.

They did not look back.

Chapter 25

"That weren't no Indian, Dusty, relax. Probably some bounty hunter looking us over." The man spoke between chewing and swallowing.

"If you're sure it weren't no Indian I'm gonna bed down. I sure as hell ain't been sleeping good and probably won't until we're through this damn canyon." He walked away, shaking his head, mumbling. He looked up the steep walls on either side. He faintly heard a coyote.

Pete Sheldon sat across the fire from Lindsay. The night air was cool. The sky was filled with stars and a half moon peaked over the canyon wall. Peter marveled at Lindsay's eyes, the firelight flickering across her face. He remembered the first time he had seen Lindsay, just two years ago. It was a cold, white, winter day. He had finished moving his gear into the bunkhouse and walked outside to see the grounds. The countryside was enveloped in a white shroud. It was difficult to tell where the fields ended and the sky began. The pine trees bent oddly under the weight of the snow. A bright blur caught his eye and he turned his head. Then he saw her, galloping swiftly through the snow, her crimson hair flowing behind her. Her cheeks were windburnt and her eyes laughed as she urged her horse on. She swept gracefully past him and his eyes were tied to her until she was out of sight. He smiled as he remembered Justin Devro walking by, snapping his fingers. The crisp sound brought Pete out of his dream and he cleared his throat in embarrassment. Justin assured him Lindsay affected everyone the same way. Astonishment. She was so beautiful and so completely natural. The sight of her riding colorfully through that white countryside was etched forever in Pete's memory. And from that day, even though he had never even said it to himself in words, he had been in love with this lady.

Sitting with her, watching her long for another man's touch, seeing her grow with another man's baby, was painful for Pete. He was shy and self-conscious but he had something important to say. And he intended to say it now. Clearing his throat he spoke.

"Lindsay," his voice burst forth louder than he had planned. Lindsay looked up from the fire, surprised.

"Lindsay, I . . . have something . . . uh . . . I want to say." His courage was slowly surfacing, like bubbles in a boiling pot. "I . . . I really don't know how to say this without, uh, distressing you. I mean, Lindsay, I understand what you're going through and I surely don't want to offend you in any way, but what I'm trying to say is . . . oh hell, damn. I'm sorry, I didn't mean to swear in your presence, but damn, I just can't talk right around you. I'm always saying the wrong thing at the wrong time." His face was red now as he averted his eyes from hers. He had wanted to be so gallant, so charming, and all he had managed to do was put his fat foot in his fat mouth.

"Pete, you are so sweet. Please don't feel so uncomfortable around me. That distresses me more than anything you could say."

He looked up, recovering his courage. Taking a deep breath, he spoke tenderly, "Lindsay, if, if the father of the baby is unable to marry you, I mean . . . like maybe he's sick or married, or, you know, Lindsay, would you marry me?" He breathed a sigh of relief at having the words out. He went on. "I mean, I'd treat you good, real good, and your baby too. And maybe you don't love me, but you could learn to, well you know."

Lindsay watched him over the firelight, her eyes compassionate as she studied the boy before her. How could she answer him without hurting him and yet make it clear to him that she would never marry another man? She searched for the words.

A crack of gunfire! A man screamed! She jumped to her feet. Pandemonium spread through the little camp. Shots were fired wildly by the men. The horses bolted and ran. Dusty came stumbling toward Lindsay blood streaming from a hole in his chest. He stumbled and fell. Pete ran to him and turned him over. Dusty reached to Lindsay, "Get her outta . . ." his head dropped to the side. A thin line of blood edged from his mouth and mingled with a tear. Pete closed the dead man's eyes and turned to Lindsay. He glanced at the clamor around him, grabbed her arm, guiding her to the wagon and lifted her in.

Drawing his gun he turned to face his unknown adversaries. There were men galloping through the camp, shooting at everything. Pete dove behind the wagon and returned the fire. For a moment the shooting subsided. He reloaded his gun. He could see several bodies lying in the dust. He turned as he heard a loud voice. Four men approached him and he recognized Michel Langroise immediately.

"What the hell are you doing here, Langroise?" Pete's gun was pointed at the man's chest.

"Making a hell of a lot more money than I ever made working for Tyler."

A shot rang out and Pete stumbled back. He felt no pain.

He tried to suck in a mouthful of air but a strange hissing sound came from his chest and he couldn't get his breath. He looked up at the men on horses. With a final surge of strength, he pulled his trigger. The explosion knocked him back and he fell to the ground. The blast from his gun hit Langroise in the face and knocked him from his horse. Langroise screamed as he fell. Lindsay opened the canvas flap and looked out. She saw Pete lying in a pool of blood and screamed. She managed to get her clumsy body from the wagon and knelt beside Pete. His eyes fluttered half open. He whispered her name.

"Pete, Pete," she cried, "can you hear me?" She wiped the blood from his mouth with a corner of her skirt.

"Pete, yes, yes, I would have married you. Do you understand me? I would have married you. I could learn to love you. Pete, oh, Pete." She rocked back and forth, sobbing and repeating the boy's name. A smile flickered across his face. He had understood. Kind, sweet Pete. She picked up his hand and kissed it softly, smoothed the hair from his face and laid his hand on his chest.

She stood and turned to face the killers. She felt a dizziness rise up in her. Everything was a blur. A great futility swept through her as she stood in the quiet canyon, the smell of sulphur and blood in the air. Her body swayed, her hands on her unborn child. And then all feeling left her and she remained standing in a half coma.

A man rode up and began issuing orders. Horses were hitched to her wagon as she was unceremoniously pushed inside. Another journey began. Lindsay was numb. Fear had not been able to squeeze in yet. She lay on the hammock her family had so lovingly made for her travels. Soon exhaustion overcame her numbness and she slept.

* * *

The wagon lurched and strained as Lindsay woke to the sound of men's grunts and groans. The memories of a few hours ago returned to haunt her as she lie in the hammock.

She was again being taken to an unknown destination by unknown men. She no longer cared for her safety. But the baby—Lucas's baby. She must do everything possible to ensure the safety of this child.

The wagon halted and the men's voices faded. She waited anxiously, but not for long. The flap was thrown back recklessly and the bright, rising sun burst into the wagon. Lindsay raised her hand to shield her eyes. Someone grabbed her arm, pulling her to her feet. She was shoved to the opening and lifted to the ground. She stood for a moment, her eyes adjusting to the sunlight. Slowly she looked around. Men gaped at her. Two men took her by the arms and led her away. She glanced at her surroundings. The terrain was hilly, juniper shrubs scattered around. Pinion pines stretched loftily upwards and corn lilies danced in the breeze. She saw hills and mountain peaks.

A small miners' cabin sat against the hillside. A broken window gleamed menacingly from the front and the door stood open, its hinges rusty and warped. Her wagon was near the horses' shelter. She could hear tumbling water in the distance. There were veiled sensory impressions in her weary mind. They meant nothing to her. She was desolate.

She was shoved harshly through the open door of the shack. She stood just inside the door facing the musty room and a voice.

"Well, well, if it ain't the elusive Lindsay Tyler. You don't look so good. Had a hard time?"

She stepped back, her hands clutching her throat, her lips trembling. Nick laughed raucously, throwing his head back and enjoying Lindsay's reaction. She stood rooted to the floor. The thought of running away, out the door and into the sun-dappled hills entered her mind but she glanced sideways and saw the men standing at each side of the door. Even if they weren't there she was sure her weak legs would fail her. She leaned against the wall and watched Nick.

"You sure have been busy since I last saw you, Miss Tyler." He rose from the bench and walked to her. She shrunk back, afraid he would touch her. He pointed to her swollen belly and smiled. "Looks like Sanger did a hell of a lot more than simply steal you. Well," he continued, sniffing loudly, "he won't be able to take you from me this time. It's my turn now." He chuckled hoarsely.

He lit a cigarette and Lindsay watched the smoke materialize from his nostrils and drift aimlessly upwards, curling and merging with the floating dust.

"What do you want?" She spoke, startled at the weakness of her own voice.

Nick frowned, the deep furrows between his eyes becoming more evident. "I want Sanger, and you, my dear, are gonna help me kill him."

"No, No. Leave me alone. Let me go. Leave me alone." Her voice was faint and she shivered when she spoke.

"You wanna have that kid, don't ya?" he pointed at her belly with his cigarette.

Lindsay sucked in her breath. Oh, God, she thought, is he capable of that? The thought of saving her child became central in her frightened mind.

"What do you want me to do?" she whispered.

Nick laughed. "You've changed, Lindsay, you've changed." He reached out and touched a tiny curl on her shoulder. "You'll be here for a time. I'll be back. Right now, I have a job to do." He threw his cigarette to the floor and crushed it with his foot. He stepped to her and reached toward her swollen belly. She winced and drew back. "You're in a hell of a mess, aren't you, bitch?" He drew his arm back and struck her face, hard. She spun and fell into the wall, then sunk to the floor. "Half-breed-lovin' bitch," he said, rubbing the back of his hand. Then he walked out.

* * *

She lay curled on the floor, voices swimming around in her head. She began to cry softly, tears mixing with blood and dirt, forming grotesque shapes on her skin. She lingered on the edge of consciousness. She felt a pair of arms gently take hold of her and lift her to her feet. She staggered back but the arms held on preventing her from falling. She looked up into warm brown eyes. They seemed to be smiling at her but she was so dizzy she thought she may be hallucinating. There was kindness here but she had fallen into a pack of venomous creatures.

She was gently but forcefully led outside, across the

clearing and up an incline to her wagon. She was helped inside and forced to lie on her cot. Her mind was beginning to clear. She could focus her eyes now, although one eye was swelling shut. Within a few minutes she heard someone enter the wagon. She heard a metallic sound and she looked at the stranger. He was sitting on a box adjacent to the hammock. He hummed softly as he kept his attention on the floor. Then he lifted his eyes and placed a cool cloth on her bruised and swollen face. He waited a moment, then removed the cloth and rinsed it in the pan of water at his feet. He did not speak, only hummed a strange tune. He repeated the stimulating treatment.

His eyes had compassion and his hands were gentle. She closed her eyes and fell asleep but the stranger remained. He shook his head at her bruised face and misshapen mouth. He continued to battle the swelling with cold water.

* * *

"We lost how many men?" Nick's face twisted in anger. He had expected to lose a few, but when he learned Lindsay's group had killed fourteen of his men, he became incensed. Marty had expected his boss's anger. He remained stoical.

"Well, Sanger sure has a debt to pay now, hasn't he?" He removed his hat and wiped his sleeve across the brim, flicked an imaginary piece of lint and returned the hat to his head.

"But Sanger wasn't there, Mr. Moriarity," said Marty. Nick's face twitched. He stared at Marty as if he was confronting a fool.

"You think you can handle her with three men?" He smiled sarcastically at the man standing before him. "I need all the others. Sanger will soon be told of his kid's tragic death. I'll need to know his whereabouts. I'll take the rest of the men and send them to find his ranch. And find it, we will." Nick's eyes squinted as he stared at nothing. Sharply he turned back to Marty, "Gotta talk to Perez's whore in Santa Fe. She'll know something. Sanger's known in Santa Fe. Somebody'll know."

Marty nodded and watched Nick ride off with his men. "You know where you can reach me if you have to," he yelled over his shoulder.

Marty walked into the shack. Soon the sound of clinking glasses and shuffling cards came from the small room.

Chapter 26

Lindsay struggled to consciousness. Her mind was fuzzy and obscure. She opened her eyes and blinked. A man leaned over her. It was difficult to see. She reached up to brush her hair from her face. Her fingers found a wide bruise over her eyes. Her right eye was swollen shut. She carefully explored the rest of her face and grimaced when she found cuts and bruises.

"Don't you worry none, little lady. Ol' Scotty will take care o' you." It was painful for her to move her lips. She wanted to speak but no sounds came. She watched him move around her. He had a white beard and stood stoop-shouldered, moving in jerks within her vision.

"You just lay still now. Ol' Scotty'll be right back."

Lindsay watched him disappear through the opening. The sun seemed to be directly overhead. It must be close to noon, she thought. She raised her arm and ran her fingers through her hair. How long had she been here? She couldn't remember. Why was she brought here? Her mind drifted in a whirl, like petals of a flower, overlapping, unable to make sense of her thoughts. She had to find out what had happened. She closed her arms protectively around her belly.

"Here I is, little lady." The scratchy-voiced man appeared at the back of the wagon and a gnarled hand reached up and took hold of the side, pulling his short, stout body into the wagon. Scotty came to her side and held up a steaming bowl. Lindsay turned her head, watching the little man. He sat on a box, still humming. He reached behind him and picked up a large cloth. Then he laid it under her chin and spread it out, smoothing the ruffled edges. When he seemed satisfied, he turned back to the steaming bowl, filled the ladle and held it to her lips.

"Now this may hurt a little but you gotta eat. You gotta get your strength. Scotty ain't gonna let no one else hurt ya. Don't ya worry none about that. Just eat and rest. Let ol' Scotty take care of everything else."

Lindsay swallowed some of the hot liquid. The salty broth stung her bruised lips. She groaned and turned her head away. But Scotty wasn't going to be put off. He persisted, literally forcing the broth between her lips. It tasted good and after a few sips, the pain subsided some and she tolerated the discomfort. It was her baby she fed.

Lindsay studied the little man as he fed her. He was old, how old, she couldn't tell. His skin was rough hewn. A moustache blended into his beard and when he smiled or talked, the great shock of white hair became animated. His hair was long and snarled—a strange combination, Lindsay mused. Skin as dark and rough as timber but topped with such whiteness. His eyes tilted down at the outside corners, reminding her of a Chinaman she had once seen. He had a craggy, almost frightening appearance at first glance but he was comforting as he doted on her. Here alone, captive and threatened, he became for Lindsay, a link to a sane and, hopefully, safe world. His brown eyes, warm, mellow, glimmering globes, surveyed her face. Lindsay felt the bond of trust he offered and accepted it. She was no longer frightened. She touched the gnarled hand feeding her and closed her eyes.

The little man kept watch as she slept.

*   *   *

"Scotty, c'mere, you old crow-bait." The voice impatiently snarled.

Scotty appeared in the doorway, his gaze cool. He lumbered to their candlelit table and set down two bottles of whiskey. "There's more o' them when you need 'em. Jus' holler and I'll get em." He turned and shuffled to the door. He stepped into the dusky-colored air and stopped. He could hear conversation coming from the shack.

"Well, the old man is good for something. Maybe after we finish off these two bottles, we can pay our guest a visit." His lips curled back in a smile, revealing broken, black teeth. The men in the room laughed. Their voices raised in agreement, arguing about who'd be first.

Scotty walked to the wagon, humming. When he reached the wagon he turned and looked back at the shack.

"I may be ugly, but I ain't dumb." He entered through the open flap, walked to Lindsay, and looked down at her swollen face. She was a child. The lines of fatigue around her eyes had diminished somewhat. Her hand clutched the cloth Scotty had left on her forehead.

"I don't care if Nick is kin. I ain't gonna let him do this. You're just a child. You ain't done nothin' to him. You're such a young mite."

He walked to the back of the wagon and looked out. The sun sat low on the horizon, bathing the countryside in blazing orange light. He leaned his head out and listened in the direction of the shack. Riotous laughter and cussin' reached him. It won't be long, he thought. I better wake her and get her ready.

"Little lady?" He gently shook her shoulder. "Little lady, wake up." Softly he urged her. "Come on, little lady."

Lindsay fought to escape the mire. She thrashed around, groaning and crying out. A man held his arms out to her. She reached for them and he grasped her and pulled her from the mist. She looked up and a pair of dark blue eyes smiled at her. "Lucas, oh, Lucas, please help me. Help me, Lucas, help me." She looked again and the hands holding her were Nick's. He laughed cruelly and pushed her back into the mist. She fought to keep her head up. Hands were holding her down, pushing her head into a fog. "No, no, let me live, please." She screamed and a hand clamped gently over her mouth. She opened her eyes. Scotty saw reality return to her eyes and he took his hand away. She shook her

231

head, as if in doing so, she would shake out the murky, sluggish sediment that had settled in her brain.

Scotty rushed to the opening at the back of the wagon and swung his head around, listening for sounds from the shack. It was quiet. Maybe the drugged whiskey had begun to take effect. He chuckled to himself. Won't they be surprised when they wake up tomorrow and find ol' Scotty duped em'? Ol' Scotty, the camp simpleton, imbecile, moron. Well, Scotty could take their cruelty, he could sit back and watch them kill each other and make fools of themselves. But when it came to a little girl who ain't never done nothin' to any o' them, that's different. And her big with child. His own kin behavin' like a rabid dog. Well, he'd get the child outa here tonight. He knew a safe place she could hide until her uncle could come for her. Hope he can fetch her before she drops her baby.

Lindsay sat on the edge of the cot, waves of nausea washing over her. Her mind spun, reeled, whirled. She moved and retched. Scotty rushed to her side and held a pan for her. When she finished, he wiped her brow with a cold rag. She gave him a weak smile, her face ashen under the bruises.

"You're gonna be fine, little lady. All this trouble has caused you to be a mite upset, but it's almost over now." He smiled into her tormented eyes. He leaned out of the wagon again, his ears tuned for trouble. Nothing. He turned to Lindsay and whispered. "I'll be back. You just sit there and relax." He climbed to the ground and she could hear his footfalls diminish.

The door of the shack still stood ajar. The candlelight bounced off the broken window and made eerie designs on the wall. It was quiet. Scotty peered through the window and smiled, tickled at himself, as his eyes found the four unconscious men. One man still clung selfishly to a bottle of whiskey. They would be out 'til morning. Scotty had made sure of that, even if they only had one drink each. He turned toward the wagon as he heard a crash. Startled, he drew a breath and turned back to the window. The whiskey bottle had fallen from the man's hands. It lay shattered on the floor. Basking in elation he put his mind to the task at hand.

Lindsay was sitting up holding the cool rag to her brow. She smiled when he entered. He reached in his pocket and drew out a match and struck it on his boot. He touched it to the stub of candle leaning in its holder and a finger of light jumped forth.

Scotty sat beside Lindsay. Taking in a gulp of air, he began talking. "Child, we don't have much time and I know you're wondering what's goin' on. So I'll tell you what I know and mebbe then you'll understand. He scratched his beard and watched the candlelight bounce off the canvas.

"You know by now that Nick is behind your bein' here. I know this. Nick is filled with hatred because of your Uncle Ned. His mind has gone loco. Anyway, when his plan to use you to get the ranch back didn't work, somethin' sort of popped in his mind. He searched for a long time for you and Lucas Sanger. Gawd, he said he was gonna do some awful things to the both of you if he ever got his hands on you again." He looked at Lindsay and she paled at his words. He touched her hand. "Anyway, after he found out about your baby and how you was gonna go back to Lucas and all, he decided he'd find you and take you again. He planned on keeping you here 'til you had the baby, then killing you both. He aimed on sendin' your bodies to Lucas. That's why he ain't here now. He and his men are searchin' for Sanger's place. Anyway, Nick figured after Lucas got your body and the baby's he'd go crazy-mad and go searching for him. That's when Nick would have the upper hand and that's when he'd have a chance at killin' Lucas." He looked at her. Tears were trembling on her lashes.

"Lissen, little gal, ain't nothin' gonna happen to you or your baby as long as ol' Scotty's around. Now we gotta get away from here fast. Think you feels good enough to walk outa here?"

She nodded. "Good, then let's get started."

Scotty stood up and reached under the cot, brought out a leather satchel and threw it over his shoulder. He walked to the opening and looked toward the shack again. Still no sound. He breathed a long sigh and turned to Lindsay, his hand outstretched. She reached for it and then suddenly pulled away and turned to the side of the wagon. She pointed to the cradle. Scotty followed her finger with his eyes, then looked back at her. "Child, we can't carry that with us. We gonna have problems enought just carrying our own weight."

Tears rolled down Lindsay's cheeks as she walked to the cradle. She turned to Scotty, her hand caressing Uncle Ned's gift, her baby's cradle. She shook her head and lowered her eyes.

"All right, if it means that much, but it's gonna slow us down, child." Lindsay looked at Scotty, her eyes brimming with tears, her mouth quivering. She reached out and touched Scotty's arm. He looked at her and she slowly closed her eyes and nodded. It was difficult to hear the very soft "thank you" that came from her lips. Scotty untied the cradle from the side of the wagon and retied the ropes around the padding. Then he walked to the entrance and lowered the cradle to the ground. He turned back to Lindsay and stretched his hand to her. She reached for it, grasped it, and squeezed it gently—an unspoken word, understood by both.

They left the wagon and headed into the mountains. The sky was now black and starless. There was no moon, only a black abyss over them. He led Lindsay up the mountain. She clung to his arm, her large belly impeding their progress. She could only walk a short distance without having to rest. Scotty frowned. At this rate they would be only a short distance from camp by morning. An idea flashed into his head.

"Lindsay, you come sit over here and rest. I'm gonna go back and get a couple o' horses. We gotta move faster if we're gonna get away. I thought we could make it on foot but I see now we ain't gonna be able to. What with carrying this cradle and holding you up, I won't last long either. I jest hope none o' those men are good trackers cause horses is easy to track." He walked off into the blackness.

Lindsay sat on the cool ground, her breathing short. She looked around. Everything was obscure. She could hear some animal snorting in the distance and the sound of bats fluttering overhead frightened her. She pressed her hand to her heart and swallowed. Her thoughts were jumbled, tumbling from fear of Nick to hoping Lucas was safe. Lindsay looked up. A few stars appeared. "Please God, please help me. Don't let any harm come to my baby." She choked and stood up. Where's Scotty? He's been gone so long. What if he got caught? She was so close to camp they could find her easily. She thought about moving on. She looked back toward camp, her eyes searching the blackness for any sign of movement. A twig snapped. She froze, her hands clenched. Beads of sweat glistened on her face, the salt stinging her eyes. She crouched and listened. She tried to be invisible. She heard the thumping of horses' hooves. She waited, her muscles taut.

"Where you at, child?" A whisper came to her ears. She breathed a sigh of relief and stood. "Over here," she replied through swollen lips.

Scotty appeared on horseback like a large shadow with a piebald mare on a lead. He jumped down to her. "Not one bit o' trouble. They was sleepin' like babies." He cackled like a prankster. He helped Lindsay into the saddle and adjusted her stirrups. Then he tied the cradle on behind his saddle. He shrugged and retied it twice more before he was satisfied, and then mounted. They began picking their way over rocks and fallen trees.

Toward safety.

Chapter 27

"What do you think, Chico?" The two men were laying on their bellies, the camp below them. They had been watching since before sunup and so far had seen no signs of life. "It's time to move, no?" Lucas nodded once.

They made their way stealthily, moving quickly, then freezing in shadows until they reached the clearing. Lucas didn't like this. No guards. Only horses by the wagon. If Lindsay was here, why were there no guards? A shiver of fear shook his spine. He cautiously made his way to the wagon. He saw Chico disappear around the side of the shack.

Lucas peered into the wagon, his gun ready. He climbed in and looked around. He opened a small trunk. He removed a shawl and held it against his face. It smelled of Lindsay. Her scent was so fresh. He put the shawl inside his shirt and turned to the small hammock. He reached down to touch the wide brownish stain. Blood. There were more stains on the quilt. A knot of anger formed in his stomach. Setting on a box at the head of the cot was a bowl and rag. He examined the rag. It, too, was bloodstained. He went to the back of the wagon and swung to the ground. He surveyed the camp. The horses that were tethered by the wagon grazed quietly. Beyond them a hundred yards away was the mining shack. The wagon was in clear view from the shack. If this was Moriarty's jail, where were the jailors? And where was his prisoner? Lucas headed for the shack. Halfway there he met Chico. They both veered into a gully, hidden momentarily out of view from the shack.

"She's been here. Looks like she might be hurt." He took his hat off and wiped his brow with his arm. He put his hat back on and looked at his friend. Chico spoke.

"There are four men in there. Looks like they got mighty drunk." He looked into the hills, scanning the horizon. "Whoever got those men in there drunk, *amigo*, has your Lindsay with 'em." Lucas looked into the mountains, to the north.

"Somebody else has her now, *amigo*."

"But who, Chico? What the hell's goin' on?"

Chico shrugged and shook his head.

Lucas pointed at the ground near the wagon. "There were six horses there last night, Chico. Now their are only four. I have a feeling if we find the other two, we'll find Lindsay."

Chapter 28

Lindsay and Scotty rode for many hours. It was painful for Linday. Her back cramped up tightly and her wounds ached deeply. But they were both more relaxed now that they had covered so much ground without any signs of pursuit. Although they probably wouldn't be found, they still covered their trail where they could and Scotty watched the horizon nervously. Lindsay wasn't sure she could ride much farther. Scotty rode slow and took the most comfortable deer trails. He gave her water and cold cloths to hold on her face. It was clear that Lindsay's time wasn't far off. This kind of excitement and hard traveling could start her in early labor and Scotty knew this.

Scotty pulled up and turned to face Lindsay. "Child, you can't go on riding like this in your condition. You know that. We've got to get some help real quick. Now if I figured right, your uncle's place is just under a hun'erd miles from here. With you along, I'll have to slow my pace but if I can go on my own I can make it sooner. I'll get your uncle and we'll come straight back to you. You'll be alone mebbe a week or more. Think ya'll be alright?"

Lindsay smiled weakly at the little man. "Yes, Scotty, I'll be fine. I'll be fine."

"Okay child, I was hopin' you'd say that. I have a place for you that's safe 'til we get back." He turned and scanned the horizon behind them. Satisfied they were alone, he turned into a narrow gully and followed a dry river bed for several hundred yards. As the gully widened he stopped to let Lindsay catch her breath. Her eyes were rimmed in purple, her breathing was labored and he knew she was in pain. Yet, she uttered not one word of complaint. In the few hours he had nursed Lindsay she had earned his considerable respect.

He spun around as Lindsay groaned. "What's wrong, child?" He stopped his horse.

"Nothing, Scotty, I'm just tired." She reached out her hand and patted him on the cheek.

"Well, it ain't much further and then you can sleep as long as you want." Scotty continued to follow the river bed. Rounding a bend he pointed up at the mountainside. "There she be, child."

Lindsay followed the direction of his finger and frowned. "What?"

"Your home for the next few days." He smiled at her and grabbed hold of the reins of her horse. "Hold on, child."

The horses pulled and prodded up the hillside. Lindsay searched for her refuge but could only see heavy brush, trees, and rocks. After several minutes, Scotty stopped and climbed down. "Jus' a minute, child," he called excitedly as he disappeared into the underbrush. Lindsay could hear him swearing and hacking away at the ground cover with his hands. Soon he returned and lifted her to the ground. She felt so weak she wasn't sure her legs would hold her. She sat on the ground, rubbing her back, watching Scotty. He unsaddled the horses and led them around the hillside out of sight. He returned carrying the cradle, satchel, and bedroll, struggling to keep them in his arms.

"Well, soon as my horse has rested awhile, I'll be off. Your horse will be fine. There's plenty o' grass and water jus' around the backside o' this mountain." He turned toward the hidden cave. "Come on, child, let's get you settled in your new home."

The climb was short but steep. After realizing that Lindsay couldn't make it without help, Scotty went on ahead, discarded his parcels and returned to her. He took hold of her arm and gently propelled her up the hillside. She groaned but she didn't complain. After what seemed hours to Lindsay, Scotty parted some underbrush, revealing a cave. She hadn't been able to see it from below. Anyone searching for her would have as much trouble spotting it as she had. This gave her a feeling of security and she smiled warmly at Scotty.

"Come on. Lemme show you around," he said, pleased at her reaction.

Lindsay walked into the opening. A musty atmosphere enveloped her tired senses. Scotty reached into the satchel, pulled out a candle and lit it. The flame reached out and danced on the eerie walls. Somewhere, far off in the distance, Lindsay could hear the tinkling of water. Scotty gathered firewood. Once he had a fire crackling, he surveyed the cave in the firelight. Picking up the bedroll, he walked to the back, a distance from the cave entrance yet close to the fire. He unrolled the bedroll and shook it. He collected tree mulch in armfuls from the cave opening and spread it near the fire. Lindsay was confused and exhausted as she watched him. Finally he picked up the bedroll and spread it over the mulch. He fussed over it until he was satisfied. Then he jumped up, his eyes sparkling. "Okay, child, see how that feels," He held out his hand and helped her to her feet. She fell on it clumsily. She stretched out, grateful for the comfort. "It's the most gorgeous feeling I've ever had, Scotty. It's lovely." Scotty beamed at her approval.

"Now, for some grub." He turned and bent over the bulging satchel and was soon engrossed in his job. Lindsay lay looking at the roof of the cave. Perhaps there was a trial in all this. Maybe, if it was so very difficult to find Lucas, maybe she would appreciate him even more. Appreciate, hell. She loved the man more than life itself. If she had to wander like this for the rest of her days, trying to find him, she would do just that. Lucas was worth any amount of pain she had to endure.

"Child, wake up. Come on, honey. You gotta eat something. That baby has gotta have food. Hands were gently shaking her. She opened her eyes. She sat up and took the plate he held out to her.

"Why, Scotty, where on earth did you get this food?" Her stomach rumbled as she beheld the plate of beans, hardtack, jerky, and a mug of steaming coffee. Scotty beamed with satisfaction.

"Shucks, little lady, I've been livin' like this most o' my life. If I can't fix a pretty little gal some good vittles, then I ain't worth much as a cook, now, am I?"

Lindsay filled her spoon with beans and put it to her mouth. Her swollen, cracked lips weren't going to accommodate her. Scotty saw this, hunkered down and taking the spoon from her, mashed the beans. Then he picked up the jerky and broke it into small pieces. He cut the hardtack in half and poured sauce from the beans over it and handed the plate back to her. "There, that should be easier to chew now. Let that hardtack soak a few minutes and it'll soften up."

Lindsay wiped at her nose with the back of her hand. A sniffle escaped from her throat and Scotty bent down to her.

"What is it, child? Are you all right?"

She couldn't stop the tears that rolled down her cheeks. "Yes, I'm . . . I'm fine. I . . . I, well, Scotty, you're such a sweet, kind man. She put her head down and attempted to smother a sob. Scotty watched her tenderly. She had been through so much, seen so much violence, been the brunt of such hatred, and yet she seemed untouched by it all. She was so gentle, so grateful, so kind.

Scotty patted her hand, picked up her plate, and pushed it back into her hands. "Now you eat that, child, you gotta take good care o' that little one."

He walked to the satchel. "Child." She looked up.

"There's several days' food in here," he said, pointing to the satchel. "Outside and round the hill is water. I stacked enough wood against the wall to last awhile." He pointed to the wood, neatly piled.

"I better git goin' now. Reckon my horse should be rested enough. I'll head straight for your uncle's place and we'll come right back to you."

Scotty," Lindsay questioned, "do you have any paper and a pencil in that satchel?"

"Yup, sure do." He reached in the satchel, searched furiously for a moment, and then produced a tattered envelope and the stub of a pencil. Lindsay took both, thought for a moment, and then composed her note. It said:

Uncle Ned: There isn't much time. The man delivering this note has saved my life. I am fine now but I need your help desperately. Trust this man and come as quickly as you can. My prayers are with you and I remain,

Your loving Lindsay

She folded the note and handed it to Scotty. He took it and placed it in his pocket, tied his scarf around his neck, and strapped his gun on his hip. He took his knife from his pocket and handed it to Lindsay.

"I wish I had a gun to leave you. I gotta take mine, child, but here, you keep this knife." He walked to the entrance. He started putting his hat on when Lindsay called. He turned and watched her struggling to her feet.

"Here now, what you doin'?" He rushed to her side.

"Oh, Scotty, I'm so big and clumsy. I hate myself." Her lips trembled as she spoke. "I . . . I just wanted to give you this." She hugged him. "I couldn't let you leave without telling you how much I appreciate what you are doing. Be careful, please."

Scotty stared at her, touched deeply by her show of affection. "We're gonna come out o' this jus' fine, child."

He walked out of the cave and Lindsay stood for a few moments, waiting, listening. Soon she heard hooves churning up the ground. "Godspeed, Scotty," she whispered.

She went to the bed and laid down. Complete exhaustion overwhelmed her.

In minutes, she slept.

Chapter 29

A gust of wind accompanied by a peal of thunder blew Lucas's hat from his head. It bounced and rolled along the ground as Lucas jumped from his horse and bounded after it. He reached down to grab it and froze. His eyes spied something on the ground. He picked up a small gold earring. He stared at the shiny piece of jewelry in the palm of his hand. It was Lindsay's. He remembered nibbling on her earlobe one night, many months ago. When he pulled a little hard on the earring she took the opportunity to jump all over him, verbally and physically. He grinned as he remembered her tiny fists pummeling his chest and recalled the pleasant way the night had ended. A sharp report of thunder interrupted his thoughts as he put the earring in his pocket, lifted his eyes, and searched for Chico. He spotted him and whistled. Chico looked up, saw Lucas and rode to his side.

"You have picked up the trail?"

"*Si.*" Lucas hunkered down, peering intently at the underbrush. He stood, looking in Lindsay's direction of flight. "They went this way." He mounted his horse and walked into the mountains. Chico followed closely.

They rode for several hours, occasionally stopping to examine a possible sign. A wisp of red hair that had caught on a branch, a recently thrown horseshoe, snatches of matetial clinging to thorny bushes—all signs of Lindsay. Lucas wondered where the stranger was taking her. They were traveling west. If they were returning to the Lazy Hat Ranch, why weren't they heading north? Maybe one of the kidnappers decided to keep Lindsay to himself for awhile. Maybe he, too, had been tempted by her beauty. Damn! Once he had Lindsay safe in his arms again he'd be he hardpressed to keep from tearing apart any man that ogled her. He smiled. If he hit each man that admired Lindsay, he'd soon be in a state of exhaustion. No man was immune to her dazzling looks.

Rain began to fall. Lucas looked at the clouds with a worried frown. "Damn! This rain could destroy the signs we're looking for."

"*Si*, but perhaps, it will also slow her down, too, yes?" Chico lit a cigarette and offered one to his friend. Lucas shook his head and reined in his horse. He jumped to the ground and walked to a rock. He picked something off a twisted branch jutting out from the rocks and then returned to his horse. He stood momentarily studying the object in his hand then looked up. The canyon continued winding through the mountains. He looked again at the object in his hand. He fingered it, then held it up for Chico to see. He pointed in the direction of the narrow gully. "They went that way."

The men traveled deeper into the gully. It was beginning to rain harder, droplets bouncing off the neck of their horses. The lightning and thunder had lessened considerably as though retreating to gather strength for the next onslaught.

They followed a dry river bed for several hundred yards. As it widened Lucas stopped and looked over the terrain. Mountains towered around them. Brush covered hills collided with barren buttes. The rain poured down now, venting its pent up fury on the men below.

They continued walking, searching the surrounding land. As they rounded a bend, Lucas stopped abruptly, cocking his head. "Did you hear that, Chico?"

"*Si.*" Chico peered at the hillside before him. Darkness had descended upon them. Rain pelted their faces, drenched their clothing, and irritated them. The only aid the weather gave them was the brief light from nature's overhead display. The men turned their horses in the direction of the sound. Slowly they traversed the hillside, listening, watching, muscles taut. They rounded a boulder and in front of them, under a tree stood a horse chewing on grass, watching them with large eyes.

Lucas smiled. Turning in his saddle he raised himself up and looked around. Nothing. Only New Mexican frontier. He swung down from the horse and began to unbuckle the saddle. Chico followed. After depositing their saddles in the shelter of some rocks, they tied the horses to a tree. They set out to search the hillside.

"*Amigo*, are you so sure Lindsay is here? Maybe that horse belongs to another."

Lucas reached into his pocket and brought out a small piece of colored material. He handed it to Chico. Chico studied it and handed it back to Lucas, his brows drawn together in a frown.

"That's a piece of Lindsay's bedroll. I wasn't sure when I first saw it. On the way to Mexico, when she was in Nick's hands, I had taken an extra bedroll along for her. When she took off, I followed. I took it along. You never know when you might need an extra one." He smiled. "She evidently took it with her when she left Colorado and has it with her now."

"Ahh." Chico wiped his arm across his face and pulled his hat down over his eyes. "Well, *amigo*, what are we waiting for? Let's go find her."

They didn't have to search long. The smell of burning wood led them straight to the cave. Had the smell of the fire not been evident, they would have had a hard search before finding the entrance to the cave. Now as they approached, brushing the foliage aside, Lucas's heart jumped in anticipation of seeing Lindsay. He couldn't believe what she had done to him. She had pierced him. She had made his hardness feel strong—not brutal. Where there had been a sore loneliness, there was now a childlike enthusiasm. She had put a glow in everything for him. And now she was here, a few feet away.

Lucas stood in the entrance, his eyes scanning side to side. A fire danced brightly, casting long shadows in the deeply crevassed walls. A plate of beans lay carelessly by the fire. A leather satchel lay against the wall, its contents strewn about. Several pieces of crumpled paper lay around the fire, partly scorched. A tattered dress lay loosely over a boulder and a lacy chemise lay by the fire.

She was laying on her side, her back to him, sleeping. The amber fireglow danced lightly over her entire body. Lucas's thoughts turned primal. He removed his hat shaking off the moisture. His heart beat furiously. He had waited so long for this and now that he was with her again he felt like a drooling school boy in love with his teacher. Chico finally pushed past him and walked quietly to the fire and held his hands over the flames. He watched Lucas.

Lucas turned and walked to the slumbering girl. He looked down at her, drinking in her nearness.

A whimper escaped her lips a she rolled over and snuggled deeper under the blanket. Her hand lay beside her face clutching the little knife Scotty had given her. The firelight reflected off her face, illuminating the bruises and swollen, cut eye. Lucas clenched his teeth in anger. Someone had hurt her. Her hair fell about her body in tangles. She whimpered, thrashing her head from side to side. Lucas bent down, took hold of her shoulders, and gently shook her. She seemed to be having a nightmare.

"Niña, niña, wake up. You're safe now." His words were barely audible.

She opened her eyes, searched his face without comprehension, then screamed. It was a desperate scream, filled with the fear of a child in the agony of a long, long night.

Chapter 30

After Scotty left Lindsay, she had slept restlessly, her mind troubled by recurring nightmares of Nick. She saw him holding her baby by the legs, laughing cruelly as he swung the baby back and forth, back and forth. She woke sweating, wiped her face with a cool cloth, then slept again. She was laying beside a pool of shimmering, cool, turquoise-colored water, filled with tiny mermaids frolicking and cavorting. Suddenly, a lifeless form floated up from the bottom. The water began to turn bloody red. The little form reached the top and turned over, bobbing inches from her face. Her baby. She screamed.

I can't go on like this. She rose, weary to her very bones. Maybe some fresh air. She wrapped the blanket around her shoulders and stepped to the mouth of the cave. There was no moon. A proud panoply of stars met her upward gaze. She sat and looked out over the dark, quiet valley. Her sense of aloneness was complete. *If I hadn't been so stubborn I wouldn't be here now.* She chastised herself. No matter how much she wanted to be with Lucas, nothing was worth endangering the baby. *That's clear now.* When Uncle Ned comes, I'll wait for Lucas to come to me. I'll write him. He'll come. I'll wait. She returned to her bed and soon was asleep.

Lucas was chasing her through a lime-green forest. The blue sky was contrasted with the oddly shaped chartreuse clouds. A breeze caressed her face, tinged with colors of olive and blue. She ducked under a lime green branch and ran through the lacy trees. Lucas caught her and swung her high above his head. He put her down and she ran off, giggling. No matter how far she ran or how often, Lucas always found her.

Lindsay opened her eyes. A hazy film kept her from seeing clearly out of her injured eye. She lay quietly, savoring the feeling of her baby moving. He kicked and Lindsay gasped, "You are an eager one." Lately the baby hadn't moved as much, but when he did it surprised Lindsay completely and moved her to smile. "You definitely take after your father. Strong and active," she said.

She rolled on her side and looked out. The sky was now leaden, dreary. The air in the cave was damp as Lindsay struggled to lift her misshapen body erect. She walked to the neatly stacked pile of wood, placed several pieces on the warm ashes, and lit a match to a piece of kindling. Soon the smell of coffee filled the cave and Lindsay smiled as she emptied the contents of Scotty's satchel on the floor. Scattered about lay containers of jerky and hardtack, bacon wrapped in paper, a delicious smelling slab of ham, a container of flour, butter, beans, and two potatoes. Six red apples were wrapped in a cloth and two more containers were filled with coffee and hard candy. Matches and utensils tumbled out from the bottom of the worn satchel. Under a towel lay a book. She pulled it out and fingered it gently. A book of poems by Percy Bysshe Shelley. She sat and thumbed through the dogeared yellow pages. She stopped near the end. There was a scrap of paper. Someone had marked the page. Her eyes moved through the stanzas of "Ode to the West Wind":

". . . . . Scatter as from an unextinguished hearth, ashes and sparks, my words among mankind.

Oh, trumpet of prophecy, if winter comes can spring be far behind?"

She was confused. Was this Scotty's? No, it couldn't be. But the page was marked and the passage spoke of fresh changes coming after difficult times. It held a purifying feeling for her. It was a statement of newness and, for a moment, she didn't feel alone.

She poured a mug of coffee, got comfortable on her makeshift bed, and spent the remainder of the morning reading through the yellowed pages of this treasure. Thunder peeled. She raised her head and looked outside. It was raining. As the wind buffeted the trees and whistled past the mouth of the cave she laid back and closed her eyes.

* * *

She awoke startled. The storm continued its assault. The wind was fierce. She ran her fingers through her hair. She was hungry. She moved to the scatterd contents of the bag and picked up the slab of ham. She warmed the coffee, cooked the ham, and ate ravenously. Then, she decided to heat some water for a bath. She felt dirty, ugly, and ponderous. She stood, breathing heavily. She sipped her coffee and gazed into her cup at her reflection. She looked hideous.

Damn! Damn! Some present for Lucas, I am. Ugly, ugly, ugly! She flung the cup at the wall and prodded the fire. She touched the bruise on her face as she crossed to the cave entrance. She walked out. A rain-soaked gust peppered her face. The rain water mixed with her salty tears and Lindsay offered her face to the sky and indulged the rain completely.

She turned back into the cave, picked up the coffee pot, and walked outside into the heavy rain. She groped her way around the backside of the mountain. Scotty told her there was water here.

Thunder rumbled in the distance and lightning tore at the sky. The cool rain felt good on Lindsay's tired, sore body. She walked slowly, following the rocky pathway. Soon she came to a grassy slope where a rivulet undulated through the trees and rocks. Her horse snorted and watched her warily. She spoke, reassuring him. She walked to the creek, rinsed the pot, and filled it with fresh water. Then she turned back to the cave. The wind whipped her skirt, causing it to tangle at her ankles. She set the pot down, bent over, straining, and reached for the hem of her skirt. If she could hike it up and hold it in her free hand she could walk easier. The rocks were wet and if she wasn't careful she would end up falling. She stood up, holding the clinging skirt above her knees and turned to pick up the pot of water. She stepped sideways and, as her foot came down between two rocks, she lost her balance. She grasped for a large branch but the momentum of her fall carried her backward, her hands slipping from the branch. She tried to break her fall by twisting her body. With thoughts of the baby foremost she wrapped her hands around her belly. She crashed to the ground, landing on her back. The toe of her boot had slipped between the rocks and lodged there. The wind knocked from her lungs, she heard a muffled snap. She lay on the wet ground, struggling to gulp air into her lungs, her eyes misty with pain. She struggled to sit. Angrily she brushed the hair back off her face. "Damn-it!" She hit her fist on the ground. "Damn! Damn! What else is going to happen?" She looked up into the sky, the rain pelted her skin and soaked her dress. "Oh, God, no more. No more, please."

Her ankle throbbed. She tried to move it. A bolt of pain shot up her leg. She gasped. Tears of pain and anger began to fall. She had to get back to the cave. She was wet and cold and in pain. If she lay out here much longer she would be sick for sure. She looked around for something to lean on. Tendrils of fright began to gnaw at her. A stick lay a few feet away. If she could reach it she might be able to use it for a crutch. She reached sideways, stretching, groaning, pushing. Just a little farther. But she couldn't reach it. She looked down at her ankle. I've got to get to the cave and walking on you is the only way I'm going to make it, she thought.

With her good foot she pushed against the rock that held the boot of her injured ankle. She grabbed hold of her knee and pushed the rock with her foot and pulled on her leg.

After a few seconds the imprisoned foot was freed but the movement caused her to cry out in pain. Taking a few deep breaths, she looked up, letting the rain cascade over her face. After the waves of pain subsided, she spoke to herself again. Gather your strength and do it. Just force yourself to do it. She was only a few hundred feet from the cave, but it might as well have been a mile.

After several tries she managed to get on her knees and grabbed the coffee pot. She bent forward and slowly inched her way along, resting most of her weight on her good leg and dragging the injured one. She finally entered the cave. Her teeth chattered. Her skin was cold and covered with scratches and bruises. She crawled to the fire and placed the pot of water in the hot coals. "I went through all this for a bath and I'm going to have one." She crawled to the piled wood and threw several pieces on the flames. Then she turned to the scattered contents of the satchel. She threw everything on her bedroll. Once she got down, she wasn't getting up again for anything. After the water began to bubble, she grasped the pot, and again using it for support, she crawled to the bedroll. She lay on the rumpled bed for several minutes. She was really scared now. How could she spend several days alone like this. The pain in her ankle was becoming severe. She wouldn't be able to cook. "Oh, God, my baby." This thought suffused her senses with reasoning. She would make it. No matter what happened she would be strong, for her baby's sake.

She sat and leaned against the wall and removed her dress. She wrung it out and tossed it over a boulder near the crackling fire. She took off in her chemise and looked around. "Oh, hell!" She spat, throwing it angrily toward the fire. She was naked and chilled to the bone now. She rolled over slightly, pulled the blanket from under her and wrapped it around her. With the wet clothing off she began to warm. The fire crackled brightly and an aura of safety filled the interior. Lindsay was sure her ankle was broken. She wasn't sure if she could remove the boot or, as Lucas had done long ago, leave it on for support. She could feel the foot swelling and the pain worsened. She decided to remove it. She sat up straight, her belly impeding her every move. She wrestled with the boot on her good foot and after a few grunts and groans, pulled it off. With the pain and swelling she might not be able to remove the other boot. The pain was so intense and she could feel the bulging, swollen skin straining against the leather. She bent her leg and rested it, Indian style, across the other leg. The painful foot was accessible now only partly hidden by her protruding stomach. She leaned against the wall, took several deep breaths, and straightened her back. She grabbed hold of the boot and began tugging. Pain shot up her leg and exploded into sparks of nausea. Sweat popped out on her brow. She relaxed a moment. She knew it wasn't going to be easy, but damn, this was ridiculous. She tried again and again but the gut-wrenching pain stopped her. She lay back, lost in agony. Then she saw it—her knife. She reached for it and ran her finger across its edge to test the sharpness. She leaned forward and carefully slide the blade inside her boot. She cut it slowly, its full length, until the knife could no longer wedge between her boot and the swollen ankle. The boot finally slid off in her hand as lights flashed in her head, stars bounced off the walls, penetrating her eyes. She fell forward, her face landing half on the blanket, half in the dirt. Mercifully she had fainted.

As she came to, dust swirled around her nose and mouth with each breath. She raised herself up onto her elbow, fighting back a wave of nausea. Swallowing several times, she pushed herself back, sitting against a wall. The cool rock somewhat alleviated her lightheadedness.

She relaxed and looked at her ankle. It was twice its normal size. A large purplish knot covered the instep. Maybe tomorrow she would be able to bind it and put some weight on it. She reached for a cloth and dipped it in the coffee pot. The hot water felt good to her cold hands. She took her time washing herself, enjoying the clean, hot cloth against her cold, sticky skin. She scrubbed until the water was cool, then turned her attention to her hair. Hopefully she would be able to wash it soon. Another few days without soap and water and a comb wouldn't pass through the snarls. She felt better after she finished her makeshift toilette. She looked outside and was shocked by the blackness. The rain continued to pelt the earth and lightning rent the sky followed in seconds by peals of thunder.

Lindsay snuggled into the blanket. She was hungry but not enough to go through the pain of crawing on her hands and knees to cook. She looked at the wrapped cradle. She smiled. "Well, my precious child, you will at least have a comfortable bed." She looked outside again and watched the lightning dance across the sky. I'll write Lucas a letter. I'll explain everything that's happened and ask him to come and get me. She would post it at Uncle Ned's. She was excited at the thought that Lucas might arrive at her uncle's ranch soon after the baby's birth. She desperately wanted him to see his child then.

She reached for the pencil and the paper that had been wrapped around the bacon and began to write. After a few sentences, she tore off the part she had been using, wadded it and tossed it to the fire, unable to write the words she felt. She tried again, and again she discarded the letter. In moments, the bunched-up, unfinished letters were strewn about the cave like rocks. She gave up. Maybe tomorrow. She laid her head down, her eyes getting heavy. The knife. Her eyes darted in search. She found it and lay back down holding it tightly. She made a silent plan. If she was found by Nick or any of his men she would kill herself. She would not birth her baby for his insane pleasure. With this knowledge tucked safely in her frightened mind, she slept.

But she hadn't been asleep long when the nightmares spun from her subconscious. She had just given birth and someone was holding her baby, tempting her with the tiny body, holding it close to her face, then running into the hills laughing, the baby's mewling sounds slowly disappearing. Then suddenly Lucas was standing over her holding their baby, smiling warmly, holding out the small bundle so Lindsay could see the child's face. She struggled to see but the only thing in the blanket was a skull. She looked up at Lucas. He was gone. Standing before her, holding the little bundle was Nick. His eyes were glassy, his lips covered with blood, his tongue flicking over them like the devil. She reached for her baby but Nick turned slightly, threw the bundle into the trees and then began shaking Lindsay. "I'm gonna kill you and your baby." He was a madman. His breath was hot against her face. She began to cry for help trying to break loose from his grip.

* * *

Opening her eyes she looked into the face of a man. Nick! He had found her. Now he would kill her and her baby. She began to scream. Loud, piercing, agonizing screams rent the air. The hands continued to shake her. "Please, oh God, please don't kill my baby. I'll do anything, only, please, don't kill my baby, please, please . . ." She bent her head and saw the knife, shining, glistening by her hand.

The strong hands continued to hold her imprisoned in their grip. She pushed with renewed strength against her captor, kicking at him with her strong leg, falling backward slightly as she realized she was free of the restricting hands. She scrambled to her knees, clutching the blanket to cover her nakedness. She backed away from the man, placed the knife against her heart and through swollen lips said, "If you come one step closer, I'll kill myself."

Lucas watched the trembling naked girl with the flashing knife. He didn't move, afraid of her frantic delirium. From the corner of his eye he saw Chico approaching Lindsay from behind. She was shuddering and wavering, the knife poised over her belly.

"Lindsay, Lindsay, it's me, Lucas. I've come to take you home." His hand went out to her.

She backed away. "Don't you come near me," she screamed. "I won't fall for your schemes again. Lucas doesn't know where I am, he thinks I'm with my uncle, but you, you . . . you've fooled me for the last time. If I die it'll be at my hands not yours." She squinted into his face, her mind frightened in the confusion of mistaken identities.

Lucas studied her distorted face. It was discolored with bruises, her eye partially closed, and her hair fell around her shoulders in unkempt fashion. Tears spilled from her eyes, rolled down her cheeks and splashed onto her breasts. Her lips were swollen, dried flecks of blood touched here and there. But her eyes, her beautiful green, luminous eyes. Lucas had never seen eyes so filled with fear and hatred. What had happened to his niña? If Nick was so concerned in getting even with him, why didn't he come to him and leave Lindsay out of it. Why pick on a helpless woman carrying a child? But then, who knew what a madman thought. One thing for sure. No one will ever hurt Lindsay again. No one.

Chico was directly behind her now. Her back was near the cave wall so he had to come around her left side to surprise her. If she saw him she would act quickly to destroy herself. Lucas had to keep her attention riveted on him. So he began to speak, slowly, softly, "Lindsay, niña, look at me." He touched his chest with his finger. "It's me, Lucas, father of our baby." She watched him warily, imploring her mind not to fall for this man's shrewd speech. How many times had he convinced her he was Lucas only to turn into Nick when she let her guard down? Lindsay's mind was so filled with fear she was unable to decipher the nightmare from reality—wondering whether she would make it back home alive, injuring her ankle, seeing so many young, innocent men die because of her, being beaten, and fearing for her unborn child's life had caused something to click in her mind. It was as though Nick was everywhere. He had become everyone. Until she was home safe with her baby, she would trust no one. This man kneeling before her, talking softly, was obviously another of Nick's shifty tricks. Well, she wouldn't fall for it again. She wouldn't be taken alive by him.

Her eyes watched him intently, glazed and hazy with uncomprehension. Lucas watched her closely, if she started to plunge that knife into her chest he would grab it, hopefully before she had done too much damage.

Time stood still in the cave as the only audible sounds were those of breathing and rain falling heavily to the ground. A bolt of lighning seared the sky, thunder roared. The noise gave Chico the cover needed to make his final approach. He lunged forward, wrapping his arm around her shoulders and pulling her backward. Lucas reached for the knife and wrested it from her fingers before the peal of thunder had abated. Her eyes grew large and beaten. She fell onto her side, sobbing pathetically. She might have been able to defend herself against Nick . . . but two men. No, she was beaten. Lord knows how many more men are waiting outside the cave. She raised her head slightly, looking up. She spoke through sobs, "I'm sorry, Lucas. I tried. I tried to save our baby. She laid her head on the blanket and cried. She could fight no more.

* * *

She was in pain beyond caring. The blanket had fallen, exposing her soft white shoulders. Lucas tenderly wrapped the blanket around her tucking it under her chin. He did not leave her side. He stroked her face gently as she cried. He spoke softly, almost cooing, he mixed English with Spanish.

Chico stoked the fire, put a pot of coffee in the flames and began to cook some food. He brought Lucas a wet cloth, looked down at Lindsay, and shook his head in concern. Lucas wiped gently at her tears, all the while urging her mind to believe his presence. Eventually her crying stopped but every few seconds a sob escaped.

She rolled onto her back, brushed at the curls on her cheeks and opened her eyes. She looked up into the ice blue eyes of the man bending over her. Her lips formed his name but no sound came out. "Lucas!"

Groping, as one who is blind, she reached a hand, caressing his lips, moving to his cheeks, across his nose and down his chin. She sat up slightly, reclining on her elbow. The blanket fell from her and exposed her pink-tipped breasts. Excitement bubbled up from, what moments ago, had been depths of despair. "Lucas, oh my God, is that really you?" With difficulty she shifted her weight, trying to get closer to him. A sudden smile came and she glowed with happiness. The smile touched her eyes and even with the bruises and cuts, dirt and tears, Lucas marveled at her beauty. "Lucas," she breathed the name again and again. "Lucas . . . Lucas . . . Lucas." She folded her hands together, holding them in front of her, staring at him. She drank in every inch of skin, every black hair, every lash, every twitch of his muscles. With a startling shriek, she threw herself against him, wrapping her arms around his body, inhaling his manly smell. They embraced tightly, neither willing to let go.

Lucas reached for the fallen blanket, pulling it around her, shielding her naked body from Chico. Shortly he pried her fingers loose and pushed her away from him, lovingly. He held her hands and began asking her what had happened. Why had she left her uncle's ranch so close to the birth? How had she gotten to this cave? On and on he questioned. Lindsay answered, caring about nothing except his nearness.

Chico called to them. "*Alimento, mis amigas.*" The food was ready. Lindsay's mouth watered as the aroma of the sizzling ham assailed her nostrils. She was starved. Lucas stood and reached to help her up. She held the blanket securely around her and began to stand. She cried out and fell back onto the bed. Her eyes filled with tears as she looked up at Lucas. Her lips trembled and a lump formed in her throat as she tried to speak. With the excitement of seeing Lucas she had forgotten about her ankle. Lucas bent down, his eyes questioning. "What is it, niña? What's wrong?" She pointed to her ankle.

A deep audible breath escaped from his lips as he examined the ankle. Then reaching down, he held her foot in his hand and gave her some instructions which she was unable to follow. After probing the swollen flesh he said, "You know it's broken, don't you, Lindsay? How in hell did you expect to survive out here with a broken ankle, a baby due any minute, and a maniac searching for you." He paced gruffly and kicked his hat. Then he returned to her side, seething.

Lindsay laid her arm across her eyes, attempting to shut out his fury. Tears of shame bubbled over and ran down the sides of her face. "I only wanted you. I wanted you to be near for the birth of your child. I wanted to see your face when your son was born, I . . ." she stopped, unable to continue. Lucas reached for her and gathered her in his arms. After a few minutes he tilted her face up, wiped away the tears with a corner of the blanket, and kissed the tip of her nose. He went to the fire, fixed two plates of ham and beans and returned to her with their food. He sat beside her as they ate in silence. Chico sat across from them. After they had finished Chico took their empty plates.

Lucas stood and looked at the scattered contents on the floor of the cave. He spotted the towel, picked it up, and ripped it into long narrow strips. Then he gathered some long, thick sticks of wood and returned to Lindsay. "Honey, I've got to bind that ankle. This is going to hurt but if it isn't done right away your bone will heal crooked. He looked at her, feeling her pain. She nodded.

Chico came to her side as she lay back and he drew the blanket up to her knee. He placed his hands on her thigh, holding the leg prone. Lucas picked up the sticks and laid each one against her ankle, comparing their size. He selected two and turned his attention to wrapping her ankle with the towel strips. He wrapped two strips around her ankle, pulling them securely. He grimaced when she moaned. Chico held her leg and smiled at her. Lucas placed the sticks along the inside and outside of her ankle. They extended almost to her knee. Then he wrapped them tightly to the leg with the strips of cloth. When he had finished, he wiped the sweat on his brow and looked at her. Her eyes were closed and wet. He knew the pain had been unbearable but she had not uttered a sound or attempted to move. He wiped her face with a cool cloth. He removed his boots and lying beside her he took her in his arms and held her. She finally slept in the protective circle of his arms. For the first time in many weeks she slept without suffering the recurring nightmares. A smile touched his lips and he looked down at her and whispered, "Tomorrow, I'll take you home."

* * *

The sun smoldered on the horizon, trying to creep into the morning sky. Lucas opened his eyes. Lindsay's deep, regular breathing continued undisturbed as he lay watching her. The swelling around her eyes and her lips was down a little—not quite as bad as yesterday. Her hair fell over her breasts, wisps of curls hugging her white skin. He touched a curl, rolling the hair in his finger, savoring the feel of its softness. Her stomach was swollen. So large, he thought, for such a little girl. As he lay looking at her belly a movement caught his eye. He laid his hand on her stomach and smiled proudly as the baby kicked. "Soon my fine, strong child, soon you'll be free to enjoy the world, to gaze upon your beautiful mother, to learn your heritage." His heart filled with pride, his love overflowing as he held his woman in his arms.

* * *

The sun burst forth, spreading glowing warmth on the land. The storm had passed on during the night. It was going to be a beautiful, sunny day. Wisps of clouds skittered through the sky in chase of the storm. Birds began their morning chirping, waking their families, preparing for their search for food.

Chico stretched, stood and walked outside. Lucas listened as his footsteps diminished, then shortly returned. Lucas watched Chico start the fire and soon smelled the pleasant aroma of freshly brewed coffee. Lindsay opened her eyes and yawned. She looked at Lucas and snuggled closer to his muscular body. "Ummmm . . ." she placed a warm kiss on his cheek.

"Good morning, niña. Did you sleep well?"

"What do you think?" She began to tug playfully at the mat of hair at the base of his throat.

He grasped her hands and said teasingly, "I've been told it is not good to make love to a woman far advanced with child. Continue and we'll find out if that is true."

She giggled, rolled away from his grasp, and attempted to sit up. The pain in her leg made her groan and Lucas reached out to her. "Your leg, niña?" She nodded. Tears of pain were evident. He motioned to Chico who came to them holding a flask. Lucas opened it and held it to her lips, instructing her to swallow a mouthful. "The whiskey will help numb the pain, niña. It's all we have with us." Lindsay took a mouthful, swallowing the strong liquid quickly. Her eyes widened as the fiery fluid burned her throat, causing her to gasp for air. It took several seconds for her to speak and when she did, she glared at Lucas. He laughed. "Just relax a minute, niña. Soon the whiskey will help ease the pain."

She lay back, watching the men prepare for their departure. She was suddenly certain she was safe. She felt warm and secure. She wrapped her arms around her much enlarged belly, hugging the unborn baby.

The fire was extinguished, the scattered contents of the satchel picked up, the blankets rolled into neat rolls, and the scraps of food thrown to the birds.

Chico left to bring the horses as close as possible to the entrance of the cave. Lucas turned to Lindsay.

"Now, niña, if we can get you dressed, we'll start for home." He walked to the dress laying on the rock, picked it up, and bent to retrieve the chemise. He returned to her, sat down, and reached to pull the blanket from her body. But she held on.

"No, Lucas, let me dress, alone, please."

He looked at her. "But niña, I can help you. After all you have nothing to hide from me. A warm smile touched his eyes. She blushed, lowering her eyes to her hands.

"I know, Lucas, but . . . but, well, I can dress myself. I would rather dress alone, please."

Lucas understood.

"Lindsay, if you think I will find you less than beautiful because of your large stomach, you're wrong. You're the mother of my child, soon to be my wife, the reason I live, the reason I would die. I am a sandy beach, you are the waves that wash over me constantly, cleansing me, refreshing my soul. Lindsay, I love you more than anything I have ever known." He kissed her tenderly. His lips hungry for the touch of hers.

Tears of happiness fell from her eyes. Tears of wonder at the words he had spoken. She removed the blanket and Lucas helped her dress. He picked her up to carry her outside when she spoke. "Lucas, the cradle . . . don't forget the baby's cradle." She pointed at the wrapped bundle standing against the cave wall. Lucas looked at the cradle and back at Lindsay. A frown touched his brow. "Uncle Ned made it, Lucas, he gave it to us. I won't leave it. Please," she pleaded.

Lucas nodded and as they walked outside he asked Chico to carry the cradle out and tie it on Lindsay's horse. He placed Lindsay on his horse and turned to look at the countryside. The sun bathed the hills in yellow light. Lucas turned to mount behind her when she again spoke.

"Lucas, I nearly forgot. Scotty and Uncle Ned will be returning here in a few days. If they find me gone, they'll worry. I have to leave them a note. I'll explain you came for me and they can meet us at your ranch, for our wedding." Lucas fumbled through the satchel and finally found some paper and the pencil Scotty had brought for her. She wrote:

"Lucas has come. We are heading for the ranch today. We'll be moving slow as I have a broken ankle. But all is well. Join us at home—Lucas's home for the wedding."
                                            Love, Lindsay

She drew a map and instructions to the Sanger ranch. Chico sandwiched the note with rocks near the firepit. Lindsay took another swallow of whiskey and the trio made off, winding their way down the mountain into the dry river bed and through the narrow gully.

They rode for several hours. The warm sun helped to heal Lindsay's cut face, the nearness of Lucas helping to heal her fears.

Lucas held Lindsay close, talking to her frequently, kissing her brow and reassuring her constantly.

Lucas figured they were about three days of hard riding from his ranch but they would travel slowly, avoiding the steeper and rougher terrain. The trip would probably take at least six days. He looked down at Lindsay's protruding belly. She was due any time. She had said she had another two weeks but with the ordeal she had suffered, well, he just might be delivering their baby real soon. Thank God, he had seen women give birth. At least he wouldn't be shaking in his boots when the time came. He knew what to do and hoped when Lindsay's time came he would be able to do it with some of the ease he had seen in the old Indian women at the reservation.

* * *

The sun was setting, reflecting brilliant colors from the tops of the red plateaus. They had traveled slowly but steadily, stopping only once to eat. Lindsay hadn't complained of pain during the day and Lucas marveled at her strength.

They camped on a grassy area, ponderosa pines and cedars surrounding them. There was no water around but they had ample drinking water in their canteens. Lucas carried Lindsay to the campfire Chico had started and set her on a blanket, careful to keep her leg straight. He set her satchel beside her and she dug through it searching for her comb. After finding the precious item, she began tugging at the snarls and tangles in her long, dirty hair. It was hopeless and she desperately wanted to be a little pretty for Lucas.

"Lucas, can I please bathe tomorrow? I mean, if we should pass a stream or river. I don't think I can stand another day without a bath."

He smiled. "I think that can be arranged, niña."

The horses were hobbled for the night, eating from their oat bags. Chico had prepared a meal and they were sitting around the fire, watching the flames leap and flicker.

"I'll keep watch tonight, *amigo*." Chico stood, scanned the horizon and walked off. Lindsay watched him. She could see nothing around her. A few stars blinked but there was no moon to aid his watch.

"How can he tell if anyone is out there?" she frowned.

"When you have spent your life watching, waiting, you soon need only your instincts, little one. Eyes only help at the last minute." Lucas wrapped his arms around her and laughed. "Don't worry your pretty little head, niña. If anyone gets too close, Chico will wake us. Take my word, no one will surprise us like they did your group."

At the mention of that, she lowered her eyes. Thoughts of Pete dying in her arms came back vividly. She began to shiver. So many deaths because of her. Lucas laid back beside her, tucking the blanket securely around her.

"Do you want to talk?"

"I, I don't think I can. I mean, I don't know what to . . . oh, Lucas, they killed every one of the men, every one shot before he even knew what was happening. All because of me." She began to cry. She buried her face against him. He let her cry and finally she slept quietly.

He looked at her. Dried tears hed left streaks of dirt on her cheeks. Her wounds were healing. The swelling had gone down. He ran a finger down her cheek, around her mouth and down her throat.

"I'll kill Nick Moriarity, niña. Until he's dead you'll never be safe, not completely safe. I swear, I'll kill him, niña."

* * *

Chico lit a cigarette, the flame from the match illuminating his face. He inhaled the sweet smelling tobacco and looked at the sleeping couple, "I hope, *amigo*, your senses have not dulled since love has changed your thoughts. Now, more than ever, you need a sharp wit."

He looked into the heavens. A few more stars glimmered down at him. "Ah, but I guess like Lita, she is worth it friend. Yes, a good woman is worth it."

Chapter 31

Dawn burst on the little camp. A bee buzzed around Lindsay's face, her lingering scent attracting him. She rubbed her nose and turned on her side. Lucas sat up, surveyed the countryside and nodded to Chico. He let Lindsay sleep while he and Chico prepared a meal.

They had ridden several hours when Lindsay's back began to bother her. At first she tried to ignore the irritating little twinges of pain. As they increased in strength, she rubbed her back and finally asked, "Can we stop for a few minutes, Lucas, I don't think I can go much farther with my back aching like this."

Lucas looked down at her, apprehension washing over him. He glanced at Chico who returned the look. "Just a little farther, niña. We'll stop at the river." She smiled wearily. Lucas lowered his hat over his eyes and placed a hand on Lindsay's stomach.

Finally they reached the river. Lucas spread a blanket under a small pine and helped Lindsay get comfortable. Chico watered the horses and hobbled them in the shade, oat bags over their faces.

Lucas walked to Lindsay, knelt down, and put his hand on her stomach. He felt the beginning labor pains tighten and relax.

"Lucas, I don't know if I can ride much farther. My back is really bothering me."

"Niña, you're in labor." Her eyes and mouth flew open. She stared at Lucas incredulously, then looked down at her belly. Lucas held her hand and finally she spoke.

"Well, at least my dream will come true. You'll be with me for the birth of our child." She rested her arm across her brow and laid back.

"Are you frightened?"

She nodded and tears began to fall from her large questioning eyes.

"Niña, don't be. I'll be here to help you," he said reassuringly, his finger tracing the path of one of her tears.

She looked at him. "I love you, Lucas."

He bent and kissed her. "And I love you, Lindsay."

Lucas looked at Chico. "We won't be riding any more today, *amigo*." Chico nodded and began gathering fire wood. Soon a fire burned and a pan of water bubbled in the coals.

Lindsay's pain grew stronger each hour and blood droplets appeared on her lips where she bit them to keep from crying out. Lucas and Chico spent the morning preparing for the birth. Lucas sat with Lindsay, sponging her face with a cool cloth, talking, kissing her fingers, and reassuring her. Chico kept watch on the horizon. His eyes seeking out dust clouds that could foretell trouble.

Lucas pretended to be calm and hoped that Lindsay couldn't tell of his fears. He had been present at two births, assisting at both. But Lindsay. This was his woman giving birth to his child. He felt so helpless as he watched her writhe in agony. The pains tore through her body and she panted and groaned. The pain from her ankle was nothing compared to this. She had been afraid she wouldn't be able to move freely with her injured leg. But the pain of labor wiped out all feeling in her leg. She tossed and turned as though her leg was not bound with splints. She bit her hands, clawed the ground and finally she screamed. Sweat soaked her dress, her hair was plastered to her skin and her face was white as she strained to give birth.

Lucas wiped her dry lips with a wet cloth. "Relax, niña. Try to breathe with the pains, not against them. Honey, please, it's going to get harder. Try to save your strength."

But Lindsay's mind was blurred with pain. She pushed with each contraction, pushed until her lungs had nothing left. She pushed until she felt as though her brain left her body and hung suspended above her. No matter how she turned and pushed, she felt more pain.

Chico brought two round, smooth sticks and pounded them in the ground beside her arms. He took her hands and placed them on the wood. "When you need to push, these will help, *chica.*" He looked down at her momentarily, remembering another girl, another birth. Lindsay shut her eyes and smiled weakly at Chico. He nodded and walked away.

She wrapped her hands around the sticks and pushed with all her strength when the pains came again. She pushed so hard she bent one and Lucas straightened it and pounded it deeper into the earth.

The afternoon lumbered slowly while the sun beat down relentlessly. There was no breeze to cool her and Lucas wiped her skin continuously with a cold cloth. Lucas brushed away the fly that buzzed irritatingly around her face.

"It's so hot, Lucas," she whispered weakly, "so hot, so dusty, no place to have my . . ." A scream tore from her lips and grew in intensity as she flailed in agony.

Lucas checked her and began issuing orders. Chico held a knife in the flames as he watched Lindsay and wondered how much more she could take. Lucas grabbed a pan of water and set it beside Lindsay's hips. He gathered the pieces of blanket they had torn up for the birth and began talking to Lindsay in an even tone. "Okay, honey, here we go. When I tell you to push, you push. Our baby's ready to be born, niña, he's almost here." Lucas wiped her face. "Push, niña, push, push!"

Push, push, push . . . the words slowly diminished, disappearing.

* * *

She opened her eyes but couldn't see anything except a white, hazy fog. Her arms were so weak. Too weak to grab onto the sticks. She tried to move her hands, move them to her face, but she couldn't feel them. Groggily she thought about searching for her arms later when she felt better. She heard a baby cry a long way off. But Lindsay's mind was not comprehending anything right now. She had suffered so much pain her mind had retreated and now she floated above the ground, a long way up. She felt disjointed, uneven as though she were very, very drunk. She closed her eyes. She thought she heard Lucas talking but she was too tired to care. She couldn't remember ever being this tired. Dried tears mixed with sweat, and blood from her cracked lips clung to her pale skin.

Lucas bent to her. "Niña, it's a boy. A beautiful boy. Thank you." He kissed her tenderly as he covered her with a blanket. He kissed her tenderly as he covered her with a blanket. Lucas carried the bundle to Chico and proudly displayed his son to his friend. They sat together talking, touching the child, amazed at the whole thing. Chico held the baby as Lucas checked on Lindsay. He wiped her face and watched her breath as she slept peacefully. He walked back to Chico.

Lindsay woke slowly, awareness filtering back. She tried to sit up. Lucas pushed her back gently on the blanket.

"Rest, niña. How does it feel to be a little mother?"

"Does he look like you?" she questioned.

"How did you know it was a boy, niña?"

She smiled faintly, her eyes half closed. "What else would your first born be?" She raised her arm to point at Chico, but it fell weakly back to her side.

Chico walked to her, knelt and moved the blanket from the baby's face. He held the little bundle in front of her and the men watched Lindsay's eyes widen as she looked at her child. Chico laid the baby in Lindsay's arms and she stared unbelieving at the tiny face. She pulled the blanket down and gazed at her red, wrinkled son. The baby rooted and fussed, then found his fist and sucked contentedly on his fingers. Lindsay's eyes closed and Lucas watched her sleep peacefully, holding their son.

The smell of sizzling meat invaded her senses and Lindsay woke. The sky was black, laced with stars and a quarter moon rocked above her. She brushed her hair from her eyes then jumped at the sound of her son crying. Lucas walked to her, smiling broadly and carrying the baby. He hunkered down and laid the baby in her arms. She smiled as she eagerly accepted her son. Lucas watched as she lowered her dress and shyly put the baby to her breast. His little mouth rooted, searched almost in a frenzy, then found a nipple and began to suck. Her breath came out in a low, long gasp as the baby clamped down hard and she laughed. "His jaws are strong for such a little thing."

Lucas threw his head back and laughed deeply. He was content in his new role. Lindsay moved the blanket from around the baby and checked him over. She checked his fingers and toes, touched his ears and nose. She caressed his hair and ran a finger down his cheek.

"He's so beautiful, Lucas, so beautiful. He looks like you, Lucas, his hair, his eyes—just like his father." Lucas bent and kissed her long and soft on the lips. When he stopped, he looked into her eyes, searching her soul and she returned the look.

After the baby had been fed and lay sleeping by Lindsay's

side, Lucas brought her a plate of food. He sat beside her and helped her eat. She was very weak and he watched her for several seconds, then frowned. She saw the frown and asked, "What's the matter Lucas, is something wrong?"

"You, niña. How are we going to travel with you so weak?"

She lowered her eyes to her baby. "I'm fine. By tomorrow I'll be ready to move on, just you wait."

Lucas nodded as he thought. How can I make her ride the day after giving birth? After she finished eating, Lucas kissed her and went to sit with Chico. They sat by the fire drinking a mug of coffee and their voices carried to Lindsay as she nursed her baby.

"Chico, I can't take Lindsay on a horse tomorrow. I can't expect her to ride mile after mile after just giving birth." Lucas looked on the horizon and squinted. "But we can't stay here either. The longer we delay leaving the better chance Nick has of finding us."

Lindsay silently vowed she would be up and walking in the morning. She would ride if it killed her. She would not endanger her baby or her man.

Lucas walked to her and looked down on the baby nestled in his slumbering mother's arms. He folded his arms over his chest and smiled as he heard Chico.

"Well, *amigo*, you did a good job. Course she didn't do too bad either."

"*Gracias*, friend," Lucas replied. "Now to get them home safely."

"Let's have a drink, *amigo*. We deserve one, no?"

They sat by the fire and drank from the flask of whiskey.

"Damn, Chico, Lindsay's in no shape to travel. Her leg needs tending by a doctor. She should be checked to make sure everything's all right from the birth. We have to watch for Moriarity and his men." His voice raised, "And you know damn well he's waiting out there." His eyes looked at the surrounding countryside. "How many men will he have this time? How do we hide with a baby? A baby that cries and needs to be in a home and oh, shit, Chico." His voice trailed off and he took a gulp of whiskey.

Chico looked at the ground, his hands resting on his legs.

"Lucas, I have known you many years. Now we have a problem we have not had before." He looked at Lucas. "*Amigo*, we will make it. We will get them," he pointed to Lindsay, "safely home. Fighting isn't what worries me, it's her." Chico stood, stretched and walked into the darkness. "I'll be close, *amigo*."

The stars shone on the desert in lavish numbers as Lucas stood and peered into the darkness, searching for Chico. "Thank you, *amigo*, thank you."

He went to Lindsay and lay beside her, snuggling close. The baby whimpered but Lindsay slept undisturbed. He could hear her soft, even breathing, feel her heart beating. He drew her closer to him, wrapped his arm around her and kissed her brow. "Nothing will happen to you, niña, nothing."

The morning sun rose with grays and reds. A hot breeze touched Lindsay's face and she threw her arm over her eyes to block out the sun. Then she opened her eyes and reached for the baby.

"Morning, niña," Lucas smiled from the fire as he held his son on his lap. The baby cooed and gurgled. He brought the baby to her and she put him to her breast, gasping again as he gripped a nipple. When his tummy was full and he had been diapered, she laid him on the blanket and began to stand.

Lucas took her by the arms and helped her up. She stood weakly in his embrace for several seconds, her head spinning dizzily. After a few minutes, she straightened and smiled. "I'm okay. I think I need to bathe, Lucas. I would feel so much better if I could clean up a little." She saw the hesitation in his eyes and added, "Please, Lucas, please."

Lucas frowned, "I don't know, niña, I don't know if a bath would be good so soon."

Her shoulders slumped wearily and she lay against his chest.

"Lucas, I have not bathed for so long. I'm going to take a bath with or without your help." She hugged him, "but it would be easier with your help since I can't walk with this splint." She tilted her face and peered at him pleadingly. "Please."

"All right you little baggage, but I'm warning you, if you so much as move without my help I'll take you over my knee and wallop you good . . . after you're well." She giggled and hugged him again.

He picked her up and called over his shoulder, "Chico, watch my son, will you? I'll be back shortly."

"*Si.*" Chico walked to the sleeping baby and sat beside him.

Lucas carried Lindsay to the river. He laid her on the sand and helped her strip. Although she had given birth less than twenty-four hours prior, her body had already begun to return to normal. Her belly was flatter and she giggled as she looked at her toes and saw them.

Lucas removed the splints and frowned.

"What's the matter, Lucas,"

"Lindsay, your ankle isn't healing right. There's something wrong. I think we should stop in Santa Fe and see the doctor." He threw the splints on the ground and lifted her naked body into his arms.

"No, Lucas Sanger, I'm not going into Santa Fe. You know very well Nick will have men waiting there for some sign. I'll be fine. Just give me a little time to heal. Lucas, you are not going to take me or my baby into Santa Fe." She looked at him with fear in her eyes.

When he reached the river's edge he laid her in the cool water. She gasped. Then as she got used to the coolness, she relaxed, laying back, letting the water cascade over her body, over her face and over her hair. She laid several minutes reveling in the feeling of being cleansed. Lucas hovered over her, ready to grab her if anything should happen. She opened her eyes and peered up at him.

"Why, Lucas, you act as though I'm going to float away, in six inches of water," She laughed gaily and he laughed with her.

Finally, after he felt she had bathed long enough he reached down and picked her up. He dried her body with a piece of blanket and put the soiled dress back on her.

Don't worry, *niña*, at the first chance I'll buy you a new dress." He smiled at her despair at having to wear the same dirty dress. He placed the splints on her leg and carried her back to the blanket. As she snuggled the baby, he walked to his horse and returned to her carrying her shawl. He tossed it to her. "Here, niña, this will cover some of the soiled dress." She picked up the shawl and held it in front of her.

"Where did you get this, Lucas?"

"From my saddle bag," he grinned. She looked at him then sighed.

"Oh, you. Well, it isn't important now but you better tell me later." She wrapped it around her and spent the next several minutes struggling to comb the snarls from her hair.

Chico prepared a light breakfast and they leisurely sipped their coffee. The sun moved higher and the ground warmed. Finally Lucas stood and announced.

"I think we should try riding a ways. Lindsay, we'll make a special pad from a blanket for you to sit on. We'll ride for a few minutes and then stop and let you rest." He hunkered down in front of her. "Niña, if you tire or hurt, tell me. We'll stop whenever you need to." She smiled and nodded.

That's the way they traveled for the next several days. Slowly. Lindsay was made as comfortable as possible, but her leg banged and bounced and the pain became more and more severe but she didn't complain. When the horse would lurch or stumble, she winced, bit her lower lip, and gasped but she said nothing. She knew if she did Lucas would take her to Santa Fe and she didn't want to go there. She was frightened of Santa Fe. Nick Moriarity would know they were there.

Lucas watched Lindsay closely. She seemed to feel fine from the birth. The baby ate hungrily when put to her breast and she had no problems with her body following the delivery. But her leg was not healing. The swelling and discoloration had worsened.

After debating as to the dangers of taking Lindsay into Santa Fe to a doctor and being seen by Nick versus the very real possibility of her losing her leg, Lucas made the decision to ride into Santa Fe.

They were a few hours from town when he announced his decision to change direction and head in for help. Lindsay was adamant against going into Santa Fe. Chico said nothing. They had stopped under a clump of trees to rest. The horses were pawing the ground, angry at the lack of sweet grass. Lucas lifted Lindsay and the baby to the ground, setting her next to a tree where she began to nurse the child. Lucas stood over her, watching his son suckle. "He sure has a big appetite for such a little mite."

Lindsay looked at him with icy eyes, her voice cold.

"If you think I'm going into Santa Fe and risk the life of this baby just so a doctor can check my leg, well, you are utterly mad. I will not take the chance. I'll wait until we're at your ranch. I don't want to discuss it anymore." She looked at her baby, her eyes softening.

Lucas rested his arms on his hips, his feet wide apart.

"There may be some people you can order around and some who'll listen, but get this straight, I don't intend to repeat it. You will do as I damn well tell you. No back talk. You're going into Santa Fe. You're going to have a doctor tend you and you are going to be a lady while doing it, mouth shut, understand?" His eyes were dark, his brows drawn together.

Gooseflesh popped out on Lindsay's skin. She remembered when he used to talk like that so long ago.

"Go to hell." She didn't look up.

He bent to her, placed a finger under her chin and turned her face up to his. "We shall see, niña, we shall see." He turned and walked to his horse.

Damn her, he thought, damn her ability to irritate me, but damn her most for not trusting me enough to think I could protect her and the baby. Damn her! He jerked the saddle from his horse, startling the animal which shied away in fright. "Sorry, boy, just my nasty temper." He attempted to soothe the skittish animal.

The sun hung low in the sky now, a big yellow ball, clouds hugging its sides like waves washing over its flatness. The day had been warm, a promise of hot summer days to come. The air was still. Beads of perspiration glistened on Lindsay's face and she wiped her brow with her sleeve.

Chico walked off, searching for a place to better survey the countryside, always on the watch, always aware of his surroundings.

Lindsay longed desperately for a cool bath. Her temper was short, her body sticky. She caressed her son's face as he sucked greedily on her nipple. She glanced up and her eyes rested on Lucas. She watched his muscles rippling under his damp shirt, the material clinging tenaciously to his skin. She watched him remove the saddles, easily tossing them to the ground. He lifted the cradle down and rubbed his knuckles along the padded side. He turned to look at her and smiled as he realized she had been watching him. Blushing, she quickly returned her attention to the baby

He came and sat beside her. "Niña, have you decided on a name for our son?" He leaned back and rested his head on his arms. She didn't look up.

"Yes, I meant to talk with you before, but, well, I wanted to see if you brought up any names. Would you mind terribly if he were called Lucas Theodore? We could call him Neddy until he gets older, then Lucas or Ned."

He turned on his side, resting his head on his arm and running his free hand down her thigh. "Lucas Theodore. That sounds fine to me. I was afraid you'd have some high fallutin' name like Clovis," he laughed. "Lucas Theodore." His hand traveled up her body, his finger caressed her breast.

"Stop that, Neddy's nursing." Her voice was unconvincing.

"I'm sure he won't mind, niña, the only part he's interested in is in his mouth." He smiled as his fingers moved around her breast and up her throat. His fingers felt hot to her skin, burning a path as they continued to fondle her. She began to feel helpless, melting, bending to his will. She pulled Neddy from her breast and quickly covered herself. She handed the baby to Lucas hoping this would stop his growing ardor. It was too soon to lie with Lucas. As much as she wanted to feel his body on her's, his manhood deep within her, she could not.

"Here burp your son. Maybe that will keep you occupied for awhile."

Lucas laughed. The sudden movement frightened the baby and he began to cry. Lucas held him close and comforted him, patting him on the back. Lindsay pulled herself up and hobbled to the horse, dragging her splinted leg, leaning on a long stick for support. She wrapped her arms around her waist and smiled as she gazed upwards. A big white cloud slowly floated by. She watched it, leaning against the side of the horse. Finally she turned to walk back to Lucas. She stumbled and caught herself, putting her weight on her broken leg. A pain shot up her leg and into her stomach. She reached out to grab for the horse but he shied away. The ground loomed closer as she fell. She lay on the ground, gasping for breath, her face wet with perspiration, the pain bringing waves of nausea. Lucas laid the baby on the blanket and bounded to her.

He rolled her over and smoothed the hair from her face. She was white, her eyes shut tightly, her breathing uneven. He started to move but her hand gripped his arm.

"No, please, just hold my hand a few minutes." Lucas knelt by her side, one hand gripping hers and the other smoothing her wet brow. This is how Chico found them.

"What happened, *amigo*?"

"We must get her to a doctor fast." Lucas's voice was filled with worry.

Chico saddled the horses, wrapped the sleeping baby in a blanket and mounted his horse, holding the infant close. Lucas looked at his friend, a sigh of appreciation coming from his lips. Lindsay attempted a weak protest but Lucas had her in his arms and on the horse before she could speak. Chico led the extra horse and they rode off swiftly, faster than they had ridden since the birth. The jarring caused Lindsay to scream in pain. They slowed at intervals to allow her to rest but they didn't stop.

Toward dusk they spotted Santa Fe. Wagons and horses riding through town lifted large dust clouds to float over the area. These dust clouds mixed with the gold sunset portrayed an eerie picture. Lindsay shivered as she opened her eyes and gazed down. Something in that town was evil, something that would hurt them. She spoke shakily, barely audible, "No, please don't take me . . ." But Lucas ignored her, squeezed her once and kept riding.

Before entering the main street, they veered to the left,

entered a dusty alley and continued. They hadn't gone far when they stopped and Chico tethered the horses. Lindsay opened her pain-filled eyes and looked around. It was hard to see anything as shadows bathed the buildings but she could see they were next to a large, freshly painted building. Music came from some far off interior room and a flickering light bounded off the window above her head. Lucas disappeared inside, leaving Chico holding the baby and supporting Lindsay, his hand on her back. She smiled weakly at him but when she tried to raise her hand to motion to the baby, she couldn't. Everything had become so difficult, every movement brought pain.

Chico whispered, "*Chica*, soon you will be well, your body as well as your spirit." She had no strength to answer.

Lucas returned and gathered her in his arms. He walked to the open door and Lindsay saw a woman standing partially in the shadows holding the door for them. They entered and the woman closed the door, gathered her billowing skirts and pushed in front of them. She led them down the hall, through a door, down the stairs, and into a dark room. A match struck and a flame pierced the blackness. A lantern soon bathed the room in soft orange light. Lindsay's head lay against Lucas, her face white and beaded with sweat. The woman felt her brow. "She's burning up with fever, Lucas."

She walked to the bed and drew the quilt back, exposing white, fresh sheets. Lucas laid Lindsay on the bed. Her eyes were closed and her face was so pale she looked as if she were made of porcelain. Chico said he would go get the cradle and walked out the door.

"Thanks, Millie," Lucas smiled.

She nodded and turned to the door. "Your horses have been taken care of. The doc has been sent for and no one knows this room is here except me." Opening the door she continued, "I'll be back shortly." Then as though she had forgotten something she nodded at the baby, "How old is it?"

Lucas looked at Neddy and then Millie, "I . . . he's five days old."

Millie shook her head, her curls bouncing, "My God,

Lucas, no wonder she's in that condition. Traipsing around the countryside. Five days old." She walked out.

Chico knocked softly and after announcing his name he entered. He set the cradle at the foot of the bed and began unwrapping the blankets. Millie came back with an armful of clean bedding and a pitcher of water. She watched Chico unwrap the cradle and when it stood exposed they all stared at it. The carving was so intricate, so delicate. Millie fixed a blanket in it and lifted Neddy, holding him a few seconds before she laid him gently in the cradle. She turned to Lucas, straightened her shoulders and spoke sharply, "Five days old, why she's in no condition to be . . ." A hand clamped over her mouth as Chico bent to her and said, "Come, *chica*, I'll buy you a drink."

Lindsay lifted her head weakly. "But, Chico, you can't. What if someone sees you?"

"Don't worry your pretty little head, let me do the worrying, *si*?" He walked to the door, his hand on Millie's elbow and guided her out.

Lindsay struggled to sit. "Lucas, where's the baby?"

"Niña, he's alseep in the cradle, right there," he pointed, "and in a very lovely cradle, I might add." Lindsay laid her head back and smiled weakly.

"What do you think is wrong with me, Lucas?"

"I think you have an infection, niña." A touch of anger laced his voice. "Next time you're injured, you'll not stop me from tending to you. If you hadn't been so damn stubborn this wouldn't have happened. You'll have no more chances to defy me, niña." He bent close to her and she felt his breath on her skin.

A knock startled him and he pulled his gun and cocked the hammer, "Who's there?"

A muffled voice answered, "I have the doctor, *amigo*."

Lucas went to the door and opened it slightly, peering out. A tall, thin grey-haired man with glasses resting on his nose stood in the dark hall. His face was tanned and wrinkled with years of hard work. Chico stood beside him and Millie behind them. Lucas opened the door wide and they entered. The doctor walked to the cradle and gazed down at the sleeping baby then went directly to Lindsay. He placed a hand on her forehead. "How long has she had this fever?"

"I don't know, about a week, I think."

The doctor wasted no more time. He laid his bag on the bed, threw his jacket over the back of a chair, and rolled up his sleeves. He pointed to Chico and Lucas.

"I may need your help." He pointed to Millie. "You keep hot water and clean sheets handy, please."

He reached down and gripped Lindsay by the shoulders and turned her to him. She groaned and opened her eyes. Lucas rubbed her cheek. "It's all right, niña, the doctor will help you."

"You hold this leg up so I can take the dressing off." He pointed to Chico who bent to the task. Lucas stayed close to Lindsay's face, talking softly, smoothing her hair from her glistening skin.

The doctor proceeded to remove the makeshift splints and although he worked fast, he was gentle. Soon the leg lay exposed. A large, black, swollen sore on the top of her foot oozed and streaks of discoloration ran upward, some reaching as far as her knee. The odor was strong and Millie made a face. The doctor lifted the leg, examining it closely, probing and touching. Lindsay lay quietly biting her lower lip, gripping Lucas's hand but uttering no sound.

"She has an abscess. It needs to be lanced and drained. The bone is healing nicely. Whoever set it did well."

The doctor opened his bag and laid several surgical instruments and jars on the bed. He handed a couple of strange-looking devices to Millie with instructions to immerse them in boiling water for five minutes. He worked steadily. He prepared tools, checked solutions, and laid a clean sheet under Lindsay's leg. Then he ripped another sheet into small squares and set them beside her. After he was satisfied that everything was in order he looked up and smiled crisply.

"Lindsay, that is her name, correct?" He looked to Lucas for confirmation. "I'm going to cut open the sore on your leg. It's filled with infection. That's why you are having so much pain. As soon as it's drained you'll feel a great relief. Your fever will break and you will heal." He walked to the washstand and scrubbed his hands. Turning back to the bed he said, "This isn't going to be pleasant. If any of you have a weak stomach, I suggest you leave now." When no one moved, he continued, "Okay, then I'll need your help." He pointed to Chico, "You hold her leg steady for me. Don't let her kick or I could slip with the knife, understand?"

Chico nodded as he sat beside her, gripping her leg. To Lucas, "You keep her occupied, talk to her. Don't let her sit up."

Millie cleared her throat and softly called to Lucas. When he acknowledged her she held her finger to her lips as though to silence him and pointed to Lindsay. Lucas understood. He would not let Lindsay scream. Millie had sneaked them down here. A scream would arouse suspicion—something they didn't need.

The doctor bent to his task. He worked with a flourish. Millie had to stifle a giggle as she watched him. I bet he wanted to be an actor when he was young, she thought.

Lindsay's eyes were squeezed shut, she gripped Lucas's hand with all the strength she had. His face was close to hers and she could feel his warm breath. The pain was bad but nothing like childbirth. When the knife cut through the diseased tissue a scream came to her throat and she swallowed hard several times attempting to extinguish the sound. Because of her stupidity and stubbornness they had had to come to Santa Fe, possibly risking all their lives. If anything happened to Neddy, Lucas, or Chico, she would never forgive herself. She swallowed the screams that tried to escape.

The doctor straightened. Sweat dripped from his brow onto the bedding.

"There, I think that'll do it. She'll be fine now." He walked to the washstand and splashed water onto his face and neck. Then he turned back to the bed and wiped his hands on a towel.

"You have a healthy looking baby there." He nodded in the direction of the sleeping child. "Don't look to me like you need any help there." He smiled at Lindsay, tossed his instruments into the bag and closed it. He ran his fingers through his hair, put his hat on and walked to the door. Reaching for the handle he spoke, "On the table there's a bottle of medicine. Give her a teaspoon every four hours. It should help the pain." He walked out and closed the door.

Lucas sighed and turned to Lindsay. She opened her eyes. Millie bustled around cleaning up and ordering Chico around like a houseboy. After she was satisfied, she went to the door. "Don't anybody leave. I'll be back in a minute with food." She left the room, the sound of her footsteps disappearing on the stairs.

After they had dined on flour tortillas, tomatoes and beef, the men and Millie enjoyed a glass of brandy while Lindsay nursed Neddy. Chico said, "I'm going to take a walk, look things over."

Millie admonished him to be careful. Several of Moriarity's men had been seen earlier in the saloon. Millie walked to the bed and looked down at the baby. "Can I hold him, Lindsay?" Lindsay nodded. Millie picked up the tiny bundle and sat in the rocking chair. The baby had a full tummy and dry bottom. As he lay in Millie's arms he opened his eyes, attempting to focus them on the face above him. His eyes would cross and straighten and Millie giggled delightedly at his antics. Lucas and Lindsay watched the bond of friendship forming between their son and this warm lady. Millie raised her head, her eyes moist. Lindsay liked this happy, carefree woman who had given them shelter. It was obvious that Millie was in love with Lucas, yet she showed no animosity toward her. Perhaps Millie knew her love for Lucas was meant only to be a sister-brother love. Whatever Millie felt, she didn't show it and Lindsay grew fond of her during the few days the woman offered her hsopitality.

One morning Millie swept into the bedroom without knocking, startling Lindsay and Lucas. Her bright yellow satin dress was fringed with yellow roses that almost matched her blond hair. Her curls bounced and jumped as she walked to the bed, smiling.

"*Chéri*," she spoke to Lucas, "I'm going shopping. I stopped to see if there was anything special you would like." She played with the fan tied at her wrist and stared at Lindsay's hand resting on Lucas's leg. The sheet covered only his hips and his legs lay crossed on the bed. Millie's eyes swept him boldly, then taking a deep breath, she looked away.

"What else did you want to tell us, Millie?" He knew her well enough to know she was stalling. Lindsay held the blanket under her chin watching Millie with a touch of pity.

Millie looked down at her dress, plucked at a piece of lint and sighed. "Well, I just thought you should know . . . Nick's in town." Lindsay's eyes opened wide. Millie's fan stopped. Lucas stood and walked to the table holding the sheet around his waist. Suddenly he raised a clenched fist overhead and brought it down quickly on the table. The resounding crash startled the baby and he began to cry. Lucas stared at the wall, his thoughts a jumble. If he made his move here, would he have many men to deal with? If he baited Nick and set a trap, would he fall for it?

Millie's hand shook him, disturbing his thoughts. "Lucas, I'll talk to him, find out why he's here and where he's going." Lucas looked at Millie. Her face reflected the concern she felt.

"No, Millie. It might make him suspicious. I'll think of something."

She patted her curls and turned to the door. "I'm not lucky like some people I know staying in bed all day." She opened the door disguising her concern with a gay theatrical flourish. "I have shopping to do."

Chapter 32

"I tell ya, Nick, that's him. That's the lousy bastard that was riding with Sanger." His voice was agitated. "I'd know him anywhere, even in a drunk room and me drunk on my ass, I'd know him. Sanger must be here. Let's find him, let's find the bastard."

Moriarity's eyes fastened on the drink before him. The

amber liquid sloshed over the sides of the glass as he slammed it down on the bar. "Okay, gather the man and meet at the river." His eyes narrowed as his thoughts went to revenge. He ordered another drink and moved to a table. He sat and rested his feet on the table, his thoughts wandered to Lucas Sanger and the woman.

* * *

"Tony, Tony Perez." The voice pierced his consciousness as Tony walked from the bar to his horse. He turned and watched Millie approach, her hand outstretched to him. She placed her hand on her heart. "Mercy sakes alive, I'm almost out of breath from chasing you." She smoothed her dress and continued. "Tony, how are you? Why, I heard you had an accident and I thought we would never see you again." She stopped and looked at his face. When he didn't speak she continued, "Why Loralee was so upset after that night she had an attack of the vapors just talking about it. Finally, she quit and left for California. Said she couldn't stand the memories. Hated to lose her. She was a good girl." Millie's voice trailed off.

Tony looked at her then up at the sky. "Yeah, she was a good little doxy."

"Loralee told me some halfbreed took you away, right out from her bed. Why, I was so shocked to hear, I nearly fainted away."

Tony looked at her then turned to his horse and mounted. "Keep the beds warm, Millie. I'll soon be back." He smiled at her and rode slowly out of town. A frown touched her brow as she walked across to the general store. She was loading up with supplies when she saw Nick Moriarity climb on his horse and ride after Tony.

I have a bad feeling, she said to herself.

* * *

Lucas stared at the floor, Millie's words penetrating his brain.

"I just know they're planning your ambush, somewhere

out there." She waved her hand in the direction they left.

"Oh, *chéri*, a man who called hîmself Johnny Diego was in the general store buying tobacco. He asked Tom, the storekeeper, how far it was to your ranch. Tom didn't know. I followed him outside and stopped him. He told me he had to find you because he had an important note from a Ned Tyler that had to be delivered to you as soon as possible. I told him your ranch was not far from here but that maybe I could help him. Of course, I had to bat my lashes at him," she chuckled. "Anyway, he was trying to find you to tell you Lindsay was on her way. He wanted you to know she was coming and be prepared. I told him that information was mighty important and he should start right out. He had a map but he didn't know how much farther. I figured you didn't need his message and sent him on to your ranch." She laughed and Lucas was amused.

"I wonder why Uncle Ned sent him to tell you?" Lindsay looked at Lucas.

"Why, niña, I have no idea," he said and threw his head back and laughed. Chico joined him. Lindsay stared at them perplexed.

"Well, what do you plan to do about Nick?" Millie interrupted.

Lucas smiled at her and touched her cheek. "Don't worry, *chica*, I've been in a lot worse situations." The statement was true but never before had he a woman and baby with him.

Chico was leaning against the wall, his arms folded across his broad chest. "He's the only one that could have recognized me. Nick never saw me in Durango. Damn."

Lucas stood abruptly. "Well, we better prepare to leave right away. The sooner, the better. Give's him less chance of getting ready."

Lindsay sat on the bed holding the baby. Her eyes were large and frightened. Lucas walked to her and leaned down, putting one hand on each side of her hips. "Niña, don't look so frightened. I've fought with men far more cunning them him." He tossed his head backwards.

Millie gave Lindsay a pair of pants and shirt and moccasins which fit over the bulky dressing on her ankle. Lindsay asked Millie to dispose of the dress she had worn so long, the bloodstained, dirty dress. She wanted no part of it. She braided her hair in two long braids, letting them hang down her back. Then she turned her attention to Neddy. She took a blanket and knife and began working diligently on the bed. She asked Millie for a needle and thread.

Lucas and Chico saddled the horses, rewrapped the cradle and checked everything. They stopped to watch Lindsay, puzzling over her labors.

The sun was leaving the sky. Streaks of red filtered through the clouds when they finally finished eating and prepared to leave. Lindsay wrapped the remodeled blanket around her neck and tied it at her waist. She picked up Neddy and put him in it tying him safely. His arms and legs hung free but his body was held against Lindsay's.

"I saw the mothers at your camp carry their babies on their backs. Why can't I carry mine in front?" She looked at them as they stood watching her, surprise plainly on their faces. Lucas walked to her and kissed her brow, "Just like a little Indian mother." She limped to the door, saucily swinging her hips. "There are some attributes I possess that you can't see, Lucas Sanger." She opened the door and walked out. Chico lowered his eyes, trying to suppress the merriment as Lucas walked past him.

"Hmmm," he said to his friend.

They joined Lindsay on the stairs and Lucas helped her up them and down the hallway. Suddenly a door opened and a voice spoke.

"Lucas, Lucas, you stop right now." Conchita stood at the open door, her feet apart, her hands on her hips. Lucas and Lindsay both turned to her.

"*Querido*, how long have you been here?" She walked slowly to him, swinging her full hips.

"Not long, why, Conchita?" he replied easily.

"Don't play games with me, *querido*. Did you just get here? Are you leaving? What's going on? I think you owe me an explanation?" She looked at Millie.

"I'll see you later, Godspeed." Millie kissed Neddy's brow and walked down the hallway.

"Millie, thank you for everything," called Lindsay.

"Anytime, Mrs. Sanger, anytime." She didn't look back.

Conchita's eyes widened and defiance crept into her eyes. "Mrs. Sanger?"

She looked at Lindsay, her eyes staring intently into her face and then she noticed the baby. She stared at Neddy.

"Who is this Indian woman? This baby?" She walked a few steps closer to Lucas.

"This is Mrs. Sanger and our son Lucas Theodore. Lindsay, this is Conchita." Lucas spoke lightly, smiling at the lie. Neither woman spoke. They continued to stare at each other, each seeing in the other an enemy. The hatred emanating from Conchita's eyes was almost tangible. Lindsay unconsciously backed up, trying to escape her eyes. Lucas's hand on her back stopped her. He looked at Conchita. "Did your rich man take you to his *hacienda*, chica? Last time I talked with you, you were excited about having such a rich boyfriend. Are you still planning the wedding?" His words were mocking.

He guided Lindsay to the door, his hand possessively on her. "We have to go. Send us an invitation to the wedding, Conchita." They walked outside, the air cool on their skin. He stopped beside the horse, "Conchita, I wish you all the luck in the world. I mean that." He looked at her. She stood defiantly in the doorway, her hands at her side, gripping her skirt. After Lindsay was secure on the horse he walked to Conchita and placed a finger under her chin.

"Chica, you knew it would never be anything more for us than what it was. You knew that. I never told you any different. Don't play with me, Conchita, I know you too well. You only wanted my money." He turned back to Lindsay then stopped, "I wish you much luck, Conchita." He mounted his horse and slowly they rode down the dark alleyway.

Tears coursed down Conchita's face and she brushed at them angrily. "*Puta, mentirosa,* damned *puta,* I hate you Lucas, you're *horrendo,* you and your *puta.*" She slammed the door, leaned against it, and wept. The sound of horses hooves diminished long before she stopped crying. Then, straightening her skirt and brushing back her hair she walked down the long empty hallway.

Chapter 33

They rode quietly before Lucas finally spoke, startling Lindsay who was buried in her thoughts.

"Are you frightened?"

Yes, she was afraid, but not for herself. She was afraid for Neddy and Lucas. She had seen what Nick was capable of. She was sure he wouldn't hesitate to kill them.

The tone in her voice belied her true feelings. "If I said I weren't frightened, I'd be lying and you'd know it. I know you, I know what you're like." Lucas's hand, which had been resting on her thigh, squeezed it gently.

"Lucas, who was that girl?" She tried to keep her voice light but there was a note of concern in it.

"Niña, she is no one to concern yourself about. She was around before you and she'll be around for many more men." He kissed the top of her head and the words reassured her.

They made camp before dawn. Now they would travel at night and sleep during the day until Nick's plan became clearer and they knew how many men he had. Until then, they would keep hidden. Lindsay fell into an exhausted sleep the instant her head touched the bedroll. She slept undisturbed for several hours, waking to the baby's cries of hunger. Drowsily she put Neddy to her breast and looked at Lucas. He was standing with Chico, gesturing at the horizon. They were discussing something fervently and Lindsay's curiosity was piqued.

Lucas turned, saw she was awake and walked to her. She admired the graceful, catlike way he walked. He knelt to her and brushed her cheek with his hand.

"Niña, we must leave. We've changed our plans." Her eyes widened in concern. "I know how hard this is for you, Lindsay. I know how frightened you are but it's going to be all right, trust me."

She reached out and laid her hand on his shoulder. The feel of his muscles under her fingers caused her to tremble with desire and a taut bowstring snapped in her belly.

"Darling, I do trust you. Oh, I do." She kneaded the flesh under his shirt, causing his blood to stir. The fire he constantly felt for her leaped up, flaming. He bent forward, his lips brushed hers. She laced her fingers through the black curls that grew unkempt down the back of his neck. When his lips left hers she grabbed his arm and pulled him down to her. She kissed him again, hungrily, longingly. A grunt of surprise escaped his lips as Lindsay's tongue probed his mouth, seeking, yearning for those past memories of their feverish lovemaking. Lucas's tongue searched her sweet mouth, his fingers twining in her braids. He was leaning close, the baby between them, completely forgotten for the moment. Suddenly Neddy stopped nursing and let out a squawling cry, displeased at being crushed between his parents. His startled parents looked down at him. Lucas backed away, his gaze lingering on Lindsay's soft, inviting lips. He ran a finger over her mouth and down her throat, stopping at the base where a pulse beat wildly. Tearing his eyes from her face he looked down at the unhappy baby. With a lazy smile touching the corners of his mouth he smoothed the soft down on Neddy's head.

"I have never seen such a young chaperone," he said, his voice thick with passion. He stood and looked down at Lindsay, her face flushed.

"I certainly am marrying a hotblooded bit of baggage." And turning he strode gracefully back to Chico who discreetly had his back to them.

Lindsay soothed her unhappy son as she thought, soon my magnificent man, soon you will not be able to walk away from me. She looked down at Neddy and ran a finger over his cheek. And you, my fine little interloper, you will definitely have your own room. She smiled and hugged him close as his eyes closed in needed slumber.

The group had eaten and when the sun began its descent they rode on, changing direction. They rode through pine trees scattered among juniper shrubs and wild grass. They rode for two days, the scenery changing constantly but always beautiful. They climbed into the mountains, where the weather cooled slightly and the trees got thicker. They again slept at night and rode during the day and Lindsay wondered how much longer she could take this abuse.

They traversed lava-capped mesas and canyons cut deep by rivers. They climbed high peaks until Lindsay thought she could reach up and touch the clouds. Then they dropped down into green gullies with a ribbon of silver water flowing through them. Lindsay never tired of the constantly changing scenery but she did tire of the endless riding. Her bones ached, her leg ached, even though Lucas made sure it was healing and gave her sips of the medicine the doctor had given them. She longed for a bed, longed to lay with Lucas in private. Although it was her stubborn, willful choice that brought her here, she nevertheless felt entitled to one night in a bed. At least, Lucas had been with her when she had Neddy. One consolation for all this, she mused.

They crested a mountain and were dropping down into another canyon. The trees were a thick carpet beneath her eyes. She could see nothing but pine trees reaching upward. They continued down and then turned back, hugging the mountain following a trail. They rode for a few hours and Lindsay sagged wearily against Lucas's chest. She had just closed her eyes when she heard the bubbling of a brook. Water! She opened her eyes and a shiver of anticipation at bathing ran through her blood. She opened her mouth to speak when Lucas reined in the horse, stopping quickly. She turned her head and looked at two Indians standing several yards in front, their rifles pointed directly at Lucas and Chico. Their eyes were cold and unwavering. Lindsay gasped in fear, her eyes wide as she held her baby close to her chest. Lucas, hearing her gasp, laid his hand on her shoulder and squeezed it reassuringly. Soon the strange Indian faces relaxed, their eyes softening as they recognized Lucas. Raising their rifles in the air, they turned making a sign for Lucas to follow. The Indians mounted their horses and they rode off slowly.

Again they rode for what seemed to Lindsay, hours. Just when she was ready to scream out that she could take no more she spotted a ribbon of smoke. She raised her head, her eyes studying the dense grey smoke as it lay in the sky thickly, then dissipated. Soon she heard the sound of voices, children laughing, horses snorting. They wound their way through trees, around rocks, across a brook and then, Lindsay's eyes widened, as she took in the Indian camp. Tepees were scattered around a broad, flat area. Children played, dogs barked, horses pawed the ground. The smell of cooking meat lay over the area and several Indians watched their approach. They rode through the camp and stopped in front of a tepee set to the side. The children stopped their games and watched them with hooded, dark eyes. Five braves followed them, speaking in their guttural tongue. Lucas lifted Lindsay down and held her hand as he talked with the men. A young boy led the horses away and Chico carried the cradle into the tepee. Lucas pushed aside the flap and helped Lindsay inside. A stream of light came through the open smoke flap. A bedroll lay against one side and a circle of rocks, blackened by fires lay in the middle. A deerskin covered part of the dirt floor. Lindsay looked at Lucas frowning.

"This tepee is kept for the chief's son," he smiled at her. "I am the chief's son, niña."

"But Lucas," she pointed a finger, "I thought your family lived that way."

"They were forced to move again, niña."

"Then, since you have not been with them, how did you know where they would be?"

"Niña, I always know where my people are. They have been forced to move for many years. They leave signs for their lost children. That part of me that's Indian always knows his way home." He sat on the bed. The grass underneath him smelled sweet. He motioned for her to sit beside him. He laid the baby in the cradle and sat down, resting her head on his shoulder. The baby gurgled, found his fist and fell asleep. Lucas and Lindsay sat quietly, holding each other and soon, they slept, too.

Lindsay's eyes flew open as she rolled over and reached for Lucas and found he was not there. She listened. The camp was quiet except for an occasional dog barking. She got up and checked on Neddy. He still slept, his fist in his mouth. She laid back on the bed and turned her head when she heard footsteps. Lucas walked in, smiling at her when he saw she was awake. His eyes glittered like blue diamonds as he studied her face. The way he looked at her. She felt shivers of icy delight run down her spine. Lucas came and sat beside her. The corners of his eyes wrinkled and Lindsay reached a hand up touching his face. He held her hand against his cheek, then to his mouth and pressed warm, lingering kisses in her palm. His lips moved to her brow, her nose, her lips. He kissed her lightly, then impatiently kissed her harder, his tongue deep in her mouth. His lips moved to her throat and he kissed the pulse there. His fingers unbuttoned her shirt and her white breasts gleamed in the diminished sunlight filtering through the smoke flap. They looked ivory. His tongue played with her nipples making her gasp with delight. He kissed her breasts, then sought her mouth again. Suddenly, as though he had been struck by lightning, he stood, looked down at her and spoke in a thick voice, "Niña, I'm sorry, it's too soon. It's not good this soon after birth." Lindsay reached her hand to him, smiling impishly. She pulled him back down beside her and laid her head against his chest and moved her hand down, down to his legs. And there she found him, hard and hot, moving rhythmically now and willing. Lucas smiled, "What a devilish creature I have for a squaw." He laid beside her, holding her close, crushing her to him when he climaxed. She ran her fingers over his chest, playing with the mat of hair, planting kisses on his hot skin.

"But what a wonderful squaw.'

Afterward they lay entwined together, enjoying the closeness of each other. Lucas spoke, touching her face with his fingers. "Soon, my love, soon we will share what you have given me tonight."

Lindsay slept, content in her man's arms and content in the knowledge she had satisfied him.

* * *

Lindsay's mind slowly climbed to awareness as a thick, wet fog leaves a marshland. Dully she groped to a waking state. Suddenly, as though doused with a bucket of cold water, her eyes flew open. The baby's crying made her jump up, wincing as she put too much weight on her ankle. Lucas was gone again and the rising sun cast shadows on the tepee. She had slept undisturbed through the entire night. Something she had not done for many days. After Neddy was fed and changed she laid him in the cradle, gently caressing his head as she talked to him. His eyes closed and she walked outside. The brightness caused her to close her eyes and she raised her arm as a shield. She stood like this for several seconds looking like a beautiful Indian maiden.

Standing in front of a tepee across the camp, Lucas stood talking with Spotted Fawn. The moment Lindsay stepped from the tepee, Spotted Fawn's gaze left Lucas and fell on her. With a venomous voice she asked.

"Why did you bring her back?"

"This is my home. I see no reason not to bring my woman, my wife, and son here."

His gaze followed Spotted Fawn's and on seeing Lindsay, her golden hair, her tawny skin shining brilliantly, his eyes softened. His face filled with pride. But this moment was pregnant with tension. Spotted Fawn looked back at Lucas and seeing the change on his face stared cruelly at Lindsay, aiming her hatred at this woman who stood now, perhaps forever, between her and her warrior.

Lindsay spotted Lucas and smiling broadly started walking to him. He wore a buckskin shirt open to his waist, leather pants, and high topped moccasins. His hair grew down the back of his neck, curling up, and the stubble on his face had become a short beard making him look quite savage. Just before Lindsay reached him, Spotted Fawn turned away, a contemptuous sneer to her voice.

"You should not have brought her back here." She stomped off.

Lindsay, hearing the venom in the woman's voice,

stopped in her tracks. She watched the receding back of the woman she hardly knew. As she stood watching Spotted Fawn walk angrily away, Lucas came to her and wrapped his arm around her waist.

"Don't worry, niña, Spotted Fawn is inappropriately named. She has never been tranquil like a fawn, but tempestuous like a raging wind. Come, we have no time to think about Spotted Fawn."

Spotted Fawn watched as he led her away. "You will be sorry, Lucas. You have made me a fool. For that you will be sorry." She flung the words bitterly at the back of the man she thought would marry her. Lindsay shivered slightly.

"Are you cold, niña?"

"No, but I have a feeling that girl means to cause me trouble, Lucas."

Lucas laughed. "Niña, you worry too much. Come, let's go eat. I'm hungry and don't intend to let anything ruin my appetite."

The day was a quiet, enjoyable respite from the constant riding they had done. Lindsay spent most of the afternoon visiting with Little Bird, catching up on all that had happened. Little Bird played with Neddy and she smiled, her eyes moist, when Lindsay nursed him. "I don't mean to be foolish, but he's so beautiful."

Lindsay touched her arm. "Little Bird, I don't think you're foolish. I think it's important you can feel so deeply. When a person can cry over a loved one or cry when she's happy, well, to me that person also loves deeper, and lives life fuller. Well, Little Bird, to me you are one of the warmest and most gentle persons I know."

Little Bird smiled shyly at Lindsay's words and when Lindsay had finished nursing Neddy, she took him from her and cuddled him, talking softly to him. Lindsay buttoned her shirt and watched Little Bird.

"Why have you never had a baby, Little Bird? If I'm stepping out of bounds by asking, tell me, but you are so natural with children, so loving. I should think you would have a dozen by now."

Little Bird looked at Lindsay, a smile touched her lips, then she laughed, her eyes twinkling. Lindsay was puzzled.

"What's so funny?"

"I'm not laughing at anything funny, Lindsay. I'm laughing because I'm happy. War Eagle and I are going to have our first child this fall."

Lindsay stared at Little Bird momentarily, and then shouted, "Oh, Little Bird, that's wonderful, that's just great." She hugged her and Neddy squirmed. "I'm sorry, Neddy." Lindsay grinned as she patted the baby's back.

The women talked about the coming arrival and Neddy for another hour and Lucas stood and watched them after he left his father. He smiled as they talked and gestured. The baby slept between them on his stomach. Motherhood became Lindsay. She glowed with accomplishment.

Lindsay jumped when Lucas placed his hand on her shoulder. "Sorry, niña, didn't mean to scare you." She touched his hand and smiled.

"Well, have you two had a pleasant day?"

Little Bird nodded and excused herself. It was time to prepare a meal for War Eagle.

"Well, niña, are you ready to visit my father?"

Apprehension washed over her. She remembered Grey Wolf well, remembered his inscrutable look which had brought color to her cheeks. She felt overwhelming shame at having to face this man with a baby and no husband. Her fears were unfounded however for Grey Wolf showed no emotion, his eyes veiled during their visit until Lindsay handed him Neddy. Then the stately old man smiled. Grey Wolf gazed on the child's face and Lindsay was sure Neddy smiled at his proud grandfather. They left Neddy with Grey Wolf and went to eat. When they returned to pick up the child, Grey Wolf looked at Lindsay, nodded his head, and smiled. He held the baby close and spoke.

"He will have two names. A white man's name and an Indian name. He will be called Little Hawk by his father's people. He is strong and his eyes see much, like the hawk."

Lindsay said nothing but her heart quickened at his words. Lucas nodded in approval.

Grey Wolf looked at Lindsay. "You are the mother of my grandson. You will be called Little Fire Woman." Lindsay looked surprised and Lucas grabbed her hand and squeezed it. "Father, the names you have chosen for both suits them well. I am honored."

Grey Wolf continued to stare at his grandson. Finally Lindsay bent over and reached for the baby. "I must feed him." She smiled but her eyes mirrored a little fright. Grey Wolf handed her Neddy and motioned for her to come closer. She did. He lightly kissed her cheek and Lindsay gasped in surprise. Her eyes widened and she looked at Lucas. He shrugged. She turned back to the Indian and kissed his cheek. "Thank you for the name. I'll be back tomorrow." She turned and walked out of the tepee. Lucas touched his father's shoulder and followed her.

Dark shadows crawled over the camp. The sun sunk below the hills and the tepees became quiet as the families ate and the children were put to bed. Lindsay settled Neddy for the night and sat beside Lucas who was wiping his revolver with a cloth.

"Lucas, we can't stay here forever. I mean it is your home but Uncle Ned will probably be at your ranch any day, desperately worried if we aren't there."

"We'll leave as soon as the information I need arrives." He returned to cleaning his gun.

"But, Lucas, surely Nick has given up looking for us by now. It's been so long, he'll never find us. Let's go home. Let's go to your ranch."

"Lindsay, Nick will search for us until the day he dies. He won't stop until he's killed us whether it be today or years from now. Take my word, niña, I know him. He'll stop at nothing. I can't take that risk with you and Neddy, Little Hawk. We'll wait and solve this once and for all." His voice was controlled and Lindsay knew if she went on she would make him angry. She turned her attention to straightening the bed, glancing at him while he continued cleaning his weapon. Both were engrossed in their separate thoughts and neither heard the soft footfalls diminish. They were unaware of the figure who stealthily crept away from their tepee, hid in the shadows, and then disappeared into the night.

Chapter 34

"I don't know, Nick, this could be a trap." The man pushed his hat back on his head and suspicioulsy eyed the girl sitting by the fire.

Nick Moriarity rested his chin in his hands, his eyes glancing from the fire in front of him to the girl across from him.

"What's your name?" he asked coldly.

"I am Spotted Fawn."

"What do you expect to gain from this?" He leaned forward, "and why do you want to see Lindsay dead?"

Spotted Fawn lowered her eyes. "Money, I want money."

Nick laughed loudly. "What the hell do you want money for?"

Irritation bubbled up as she spoke. "Why should I not have white man's money. There are things I, too, would like."

"A damn Injun. Shit. What do you want except guns for killing and knives for scalping?" Amusement gleamed in his eyes as he taunted her.

Indignation welled up in her. "I came here free. I can leave here free. If you are not interested in what I have to say, tell me. Do not treat me foolish."

"Nick," Tony called from the rock he was sitting on. "Can I see ya over here?"

Nick rose from the fire, his eyes studying the girl. He walked to Tony and turned to watch the Indian girl.

"Nick, listen, she just may be on to something. I mean, Lucas does go to see his pa. Well, if he's there now maybe we just oughta see about making our move there."

Nick looked sharply at him. "Are you crazy? Those goddamn Indians would kill us before we got within half a mile of that camp."

"Not if we have her help. Don't ya see, Nick, she could cover our approach for us. I think we oughta look into this real serious like before we make any decisions."

Nick rubbed his hand across the stubble of beard on his face. After several moments of silence he raised his head, looked at Tony, and spoke.

"Okay, we'll hit Sanger, his kid, and ol' lady in the camp in the middle of the night, with knives, no guns, no noise. We'll sneak in with her help. She can lead us through where no guards will be posted. We'll have a better chance if only a couple of us go, though. You, Ben, and I will go in. Let's go talk to her." He nodded his head at the girl and the two men walked to the fire.

Tony smiled broadly, his white teeth gleamed in the firelight. He had waited long and patiently for this. Damn! He might even sample Lindsay's charms while Sanger lay dying. He rubbed his hands together, anticipation emanating from each pore as his mind slipped into thoughts of bittersweet revenge.

Nick grabbed Spotted Fawn's arm and pulled her roughly to her feet. He bent close to her face, his breath hot on her skin.

"Now, I'll tell ya whatcha gotta do, little gal. And if you think o' double crossing me, well, you'll wish your death was as easy as Lindsay's is gonna be."

Spotted Fawn shivered as she watched Nick's scowling face. His fingers dug into her flesh and she flinched.

"That ain't nothin' compared to the pain you'll feel if you don't follow my orders exactly."

"Do not kill Lucas, only the woman and baby." She spoke softly as she stared coldly into his face.

He pulled her to a tree and shoved her against the rough bark, leaning one arm beside her and bent close to her face.

"You don't tell us who we kill and who we don't. All you gotta do is make sure we can get into that camp with no one seeing us. We'll show you a signal and you take us to Sanger's tepee. Then, you lead us back to our horses. If anyone does see us or anyone tries to stop us, I'll kill you."

Spotted Fawn had no doubt he meant what he said. Maybe she had gotten herself into something more dangerous than she had anticipated. Her palms were sweaty and she rubbed them on her skirt.

"Well, you got the orders straight, gal?"

She nodded.

"Good." He walked to the fire. "Tony, take her to her horse and tell her the signal. I'm gonna get some shuteye."

Spotted Fawn relaxed slightly but she tensed as she looked into Tony's face. She flinched as Tony reached out and grabbed her face, pinching her cheeks.

"Ben," Tony smiled cruelly, "Ya know this little gal ain't too bad lookin'. Maybe she should taste a real man. Ya know what I mean?"

Spotted Fawn began to struggle as his words penetrated her numb brain. Ben smiled, his broken teeth exposed to view. "Well, now that ain't a bad idea. No sirree, that just may be what she needs." He grabbed her other arm and the two men pulled her along into the trees.

* * *

She hadn't expected to be treated so badly. She had offered them information they were only too anxious to get, but no amount of money, no amount of hatred was worth what they had done to her. She knew she had to do something before it was too late. But what? What could she do now that would help? She had gotten into something she couldn't get out of. She had hurt her people. The white men would kill Lucas as well as any other person that got in their way. Lindsay was only the beginning of their killing. Why had she let her jealousy cover her senses? Nothing had become as important as getting even with him. Now she would have to answer for many deaths, not just the white woman.

She fell forward, her head on the horse's neck. The cruel way those man had used her was something she had not thought about. She was so stupid to have expected to ride to them, sell them her information, and ride back to camp untouched. She shuddered as she remembered crawling back to her horse. It took her so long to climb on. She kept falling to the ground, lying in her blood, sobbing. The things they had said about her, their laughter finally gave her the determination to mount her horse. Now she was picking her way home and each bump from her horse caused pain to slice her body. She could feel the blood dripping onto her feet, feel it run down her legs and over her toes.

She shuddered as she recalled the rape. Thankfully her mind had filled with smoke, curling, soaring, escaping the pain. She had never completely passed out but her mind blocked out the torture, the tying of her arms and legs to the stakes, Injun style the men had said. They ripped her clothes from her body and that hurt. She cried as she remembered the entry of the first man, his hot rancid breath on her face. Then there were the others. She lost count after four. One had screamed at her to kiss him and when she didn't his fist slammed into her face. She could feel her lip split and taste the blood as it mingled with her tears and ran down her face. When she finally opened her mouth to scream, he had hit her harder. She waivered on consciousness. Her mind struggled to escape the pain but the men kept throwing water on her. They wanted her awake, fighting, enjoying. It's an honor for an Injun woman to have a white man they kept saying over and over and over.

Tony kept calling her Lindsay. His face was buried in her hair and as he moved in her he kept repeating Lindsay's name. He plunged deeper and harder and Spotted Fawn could feel the blood begin to run down her legs.

The moon lit her way as she continued to climb the hill. The horse walked slowly, picking his way carefully. The pain was beginning to shred her brain. Lights flashed in her mind and colored spots danced before her eyes. She had to make it to camp before she bled to death. She had to tell them. She glimpsed a beam of silver light reflected from a fire in a tepee. As though the horse knew his rider was badly hurt, he broke into a gallop, rushed directly into camp and stopped abruptly. She fell to the ground, landing in a heap in the dust, groaning and writhing in pain. She opened her eyes when she heard voices. Gently, hands turned her over. When her face was exposed, she heard gasps. She tried to smile but nothing moved. Her mouth was filled with dirt and blood, her lips were raw. Blood pumped ominously from between her legs. She was lifted, carried, and laid on a soft bed. She was safe. Cool cloths were laid on her face. What was left of her clothing was removed and she was examined carefully. After she had been cleansed and wrapped in a clean blanket, Little Bird placed a poultice of herbs on her face.

Lucas and Chico entered her tepee. Lucas bent to her.

"Spotted Fawn, who did this to you?" She opened her eyes but it was hard to see. A thick wall of fog stood between her and Lucas and she raised her arm to brush it away. Her hand fell back weakly. "Who did this, Fawn?" Lucas's voice was touched with anger and worry. Fury suffused his entire being, anger that anybody could do this to a woman, anger that she left the safety of the camp, anger that she wouldn't answer him.

"I'm sorry." Her words were barely audible.

Lucas touched her shoulder, "Who did this?" His voice was raised.

* * *

The sky was a light pink, slivers of orange touching the somber faces of the people standing outside the tepee. Lucas walked out and looked up at the waiting group. His face was grim, his arms hanging at his side. His fingers opened and closed, flexing and relaxing, as though he were choking someone.

Lindsay walked to his side, touched his shoulder and waited. He looked down, his eyes rested on her upturned face.

"Spotted Fawn is dead."

Lindsay looked at Lucas, a myriad of expressions crossed her face before he spoke again.

"Before she died she told me what she had done. She gave up fighting, willed herself to die."

He pulled Lindsay into his embrace, holding her tight for

a few moments, then, "We must talk." He looked at Chico and the men. They nodded. "Niña, you go back to the tepee with Neddy." He turned her toward it and patted her on the rump.

The men started gathering in front of Grey Wolf's tepee. There was to be a meeting and it would be a long one. Lindsay was worried. If these men were capable of doing what they had done to Spotted Fawn . . . she shuddered. She lay on the bed. There was absolutely no doubt in her mind. She would kill herself before she would let those animals touch her. She rolled onto her side and rested her eyes on the cradle. How much Neddy was like his father. Could she take his life too if they were threatened?" Nothing must destroy her family. She closed her eyes. She would stand and fight the same as her man. She would not hide. She would not cower. These men would have a bigger battle on their hands than they had ever had.

Chapter 35

The sun was bright and hot when Lucas entered his tepee. He stood momentarily letting his eyes adjust to the diminished light and then walked to Lindsay. She lay sleeping, holding the baby. Neddy had been nursing and her breasts were exposed. The baby lay contentedly in his mother's arm, sucking on his tiny fist. Lucas looked down on them. His heart filled with pride as he gazed at his son and woman. He hunkered down and touched his son's fuzzy head. The baby opened his eyes and tried to focus on his father. Lucas chuckled. Lindsay opened her eyes. Lucas reached for an unruly curl and twisted it around his finger. His eyes were dark and unreadable.

She reached out a hand and touched him on the cheek.

"Is it going to be bad, Lucas?"

"Not for you, niña."

She sat up, buttoning her shirt. The baby cried in displeasure and she soothed him. She turned to Lucas.

"What do you mean, not for me? Where in the hell will I be?" She laid the baby in his cradle and turned back to Lucas. "If you think I'm going to be hiding while you're fighting, well, you think again, Lucas Sanger. I have a right to defend my own too. I'm fighting by your side." Her face was white, her lips grim.

Lucas threw his head back and laughed for several seconds and then ran a finger lightly up and down her arm.

"Niña, you will follow orders. You will be with the women. There is nothing else to say." He tilted her chin with his hand. "You're such a beguiling bit of baggage, I don't intend to risk you again. No, niña, you'll do exactly as I say and if I have to tie you again, I'll do so."

Lindsay sucked her breath in, anger making her clench her fists. She walked to the opposite side of the tepee and faced Lucas.

"Listen, you stubborn man, I can shoot as well as any man, I can ride a horse as well and better than many. I can help, Lucas." Her hands went out in a supplicating gesture. "Please, let me . . . let me stay with you."

"And what do you suggest we do with Neddy while we fight?" He took several steps toward her. "Niña, what would happen to the baby if we were killed?"

She saw her opportunity and pounced on it. "If anything happens to us I want your father to raise him."

Startled, Lucas shifted his weight, his arms akimbo. "Lindsay, do you realize what you're saying? Do you have any idea what kind of life that baby would have here? Oh, honey," he shook his head several times. "Someday I'll have to explain a few things about these people." He swung his hand wide in an arc, "Niña, what you see now isn't the way it always is. If Neddy were to be raised by my father his chances of reaching manhood are slim. White people don't like Indians, that includes babies and women and children. Niña, you saw what happened to Spotted Fawn. White men treat Indian women like that commonly. I could tell you things that would make you retch. No, honey, this is not what our life is like all the time. Soon, we will move again as the white man decides he wants this land. And if we fight, he'll kill us all."

Lindsay shuddered as Lucas took her in his arms. "Honey, I know how you feel, I know why you want to help and believe me, if I thought you wouldn't be hurt, I'd let you stay. But, I don't know who these men are. I suspect they're Moriarity's but we can't be sure of anything yet. I will not endanger you. I can't fight and keep an eye on you. I have to know you're safe. Please, niña, try to understand." He tilted her chin up and kissed her nose. His mouth brushed hers and then he kissed her hard, his tongue searching her mouth, probing. His hands caressed her hips, her thighs, her breasts. Lindsay's breath came in shallow gasps as she fought her mounting fervor. But as always, the minute he touched her she lost her will. Exasperating as it was, she smiled to herself. It was nice to have a man who could make you have such feelings.

The camp was quiet the rest of the day. Spotted Fawn lay swaddled in a blanket next to her tepee. She would be buried after the battle. Little Bird prepared the body as best she could. Spotted Fawn would be buried with respect and honor. Lindsay had said no more to Lucas about staying with him but she had not given up hope.

Many of the warriors had ridden out earlier in the day and were now returning. The women had been moved into the hills, their bewildered, frightened children in tow. Only two women were still in camp—Lindsay was one. It seemed so strange not to hear the children playing and laughing and the women talking and giggling. Lindsay stepped out of the tepee and looked around. The sun peeped on the horizon, hanging quietly before descending for the night. Rays of red and purple danced on the tall trees making black shadows dance across the camp. Everything was so quiet. Even the birds seemed to sense the impending battle. They did not sing. She shivered. A feeling of doom hung over the camp, an invisible cloud filled with hatred seeped its contents on the land surrounding her. She looked up, startled, as Chico approached her. He had such a menacing look about him. If she didn't know him she would be terrified. Yet for all his expertise at fighting and killing he had a rather intriguing look, almost savagely handsome. He tipped his hat and smiled, "Chica, are you ready to go?"

Lindsay blinked, her voice soft, "Go where, Chico?"

"Come now, Chica, you have been told. I am here to escort you. Please." He pointed to the tepee. "Gather your things, let's get Neddy. I have little time to argue." It was a clear statement of fact. This was a one that would tolerate no argument.

Lindsay walked into the tepee, gathered the satchel that she had packed earlier and picked up the baby. She'd think of something yet. She couldn't sit idly while her man was fighting, possibly dying. She trembled. Life wouldn't be worth living if Lucas wasn't with her. She walked out. Chico helped her mount and placed Neddy in her arms. He led her to the edge of the camp where she saw Lucas talking with an Indian girl. She didn't know who the girl was but she noticed she was pretty. As she approached them a pang of jealousy pierced her. She stiffened as Lucas looked up. Chico stopped, reached out and grabbed Lindsay's horse by the reins. Lucas smiled lazily, "Why, niña, you look jealous." His mockery irritated Lindsay and she spurred her horse but Chico held the reins and the horse stopped. "Niña, let's not part like this. I want to remember those green eyes full of laughter."

Lindsay tucked the blanket snugly around Neddy, a little embarrassed. With red cheeks, she smiled. Her eyes downcast, she whisperd, "I love you, Lucas." She turned to Chico and he nodded. They rode slowly into the hills.

Lucas watched her ride off and when she was out of sight he turned his attention to the girl.

* * *

Chico led Lindsay deep into the surrounding hills. They hadn't ridden long when Lindsay began to hear sounds of children giggling and women talking. In moments she could see the Indian women and children together. Against the dark sky she saw armed men standing tall and ominous, guarding the group. They were at the end of a high, walled canyon and with the guards it appeared impossible for anyone to surprise them. Clever. She would be only too proud to have her son raised by these people.

After Chico had delivered her, he took her horse to a guard and walked back to her.

"Well, chica, we shall return soon." He pushed his hat low on his brow, rested his hands on his hips and winked at her. Then he turned and strode off. Lindsay followed him. As he reached his horse she called to him, "Chico, wait, please." He turned and waited. She stopped in front of him, her eyes searching his face, her lips trembling. Chico reached out and patted her on the head. "Don't worry, little one, I'll keep an eye on your man." Lindsay relaxed slightly, her eyes softening as she stood on tiptoe and placed a kiss on his scarred cheek. Turning she walked back to the baby, her hips swinging saucily, a bounce in her walk. Chico watched her bend down and pick up Neddy. Then he turned and mounted his horse. "*Mio, dios!* She is a woman!"

Chapter 36

Darkness fell suddenly, like a curtain, covering the countryside. A fire burned in the center of the camp. The flames reached upward, higher and higher as more wood was thrown on it. Several figures danced around it with large, elaborate headpieces. Directing the dancers was the gahe dancer. He wriggled, writhed, thrashed, flailed, and jerked around the fire, chanting and praying to the spirits. Without speech he led the other dancers. Lucas, Chico, and several warriors sat in front of Grey Wolf's tepee watching intently. The men had been dancing for a couple of hours and none seemed inclined to stop. A few stars hung lazily in the dark sky but the moon had not made its appearance. A girl slowly approached the group of men sitting on the ground. Lucas looked up as she stopped in front of them.

"Are you frightened, Nalin?" he asked.

"No, I don't think it is fear I feel. I have asked the spirits to give me strength. It is that the white man is so, so changeable, so unkind. I only hope we are prepared."

Lucas stood and rested his hands on her shoulders.

"Are you sure you want to go through with this? You don't have to if you don't want to." She nodded as she looked at her trembling hands.

"I will not back out now."

"Well, are you ready, then?" Lucas asked.

She looked at him, her mouth set in a grim line.

"Yes, I am ready."

Lucas looked at her as she stood there, trying to be so brave. He thought of his Lindsay. He chuckled as he thought of the differences between these two. Lindsay would be charging and gnawing at the bit to get started, to help fight whereas this girl was quiet, withdrawn, and frightened. Her eyes reflected the firelight and flecks of yellow shone in them. Her long, dark hair hung straight down her back with a leather strip wound around her brow. Her tawny skin glistened with beads of perspiration. Lucas smiled. The men guarding her would stop anything from happening to her even if it meant warning the enemy.

A long shawl was handed to Lucas and he gently wrapped it around the girl's shoulders, drawing it over her face, hiding everything except her eyes.

"You look much as Spotted Fawn did. They won't be able to tell. Remember, your face was bruised and you wish to keep it covered until it heals." He put a finger on the tip of her nose. "Can you remember everything you have been told, Nalin?"

She nodded, her eyes large, the firelight reflecting off her skin.

"Remember, Nalin, these men are killers, do not underestimate them." He took her arm and led her toward the four waiting men and lifted her on her horse. The four men surrounded her and they rode off silently into the night. Lucas watched them and then strode toward the dancing men. He raised his arm high and the dancing stopped.

"It is time." He walked into his tepee. He was sitting on the bed, deep in thought when Chico entered. Lucas looked up and nodded.

"She is safe, *amigo*," Chico smiled, "as safe as she could be." He sat beside Lucas. "What is bothering you?"

Lucas took a deep breath. "I have a feeling Lindsay is going to do something. She's so damn stubborn and she fought me fiercely when I told her she was to go with the women. I just don't know, Chico. She's not the type to sit back and watch. You know that, Chico."

"*Si*, but she won't be able to sneak away tonight. I warned the men to watch her closely. Do not worry, friend." Chico smiled. "We have a long night ahead, a night we have long looked forward to, no?"

They stood and walked out. Everything was silent. The fire burned brightly, crackling, sending shards of flame upwards. To the outside world it looked as though nothing were amiss, but to the men in the camp, anticipation of the forthcoming battle welled up in each belly. A great moment was at hand. Fighting was their greatest triumph.

Lucas returned to his tepee to prepare for the fight. Chico went off to his specified spot and now began the hardest part of any battle.

Waiting.

Chapter 37

"Okay, men, let's get the hell out of here and kill us some Injuns and white folk." Nick laughed heartily, confident that at long last he would witness Lucas Sanger's death.

"Remember, you guys give us two hours then split. If we ain't back by then, something's wrong and I want to know there's someone left to help me. Perez, you and Ben can have any Injun you want, but Sanger is mine."

"Goddamnit, Nick, Sanger's mine. You can have the girl and Scotty, that little sonofabitch. Maybe I should get him too." His eyes drifted to the dark sky, then he came back to the present.

"Them's my orders. You don't like 'em, someone else can go with me instead o' you."

"Well, I don't like it but I'm not staying here." Tony's irritation was evident in his face as he tried to keep calm.

"If there's a problem, take the girl—only keep her quiet. If we have her, Sanger will follow." He walked into the trees. Tony and Ben followed. Tony's thoughts were filled with Lindsay. He lived for the day he would taste her flesh, feel her body under his, relish her lips again. Goddamn!

They had ridden an hour. A crescent moon hung in the sky and stars filled the sky. A coyote howled and bats could be heard, fluttering overhead. The men had traversed a butte and rounded a bend when Nick stopped his horse sharply. Standing several yards ahead was the girl. She held a torch in her hand, the signal. Nick's heart began to beat rapidly. He took several deep breaths.

"Okay, men, this is it." He approached the girl, his eyes studying her closely. When he was a few yards from her she dropped the torch and kicked dirt on it until it was dead.

"Well, you *can* follow orders, huh?" He bent forward in the saddle. "How far?"

She pointed behind her. "That way, follow me."

"Why are you wearing that thing across your face?" Nick asked suddenly.

"I suffered some bruises at the hands of your men. I had to cover them. My people would have asked questions." She turned toward the camp.

Nick relaxed slightly. "Oh, yeah, I heard about that. Well, men will be men."

Nalin's hands were sweaty and she wiped them on her skirt. From the corner of her eye she could see an Indian standing on a hilltop, a rifle in his arms, his feet spread. She smiled quickly. When she looked back the man had disappeared. She lifted her head proudly and walked to her camp. Her thoughts were filled with hatred for the men that followed.

They stood for several minutes looking down on the camp. The fire burned brightly, flames leaping high but no life was visible.

"Where is everybody?" Nick asked.

"Many warriors have gone on the hunt. They will not return for many days. A few are guarding the camp." She pointed her finger in the other direction. "The people are sleeping. Indians sleep at night, too." She smiled at Nick coldly.

"Well, ain't that nice, hunting, huh?" He rubbed his hands together. "Okay, men, tie the horses and let's go." He climbed down and handed his reins to Ben, studying the camp while the horses were being tied. His eyes moved back and forth, searching.

As the edge of the camp Nalin stopped and turned to Nick. "That is Lucas's tepee." She pointed her finger and then backed into the shadows. Nick stared at the tepee and when he turned back to Nalin she was gone.

"Damn, I hope she remembers to lead us outa this goddamn place," he whispered through clenched teeth.

"Nick, I ain't got a good feelin' about her. I mean I was with her, remember? She had swollen eyes. This one, well, her eyes don't look like they even been touched." Tony spoke uneasily, quietly, suspicion nibbling at his mind.

"Goddamnit it, Perez," Nick whispered. "Don't start none o' that shit with me now. I got enough to worry about without wonderin' about a damn Injun's eyes. She led us here, didn't she. She knew the signal, didn't she? Who else woulda known?"

"Hell, Nick, she coulda led us right into a trap. Just cause she fed you some bullshit about men off hunting and all that don't mean a hill o' beans. She coulda been lyin' through her teeth. And I think she was." Tony spoke to the red-faced man in front of him. "I ain't goin' with you. I'm gonna nose around. If anything's wrong I'll be watchin'." Tony touched his hat and disappeared.

"Shit, I never shoulda trusted that guy. Well, I ain't got time to think about no yellow-bellied snake now. Let's go, Ben." Nick whispered to the tall man standing beside him, an evil smile on his lips.

Nick walked to Lucas's tepee and Ben hid in the shadows watching for movement. Satisfied that Lucas and the girl were sleeping Nick cowered down and slowly raised the flap. He surveyed the interior of the tepee. White puffs of smoke touched the top, then drifted away. Smoke covered much of the camp from the huge fire. Nick wondered momentarily why such a big fire burned when no one was around. But he was engrossed in other things now. Burning fires were not important. He moved into the tepee and knelt in the doorway, closing the flap behind him. His eyes shifted from one side to the other and then fell on the sleeping occupants across the teepee. He watched them for several seconds. They were covered in blankets and he couldn't make out which one was which. A cradle hugged the side of the tepee a few feet from them. Nick smiled. He'd kill the baby first, relishing the look on the parents' faces when he held the tiny lifeless body over theirs. He must be careful and plan everything just right. There was no room for error now. He walked to the cradle and pulled his knife from his belt. The steel glinted coldly in the shadows. He gripped the knife with a frenzied madness as he stood over the cradle. He lifted his arm. Quickly, heavily, he brought the blade down. The babe must not cry. He had to have time to get his gun drawn and be ready for Lucas. His blade plunged into the bundle through the material and into the hidden body. He brought the knife up. No blood! He tore the blanket from the body and threw it aside. Straw! Only straw in the cradle. He raised his eyes and looked at the bed. He leaped up and tore the blankets from the bodies. The same thing! Straw and hides! A grunt of anger escaped from his throat and then he froze. He turned slowly toward the laugh and looked into the hate-filled face of Sanger. Nick's eyes closed to slits, his breath came in jagged gasps, his face white with anger.

"Very clever, Sanger, very clever."

Lucas was leaning against a frame pole just inside the

entrance. His arms across his chest, his expression cold.

"A girl named Spotted Fawn came to your camp. I grew up with her. When we were young we played in a stream together not far from here. Now I see you holding a blade over my family's bed." Lucas straightened. "Pray, Moriarity. Pray to whatever God you believe can save you." Lucas wheeled and left the tepee.

Nick wasn't prepared for this. He'd had no qualms about sneaking up on Sanger and killing him, but face to face? Sanger was nothing to laugh at. Nick walked to the flap, opened it and walked out. He sucked in his breath as his gaze fell on Ben. Chico stood over Ben's body, blood pulsing from his throat, Chico's knife dripping on the man's face. Several dark-faced Indians stood staring at Nick, cold hatred thick in the air. Lucas stood in front of the fire, stripped to the waist. Leather pants and knee-high moccasins laced up the side were all he wore. He gripped a gleaming knife and Nick shuddered when he realized he had walked into a trap.

"I'm giving you a chance, Moriarity. If you don't want to fight like a man, you'll die like a coward." Lucas stood, giantlike, the fire reflecting off his cold, blue eyes.

"What do you mean, fight like a man. Shit, even if I kill you I'll never leave here alive. I ain't the coward here, Sanger." He swung his arm at the surrounding men.

"You're right, Moriarity. You won't leave here alive. Drop your gunbelt."

When Nick laughed he was grasped from each side and held firmly while his gunbelt was removed. Then he was released.

Lucas approached him slowly, menacingly. Nick shuddered. Lucas brought the knife up, caught Nick's shirt front and ripped. The blade left a long, red scratch on Nick's belly and blood began to trickle from the wound. Nick looked down, astounded. Then anger began to suffuse through him and he jumped Lucas, stabbling wildly with his blade. Lucas stepped aside and reached out again, ripping the sleeve of Nick's shirt, drawing blood to his arm. It was a battle between a cat and a ferret. The cat, lithe, sinewy, and lightning quick, the ferret frenzied and predictable. It was no battle at all. Nick had never fought with a knife unless his victims were helpless. His choice had been to shoot a man in the back. Lucas was playing with him, making him look like a fool. Desperate at the turn of events he spat, "You may kill me, Sanger, but Perez will get you and that woman of yours. Perez will be a real match for that redheaded bitch and plow her like she deserves."

Lucas looked at him, his eyes slits. "Did you think we didn't know about the others? Where do you think the rest of the camp is, Moriarity? Don't ever underestimate an Apache."

As the meaning of Lucas's words sunk into Nick's frightened brain, he lunged again, his knife glimmering in the firelight, dancing, vibrating. Lucas leaped back as Nick fell face down into the dirt. He lay there for a second waiting for Lucas to approach. When he glimpsed the moccasins he reached out, grabbed Lucas's foot and pulled him down. But the second Lucas fell he rolled to his side easily, dodging the knife. Lucas stood looking down at Nick, taunting him, "Stand up." Nick began to stand, then stopped momentarily on his knees, his hand in the dirt. Lucas reached out and kicked his arm. The concealed dirt in his hand flew out and Nick grunted. "Stand up," Lucas said.

Nick stood, his knife poised for assault, his eyes slits of anger, his lips curled back. The two men circled each other, two dangerous animals, lashing out with their knives, antagonizing each other, teasing, and cajoling. Lucas clearly had the upper hand.

Lucas tired of playing with Nick and kicked the knife from his hand. It tumbled into the dirt out of reach. Startled, Nick glanced at it, watching it land.

Lucas struck, his knife sinking into Nick's large stomach. Nick's hands reached for the knife, his eyes large, filled with pain. He fell to his knees. "That's for Spotted Fawn. This is for Lindsay." He sunk his knife into his chest, into his heart.

Nick fell forward, bubbles of blood oozing from his mouth, his eyes closed in death as he landed in the dirt. Lucas turned to the surrounding men. All was silent. He looked down at the man lying at Chico's feet.

"There is only one left now, friend."

Chico nodded. His eyes stared coldly at Ben.

"I have waited so long to see Lita's killers. I never thought they would be working for him." He nodded at Nick's body. Lucas looked into the darkness.

"There are more out there, Perez and this one's partner. Where are they, Chico?" Chico wiped his blade on his pants and gazed up. "One thing for damn sure, they won't come looking for us. Let's go find them."

They walked to their horses and mounted. They rode into the darkness but had gone only a short distance when a group of warriors rode toward them leading several horses with bodies strung across their backs. Chico jumped down and walked to the group. He walked to each body, grabbed them by the hair and pulled their face up to his view.

"Here he is, amigo, the other man I have searched for." He looked up at the warriors. "Who killed him?" An Indian nodded. Chico looked at him, said nothing for several seconds, and then nodded. He walked to his horse, stood for a moment, and then mounted. Lucas watched him. Lita's death was avenged, but for some reason it wasn't as sweet tasting as he thought.

"Well, *amigo*, let's go tell your woman." Chico looked at Lucas.

"Where's Perez? Nick said he was here. His body isn't one of those," he stated, pointing.

"Chico, Lindsay!" Lucas kicked his horse and galloped off. Chico followed.

Chapter 38

"Lindsay, we have been forbidden to leave here. I cannot do this," Little Bird pleaded, her eyes bright.

"Little Bird, please, just this once, do this for me. I must go to him. Because of me, he may be in danger. Please?" Lindsay's eyes begged as well as her voice.

Little Bird's head lowered. She finally agreed to take care of Neddy and followed Lindsay to the sleeping baby. She turned to Lindsay before she walked away.

"Lindsay, do not turn into another woman chief. She became as good a fighter as the Crow Indian men but never found a man to marry her. She had to choose between being a wife or a chief. She chose the latter. Do not do the same." She turned her back on Lindsay, a signal the conversation was over.

Lindsay sighed and walked off. She was not going to stay here and wait to hear from Lucas. She was going to him. And nothing was going to stop her.

Sneaking away from the camp wasn't easy. The guards watched her closely, as though they read her thoughts. Every time she walked too close to the opening she was forcefully led back. She sat on a rock, her chin resting in her hands, musing over this problem. Suddenly an idea struck her. Why sneak out? The men wouldn't leave the camp unguarded to follow her and she wouldn't stop riding until she reached Lucas.

She turned to the tethered horses, striding casually in the shadows to a fleet pinto mare. She petted the mare's neck, reassuring the skittish animal. The horses were tied well within the confines of the camp so when she began to ride out, she would have to move fast to get past the guards before they could act. She untied the horse and led her to a rock. She had not been seen as yet but she would have to work fast. She stood on the rock and jumped on the horse's back. Her heart beat furiously and her shirt was wet with sweat. She turned the horse to the trail and kicked her hard into a full gallop. The mare's dainty hooves churned up the ground as they thundered past the startled guards. As she suspected, the guards wouldn't leave the women unprotected to follow her but they sent a young boy, Fox Hunter, back to camp to tell Lucas. Lindsay saw no one following her. Smiling smugly at her successful escape, she rode swiftly into the night. She thought she remembered her way to the camp and continued to gallop. The horse and the rider began to tire before she slowed up. Soon she would be at her man's side.

She should have reached the camp by now. At least she should be able to see the fire. She reined in the horse and scanned the horizon for a glowing fire. When she saw nothing, she turned the pinto. She frowned. God, where was she? The camp should be around the next bend. That's it. Maybe she hadn't realized how far they had been taken into the hills and now that she was in a hurry . . . she jerked on the horse's reins. The pinto reared up, throwing her head back. A man stood several yards in front of her. There was something vaguely familiar about him as he stood there in the moonlight. She turned her horse, ready to gallop off when an arm reached up and grabbed her leg and jerked her to the ground. She landed with a thud and screamed. She lay on the ground and raised her eyes to meet Tony's lusty gaze boldly sweeping her body. She wiped her hands on her pants and then clutched the top of her shirt. Tony reached out, grabbed her by the shoulders, and pulled her roughly to her feet, all the while his eyes feasting on her body. Lindsay shivered at his touch, her eyes wide and frightened. Tony chuckled as he felt her shudder.

"So, I still ain't good enough for you, huh? Well, this time I aim to show you what a real man can do." He ripped the front of her shirt, exposing her breasts. He caressed her white breasts with his eyes as he silenced her struggling with increased pressure on her arms. Tears of pain and fear clung to her lashes. He stood for several minutes gazing on her and then grabbed the front of her pants and pulled them roughly down to her feet, hurting her. His tongue licked his lips as he searched her body with his eyes. His free hand began caressing her skin, down her belly, around her thighs, then between her legs. She gasped and began to struggle but he only gripped her arm tighter and laughed. Then suddenly, he began dragging her. He stopped and Lindsay saw his horse under a tree. Tony pulled her roughly to the animal, flung open his saddle bag, and pulled out some rope.

"What . . . what are you going to do?" Lindsay's fear was tangible. She was prepared to do anything to keep this

311

man from hurting her.

He shoved Lindsay to the ground and she lay in the dirt, sobbing quietly. He grabbed her ankle and twisted her onto her back. She tried to struggle and he hit her in the face. Bright lights shot out, dancing in front of her eyes. The stars in the sky descended upon her, gnawing at her brain as she lapsed into unconsciousness. Somewhere in the distance she could hear a horse pawing the ground anxiously. Someone was humming and moving above her but she couldn't see. Her jaw hurt. She tried to touch it but her arms were tied. She tried to move her legs but they, too, were tied. Tony sat beside her chewing on a piece of jerky.

"Well, did you finally decide to join the land o' the living?"

She blinked several times trying to clear the fog that filled her mind. Finally she looked down and saw her legs spread and tied to stakes. Her arms were tied above her head.

"Is this the only way you can make love to a woman, Tony? Tie her so she can't run away." She whispered the words.

Tony stood and strode to his horse. She followed him with her eyes. He returned to her side, standing over her, his eyes raked her body, lingering on her inner thighs. She squirmed but the bonds held her securely. Tony chuckled. He bent to her, his hands touching her body, searching, probing intimately. She bit her lip to keep from screaming. After several minutes of fondling Tony stood and with his eyes glued to her, he began to strip. When he stood naked over Lindsay, his manhood stiff and throbbing, he whispered, "Now, now you'll feel a real man."

He lowered his body over hers, his eyes glistening, his hands holding her face, his manhood hot against her stomach. His lips traveled to a pink-tipped breast, then back to her throat. A tremor of repulsion shot through Lindsay as she stifled a scream. Tony's lips smothered her mouth and she groaned in pain as he roughly kissed her swollen jaw. When he finally stopped kissing her, she screamed. He clamped his hand over her mouth and she bit him. He pulled away in surprise and she screamed again. He grabbed her kerchief and gagged her.

"Well, I don't need to kiss your lips, anyway. There are other parts I can kiss," he said wickedly. He perched over her body ready to enter her, his manhood hot against her and she began to cry.

"Now, my pet, you will learn . . ." he gasped, his arms no longer held his weight as he fell forward, smothering her, his face in her hair. Then she saw the knife buried deeply in his back. His final breath came from his lips in a long, agonizing sigh and she gagged. His body was lifted from her and she looked up at Lucas. He threw a blanket over her naked body. He bent over Tony's body and removed his knife, wiping the blade on Tony's shirt. Then he looked down at Lindsay.

"Doesn't it get tiresome being tied all the time, niña?"

A sob escaped her throat and came out muffled. Lucas removed the gag. He touched her swollen jaw.

"God, you seem to hurt yourself a lot. I just don't know about you, niña, I'm beginning to wonder." He smiled as she clenched her teeth. He cut her loose and she sat and rubbed her wrist and ankles, her lashes spiky from dangling tears. She watched Lucas as he tossed Tony's body over the back of Chico's horse. The he came to her, hunkered down, and studied her face silently. After several moments he stood, reached down and pulled her into his embrace. She relaxed against him, tears spilling down her cheeks. He carried her to the horse and held her close as they rode off.

Chapter 39

Lindsay luxuriated in the tub, the water silky against her skin—a marvelous finish to a wonderful day. She stood, dried her body with the big towel Manuel left her, and wrapped her robe around her. She ran a brush through her hair and walked to the patio doors. It was as lovely as she remembered. Pots of gardenias hugged the walls, their perfume permeating the air. The fountain tinkled, droplets of sparkling water landing on the tile, shimmering like diamonds. The lanterns hung, flames flickering in their blackened glass.

The trip back to Lucas's ranch had been uneventful. They had spent two days at the Indian camp helping Little Bird bury Spotted Fawn and Lindsay spent many hours visiting with War Eagle, Yellow Cat, and Little Bird. The Indian camp returned to normal. When Lindsay asked Lucas about finding her and Tony, he shrugged nonchalantly, throwing out something about Fox Hunter finding him and telling him what she had done. It was easy tracking her even though she was going in the wrong direction.

Uncle Ned, Scott, Jonas, Ricco, and Zuni were waiting at the ranch. After Ned stopped crying, he told her they were getting ready to ride out and search for them. Scotty commented on how well she looked, her face healed and golden.

But the most poignant moment in their reunion was when Lindsay placed Neddy in her uncle's arms. Ned couldn't speak. His throat was thick, his eyes misty as he gazed on his namesake. Lindsay and Lucas had left them alone. She was anxious for them to get acquainted.

Slipping away, she had made her way to the bedroom, gazing at the room that held so many memories. Lucas came up behind her and wrapped his arms around her waist. He kissed her neck and shoulders. She turned to him, her eyes loving. They kissed long and passionately. Lucas carried her to the bed, laying her on the soft quilt. He undressed her and after stripping, he lay beside her, his hands searching her body. After several minutes Lucas took her hand and placed it on him, waiting for her to wrap her fingers around him.

"Uh, uh . . . it's my turn . . ."

* * *

The tall white-haired priest from the Solano Parrish had

performed the ceremony in the afternoon under a cobalt blue desert sky which played host to ponderous, white desert thunderheads. He was an animated man, whose long, sweeping arms gesticulated comically while he sang his sincerest Mass in a disjunct mixture of Spanish and Latin.

Lucas and Lindsay had stood in the shade of the proscenium arch while the guests who had come from as far as Santa Fe, the neighbors, children, and brightly dressed vaqueros leaned over each other on tiptoe to see the wedding couple. Children scampered beneath their mothers' flowing dresses and giggled at one another.

Ned had given her away, the crowd opening and closing behind him and Lindsay. In their wake the hums of admiration hung in the air like a soft song.

Lindsay wore an ivory muslin dress with an intricate lace bodice. She carried a single red rose. When Lucas turned to receive her, all eyes moved to him. He wore a black charro suit. His beard and moustache were neatly trimmed but the same unruly curls laid on his neck. He had winked at Lindsay.

When they turned to face the old priest, Ned took it as his cue to dash to Zuni who was holding little Neddy. There was a whispered to-do about who was going to hold him. Zuni argued that the child was asleep and that Ned would have to wait until he woke up to hold him. Ned's face contorted like a puerile orphan and squared off at the great, round Zuni who was now beaming like a triumphant picador. Although their rift was in whispers these sounds contained all the inflections and emphasis of a full brawl so that the crowd could hear an occasional word. Finally Zuni acquiesced and Ned scooped up the sleeping baby from the recesses of the rotund woman's sagging arms. As he did, there was a great cheer. Even the band joined in with a triumphant trumpet flourish. Zuni stood with her hands placed where her hips should have been and scolded them all with her deepest scowl. When the hoopla died down, Ned pivoted to face the ceremony again. With his "grandson" now securely in his arms, he found himself facing the surly face of the old priest, arms folded, clearly distressed at the interruption. Ned looked sheepish. Lindsay and Lucas were smiling proudly and not in the least upset at anyone.

The old priest continued. Soon the incantation of the Mass made everyone's mood contemplative again and involved in the spiritual magic that the Mass held for them.

"Dominus Vobiscum . . . . ."

Lindsay stood in the scent of her man like a stone. No one could know the force of will required of her to remain still and not turn to embrace Lucas. When she spoke her vows, her own voice sounded distant and alien to her, as though the promises, the words were nothing. All this circumstance, beautiful as it was, seemed too earthbound for her unexpressable feeling of joy.

"et cum Spiritu tuo . . . . ."

When the ceremony ended, there was another great cry and the band produced a series of festive chords as Lucas and Lindsay scampered to the patio by the fountain. There they kissed and the voices of the crowd roared in approval. Then the dancing began. Lucas and Lindsay danced slowly under the fading purple and orange desert sky.

* * *

Overhead a single red-tailed hawk glided against the western sky. It floated easily on wide wings in a great circle. The flash of sun on its wings revealed another who joined the first in the great arcs.

The rhythm of their wings matched for a moment and they soared side by side. Then suddenly, as if the same notion had struck them at precisely the same instant, they dove several hundred feet. With new speed they turned and glided over a shadowed arroyo to the shoulder of the hill beyond the husky sage and out of sight into the heart of the desert.

The biography of Libby Holman, the torch singer accused of murdering her millionaire husband! Solved at last! The most sensational case of the 1930's!

Milt Machlin

PRICE: $2.75   T51533

LIBBY
By Milt Machlin

She was Broadway. She was the 30's. Libby Holman possessed an allure irresistible to both men and women, and numbered among her lovers Tallulah Bankhead, Jeanne Eagels and Montgomery Clift. Though Libby was accused of murdering her millionaire husband, no conclusion was ever reached. That uncertainty shadowed the rest of her tragedy-haunted life. Award-winning author Milt Machlin has unearthed startling evidence that sheds new light on the most sensational murder case of the 1930's, and on this dazzling woman who still occupies center stage! ILLUSTRATED

THE LAST OF THE LATTIMERS
The Silver Web (Vol. 1)
Jean Nash

PRICE: $2.25—BT51473
CATEGORY: Historical Romance (Original)

The lovely Victoria, orphaned at 17, goes to live with her cousin Nicholas and his wife Elizabeth in their handsome New York townhouse. Victoria falls in love with Nicholas. Elizabeth dies from a miscarriage after an affair with Morgan. Then Nicholas and Victoria are married, though she fears he does not love her. In the next volume, Victoria enters into the elegant social and business milieu occupied by the fabulously wealthy.

Vol. II, "The Golden Thread," to be published in <u>April</u>, 1980.

(The completion of the two-part story "The Last of the Lattimers")

THE GOLDEN THREAD
Jean Nash

PRICE: $2.25 T51483
CATEGORY: Historical Novel

Married at last to Nicholas Lattimer after his first wife's death, the happiness she sought still eluded Victoria. Wealthy, protected, and secure, she nonetheless suffered loneliness and frustration as Nicholas' far-flung business empire continually took him from her side. Fearful that Nicholas had married her out of pity, Victoria desperately yearned for proof of her husband's love. Doubt, fear, and tragedy finally bring the Lattimers together in reconciliation.

OTHER TITLE:
THE SILVER WEB   T51473 — $2.25

SEND TO: **TOWER PUBLICATIONS**
P.O. BOX 270
NORWALK, CONN. 06852

PLEASE SEND ME THE FOLLOWING TITLES:

Quantity	Book Number	Price

IN THE EVENT THAT WE ARE OUT OF STOCK ON ANY OF YOUR SELECTIONS, PLEASE LIST ALTERNATE TITLES BELOW:

Postage/Handling

I enclose...

FOR U.S. ORDERS, add 50c for the first book and 10c for each additional book to cover cost of postage and handling. Buy five or more copies and we will pay for shipping. Sorry, no C.O.D.'s.

FOR ORDERS SENT OUTSIDE THE U.S.A., add $1.00 for the first book and 25c for each additional book. PAY BY foreign draft or money order drawn on a U.S. bank, payable in U.S. ($) dollars.

☐ PLEASE SEND ME A FREE CATALOG.

NAME_____
(Please print)

ADDRESS_____

CITY_____**STATE**_____**ZIP**_____

Allow Four Weeks for Delivery